THE CLOCKMAKER'S SON

BOOK ONE OF THE TWISTED WOLVES DUOLOGY

YURI SHARKEY

BOOK ONE OF THE TWISTED WOLVES DUOLOGY

YURI SHARKEY

For the ones who love a wolfish smile and a warm heart. Thank you for taking a chance on a small indie author.

Chapter 1

Helm Castle

As I stared at my reflection in the bloodied water, death stared back at me with a vengeance. My foot met the side of the rusty bucket as I let out a string of curses. *I need to escape this damned castle. Escape Sullivan.* I snatched the old mop head and squeezed the excess out with the heel of my boot, mulling over my options.

Fang stood in the dark corner of the room, tending to his wounds as I mopped up the rest of the blood. *Our blood.* Waning purple light filtered in through the large window, illuminating his profile.

He sighed, shoving his curly black hair out of his face. "That's good enough for now, Rue."

Despite our injuries, Fang offered that familiar warm smile I'd grown to love over the years. "You've cleaned this room at least six times now. It can't get any cleaner."

"Nothing is ever good enough for Sullivan," I reminded him with a pointed look. He didn't argue.

I glanced down at the stinging cut on my left forearm and grimaced.

Fang came to my side and grabbed my arm. "Here," he said, taking my wrist and carefully wrapping a few layers of gauze around it. "That should hold for now, but Arthur should take a look."

Arthur's famous concoction will do the trick, he conveyed with his always readable expression.

I shrugged, but all I could think about was Sullivan's last words to us, repeating over and over in my head: *Clean the floors. Scrub those walls until your fingers bleed. Get it all. There'd better not be any mess left by the time I return or there'll be hells to pay.*

Sullivan had caught us training with knives we'd taken from the kitchen quarters earlier today. We'd been extra vigilant by taking our training escapade to the dungeon, but Sullivan's hyper-sensitive hearing must have pinpointed us. He swooped down like a bat out of Vol , dragged us up to one of his dingy, oversized closets, and delivered his usual punishment, a rare form of dark magic he used to inflict pain or wounds. Afterward, he'd called on his magic to drain our energy, taking it for himself, aiding his own strength.

I frowned, recalling Arthur's screams from earlier, begging Sullivan to stop, to have mercy, but Sullivan locked him out of the room. It didn't matter, though. Arthur's screams eventually faded from my hearing and I took my punishment without fighting back, as Fang and I always did to protect Arthur. I'd take punishments every day if it meant saving Arthur's life.

Next time, I'll feed you to the Volings. Sullivan had warned, a sinister smile ghosting his lips as he knelt down and ran his fingers through the blood on the floor.

I gripped the mop handle and shuddered, recalling the fresh memory.

"Hey, are you okay?" Fang placed a finger under my chin as he surveyed my face with a worried expression.

I shook my head and pointed to a reddish-brown area on the stone floor by my feet. "I missed a spot."

Fang took the mop from me. "Go take a break. I imagine Arthur will be down soon."

Taking his advice, I limped to the side of the dark room. The sky outside was shifting into a darker blue-purple color. We'd need to wrap the cleaning up soon before it was completely dark. I sank against the wall and brought my knees to my chest, drawing in a few deep breaths, but I couldn't stop trembling.

Arthur returned to us by the time Fang finished mopping, his long gray hair slick with sweat and his eyes rimmed in red. Without saying anything, he sat beside me on the floor and took my left arm, unwrapping the gauze with ease. More blood dripped out, staining my brown trousers.

Sadness clouded Arthur's features as he examined the jagged cut. He retrieved a tiny glass bottle from his coat pocket. *His famous concoction.*

An exhale escaped my lips when he applied the strange ointment to my wound. The cut audibly sizzled and closed as I watched in amazement, grateful for Arthur's alchemy skills.

"That stuff never ceases to amaze me," I said, twisting my arm back and forth as the magic patched me up. "And the pain's gone."

Arthur pocketed the bottle, surveying my healed wound with a pinched expression. "I added a painkiller to the concoction. Should help."

Fang stared out the window, his eyes distant. "Sullivan went too far this time."

Arthur shushed him. He gestured to Fang and made a weird expression. Fang nodded.

"Can I blink us to the garden?" Fang whispered, his figure blinking in and out of existence as though he was ready to evaporate right that second.

Arthur shook his head. "Not without alerting Sullivan." He paced across the floor, his dark blue eyes narrowed. "We don't have much time, but we're getting out of Helm Castle soon. All of us."

"He'll find us," I said, my stomach churning. Sullivan was a known hunter—he'd trail us, and when he found us, we'd all be Voling food, and from what I'd heard, the Volings enjoyed taking their time with their prey. A slow and painful death while being skinned alive was something I'd like to avoid at all costs.

"He won't," Arthur assured. "I know you're scared, but we can do this. Hold tight. This nightmare will soon be over," Arthur said as he caressed the top of my head. "Trust me."

"Of course we trust you, Arthur," Fang said.

I gave a hesitant nod, unsure if it was possible to escape Helm Castle, but there had to be a greater purpose in life than running away from the Volings and reliving the horrors of Sullivan's dark magic every day.

Arthur squeezed both of our hands. "I'll get us to safety. To where Sullivan will never find us." His voice was shaky with emotion. "I love you both. Never forget that."

I released a breath, a trickle of warmth dancing along my spine. "I love you too, Arthur."

"Likewise," said Fang with a grin, his cheeks reddening as they always did when either Arthur or I became emotional.

"I've gotta go. There are some bodies that need tending to before Sullivan gets impatient with the burial proceedings," Arthur said. He gave a small smile before departing, leaving us alone in that dreary closet inside the old, haunted castle.

Sullivan arrived shortly after to check our work, scrutinizing every inch of the room for any errors. My breath caught, and I held onto Fang's hand as tightly as I could.

A suffocating pulse of heat and ice flowed from Sullivan, so powerful that it made me nauseous. He towered over me, clad in a fresh change of burgundy robes and hands clean of our blood.

Sullivan extended his palms outward, and I gritted my teeth as he relentlessly drew energy from my body, nearly bringing me to my knees, but I kept my chin up as I calmly held his cold gaze, refusing to show fear. Fang shifted on his feet beside me, his face pale as his energy depleted, but he said nothing.

When Sullivan was done, he glanced around the room once more, his hooked nose scrunched at an odd angle. He snapped his fingers at us with impatience. "Outside. *Now.*" His harsh tone washed over us, and I flinched like I was being held at knifepoint.

Fang and I raced up the steps, panting heavily as we passed stone walls decorated with tapestries of dragons and paintings of the old kings of Fogstone. Sconces spread dim light onto our path leading towards the wrought-iron gate. I held Fang's hand as we stepped outside of the castle, where two moons greeted us from above, bathing us in moonlight.

Sullivan prodded my back with the hilt of his dagger as we put more distance between us and the castle. "Keep moving."

I swiveled to steal a glance, catching sight of his outstretched hand. He pointed a finger towards Hanging Forest, past the garden of stone henges and blue, carnivorous plants. I kept my distance from the plants, their limbs striking out like thorny snakes trying to catch their prey. While passing by, one lunged close to my foot and I back peddled, crashing into Fang's side.

Fang grabbed my arm, steadying me. "You okay?' He pulled me close, wrapping an arm around my waist.

"Keep quiet!" Sullivan ordered, and we both snapped our heads forward, glaring at the moons as we trekked towards the twisted woods.

Once we made it to the forest's edge, Sullivan marched us a half a mile inside its depths.

I lowered my eyes, shivering, not wanting to see the horrors the forest held within. The legend told that Hanging Forest was notorious for stealing souls when anyone so much as laid a toe inside the thick wood. Trees would awaken, their branches snatching up trespassing mortals before devouring their souls through cracks in their trunks. Whatever remains were left afterwards usually hung from the tree boughs.

"I'm right here, Rue." Fang whispered, dipping his head close to mine as we pushed forward. "Always right here."

I gave him a tiny smile, though my shaking hands betrayed my worry.

"Stop!" Sullivan snapped, raising his hands. He bellowed something in a guttural language I couldn't understand, opening a funnel cloud of magic that dumped two shovels onto the ground.

Ah. Conjuration magic. Every day, I learned something new

about this monster. I stared at the shovels as the funnel cloud evaporated. What the hells were we supposed to do with these?

Sullivan snatched me by the collar of my shirt, then shoved me onto the ground. "Pick up the shovels and start digging. Both of you."

"Why?" With narrowed eyes, Fang squared up against Sullivan.

Sullivan flicked his wrist, sending Fang crashing into a tree stump nearby before his gaze snapped to me.

I winced, my chest throbbing as I resisted the urge to cry out for Fang, but he got up as quickly as he was thrown, a hateful glare spreading across his features.

"Pick it up and start digging." Sullivan commanded.

My fingers gripped the rusted shaft, and I dug a hole alongside Fang as fast as I could, sweat pouring off of my forehead while Sullivan paced between two winding trees as he watched us.

The moons dipped closer to the horizon as each hour ticked by. When me and Fang finally dropped the shovels, we were panting like we'd just finished a marathon. That hole had to be at least six feet deep, if not more. I was covered head to toe in sweat and mud, my hands shaking as the smell of damp earth assaulted my nostrils.

Sullivan gave us a cruel smile, approaching us as fresh sunlight peeked through the trees.

"Get in. Don't you dare move until I get back." Sullivan ordered. "If either of you so much as move an inch before I return, consider this your graveyard."

We descended into the hole, exchanging worried glances, and waited until we could no longer hear his footsteps. When he was gone, I groaned, my skin crawling when I saw all the skittering bugs around us.

"I'm done with this," Fang said, and his body began blinking as he reached for my arm.

I smacked his hand away, panic building inside me. "Don't!" There was no way he could blink us out of here without alerting Sullivan. We'd be dead before we could even taste the word *freedom*.

Fang clenched his teeth, his brows furrowing. "We should still try."

"Not without Arthur," I said. Hopefully Arthur's plan of escape wouldn't take much longer.

"Fine," Fang replied with a scowl. "But Arthur better hurry it up."

"Do you think Sullivan is working with the Volings?" I asked, shuddering as that thought consumed me. Volings terrified me, especially the ones resembling tall hyenas with bulging eyes and long snouts encasing sharp teeth. Those teeth were perfect for tearing into flesh, something I'd witnessed on too many occasions.

"I'm not sure," Fang replied, chewing on his bottom lip.

My chest rose and fell with rapid breaths as we continued waiting for Sullivan's return. The trees rustled with the wavering breeze and branches creaked and snapped, sending chills down my spine.

"The trees won't eat us, Rue. It's just a myth," Fang said after a tense moment, his breath hot against my ear.

I grimaced, wrapping my arms around myself. "Arthur said he's seen bodies in the trees."

"They were probably put there by Volings," he replied. "Besides, how could a tree suck—"

I held up my hand, straining my ears. Footsteps were approaching. "He's coming back," I warned.

Fang snapped his mouth shut as Sullivan's head poked over the dirt. "Come out."

I didn't have to be told twice. I hopped to my feet and scrambled towards the dirt wall. Fang held out his palm and hoisted me up, then I extended my hand towards Fang, though he didn't need my help. He was as long as the depth of the hole, if not taller.

Sullivan glared at Fang. "Blink us back to Helm Castle."

Fang pursed his lips as he took our hands. Within the next second, we were standing inside Helm Castle's common room. I found Arthur sitting at a round table nearby shining his boots. The apron he wore over his clothes was bloodied, as though he'd recently finished preparing bodies for burial. He glanced at me, his skin paling as his mouth fell open.

Sullivan smacked me across the side of my head, sending stars through my vision. I clenched my teeth, rage bubbling under my skin.

"See yourselves to your cells. Ulroc will await you there," Sullivan demanded, sending us on our way as he blocked Arthur from view. Fang and I stalked to the cell block, located on the lowest level of the castle.

A hunched man with missing patches of white hair met us there, key already in his hand. He ushered us into our own cells, then taunted us through the bars once we were locked in, sending Fang into a fit of curses and threats, but the hunchback only laughed at him.

I side-eyed Fang through the bars, ordering him to shut up before Sullivan came back, and we waited for Ulroc to leave.

Once he was gone, I pressed myself up against the rusted bars of our joined cells and reached for Fang.

"We're going to be okay, Rue," Fang whispered, pressing his palm to my cheek. "We'll get our payback soon enough."

"How are we supposed to do that? The weaker we are, the stronger he gets," I bit back with a sour tone. It wasn't news that Sullivan drew on the energy of weaker mortals. He'd made that clear during each punishment we'd received. But why had he singled out me and Fang? It was always the two of us.

I couldn't stop the tears from falling as I finally released the sobs I'd been holding back. Fang offered soft words of reassurance, but the only thing keeping me sane was Arthur's promise to get us out of here. As Fang reached his arms through the bars, wrapping them around me, I silently promised myself that better days would come, and we would soon be free.

Chapter 2

Escape

Blood dripped down my eyelids, painting the darkness red as I squeezed my eyes shut, an attempt to block out the horrors within the castle. Screams reverberated off the surrounding walls as I covered my ears with my palms. All hells had broken loose in Helm Castle.

When my eyes snapped open, I scooted myself backwards until my back met a stone wall. Something monstrous hovered over me, yipping as its bulging eyes tracked my movements. *A Voling.*

"Fang?" I called, but no response came.

The monster's rancid breath flooded my senses as it crept closer, its bloody jaws snapping at my face. I shoved it as hard as I could and screamed for help, but it overpowered me, its sharp claws slicing into my skin.

Disoriented from pain, I lolled backwards. The gray-skinned creature climbed on top of me, a wide grin spread across its hyena-like face as it plunged its other spindly hand into my thigh. Pain ripped through me as I released another cry. A flash of silver caught my eye before my vision faded into darkness.

"Rue!" a voice called out from the darkness. A voice that sounded miles away. I thrust myself into the depths of the dark pool, forcing words to emerge from my lips, but nothing came out.

"Rue, get up!"

I attempted to claw my way out, delirious and exhausted.

"Wake up!" the voice snapped, loud and sharp, tearing me back into reality. The sound of scraping metal rang through my ears, indicating that my cell door had been opened. I glanced upward, pain shooting through my limbs, and recognized the mop of gray hair standing over me.

Arthur's hands and clothes were dirty with blood and viscera. I released a shuddering breath when I caught sight of the horrifying monster beside me. It was dead, black blood oozing from its leathery neck.

"What's going on?" I coughed, my hands scraping against cracked stone as I pushed myself into a seated position. Cold air stung my skin, aggravating the cuts that were already there.

"The castle's under attack." Arthur's attention shifted to my body. "Rue, your wounds. Your eyes are bleeding," he said, his voice breaking as he knelt beside me. He retrieved his healing concoction and began lathering it over multiple wounds. He worked quickly, with urgency. "That should do it."

"Thanks," I said, my wounds healed as if they'd never happened.

When the pain dissipated, Arthur grabbed hold of the front of my beige blouse and yanked me upwards. "Quietly." He held a finger to his lips, the stubble around his chin and lips dirtied with grime.

I didn't argue as I held onto Arthur's arm and followed him up the winding steps away from the cramped prison ward.

When we reached the ground level, I slowed my pace and swallowed hard, my heart racing as I observed my surroundings. Helm Castle had been torn apart. Everything lay in shambles around us, even the ceiling mostly gone, revealing the twilight sky and two half-moons above. The decayed skeleton of the broken castle loomed over me, the trees outside casting ghostly shadows across the wretched walls.

I shuddered. Wind whistled through the cracks of the open ceiling, causing goose bumps to prickle my skin as I forced myself forward alongside Arthur. Shards of glass and stone blew past my feet, the wind carrying them into the fog out of my sight.

Teeth chattering from the cold, I covered my nose with the sleeve of my blouse, blocking out the pungent smell of iron and decay the wind carried with it. When we turned a corner, I caught sight of multiple bodies, most missing their skin. A typical sign of a Voling attack.

Nausea tore through me. I doubled over and vomited on my own feet, trying to wrench my gaze away from the gruesome scene. I pressed my palms into my knees and held myself there, supporting my upper body. My breath came in heavy pants while I lingered, staring at the ground to avoid looking at devastation surrounding us.

Arthur bent down beside me, placing his arms on my shoulders to steady me. "Breathe through your mouth. It helps."

I coughed. I was never one that dealt well with dead things. Or dead smells, for that matter. Thankfully, Arthur kept his hands on my shoulders until I found my balance.

"We need to hurry. Rorik is waiting for us. I'll explain everything later." He spoke quickly, his tone serious. I nodded, wiping the remaining vomit from my lips as I righted myself.

"Do you still have your dagger?" Arthur asked.

I patted my thigh in confirmation, my fingers brushing against the hard silver concealed underneath my trousers. Arthur's hand remained on the hilt of his sword as he cautiously surveyed the area. Trembling, I, too, observed the ruins as we quietly crept through the stone halls, but the twilight sky grew darker, and that darkness swallowed us whole. The fog thickened, blurring the environment, but I sensed something was lurking nearby, watching us. I strained my eyes, frustrated that I couldn't see much of anything.

As we rounded a corner, I slowed to a stop, dread pooling into my stomach as realization set in. The cell next to mine had been empty.

"Fang!" I cried out, turning in all directions, scanning what I *could* see. "Fang?!" I started back in the opposite direction, but Arthur caught my arm.

"Rue, we can't," he whispered. His expression was tainted with something I didn't recognize.

"Let me go!" I snapped, trying to wrestle out of his grasp, but Arthur was strong. "We can't leave without him." My heart erratically thumped against my ribs. Despite the cold, sweat formed on my skin.

"Fang!" I called out again, my desperation rising to a crescendo.

Arthur grabbed hold of my shoulders with such firmness that I stopped struggling and looked at him.

"He's gone," he said with an eerie calmness. He shuffled us to the side of the wall and peeked around the corner, his movements fast but careful. There was a brief pause as Arthur and I stared each other down, but he didn't release my shoulders.

Something wasn't right. I couldn't seem to form any words as I searched Arthur's face for any hints of Fang's whereabouts. The sound of footsteps echoed from somewhere behind us.

He drew in a shaky breath and averted his gaze. "He disappeared. Might've blinked out of the castle, but I can't be sure. I haven't been able to find him anywhere." His grip on my shoulder tightened, his fingers digging into my skin.

"Wh-what?" I stammered. A lump hitched in my throat, blocking any words from escaping.

"It happened too fast. He was surrounded by the monsters, then he was gone."

I shrugged out of Arthur's grasp, nausea bubbling in my gut. "No, you're wrong. He wouldn't just leave us. He can't... He isn't—"

"He's gone, Rue," Arthur interrupted, "and we *need* to go now. It's our only chance."

I shook my head, backing away. Fang couldn't be gone. He just couldn't. He'd always been right here. *Right beside me, and—*

All inhibition left me as I reared my arm back and snapped it forward, but Arthur deflected my fist and tightened his grip on my arm. I sensed a familiar presence and we both turned as Rorik emerged from the fog, his wand raised and electricity sparking in the air surrounding him.

Parazio! The incantation left his lips before I registered what was happening.

A searing heat smacked into the side of my skull, and I fell to the ground, unable to move or speak.

CHAPTER 3

JOURNEY

Arthur locked eyes with me briefly before averting his gaze, his bottom lip quivering. Helm Castle groaned and creaked as he carried me from its torment. The castle walls curved outward, as if reaching for us, beckoning us to return to its dreary depths. Through my blurred vision, I saw a dark shadow standing before the castle ruins, extending a long arm above its head. A voice boomed something unheard, and clouds of smoke enveloped the ruins, fully encompassing the structure. With a drawn-out *whoosh*, the castle crumbled into nothingness, taking the lone figure with it. Just like that, it was gone.

After Arthur had carried me into the steamcraft and set me down, Rorik put me to sleep with a different spell. When I woke sometime after, my head throbbed, an unfortunate consequence of Rorik's magic use.

"Ow," I complained, rubbing the sore side of my head. *Damn Rorik for using his magic on me.* The cool silver of the dagger strapped to my thigh pressed into my sensitive skin as I stretched my legs.

"Glad you're finally conscious," Arthur said.

"Real funny, Arthur." As I straightened myself in my seat, I picked my brain, trying to remember the events that led to our departure from Helm Castle. The only details I recalled were rotting away in that cell with hardly enough food to sustain me and the stench of death constantly smothering me, followed by a period of unconsciousness before being freed by Arthur, and making a quick escape. After, the rest of the night was a blur, and the time before my breakout was something I'd like to forget. Still, my head was fuzzy, like not everything was there. Maybe Arthur had used one of his memory charms.

"Glad we finally got this craft up and running," Arthur said. "We wouldn't have made it if it weren't for this piece of junk." He looked at me as he said *junk*, reminding me that I'd referred to it as junk a couple of weeks ago when he'd shown it to me.

I held up my hand in surrender. "I get your point."

The steamcraft was special to Arthur. He had discovered it while patrolling the outskirts of Helm Castle one day a few months ago and took an immediate liking to it. The craft, a rare relic of the past, was covered in a tumble of bramble and wood outside the walls of the Helm. It was in decent condition, much to our surprise. Claude, the mechanic, had helped with repairing and replacing the rotted and rusted parts of the craft, and he got it in working order... before he was brutally and publicly executed for some unknown reason. I forced my eyes shut and cursed under my breath, trying to push that grim memory aside.

"Where are we?' I asked. "Where the hells is Fang?" I scanned the cramped craft, but there was only us. And Rorik at the front, hidden behind a metal door. It was a miracle the three of us could fit in this thing.

I crossed my arms out of frustration, half annoyed because I hated tight spaces, and terrified because Fang wasn't with us.

"I don't know," Arthur said.

My stomach trembled with the rage of a thousand angry bees. "We can't leave him!"

"It's not safe to go back." Arthur draped a blanket over himself. His cheeks were flushed more than usual, and his skin was sunken into his face, accentuating his bleary eyes and his thick eyebrows.

"Arthur!" I yelled, slamming my fists against the bench.

"We'll find Fang, but for now, we need to keep going," he stated, ignoring the blatant anger on my face. "We're very lucky we made it out alive. If not for Alden, we wouldn't have made it this far."

I raised an eyebrow. "Alden?"

Arthur nodded. "He's invited us to live with him. Somewhere safe, away from Sullivan and the Volings."

My brain was beginning to feel as scattered as Arthur's vague descriptions.

"Somewhere where you won't ever be locked up by Sullivan again," he added pointedly, his expression pained.

"Alden who? What are you talking about?"

Arthur drew the window curtain back and took a calculating glimpse of the outside realm. "I'll explain everything when we arrive. We're headed to safety as we speak. To Fennra."

"That's a far journey away from Fang," I whined, folding my arms over my chest and angling my body away from him in an effort to get comfortable. An impossible feat when the bench I sat on was so damned hard.

Despite Fang missing, my nerves traitorously eased a little upon hearing that we were headed back to Fennra, one of the few human realms. We were getting out of Calzour. Away from Sullivan and that dirty old castle. I wanted to forget all about Sullivan's dark magic and the way he made me feel when he'd stolen my energy.

The engine of the steamcraft whirred quietly as it sped towards our destination, propelling us forward over choppy water.

Arthur closed his eyes, his body perched rigidly atop the seat. His matted, graying hair clung to beads of dried sweat on his forehead as he leaned forward and let out a heavy sigh. The craft jolted violently, then smoothed out again as it progressed forward—a cue that we'd made it back on land.

"Finally home," Arthur said, and I knew he meant Fennra.

The pitter-patter of heavy snowfall drizzled against the glass windows in a melodic, sleepy tune.

I yanked aside the curtain of the craft window and peered outside. A frozen wasteland greeted me, one that was barren, destroyed, and devoid of life. Most buildings had crumbled into piles of concrete, steel, and cement, while garbage and skeletons littered the snow-covered streets. The silence was overwhelming. Not at all what I expected to see in Arthur's hometown. He would speak of the liveliness of this place—the vivid colors, abundance of laughter and market stalls on every corner. Now it was a ghost town.

"It's gotten worse, hasn't it," I deadpanned.

Helm was attacked, Fang's missing, and Fennra is a damned wasteland. Everything's getting worse.

"You needn't worry." Arthur patted my hand. "We're going to do our best to live normal lives for as long as we can. I'll make sure of that. Besides, our new home is on the far eastern side of Fennra, far from all of *this*." He gestured towards the wasteland that I couldn't tear my gaze away from.

"Normal?" I choked out a laugh. I'd never known a normal life. Every single day was a battle to see the next sunrise.

"We'll be with other people. People your age, even. And we'll continue to *survive*."

I grunted, sick of hearing that word. There had to be more to life than *surviving*. It was only a matter of time before the Volings caught up to us again. Running away from them always led to the same results.

Narrowly avoiding death.

Finding a new hiding spot in a new realm.

Meeting new people that I wouldn't know long enough to give a Voling's ass about and watching them be torn apart and eaten.

I was sick of it *all*.

I stared at the floor, trying to rack my brain for anything else I could pick out from Helm Castle. The only picture that came to mind was Sullivan's hateful glare and his onyx eyes masked behind wild gray hair. A notable scar across his left eye. His dark magic. Punishments so cruel that they made me beg for death. *But why me and Fang?*

I grimaced, clenching my fists against my sides. It was useless trying to remember… thanks to Arthur, who was particularly skilled at memory charms and who likely made us forget certain things about Sullivan to protect us.

Something stirred at the edge of my memory.

Sullivan.

My eyes widened, and I tapped on Arthur's shoulder, having remembered another piece to the puzzle.

"Sullivan! He said something about a prophecy. Something about the Volings being forced back into Vol for good. A cracked portal that needs to be closed. Was he—"

Arthur narrowed his eyes and held a hand up, silencing me. "I don't want to discuss this so-called prophecy. Sullivan was a fool for bringing it up, especially in the presence of young ears. It's doubtful that the prophecy even exists."

"But—"

"No buts," Arthur interrupted. "This is for your own protection, Rue. You don't need the details of Sullivan's madness."

A harsh reply sat on the tip of my tongue, but Arthur shifted away from me with an annoyed harrumph.

"Everything okay back there?" The metal door slid open, and Rorik's handsome profile peeked out.

"All good here," Arthur replied without hesitation. "How's your arm?"

"Better now."

"What happened to his arm?" I asked warily.

Arthur grimaced. "He was attacked when the Helm went down. Nothing serious, but you never know with the Volings. Sometimes an injury from one of them can leave a trace of dark magic behind, particularly with poisonous effects."

I gasped. Some Voling attacks were known to leave horrid magical effects behind on their victims. Typically, the victims didn't survive, and if they did—well, they usually wished they didn't. I glanced at my left shoulder, visualizing the ugly bite scar hidden by my clothing. A Voling must've bitten me when I was too young to remember, and I suspected it was the cause of weird symptoms I'd been experiencing. The scar occasionally twinged, a constant reminder it wasn't going away.

"I'm glad he's okay," I said, turning my attention back to

Arthur. I was unable to imagine our group without Rorik. Arthur had befriended the wizard long ago, and together they'd embark on expeditions outside of the Helm in search of food and supplies. Even though Rorik was middle-aged, he still had the looks and energy of a young man. His mushroom-blonde hair had hardly acquired any gray over the years, giving him the appearance of a twenty-five-year-old instead of a fifty-seven-year-old.

The steamcraft came to a screeching halt, nearly forcing Arthur and myself out of our seats. After collecting himself, Arthur shot out of his seat with impressive speed, his hand hovering over the hilt of his sword.

Rorik slipped through the door from the front of the craft and motioned for us to get down. "I'll deal with it. Stay hidden for now." He reached up his robe sleeve and retrieved one of his dragon-scaled wands.

"What's going on?" I asked, bile rising in my throat.

"Get under the bench!" Arthur hissed at me.

I didn't have to be told twice.

Cautiously, I slipped to the floor, tucking myself underneath the bench. My heart raced as Arthur knelt down beside me, keeping his eyes on the door of the craft. I pressed my mouth into a thin line while we waited.

Fear clawed at me as I put my hyper-sensitive hearing to use. Something snarled at Rorik, alerting me that we were in the presence of at least one Voling. Footsteps drew nearer, too close to the steamcraft. Rorik bellowed a few incantations in a language I didn't recognize, but he was met with another fierce snarl. I swallowed hard, my hands clenched into fists, digging against my thighs.

We're going to be okay, I told myself, calming my nerves. Whatever was lurking with the Voling sounded large, pacing around with heavy footsteps, but Rorik was the kind of person who feared very little. I pictured his broad face: lips in a hard line and bright eyes cool and collected under the Voling's horrifying glare.

Arthur gripped the hilt of his sword and readied himself in case Rorik needed us. Another snarl sounded close by, so loud that it rattled the sides of the steamcraft. Rorik relentlessly continued his booming incantations, the old language swirling with magic so powerful that it seeped into the craft and melted into my tingling skin. Thunder cracked and the steamcraft swayed. The snarls stopped, followed by the heavy sound of two *thuds*.

Deafening silence followed.

After a few heart-pounding moments, Rorik tapped the paneling of the craft. "All clear," he said cheerily, as if nothing had transpired.

Arthur removed the blanket from over us, soundlessly stood up, and wiped the pooled sweat from the wrinkles on his forehead. "You took care of it?" he asked breathlessly, his composure somehow still intact.

"Another day for the books, I suppose," came Rorik's hearty response as he climbed back into the steamcraft.

That man has balls of steel.

Arthur caught my eye. "Are you alright?"

"Peachy," I replied dryly. Besides my pounding heart and twinging scar, I was physically fine. Mentally, I wanted to crawl into a hole.

Arthur's gaze followed mine to the front of the craft. He patted my shoulder. "I'll be right back. Get some rest," he said. He shuffled to the front to meet with Rorik, their voices low as they spoke.

The sound of their hushed conversation eventually put me at ease. I closed my eyes, only for a moment.

My vision blurred, obscuring my surroundings. Pain radiated through me. My body stiffened, and I sank closer to the ground, groaning.

Strange.

I nervously glanced from one side of the ruins to the other. Dead bodies were strewn across the cracked floors of the Helm. Tall, shadowy figures guarded the exits of the ruins, and skeletal wraiths hovered over writhing bodies, mouths impossibly wide open as they sucked out the souls of their victims, wheezing loudly as they consumed them.

My nose crinkled as my sense of smell heightened, and I coughed in response to the stench that permeated the air around me. It smelled of death... everywhere.

I turned away, searching for an exit that would lead me away from the Volings to safety, but a familiar face appeared in front of me.

Black hair fell over blue eyes as dark as a stormy ocean, a chiseled jawline that framed the rest of an angular face, and a familiar mischievous grin.

Everett Fang.

"Hey, troublemaker. It's about time you get back in your cage before he finds you, eh?" He knelt down beside me and extended his hand, ruffling my head. "How'd you escape, anyway?"

Relief washed over me, mixed with fear. Tears stained my face before I could stop them. "Fang..."

"Rue, we're home."

Arthur shook my shoulders, startling me awake. My limbs strained as I pushed myself upward and wiped the crust from my eyelashes with my free hand. Thoughts of Fang threatened to crush me. I pinched the bridge of my nose. Where the hells was he?

Arthur slid the craft door open and helped me out, the cold

penetrating me between the spaces of my shredded clothing. I shivered, wrapping my arms around myself. Snowflakes fell lazily around me, tickling my eyelashes as I gazed up at the gray sky.

My mouth parted and I let out a heavy sigh, debating whether I should jump back into the steamcraft. *Too cold.* Colder than Calzour, the realm known for windstorms and stone-built gardens.

Just great.

"There's nothing out here except trees and mountains." I waved my hand. "What are we supposed to do, live inside the trees?"

There were no structures in sight that would provide us warmth and a cozy bed to sleep in, and nothing to shield us from the Volings.

Arthur grinned. "Still got that spunk, I see."

How the hells can he smile right now?

I crossed my arms over my chest in a display of disapproval. Arthur led me up a steep hill, lined on either side with a suffocating amount of pine trees, the sun peeking over the horizon. There was nothing else around besides a murky bog in the distance, its back end leading into a twisting ravine.

When we reached the top of the hill, a warm breeze swept across me, coating my skin like heavy fog on a humid morning.

"What the hells?" I muttered, rubbing a hand across my tingling arm.

"Look." Arthur pointed his finger, his old face lighting up in a relieved smile.

My eyes widened in surprise. Rorik caught up and stopped in place beside me, awe transforming his face.

"What is this place?" I asked in wonder, my breath catching in my throat.

Rorik removed his gray overcoat, wrapped it around my shivering body, and said, "Welcome to Leavenfell Castle, our new home."

The silhouette of a massive castle, beautifully overgrown with ivy, stood on the edge of a steep, yet green and rocky cliffside, where patches of snow formed on the grounds surrounding the outer walls and drawbridge. The castle held many angular towers, turrets, connecting bridges, and a grand, intricately designed clock tower attached to the far-left side. The massive structure stood out against the dawn sky, bathed in sunlight as the sun inched over the horizon. It was much more breathtaking than the Helm: old, enchanting, and sizable enough to hold an entire nation and their king.

It was a miracle the Volings hadn't already overrun this place. Surely, they'd noticed a castle this massive by now, but it didn't take long for me to put two and two together. The heavy, warm air I'd walked through a moment ago had to be a sort of protective shield, or a cloak of invisibility.

"We're headed to the lower entrance," announced Arthur, interrupting my stares of admiration. "To first get some much-needed rest." He pulled a rusty key from his black trouser pocket. "We have a home here now, thanks to Alden. You'll meet him soon enough."

Arthur stopped walking, casting a wary glance over his shoulders. "He's... quite the character, so be prepared."

"That's an understatement if I've ever heard one," muttered Rorik from behind us.

I side-eyed them both and followed Arthur across the bridge to the base of the grand castle. We found our way to an arched wooden door, skillfully hidden by snowy vines. The door was fortified with steel across the length of it, and a padlock was attached to the end of the steel. It took Arthur a few tries, but the steel arm swung up once he was able to get the padlock off.

Inside, a wide cabin-style hallway awaited us. The oak-paneled walls held firelit sconces, lighting our path towards a few empty rooms. Rorik took the room closest to the exit and disappeared, mentioning he'd catch up with us after he'd had some rest.

Arthur yawned. "I'll be right across the hall if you need me."

"But Fang," I reminded him. I couldn't sleep peacefully knowing he wasn't here yet and found it odd that Arthur didn't seem worried. I wrapped my arms around myself tightly, as though stopping myself from falling apart. When my bones began to ache, I knew I was in for a rough morning. Not only from missing Fang, but from something else entirely. Something I couldn't control…

Arthur patted my shoulder. "We're working on finding him. Get some rest. We have a busy day ahead."

I must've looked confused, because he added, "Alden agreed that he'll meet with us after we catch up on a few hours of sleep. It's still very early."

"But…"

He held up a hand to silence me. "Don't worry. We're safer here. Try to get some rest." He closed the door, leaving me with more questions than answers.

Chapter 4

The Wizard of Leavenfell Castle

My breaths made small clouds in front of my face as I shot up in bed, clutching my gurgling stomach.

Not again.

Pain shattered through me like jagged glass. I leaned over the edge of the bed as my bones ached and creaked. I squeezed my eyes shut and held my breath, willing the churning in my stomach to go away. Despite the chill that seeped in through the cracked window, sweat poured off my skin, followed by another sharp wave of nausea that rolled through my stomach. I groaned in pain and hunched over, anchoring my head between my thighs.

A few moments passed before I was able to draw in a deep breath and sink back into the mattress, wiping the sweat from my forehead. I rubbed my temples, forcing the bile back down my throat, and waited for the remaining symptoms to pass. Once my body returned to normal, I sighed, curling back under the cotton blanket with the hopes that I would be able to get some kind of rest.

"Morning." Arthur arrived moments later, entering the room without knocking. "I hope you got some sleep."

In response, I threw a pillow at him and buried myself deeper under the blanket.

"It's about time we head up and greet our new neighbors."

"I feel like shit." I grimaced as my muscles slowly contracted back into place. My joints were stiff, locking in place as I heaved myself upward. I didn't want to act like anything was wrong, especially now that Arthur was here—not that he'd said anything about it for the past several years. He knew of my attacks but always dismissed them.

"Any word on Fang?"

"Not yet," said Arthur a little too quickly. He studied me for a moment. "Get ready. Alden needs to meet with everyone in the great hall shortly."

"Great hall?" I asked.

"It's where the people of Leavenfell gather to eat and relax, and also to get updates on the happenings from the outside realms," Arthur explained.

My stomach growled loud enough to wake the dead.

"I've heard the cooks of Leavenfell are very good," Arthur winked. "We should eat well."

The memory of old Pat's undercooked fish made me cringe. "I hope you're right."

Arthur gave me a small smile.

"Can we get back to Fang?" I asked, chewing on my bottom lip relentlessly, my nerves on edge.

Arthur's previous words came back to me. *He's gone, Rue.*

"I don't know what happened to him," Arthur replied, a hint of emotion lacing his tone.

I forced my hands into my pockets, suppressing the urge to break down. "Why didn't we stay to look for him?"

"We needed to escape. The Volings would've found us if you'd kept screaming."

"You left him alone."

Arthur bowed his head, his shoulders tensing. "I'm so sorry, Rue. It was necessary, only until we got to safety. I'm sorry."

"But Fang… we need to go back!"

"There *were* no survivors, Rue. Besides you, Rorik, and myself. I need you to understand that. I've no idea whether Fang is even alive."

My breath stilled. "Don't say that. You said you saw him blink out of the Helm."

Arthur opened his mouth, hesitating. "There was too much going on and I lost sight of him. I don't know what I saw." He averted his eyes. "But even if he blinked, Sullivan would've tracked him down."

Blood drained from my face. I placed my head in my hands, swearing under my breath. Sullivan would track him down, but if Fang was dead, I would feel it. I would *know*. Hopefully he'd made it someplace safe.

Arthur's expression darkened. "I don't know where he would blink to. There was so much chaos. I wouldn't be surprised if—"

"He's not dead," I snapped. A pit formed in my stomach, hot tears stinging my cheeks. I fell back onto the bed, my shoulders shaking with sobs. Fang was—*is* my best friend, practically my family. We'd been together since we were kids. I couldn't imagine life without him.

Arthur knelt in front of me and pulled me into a hug. I stiffened at his touch but eventually sunk into his comforting embrace. We stayed like that for a few minutes before breaking apart.

"I'll ask Rorik if he can go back and search the ruins of the castle. Maybe he can figure out where he went. Use that spell book of his," Arthur offered, eyes glistening. "If Fang's alive, Rorik will find him."

I nodded, wiping the tears from my cheeks. Calzour would be a risky trek, with all the various races of Volings stalking about seeking prey, but if anyone could handle it, it was Rorik.

"Fine," I agreed. I had to hold onto hope that Fang would return to me, unharmed. Hope would keep me sane, at least for the time being. I needed to keep moving forward.

"I promise. Now, come on." Arthur stood and gestured for me to follow him. "Go shower. You smell worse than a pig pen."

I smiled through the tears.

"We're going to be okay," he reassured me. "No matter what." Even in the darkest of times, Arthur had his way of making me feel comforted. He'd cared for me after my parents died. It happened when I was very young, and I didn't remember the details of their deaths. All I remembered was that sometime after, Arthur took me under his wing, and we'd traveled together over the years. We'd found Fang in Talem, wandering around on his own, his parents the latest victims of a Voling attack. From then on, it was only me, Fang, and Arthur, and we quickly became like a real family.

Arthur pointed to the small chest positioned against the back wall of the room, underneath a windowsill. "There should be clothes in there that fit you, thanks to Alden's preparations. I'll leave you to get ready, but best hurry up."

"Thanks. I'll get ready quickly." My stomach growled again. "Fastest shower ever," I added, hunger pains taking the place of my anxiety.

After Arthur left the room, I dragged myself over to the shower. A bar of soap lay on the floor in front of the shower head, wrapped in a soft blue cloth. I washed quickly, the hot water soothing my skin, easing my sore joints.

After showering, I gazed at my reflection in the oval mirror above the tiny sink. Stormy gray eyes stared back at me, and I hardly recognized the girl that stood there. I was much thinner than I'd remembered—my cheekbones more prominent. My freckled skin was bruised and pale. The only admirable aspect of my appearance was my long brown hair, the strands melting into a rich forest-green at the ends. A strange color that seemed to return no matter how often I cut it. Arthur always said it was because I was magic, but that wasn't true. I'd been born without any gifts, after all.

I'd finished slipping into clean, brown leather trousers, ensuring my dagger was strapped to my thigh securely, when a knock sounded at the door. I threw an off-white tunic over my head and opened the door to find Arthur impatiently tapping his foot. He gave me a once over before offering an approving smile.

"Well, I'm glad you don't smell anymore. You certainly took long enough."

"Twenty minutes isn't that long, Arthur. Fang always took an hour to get his hair perfect." *When we weren't behind bars, that is.*

Arthur laughed. "He always was the one most concerned with his looks, and always worried whether the darling Myrabell had noticed his charms."

My heart throbbed at the memory. Myrabell was a girl of our age with white hair and an elvish heritage. She was friendly with

Fang, knowing he had a massive crush on her, though I wasn't sure it was reciprocated. I prayed she'd somehow escaped after the attack. For her sake and Fang's.

I glanced past Arthur into the hallway, goose bumps prickling my skin. There were steps leading both ways, and I shuddered to think what would be at the base of the castle. Maybe a prison, like the one Sullivan had thrown me into.

Arthur placed his hand on my shoulder. "Nothing to worry about here. This is our chance at a new life, so let's try to make the best of it."

Taking my hand in his, Arthur led me through the long hallway and up a different flight of curved wooden stairs. An arched door with engraved carvings on it, written in a different language, stood at the top of the stairs. Arthur gave me a reassuring smile and grabbed the doorknob.

A blinding light flooded the stairwell as the door creaked open, and the sight of unfamiliar faces met my eyes.

A singular room in the entire castle—the *great hall*—dwarfed Helm Castle's splendor.

As I entered by Arthur's side, I stared up at the vaulted ceiling, encompassing the full size of the great hall. The walls, engraved with detailed carvings of trees and leaves, reminded me of an old fairytale. We stopped by a grand oak fireplace on the left side of the Hall, relishing in the warmth from the flames, and politely nodded at welcoming faces as they passed by. An older woman with graying blonde hair and hazel eyes heartily shook our hands. She wore a black apron covered in flour.

The rich smell of firewood hung in the air as we crossed to the right side of the vast room, searching for an empty table. Light spilled in through a row of large arched windows, casting silhouettes of swaying trees onto the walls and peppering the floors with abstract shadows.

I bumped into a boy with black hair on my way to the back of the hall, near an elaborate stage decorated to look like a lush forest hidden behind a wooden podium. A burgundy banner branded with a gold-leafed tree hung on the back wall behind the podium, partially masked by vines and garlands of leaves. Plush curtains with glittering golden foliage sewn into the fabric were drawn to the sides of the stage. There was a circular tower that was built on the back left side of the great hall.

I glanced over my shoulder, taking in the various workstations full of trinkets, clothing, pastries, and small machinery, all manned by one or two people offering their services to people passing by.

"Quite a difference from the Helm, isn't it?" Arthur asked as we made our way to a table located by the workstations.

I bet there's plenty of places to hide in this castle. Good luck hunting here, Sullivan.

"It's lovely," I replied, keeping my anxious thoughts to myself.

The great hall was full of people of all sorts of colors and ages, their voices echoing as they spoke boisterously amongst themselves. When we reached our seats, I sat across from a boy who looked to be around sixteen or seventeen years old. His hazel eyes complemented his tan, freckled skin and dirty-blonde hair. He was quite attractive, even more so than the boys I'd met at the Helm. He glanced at me in between bites of food and smiled, his grin similar to Fang's. My cheeks heated and I shoved my hands into my pockets to stop them from fidgeting.

"Hi," the boy greeted with a crooked smile, a mischievous glint behind his eyes. He ran a hand through his shaggy locks as his gaze dropped to my hair, and he paused when he glanced at my green ends.

"H-hi," I stuttered, averting eye contact. I pretended to be interested in the intricate, floral carvings on the table.

Arthur stood beside me, his attention on a rectangular table, set up outside a door that led to the kitchen. There, food was laid out on trays waiting to be eaten.

"I'll grab you a plate," he said with an air of excitement, his belly rumbling.

I gave a stiff nod, not wanting Arthur to leave me alone, and aware of the boy watching me. I wasn't shy — Fang had cured me of that — but I wasn't used to being around boys I found attractive. I didn't know what to do with myself or how to talk to them. At eighteen years old, I had very little experience in that department.

A burst of commotion drew my attention back to the stage, where an old man paced back and forth by the podium. Tall with wrinkled skin and long silvery-white hair, the man wore an exceptionally long gray robe that was thick enough to ward off the coldest of winters, and rectangular spectacles which sat at the very tip of his nose. In his left hand, he held a tall staff, the top of it adorned with a peculiar, translucent globe.

I squinted at a small creature flying inches above his shoulder — a mechanical bird. Whirring noises came from its beak as it flew around in an erratic pattern. What struck me as even more strange were the many pocket watches that hung from his pockets. Many clocks of various sizes were also fitted into the folds of his robes. Why anyone needed that many clocks on their person was beyond my comprehension.

"Typical wizard for you—they all have their obsessions, but I promise he's not as bad as he looks," the boy opposite me whispered.

"A wizard?" I asked, turning back to the man. From what I remembered, wizards usually didn't live with non-magic humans. They usually stayed within their own realm, Felroc. Besides Rorik, of course, who'd taken a liking to Arthur.

Minutes later, Arthur returned, sitting in the empty chair beside me. He handed me a plate of buttered toast, grilled sausages, and two boiled eggs. The savory scent of the sausage, a personal favorite of mine, had my mouth watering. I grabbed a spicy-looking sausage first and stuffed it into my mouth, not bothering to chew as I inhaled it. My eyes rolled into the back of my head. *This is way better than the food at the Helm.*

The wizard cleared his throat, taking his place at the podium as conversations around the great hall died down. "Good after-noon." A crooked smile spread across his withered face, slightly masked by his beard. "I'm very fortunate to have returned to Leavenfell safely. It was a long, difficult journey to Ju, as you can all imagine, but it's good to be home." His dark eyes surveyed the room. What'd he been doing in the realm of Ju? That was where the elves lived, and their kind didn't take well to wizards.

"For those of you that are new here, my name is Alden Hall. I am the builder and founder of Leavenfell Castle and, of course, our famous clock tower. I'm quite the renowned clockmaker, if I do say so myself."

His appearance started making some kind of sense. But still...

... the *clocks*.

I snorted into my glass of water.

Arthur shot me a disapproving look, and I bowed my head in apology.

Alden continued, "I'd like to welcome you into our community and hope that Leavenfell offers safe harbor, protection, and most of all, freedom. I will administer jobs to the newcomers later this afternoon. Before you disperse, I must put out a warning. Not only to the newcomers, but as a reminder to the rest of you as well. Do not stray far past these grounds. The barrier can only do so much to hide us from the Volings. I cannot guarantee anyone's safety outside the grounds, so I strongly advise you all to take caution." Alden's wrinkly eyes darkened as he cleared his throat. "The barrier has been successful in shielding us from the Volings for over a decade, but we mustn't push our luck, so it's imperative that you all take heed of my instructions."

From the undisturbed looks on several faces across the hall, not many people had encountered the Volings like Arthur and I had. I grimaced between mouthfuls of food, hoping these people would stay lucky enough to never encounter any at all. Death by the hands of a Voling was anything but pleasant—or quick.

"What about the prophecy?" A man close to us asked. His plated armor matched the deep brown of his skin. "Any word on that?"

I leaned forward, my interest peaked.

Alden cocked his head, giving the man a nervous sideways glance.

"No," Alden said.

The man slumped in his chair and resumed eating, mumbling under his breath.

Alden cleared his throat, his face softening as he scanned the room. "Before I forget, I need to see Ruby Watson and Noralei Moore for a quick discussion after brunch. The rest of you are dismissed to go about your business for the remainder of the day." Alden's eyes locked on mine, and I frowned, staring back at him.

I faced Arthur. "What could he possibly want with me?"

Arthur shrugged. "I'm sure it's nothing to be worried about," he reassured me, wiping breadcrumbs from his stubble with a rag.

There was a collective shuffling of chairs throughout the hall as people dropped off their used dishes at the kitchen window and departed. With a quick *goodbye*, the cute boy at my table left. I'd forgotten to ask his name.

When the great hall emptied, only one girl across the hall from me remained—a girl who I assumed was Noralei. She offered me an uncertain smile. Her green eyes twinkled, amplified by the flickering flames of the fire, and she had a slightly crooked nose and full, pink lips. When she pushed her long red hair over her shoulders, I caught sight of pointed ears—a tell-tale sign of the elf race. Her posture stiffened as we made our way to the back end of the great hall.

Up close, Alden looked *older,* if that was possible. He smelled like pine and lavender, and his beard was so long and thick that I half expected another mechanical bird to fly out of it.

"If I am correct, you are Ruby?" He asked, his mouth curving into a smile.

"Rue," I corrected.

"Of course. I've heard many interesting things about you."

I shot him a doubtful look.

"Good things, of course," he added. "I wanted to personally

meet and welcome you to Leavenfell." He stared at me with a hint of familiarity, as if we'd met before.

"And you are Noralei?" Alden asked, turning to the elvish girl beside me.

She nodded, her pointed ears reddening. "Please call me Nora. Everyone does."

Alden gave a sharp nod, his expression calm but friendly. "Of course. The purpose of this meeting is rather simple. I wanted to formally introduce the two of you since you will be sharing one of Leavenfell's towers."

I arched my eyebrows. "A tower room?" I grimaced, not wanting to share a room with a stranger. I wanted Fang back.

Alden's bushy brows furrowed. "Would you rather stay somewhere else?"

"No! I mean... of course not," I muttered quickly. "I'm sorry."

Alden waved off my apology. "I want you to be comfortable while you live here, hence why I'm offering it to you. I know of your history back at Helm Castle, Rue, and I intend to make your stay here quite the opposite of that place."

A blush rose on my cheeks. Alden being aware of my circumstances meant he probably heard of Sullivan. I couldn't help but wonder how *much* he knew.

Alden explained that Nora and I would be attending classes with people our age and how important it was for young people to continue their studies. Nora and I exchanged confused glances. I'd never attended school in my life, besides Arthur teaching me how to read and write while dressing a body for burial.

"I know how you must feel," Alden added. "Keeping busy is important in Leavenfell, and most of our young attend classes and assist with castle chores."

"What about Arthur and Rorik?" I asked.

"Arthur has been assigned to guard duty, and Rorik will be a supply forager. At least until we get the steambots up and working. By the way, how old are you?"

My brain couldn't compute *steambots*, whatever those were. Probably ancient relics like the steamcraft we arrived in. "I'm eighteen," I replied.

"I'm seventeen. Almost eighteen," chimed Nora.

The windows rattled from the wind as Alden let out a content sigh. "I have a feeling you two will become great friends considering you'll have plenty of time to get to know one another. We have a lot to make up for all your mistreatment in Calzour, Ms. Watson. It's a pity what Sullivan put you through, and I'm glad that you and Arthur made it out without serious injury. Not everyone can say they managed to escape the Volings."

I gave a sharp nod, blood rushing to my face. This wizard knew entirely too much about my past, *especially* what Sullivan put me through. A sense of unease rolled through me.

Alden gripped his staff. "I'll show you the way to your tower. Pay careful attention. The castle can be confusing at times if you don't know your way." He strode ahead, surprisingly fast for an old wizard.

When we exited through the main door of the great hall, Alden made a sharp left turn into a brightly lit hallway and led us up three connecting flights of stairs that circled and overlooked an antique ballroom below.

We finally reached a door that led outside onto a wooden bridge, the thin planks swaying with the wind gusts. As we crossed the bridge, I stopped to admire the scenery outside the castle walls, gazing upwards as snowflakes descended from the gray sky. The wind picked up, blowing my hair across my eyes, and I pushed the strands away. I peered up at one of the distant towers, where movement caught my eye.

A boy stood in the window of the highest tower. Whoever he was, he was looking directly at us. A rush of wind whipped my hair back into my face, blocking my view. I quickly brushed the hair out of my face, but by the time I glanced back at the window, the boy was gone.

Nora tugged on my sleeve. "Let's go. Best not to catch a cold."

I nodded and we began to move again. Once at the wooden door, I cast one last look towards the tower window behind me, but no one was there.

Alden opened the door and ushered us inside. Nora and I were out of breath as we ascended another tall staircase, meeting a white door at the top of the circular tower. Alden pulled a small key from one of his robe pockets, unlocked the door, and placed the key into my hands, along with a folded note. "Take good care not to lose this," he said as he winked at me. "Welcome to one of the finest towers of Leavenfell Castle."

CHAPTER 5

NORALEI MOORE

I FLOPPED ONTO THE MASSIVE BED ON THE LEFT SIDE OF THE large but cozy tower room, nuzzling into the thick comforter. Shadows of stars sprinkled the blanketed mattress around me, cast by the sun's rays peeking through the glittery canopy above.

I stretched my legs out in front of me and kicked off my old leather boots, thanking the gods there were two beds. I'd gone down the bed-sharing road with Fang, who'd been notorious for hogging most of the bed space, his leg always dangling over my side and his elbow persistently pushed against the back of my neck.

I unfolded the note Alden gave to me and skimmed across his elegant handwriting.

Ruby,

Welcome to Leavenfell Castle. I'm excited to see where your purpose takes you and wish you well. One of my friends will help you soon. Keep this between us. When you find what you are looking for, come find me.

-Alden

I read the note over and over again. *Where my purpose takes me? One of my friends will help you soon?* What the bloody hells he was talking about? Help me with what? Finding Fang? Because I sure needed all the help I could get with that.

"I can't believe Alden gave us a tower room!" Nora exclaimed, admiring the candlelit chandelier that hung from the center of the timbered ceiling. The warm glimmer of the flames reflected off her face, carving out her sharp features. "You must be a really important person if *the* Alden Hall offered you a room this nice."

I tucked the note into my pocket, deciding to deal with whatever *that* was later. "I'm no one special. Only a survivor, like you."

"Then you must have a special gift?"

"I was born without a gift," I admitted through clenched teeth.

Nora broke eye contact, her ears drooping as though she was embarrassed for asking.

"What about you? Any gifts?" I asked.

"Nothing out of the ordinary. I can shape-shift, but I've had a *very* hard time doing it. I've managed to er… change my breast size a couple times, but that's all." Nora hung her head, her skin reddening to the shade of her hair. "I haven't been able to change it back."

I avoided the urge to look at her ample chest.

Nora's grin faded. "I wonder why he'd put us in a room together."

"Maybe a buddy system, in case the castle is ever invaded," I answered with uncertainty. *Beats me.*

Grasping a book from my nightstand, I flipped it over, reading the description on the back.

"Does it sound interesting?" Nora asked after a moment.

"Seems heavy on romance. Not my preference, if I'm being honest."

Nora's green eyes lit up while her ears wiggled with excitement. "I'm addicted to romance novels." She held out her hand. "If you're not going to read it, I'll have a go."

I tossed the book onto her bed. "Be my guest." Despite myself, I cracked a grin. Anyone could pick up Nora's mood by watching her ear movements. Glancing over at her again, they perked right back up as she skimmed over the book description.

A heavy knock sounded at the door. Nora set the book down and glanced over at me, shrugging.

"It might be Arthur," I said, earning a confused look in return. "My caretaker."

It wasn't Arthur. Instead, a young boy with shaggy brown hair and brown eyes greeted me. A short woman stood behind him with her hands on his shoulders, someone I assumed was their mother. Nora looked almost identical to her, besides the graying red hair and the height difference. Nora was quite a bit taller than her.

"Mom?" Nora called, jumping out of her bed and running to the door. She wrapped the boy in a hug. "What are you both doing here? It's freezing outside."

"We wanted to check out your new room. Benjamin wouldn't stop asking about it," her mom replied. "What a gorgeous tower! The cabin colors are stunning."

"Where's Dad?" Nora asked, fiddling with her fingers.

"Your father went to the study to meet with that wizard... what's his name?" her mom asked as she walked around the room, observing all the intricate furniture. She stopped in front of the fireplace, her back to us.

"Alden," Nora reminded her.

"You should see our room, Nor!" Benjamin interrupted. "It's smaller than yours, but we have our own toilets."

Nora laughed. "That's great, Benny! It's important to have your own toilet." She turned to her mom while Benny darted around the room, touching every piece of furniture he could, his eyes bright with fascination.

"Mom, I'd like to introduce you to my roommate." Nora said.

My breath caught in my throat. I gave an awkward wave and made my way over to them.

"Mom, this is Rue," Nora said as I approached them.

"So I've heard." Mrs. Moore offered me a warm smile. She had the same pointed ears as Nora. "Rue. Is that short for anything?"

Benny ran up to my side. "Rhubarb?" He asked, staring at me. "I love rhubarb pie. Mom makes it the best."

Nora ruffled his hair.

"Close," I said to him. "My name is Ruby, but I prefer to be called Rue."

"Then why isn't your hair red like a ruby?" Benny asked, tugging on my trousers.

"That's enough Benny." Nora's mom huffed, walking back towards the door. "It's lovely to meet you, Rue. Promise me you'll keep our daughter out of trouble. I'm a little concerned that Nora isn't staying with us." Her mom sighed. "But it'll do for now, I suppose."

"It's very nice to meet you both," I replied, smiling down at Benny, who stared at my green ends in confusion.

Mrs. Moore's smile brightened. "Thank you. We only wanted to stop by and say hello. I was assigned to kitchen duty with Mrs. Baker, and I've got to be there soon to start the dinner shift and learn the ins and outs of the system. The oven is the strangest contraption I've ever seen." She clicked her tongue, her eyes glazing over as if she was imagining how the oven worked.

"Of course. You're welcome to come back any time," I said. "Be careful on the bridge, especially with these winds."

Mrs. Moore faced Nora, her grin fading a bit. "One more thing before I go."

A shadow of apprehension crossed Nora's face as she straightened her spine and met her mother's eyes, her thumbs twiddling behind her back.

"I'm allowing you to stay in your own room, but don't let me find any boys up here," her mom warned. "You'll move straight into our room if I suspect anything is going on. You know what your father would—"

"I know, Mom," Nora interrupted, her jaw clenched. "You don't have to worry, so please leave me be."

Nora's mom opened the door and stepped out. "I'll need to show you where our room is at some point. It's quite the hike from here, I'm afraid."

"I'll come find you soon," Nora promised as she closed the door, her face still red.

"Bye Nor!" Benny shouted through the closed door.

"Don't be a stranger," Mrs. Moore added.

Their footsteps slowly receded, and Nora let out a strained groan. "Sorry about that. Her nagging is the reason I prefer to be in my own room. My father as well."

"Seems like she only cares about you," I said as I shuffled back to my bed. A burning sensation coursed through me. What I'd give to have my parents back. Still, I was a little surprised to hear Nora's mom speak to her that way, considering Nora had said she was almost eighteen. Her little brother was funny though.

"I'm sure my father puts her up to it. He's overprotective of me. Ridiculously so." Nora's gaze dropped to the floor. "We've never had a good relationship."

"I'm sorry to hear that," I told her, not knowing how to respond. "My caretaker can be overbearing sometimes."

"Overbearing isn't a strong enough word for my dad, but it's nice to hear that you can relate a bit."

"If you ever want to go looking for trouble, without your dad knowing, you'll be fine as long as you stick with me. You won't have to worry."

Nora raised her eyebrows. "Oh? And how can I trust you to ensure we won't get caught?"

"I've had a good teacher. His name is Fang."

I sat on the edge of my mattress, hunched over a candlestick, mesmerized by the flickering flame but so deep in my thoughts that sleep felt impossible. After Nora had fallen asleep, worry crept in. Of all the things raging through my mind, I was stuck on wondering how Sullivan reacted when he found out me and Arthur were gone.

If he was still out there, *alive*, he'd stop at nothing to hunt us down and kill us. That alone was enough to keep me on edge. I couldn't fathom how he'd gone from being an ally to an enemy so quickly. It happened without warning. One day, everything was fine. The next day, Sullivan looked at me differently, as though something was wrong with me. Everything had gone downhill from there.

I clenched my clammy fists against my thighs as my mind shifted back to Fang, my heart aching. I didn't want to imagine the possibilities of what could've happened to him—I only needed Rorik to find him alive. There was also the anxiety that Alden's note brought with it. I re-read his words several times, trying to understand their meaning, but couldn't figure out what he was talking about, so I figured I'd have to ask him about it in person.

With a yawn, I turned on my side and slipped underneath my comforter, Nora's soft snoring coming from the other side of the room. A tapping sound grabbed my attention, and I glanced toward the arched window by my bedside, expecting to see the night sky full of stars.

I was not expecting the distorted, black figure staring back at me.

CHAPTER 6

THE FIRST INCIDENT

THE CREATURE'S FACE, UNNATURALLY ELONGATED, WITH gaping holes where the eyes should've been, inched closer to mine, so close it pressed up against the windowpane. A shrill sound escaped from its wide-open mouth, a sound so horrifying that I was certain it would kill me, but the creature stayed behind the glass.

I trembled, clutching my clammy hands to my throbbing chest, when garbled words sprung from its mouth.

Heed… Sull— Castle… not safe, it warned in a wheezing voice, the holes on its face shrinking and enlarging with each word. *Follow… bird.* The windowpane frosted over every time the creature spoke.

I shook my head, trying to comprehend its words, my skin crawling as its mouth went in and out of focus. A *warning* about Sullivan perhaps. But the bird… what bird?

Pro-…fae… proooo…proph.

My mouth hung open as I stared at the creature in disbelief. Was it trying to tell me about the prophecy?

The creature's mouth closed, and it fluttered away from the window, like a ghost being carried away in the wind. I scratched my head, curious about how and why it'd ended up at my window.

I rushed to Nora's side to check on her afterwards, finding her still sound asleep. After crawling back into my own bed, I replayed the creature's words over and over again in my head until restless sleep took over.

When the sun hit my face, I forced myself to get up, needing *anything* to take my mind off the creature's scary appearance. The image of it was permanently burned into my brain.

"The halflings said they needed protection after showing up at our cabin, but my father didn't like that one bit." Nora paused, searching my face as though she were waiting for a reaction.

"I'm sorry. What?" I faced her, rubbing my arms, embarrassed that I hadn't been listening.

"I was explaining why we had to move away from Ju. Are you okay?" Nora's ears drooped even lower.

I vaguely remembered the realm of Ju from long ago as being a short stop during our travels. It was a realm ruled by the elven race. We'd taken temporary shelter there before moving on to Talem, another human realm south of Fennra.

I nodded at Nora, who was busy fidgeting with a strand of her hair. "I'm sorry. I didn't sleep well last night." I said with a yawn.

Nora continued, "My dad forced us to leave our home when the halflings showed up. We had to leave other elves behind. They were like family to us, but my dad didn't care."

"I know how hard it is to leave someone behind." I swallowed hard, averting my gaze in fear that I might burst into tears. Dread trickled in, seizing my thoughts, as I worried about Fang. I hadn't realized my hands were shaking until Nora grabbed them, steadying them in her own hands.

"I'm sorry if I upset you," Nora said, "but please don't worry yourself over my troubles." She glanced at the clock and rushed over to her vanity. "We should get ready anyways. I don't want to miss breakfast."

I opened my mouth to respond, but a sudden twist in my stomach stopped me. It took everything in me not to double over in front of her. Groaning, I slipped to the other side of the room while Nora fixed her hair and braced myself against the side of the dresser. I gripped the top of the dresser with my right hand and clenched my other hand to my stomach.

I took slow deep breaths until the pain passed.

"Hey, are you okay?" Nora called out, casting a glance over her shoulder.

I ignored her question, instead focusing on rummaging through the drawers to find a decent outfit to wear.

As we passed by others in the great hall, my shoulders tensed. Quite a few people were crying and hugging each other.

I made my way towards an empty table when a wispy gray cloud abruptly appeared on the stage with a loud *whoosh*. The sound startled me, and I tripped, falling face first onto the freshly waxed floor.

I glanced up, wondering if the cloud was a figment of my

imagination, but was quickly proven wrong when Alden's face appeared in the middle of it.

"I say we go back to bed and start over," Nora suggested as she helped me up off the floor. "Honestly, if people didn't notice you before, they do now."

I smoothed the wrinkles from my green trousers. "What in the hells is that?" I asked, side-eyeing the cloud as it went in and out of focus.

Nora shrugged.

When I met Arthur's side, he elbowed my arm. "Morning. Is everything okay?"

"Besides face-planting, I'd say it's going as usual." I glanced at a nearby table. "What's going on? Why are people crying?"

Arthur, smelling of sausage, continued eating, his mouth full of food and his gaze never leaving his plate. His usually tangled gray hair was combed and out of his eyes. I glared at him. From the way his arms stiffened, and his fork slowed its path to his mouth, it was obvious he was playing dumb with me.

My gaze trailed back to the cloud, roaming over Alden, who was sitting with his hands folded over the top of a pile of papers on his desk, the mechanical bird perched atop his shoulder.

"I apologize for not joining everyone in person this morning. I've been busy communicating with our southern neighbor, Talem. They have been overrun by Volings." Alden clicked his tongue, searching the crowd in front of him as he placed a stack of papers to his side. "We need to send aid to their realm to help come up with a plan of security. I will alert those capable within the next hour."

Arthur and I exchanged worried glances. If Rorik was pulled into that journey, that would take him away from his search for Fang. I cast a glance over my shoulder and found Rorik standing by the blazing fireplace. He carried a light rucksack, full of what I assumed was food, weapons, and trinkets. I glanced at his arms, where I suspected two dragon-scaled wands would be strapped carefully and securely, hidden underneath his billowy robes. He called them his good luck tokens and had mentioned before that the wands were old family heirlooms he'd inherited when he was a young boy. Hopefully the rucksack slung over his back meant he'd be leaving soon in search of Fang.

"There has also been a terrible incident not far from Leaven-fell Castle," Alden continued, his expression unreadable. "I'm sorry to announce that we have lost a few of our own late last night to a Voling attack."

The creature outside my window. Maybe it had been warning me of that attack. It *had* to have been. *Shit.*

I shot an anxious glance at Arthur, but he put his hand over mine and mouthed *Don't worry.*

"This wouldn't have happened if your men were guarding the grounds like they were supposed to!" a stocky man with pale yellow hair wearing suspenders yelled, standing from his seat. His fork dropped to the table with a sharp clank. "How are we supposed to feel safe if this becomes a common occurrence?"

Alden waited until the man was finished. "I have taken measures to re-strengthen the barrier. I assure you that this won't happen again."

"Oh! And you're sure about that, are you?! And what about the prophecy? You said things would be moving forward to close the damned realm! The Volings are spreading further into Fogstone. I wouldn't call that *moving forward,*" the man spat. He glared at Alden and plopped back onto his seat, red-faced and shaking his head. "Bloody wizard."

Alden's eyes locked on mine, his gaze so intense that I sunk into my chair. Arthur stiffened beside me, and I snapped my head towards him. He'd gone pale at the exchange, but gave me a subtle shake of his head, extinguishing any questions I had. I wouldn't get answers from him.

I sighed, my thoughts lingering on that word. *Prophecy.* Alden had stared right at me after that angry man had said it. It couldn't be a coincidence.

"A new rule will be established from here on out," Alden continued, returning his attention to the disgruntled crowd. "No one is to leave Leavenfell Castle under any circumstances, unless you receive permission directly from myself. No exceptions."

My stomach churned. As much as I understood the gravity of the situation, I needed Fang to be found. I slumped into my chair and shivered, despite the heat of the fireplace behind me. If the rule stopped Rorik from leaving, then I would find a way to escape on my own, even if that meant banishment from Leavenfell.

Alden tapped his staff against the desk. "I have another announcement. As another precautionary measure, self-defense classes will be offered to those aged sixteen years and older. It's imperative to learn how to protect ourselves in the event of an attack. That being said, I would like to introduce you to your new defense teacher, Finnlien."

A young man made his way to the podium and bowed his head at Alden's cloud before facing the crowd. He resembled a god from a fairytale I read long ago, with his tall height, sharp features, and statue-like build. His short brown hair fell in appealing waves. When he looked in our direction, Nora's mouth parted slightly, her eyes widening with what I could only guess was admiration. I shoved a forkful of food into my mouth, shifting my attention from Nora to Finnlien, then back to the cloud.

Alden shooed the mechanical bird from his shoulder and returned his attention to the people of Leavenfell. "For those interested in participating, there is a bit of a delay since Finn will be going to Talem, so classes will start when he returns. They will be announced when he does."

"Why not now?" a grizzly man at the table beside us asked. "Why wait for *him*?" The man pointed a finger at Finn.

"Again, he is needed in Talem to aid their people," Alden answered. "Finn has the most battle experience in this castle, hence *why* we will wait for him. We are safe for now, so there is no real rush." Alden dragged a wrinkly hand through his beard, startling one of the mechanical birds inside. The bird poked its head out and snapped its beak at his hand. "If you are of age, you may sign your name on the scroll of parchment on the podium. Finn, please bring it to me after everyone signs up so that I may look it over. That is all." The cloud, along with Alden, vanished.

Sinking into my chair, I placed my face in my hands. I'd been blindsided by Arthur into thinking we were safe, only to be told a day later that we were going into combat training and that people had already died. I was worried about the people of Talem, but I secretly prayed that Rorik wouldn't be sent there. At least not yet.

And as friendly as Alden was yesterday, a part of me didn't trust him, especially after that note he'd given me and the heated look we'd shared at the mention of the prophecy. The man knew something, yet he was being as cryptic as Arthur, and that pissed me off to no end.

"Well, what do you think? Should we sign up?" Nora asked, her ears perking up.

I rolled my eyes at her. "Why? Because there's a cute guy?" I asked. "I suppose I wouldn't mind practicing my swordsmanship." It had been a while since I'd wielded a sword. Sullivan had stopped me and Fang from doing any sort of training, but before Helm Castle, we'd trained throughout our travels through other realms so much that even Arthur was impressed by our determination. I supposed a bit of practice brushing up on my old skills wouldn't be so bad.

"So, is that a yes?" Nora asked.

"Sure."

A grin spread across Nora's face. "Perfect!"

"Absolutely not," Mr. Moore, Nora's father, snapped. The man resembled Nora's brother but with sharper features and a chipped tooth.

Mrs. Moore grabbed her husband's arm. "She needs to learn how to protect herself, dear. There's no harm in it."

"This isn't up for discussion," he replied with a frown. "I won't have my daughter fighting those monsters."

Arthur stood and walked away with his plate of food. *Smart man.*

"I'm not a child anymore," Nora argued.

Mr. Moore loomed over her, his brown eyes sharp with anger. "You're still under age—"

"If an attack were to happen, I want to be able to defend myself," Nora interrupted. "What if something happens to you and you can't protect us anymore?"

Nora's father opened his mouth to argue, but her mom shushed him. Frowning, Mr. Moore stormed away without another word.

Mrs. Moore shot Nora a sympathetic look. "Go ahead and sign the parchment. I'll talk to him." She squeezed Nora's arm and rushed off after her husband. We stared after them, not daring to move until he was out of our sight.

"Let's go sign the bloody parchment," Nora muttered.

"Gods, he's handsome, isn't he?" Nora declared as she scribbled her name on the parchment. "I've never seen such soft curly hair on a man before."

I snorted. She was *definitely* visualizing running her hands through it.

"I take that as you're not interested?" Nora asked, raising an eyebrow.

"I'd rather throw myself into a bog," I replied.

Finn approached us moments after I signed my name, stopping in front of Nora and taking the parchment from the podium. He scanned the list of names and lifted his gaze to the pair of us.

"How old are you two? What are your names?"

"Eighteen, and my name is Rue."

"I'm Nora," Nora said shyly. "Seventeen."

"Neither of you look old enough," Finn replied, his eyes resting on my chest.

My cheeks heated. "Excuse me? What the hells do—"

"I assure you that we're old enough," Nora cut me off, raising her voice. "Besides, it looks like you need people." She pointed to the dwindling line behind us. Finn gave her a dimpled smile, and I swore her ears shot straight up. *Gods, this girl.*

"I'll take your word for it sweetheart, but Alden makes the

final decisions. See you later." Finn took his leave, casting a wink over his shoulder.

My mouth hung open as he sauntered off. The way he'd stared at my chest had my skin crawling.

"I can't believe he thinks we're younger than sixteen," said Nora. "I'm not sure if I should feel flattered or offended."

"That's what you got out of that conversation?" I asked in surprise.

"He's just being cautious," Nora argued.

I bit the inside of my cheek, blood rushing to my face. Nora huffed and quietly mentioned that she needed to clear the air with her dad.

I waved as she took off, thankful for some alone time. I needed to see what else Leavenfell Castle had to offer. If Alden's note meant anything, then I'd need to start searching for clues. A castle wasn't a castle without secrets.

CHAPTER 7

THE MYSTERIOUS KEY

I BUMPED INTO ALDEN ON MY WAY OUT OF THE GREAT HALL. From the way his shoulders tensed, he was either in a great hurry, or he couldn't be bothered to talk to me right now.

"How can I help you, Ms. Watson?" Alden asked.

I pulled the note from my pocket. "I need help deciphering this."

"It means exactly what it says," Alden deadpanned. "Now if you don't mind, I need to speak with my guards about Talem."

I raised a brow. "I won't keep you long. It's just… your note's cryptic. I'm going to need more explanation than that. And *what* was that back there? Is there something I should know about the prophecy?"

Alden lowered his head and opened his mouth to speak, but Arthur stepped between us, a scowl on his face. He snatched the note from my hand, read it a few times, and crumpled it before stuffing it into his pocket.

"I'd appreciate it if you didn't give Rue these sorts of notes,

Alden. Leave her out of prophecy talk as well," Arthur said, placing his body partially in between me and Alden.

Alden paused. He caught my eye, and I saw the disobedient glint in them. "Very well. My apologies, Arthur. Have a good day."

Arthur nodded his head and waited for Alden to leave.

When Alden's footsteps receded, he turned to me, his expression softening. "It's best if you keep your distance from Alden. He has too many loose screws and I don't want you getting pulled into his madness."

"But the prophecy—"

"If you know what's good for you, you will stay out of it," Arthur snapped, ending the conversation.

Like hells. Clearly Alden wanted me to find something. If that was the case, then even Arthur couldn't stop me, *especially* if a prophecy was involved.

Leavenfell Castle was a maze of endless corridors with the occasional stairwell in between them and fancy tapestries on the walls. Although the castle was beautiful, rumbles and whispers followed me. Somewhere in the distance, a bird chirped. The hair on the back of my neck stood up as I peered down a long corridor after hearing a particularly loud rumble.

"Hello? Alden?" I called out, my pulse racing. No response came. Spooked, I dashed up another staircase and stumbled through the first door at the top of the winding steps.

I was met with an unfamiliar room, a sort of storage area

with dusty books pressed against the flimsy walls on dilapidated shelves. A tiny window at the back of the room allowed a small sliver of light to filter in, illuminating a spiral staircase that stood in between towers of damaged boxes and dusty books.

There was a trapdoor on the ceiling above the staircase, and one of Alden's mechanical birds was perched on the top step, staring down at me. It was an interesting little thing, made from copper and various scrap metal, with tiny, perfectly circular eyes that looked like emeralds. Its beak clacked and whirred as it watched me, giving me the impression that it was curious about my entrance. When I moved towards it, it flapped its metal wings as though it were startled.

The bird clicked its beak and glanced at the trap door, flapping its wings impatiently as if egging me on. Maybe I was supposed to follow *this* bird.

Curiosity was going to be the death of me one day, but I was already hopelessly lost and didn't want to go back in the direction of the spooky rumbles. If Fang was here, he'd be the first through that trapdoor while scolding me to stop being a scaredy cat.

After working up the bravery, I ascended the staircase and pushed the trapdoor open, squeezing myself through it with ease. Dust smacked me square in the face as I emerged into the room above, sending me into a coughing fit. The mechanical bird landed on my shoulder and mimicked my cough. *What a strange creature.*

I wiped dust from my cheeks and looked up, spotting an impressive spider web with a rather large spider perched in the middle of it. My body jolted and I took a deliberate step backward. Spiders were my worst fear, and that fear only grew over the years because Fang thought it would be funny to chase me around with them when we were kids.

The smell of musty books assaulted my nose as I looked around, ignoring the bird's squawks and trying to see what I'd gotten myself into. Much like the room below, old books lined the small room, stacked in massive piles and covering about every inch of the room. When I turned, I came face to face with a human-shaped machine placed against the wood-paneled walls. It was covered in dust and cobwebs. Was this one of the steambots Alden had spoken of?

I froze, drawing in a sharp breath, having never seen a steambot up close before, if that's what it was. The cylinder tube on its back indicated that it was steam operated. I'd seen similar tubes on the steamcraft. According to Arthur, anything that ran off steam was considered an ancient relic throughout the realms. They derived from Windcraft City, a distant realm located somewhere in the middle of Dagger Sea, surrounded by fog. Arthur found anything related to relics interesting, and he swore that one day, he would visit Windcraft to find some for his own collection.

While examining the machine, the mechanical bird screeched and flew off my shoulder, landing on a box on the other side of the room. I began in the direction of the bird, but my foot caught on something. I fell forward, knocking the side of my head on the rounded edge of the shelf. I swore, rubbing my throbbing head, certain it would bruise later.

My gaze dropped to find the culprit, and there I spotted a very small trapdoor with a round knob fixed to the top of it. The bird landed beside it and pecked the fixture on the door.

I swatted the bird away, my heart racing as I bent over the tiny door and yanked on the knob. The mini door swung open, revealing a small compartment inside. Pushing my fingers inside, I retrieved an old leather pouch. When I tipped the pouch upside-down, a delicate skeleton key fell onto my lap with a soft *clunk*. The bird chirped with excitement, flying in circles around the room. My eyes widened in awe as I picked up the key and examined it, impressed by its fine craftsmanship. A five-pointed golden bow formed the end of the key, shaped like an intricate, curved star with elaborate crescent moon and star symbols engraved on the sides of the shaft. I flipped it over in my palm, the brass warming my skin, as if coming to life while emitting a strange energy.

Alden's note came to mind. *When you find what you are looking for, come find me.*

I rolled my eyes. Like hells I would show this key to Alden. I didn't even know what I was supposed to be looking for, but I didn't want to share a key this *interesting* with him, only to have it potentially taken away from me.

"Rue?"

I dropped the key onto my lap, my hands trembling.

"Where are you?"

Shit. That voice was attached to Nora. I hurriedly pocketed the key and rushed to the trapdoor. Nora came into view as I descended the rickety staircase.

"I've been looking all over for you!" she exclaimed, out of breath. "What are you doing?" She wrinkled her nose at the sight of me.

"I got lost."

"I can see that much," Nora replied, her gaze following mine to the trapdoor. "What was up there? Anything interesting?"

"Old books and spiders," I answered. The mechanical bird flew out seconds before I pulled the trapdoor closed, then soared out of the room, its metal wings creaking with each flap.

"You should see yourself right now," Nora said with an amused grin, looking me up and down.

"Don't laugh at me. I've had quite the adventure," I scolded, rubbing the side of my head. "Not to mention a brewing headache."

"I'll make you some tea when we get back," she promised. "My mom gave me a kettle for our room. We can hang it over the fireplace."

"Speaking of our room, I hope you remember the way there," I complained. "And I'll have to thank your mom later."

"You're lucky to have me." Nora motioned for me to follow her.

When we arrived at our tower, Nora kept her promise, hanging the kettle over the fire. We spent the night drinking lavender tea and talking about boys, a topic Nora very much enjoyed.

When Nora begged me to take her on my next exploration, I agreed… even though I'd no idea where that key would take me. If the bird I'd followed had anything to do with the warning the creature had given me last night, then I was on to something. Maybe that bird would lead me somewhere connected to Alden's note.

I downed the rest of the tea and rested my head against the plush armchair by the fireplace. Nora's giggles filled the room, and a warm, but strange sense of happiness buzzed inside of me. What I'd give for more nights like this, if only Fang was by my side too.

Snow blanketed the grounds surrounding the castle, glittering like diamonds under the approaching sunlight. Icicles melted with a gentle pitter patter against the windowsill in a sleepy melody, tempting me to crawl back under my warm covers and drift into a blissful dream where Fang wasn't missing and my parents were alive.

With Nora scarce over the weekend, Arthur busy with extra guard duty to make up for the dead guards, and Rorik officially on his journey searching for Fang, most of my free time was spent fiddling with the key I'd found and reading mystery novels by the fireplace.

It'd been more than a few days since Arthur last spoke to me, and with no communication from Rorik, dread built inside of me. I glanced at the empty space in my bed, a lump forming in my throat as I pictured Fang lying beside me.

"Ready for bed?" Nora asked that night. We were sitting on the floor by my bedside window, watching the stars.

"Just about." I yawned, picking a piece of dirt off of my white nightgown.

"When do you think Finn will be back?" She asked. "I hope soon, even though I'm sure he has a horde of girls waiting for him."

I raised an eyebrow at her. "I'm pretty sure you're going to be a part of that horde."

Nora laughed, and my mood lifted as I watched her ears wiggle with amusement.

We moved towards the fireplace and Nora hung the kettle

above the fire, ready to make our bedtime tea, but my eyes were already heavy. By the time the kettle whistled, I was sprawled across the carpeted floor, hugging a pillow to my chest while Nora's voice became a distant echo. It wasn't the first time I'd fallen asleep on the floor by the fireplace.

A dense forest full of lush greenery, surrounded by dainty willow trees and bubbling brooks—gardens upon blooming gardens occupied by peculiar wildlife. Tall, human-like beings with silky, feathery wings and beautiful faces observed me from within the trees. The woodland fae—they were said to live within Gardenia, one of the only realms safe from the Volings, thanks to fae magic. Their cozy homes were built into the willows, bridges connecting each tree and floating steps leading up to each doorway. Balls of light hung unstrung along the pathways, illuminating the trails in between the homes.

It was like a fairytale, except I was running for my life.

The harsh wind stole the breath from my lungs with every leap forward. The grass was abundant in this region, dense even, which only slowed my pace. My heart pounded furiously inside of my chest, fleeing from something that had followed me here.

Casting a glance over my shoulder, I caught the shadow of the obscured creature peeking over the tall pampas grass.

"Help me!" I shouted, waving my arms above my head. "Please!"

The fae remained rooted to their spots in the trees above, their expressions both amused and terrified.

My lungs burned and I dropped to my knees, gasping for air. Exhaus-

tion set in and I fell onto my side in the thick grass, clutching desperately at my throat.

At last, a single fae flew down from one of the trees, making a graceful landing in front of me. The onyx-skinned fae gave off a magnificent glow, as if the sun itself radiated off her. Her long lavender hair was tied back into an intricate braid adorned with various flowers and pearls, and her gray, feathery wings were folded neatly against the bare skin of her back.

When she spoke, an eerie hush fell over the woods.

"Why have you come here?" she asked, her voice softer than I expected it to be.

"I... I don't know," I said. "But something is chasing me." My bones were close to shattering into pieces. I folded my arms around myself, an attempt to hold myself together.

"What you are searching for isn't here," she stated. "What is your name, girl?"

I forced myself to look at her. "Rue."

The fae extended a hand towards me and helped me up off the ground. The instant her fingers brushed against my skin, relief washed over me, and the pain and shaking dissipated.

Only then did I realize that this fae didn't intend to hurt me. If anything, her face was twisted into an expression of concern.

"My name is Shay," she said.

"Where can I find what I'm looking for?" I heard myself ask, Alden's note in the back of my mind. Apparently, it was not a good question to ask, because an instant uproar broke out amongst all the others in the trees.

"We do not help mortals!" one shouted at me, its wings beating madly.

"She brought darkness into our land," another shrieked.

"Enough." Shay held her hand up, immediately silencing the outburst from the surrounding fae.

When they settled, Shay met my eyes, her expression softening. She brought her finger to a stunning white gem that was fastened around her neck. "This gem has a twin."

"A twin?"

"It's somewhere in the castle, and if you are to find it, it should aid you when the time arises. If you find it, you have my permission to use it. A gift."

"A gift?" I asked, my confusion growing as my gaze darted between her and the fae in the trees. "Where in the castle would I find it?"

"You must find it and its purpose on your own. Now close your eyes and leave our realm. Your presence brings darkness."

I obeyed.

Shay placed her finger on the center of my forehead, her touch making my body weightless. She spoke my name, but coming from her lips, the word sounded like a gentle breeze. "We'll meet again someday soon. Good-bye, Ruby."

CHAPTER 8

THE STEAMBOT

NORA'S GREEN EYES DULLED WITH WORRY, AND I FLINCHED when her fingers brushed against my forehead. "You're burning up," she said, her ears drooping. "Must've been *some* dream you were having."

I brushed my fingers against the spot where Shay had touched me, my heart still racing from the vividness of it. Every part of the dream felt real, including Shay. Was there really a twin gem in the castle somewhere? If there was, I wouldn't know where to begin searching for such a small item in a massive castle.

"It was a heck of a dream. Sorry I woke you," I apologized, rubbing my forehead.

"It's fine. We should get ready to go," Nora answered, tightening her beige corset. "I need to help Benny get his food since my mom is going to be helping out in the kitchen. Don't our classes start today?"

I nodded, letting out a groan. The last place I wanted to be was in class, but if I had to go, then I might as well look good. I slipped into a pair of tight black trousers, paired with black boots and a forest-green tunic that matched the ends of my hair.

After Nora took care of her little brother, we met up in the great hall and sat down by the fireplace with bowls of porridge. I wrinkled my nose at the sludge, but my hunger pains won, and I slurped most of it down in one gulp, earning dagger eyes from Nora.

"Why are you staring at me like that?" I asked, wiping warm porridge from the corner of my mouth. I set the bowl down with an echoing clunk.

"I've never seen anyone eat as fast as you do. Did Arthur not teach you any manners?" She shook her head in disapproval, her tone playful.

Huffing, I picked up a spoon. Without taking my eyes off her, I took a small bite. "This work for you?"

"Better," Nora answered with a grin. "No one is going to fancy you if they see you eating like that."

I snorted. "Don't care." Boys rarely ever crossed my mind. I spent so much of my time running for my life with Arthur and Fang that I didn't have a spare moment to give much thought to boys. Even Fang was only a friend. Well—more like a brother.

"You never know. The right guy might come along." Nora waggled her eyebrows at me, her hips swishing in her seat.

I cast a glance towards a few of the tables nearest to us. "Sorry to disappoint you, but none of these men strike my fancy." My eyes remained on a particularly stout man who lifted a leg and let one rip.

"You just haven't seen them all yet," Nora argued.

Arthur, dressed in brown, durable armor, stopped by our table, a bowl in his hands. "Mornin'."

"Morning, Arthur. You're looking sharp today," I greeted. "Any word from Rorik?"

"I'm afraid nothing yet. I'll let you know as soon as I hear anything." He said, bending down to hug me. "I wish I had better news."

My pulse quickened, and I couldn't help but feel disappointed. "Hopefully soon."

After he departed, a flicker of movement drew my attention to the back of the great hall, near the tower. The wooden entrance to the tower opened, and a boy with light brown hair slipped inside, disappearing into what I assumed was Alden's office. I didn't know why I noticed him, but something about him felt… strange, sending a chill through me. Before I could get up to follow him, Alden emerged, his posture slumped as he stalked to the podium. His mechanical bird flew in sporadic circles behind the podium, clicking its beak in a rather obnoxious manner.

Alden's withered face was unsmiling. "Don't forget that classes resume today. Ages five to eleven will meet in room twelve in the third corridor to your right, and ages twelve to nineteen will meet in room four in the corridor to your left after breakfast. That is all." With that, he returned to his office, a hollow echo resounding through the hall as he slammed the door behind him.

After breakfast, Nora led the way to our classroom. "It'll be a nice change to have normalcy in our lives, don't you think?"

"I can think of other things we could do," I said, dreading class. "Like exploring the castle."

"As tempting as that sounds, I really want to see what this class is all about. We could use the distraction from what's going on in the other realms."

Room number four greeted us as we turned a corner, and slowly, we opened the heavy door. Nora grabbed my arm, both of our jaws dropping in stunned silence. Standing inside the classroom was a steambot like the one in the storage room.

"Alden could've warned us that a machine would be in here," Nora hissed as we sat down.

The steambot was a careful patchwork of copper and iron, with barrels and pipes welded into something resembling limbs and twin spinning wheels for eyes. It walked alongside our desks, the sides of its face folding up into a smile with a creaking sound as steam rolled off it in a mechanical *whoosh*. The classroom itself was small but came with a view of the courtyard and icy gardens. More people spilled into the classroom, and I recognized the dirty-blonde-haired boy I sat with on the day I arrived at Leavenfell. He walked to a seat in front of my desk, knitting his brows as he sat down, a mischievous familiarity about him.

"Where've you been?" he asked, unzipping his black leather jacket.

"Around," I answered, smiling at him. "You?"

"Helping my mom in the kitchen. I'm Peter, by the way." He extended his hand, and I shook it.

"Rue," I replied.

He opened his mouth to respond, but the steambot interrupted him by smacking into the side of his desk.

"Good day. I am SteamBot Seventy-seven, your teacher." The

steambot sounded exactly like it looked—vintage and mechanical. The bot told everyone that they needed to reintroduce themselves since we were new to the class, and also told us to disclose our gifts, which had me biting the inside of my cheek. Being born without a gift wasn't something I was keen on sharing.

A pair of twins with black hair and bronze skin introduced themselves as Olivia and Oliver. Oliver was slightly taller, and they were fifteen years old. They had the gift of telepathy, but Olivia stated that it only worked between the two of them. Still, I couldn't help but envy them, or anyone who'd been born with a gift.

My attention shifted back to the bot as it paced around the room, drowning nearby students in clouds of smoke. Was Alden's magic involved with making the machine appear alive? Magic or not, there was something disturbingly human about its movements.

During my turn, I faced the back of the classroom and quickly introduced myself by name but left out the part about being giftless. Thankfully, the steambot didn't press for any more information.

When I turned to sit down, a boy was standing beside Peter's chair, his back to my face.

"Sorry I'm late," the boy apologized. "My name is Lance and I'm almost nineteen. This is my brother, Peter—"

"I can speak for myself," Peter interrupted, smoothing his dark studded pants as he stood up. Peter was a bit shorter than Lance, his hair a wavy mess atop his head.

"I'm seventeen and single," Peter continued, locking eyes with Nora and grinning at her, not an ounce of shame in sight. Nora's cheeks reddened as she shifted her gaze away from him.

"Peter, sit down," Lance snapped, yanking at his brother's jacket sleeve.

A strange sensation bubbled in my chest when Lance spoke, and I found myself stealing glances at the back of his head. My bite scar twinged, the ache pulsing beneath my skin like a warning.

"Before anyone asks, I don't have a gift," Peter added with confidence, like that fact had no emotional impact on him. He sat down and elbowed Lance, shaking his head at him.

I shifted towards Lance again, who'd faced in my direction. My breath caught when his wide eyes met mine, and in that moment, something primal inside me broke free. I clenched my teeth. My insides twisted as a magnetic sensation rushed through me, dragging me towards him with such unbearable intensity that I wanted to throw up.

Like his younger brother, Lance had a lean build, his toned muscles evident underneath his white tunic. A few strands of his platinum hair had loosened from his hair tie, curtaining his blue-green eyes. I resisted the urge to reach out and touch him, folding my hands into my lap instead. My cheeks burned, and I sank into my chair.

Lance sat down, barely sparing me a glance. The magnetic feeling dulled and I breathed a sigh of relief.

"You okay?" Nora asked, lightly touching my arm.

I nodded even though my scar twinged again. *What's wrong with me?*

I didn't have time to think about it too much, because Peter let out a low whistle as a girl named Liessa rose to her feet. Her dark blonde hair cascaded down her back in thick waves and mossy green eyes complimented her rosy cheeks. The pink corset she wore accentuated her curves. She refused to disclose her gift to the class and made a point to ignore Peter.

Taking the hint, Peter leaned towards Nora instead. "Hey, how about we —"

"Knock it off, Peter," Lance interrupted. "I don't wanna explain to mom why you got kicked out of class again."

Peter snapped his mouth shut and faced the front of the room, his ears turning pink. I concealed a smile behind my hand while Nora snickered. The rest of the class made quick introductions, most having normal gifts like super hearing or telekinesis. Over the years, I'd learned that most mortals were born with smaller, less useful gifts. Besides Fang, who had the gift of blinking. He'd been a rare exception.

The steambot grabbed a stack of books and placed one on every desk. Puffs of steam clouded the room as it made its way to each person. I glanced at the book and sighed. *History of Fennra*.

"Why aren't we learning about magic?" Peter bellowed, shooting up in his chair. He dropped the book from his hand like it was poison. Lance hushed him, but the steambot moved to the front of his desk.

"No magic instruction yet. Alden rules," The steambot replied.

I sank into my chair, pressing my fist to my mouth in annoyance. Fennra's geography was already burned into my brain. Years ago, Arthur had taught me that Fennra was one of the eight recognized realms within Fogstone Kingdom, and Fennra was one of the only two realms that held the human race. Every single realm in Fogstone had its own separate ruler, but most were without kings. Talem and Gardenia were Fennra's neighbors, while most other realms could be accessed by journey or portals.

"You've got to be kidding me," muttered Nora through gritted teeth. "I hoped they'd at least introduce magic."

"Wish you'd accepted my offer of ditching, huh," I joked.

"I'll skip if that means we can hang out," Peter said, facing us.

Nora's ears drooped as she gave him a skeptical look. "And do what exactly?"

"Just hang out," he said with a sincere smile. "Unless you'd rather get into trouble."

I leaned towards him, tempted to flick his nose. "I'm sure we'd rather face the Volings than get into the kind of trouble you're implying."

Lance turned towards me, his face so close that I could feel his breath on my skin. "It's best to ignore him. Attention only encourages his antics."

"I — Yeah. Okay." I stumbled over my words and averted eye contact, face flushing. "Duly noted."

The magnetic pull tugged on my chest again and our eyes locked. This pull — it was like a bond of some sort, but how in the hells could I be bonded to someone I didn't know? The room tilted, my pulse thrumming like a drum. I shook my head, my mind fuzzy. I'd never reacted to anyone this way before, not even Fang.

The steambot made its way back to the desk and bent down to sit in the chair, but it ended up freezing in a weird position. "T-t-turn to page s-s-s-seven in your b-book."

Groans echoed around the classroom as we began to study the history of Fennra.

CHAPTER 9

THE HIDDEN CORRIDOR

THE FIRE BLAZED AND CRACKLED, SPREADING A BLANKET OF heat over the great hall. Many red-faced guards huddled near the fireplace, warming their hands and their back sides.

Shortly after Olivia and Oliver joined us at our table, Arthur stopped by, muttering hello and setting a plate in front of me. He quickly walked away, his shoulders tense. I worried about him. The man had been ridiculously busy the moment we stepped foot into this castle.

"How long have you and your brother lived here?" Nora asked Olivia.

"A couple years," said Olivia. "We're from Talem, but our parents prefer Fennra. They work around the castle in exchange for living quarters. My mom helps with the farming and our dad works on guard duty. What about you?"

Nora happily relayed her life story to Olivia while I scanned the great hall for Lance and Peter. I spotted them exiting the kitchen quarters and stopping by the buffet for food. Oliver returned and listened to Nora's story with interest.

"Excuse me," a soft voice interrupted. Everyone looked up at the same time.

Willow. I'd missed her introduction in class, but from what Nora had told me, she was Liessa's younger, giftless sister. Willow's pale white hair caught the firelight, her lovely freckles soft and familiar.

"Over here, Willow!" Oliver waved at her. His beaming face said it all—he was crushing on her. Willow excused herself and took a seat beside him, and they fell into conversation apart from everyone else.

Lance and Peter joined us at our table, and my bite scar twinged, a sharp sting crawling under my skin. I muttered a curse under my breath.

"Hungry?" Lance asked, pointing to my empty plate. Arthur must've been distracted while grabbing it for me.

My stomach growled in response.

"My mom gave me an extra sandwich from the kitchen. Here, take it." He extended a large bread roll packed with various meats and cheeses.

"Thank you," I said, accepting the sandwich, the magnetic pull intensifying. *Does he feel the pull too or am I going crazy?*

"No problem," he replied.

After I finished half the sandwich and wrapped the other half into a napkin, Peter smacked his hands against the table and stood up, nearly causing me to drop the sandwich.

"Where are you going?" Lance asked with a weary tone, as if he was used to this.

Peter smoothed his messy hair back and searched the room

until he found the table where Liessa and her raven-haired friend were sitting. "To try my luck with those two."

Lance exhaled and put a hand over his face but said nothing in response.

"I'm pretty sure she was glaring at you earlier," Nora said.

Peter stared at her, his expression blank. He shrugged and wandered off mid-bite.

"I'm sorry about him," Lance said. "He's stubborn. I honestly don't know where he gets it."

"You don't have to apologize," said Olivia, her brown eyes softening whenever Lance looked at her.

"So where are you guys from?" I asked.

"We lived in Felroc over a decade ago, but after it was overrun by Volings, we ended up at Leavenfell. Alden offered us a place to stay, and the rest is history," Lance replied. Lance's family must've had wizard blood in their genes, but I didn't recall Lance mentioning a gift or any sort of magical abilities.

"What's your story?" Lance asked, his hands clasped underneath his chin.

I hesitated, unsure how to answer him. My parents were dead. Sullivan wanted me dead. My best friend was presumed dead, although I refused to believe it, and I had an old caretaker that saw to it that I didn't end up dead. It was an exhausting life, if anything.

"I was born in Fleurya, but other than that, there's not much worth telling," I finally responded.

"So you're a girl of mystery," said Lance with a thoughtful grin.

That was one way to put it.

I stopped to see Arthur, who was near the gatehouse by the entrance of the castle. He was out of breath and unorganized, dropping tons of documents to the ground and cursing when the wind carried them away. Eyes heavy, he raised his fist at the sky, his expression defeated. I offered him the other half of my sandwich, which he graciously accepted, then we hugged and separated.

Since he was busy and I had free time, I wanted to investigate Shay's claims about finding the twin gem within the castle, which I suspected was tied to Alden's note, but first, I needed to grab Nora. She'd been begging to come along on my next adventure, and I wanted the company, especially after those creepy noises followed me the last time.

"Good book?" I asked, finding her by the fireplace in the great hall.

Nora glanced up briefly before dropping her gaze back to the page she was reading. "Not my favorite, but it'll do."

"Good. Put the book down so we can explore the castle."

Nora set the book down and joined my side.

"Is that the same bird from before?" she asked, pointing towards the entrance to the great hall.

I followed the direction of her finger, spotting that mechanical bird perched atop the wooden door. Its emerald eyes were glowing.

"Yup, same one."

"I remember it flying out of that storage room. Alden should keep a better eye on his creations," Nora said.

"I say we follow the bird."

"Why?"

"Just a hunch." No way was I telling her about the creature outside our window.

When we approached the small bird, it clicked its beak and flew out of the great hall. We kept pace with it as it led us past the gatehouse, through various corridors, and stopped in front of a carved door that stood to the left of the chapel entrance. A small, odd blemish on the wall beside the door caught my eye.

The mechanical bird pecked the blemish with its beak. The blemish rumbled, strong enough that the floor began to quake, and a large crack opened in the wall, increasing in size until we stood in front of a crevice large enough for us to pass through.

"What the hells just happened?" Nora asked, her eyes widening.

"No idea." I inched towards the mysterious crevice and squeezed myself through. Once I crossed to the other side, I stumbled into a tall arched door. The crevice quaked again, expanding into a full-blown corridor, as if it had always been there in the first place.

Nora entered the space with me, her ears pointing straight up as she took in her surroundings. The mechanical bird flew to the doorknob and began pecking it. There were symbols etched into the door, resembling an old language I couldn't read.

Intrigued, I shooed the bird away, grabbed the doorknob, and twisted, but the door wouldn't budge. I knelt down to examine the knob. The keyhole was way too small to fit the key I kept in my nightstand.

"I think the bird is trying to tell us something," Nora said, her eyes following the bird to where it landed atop the door frame.

"Wouldn't be the first time," I admitted, briefly explaining how the bird led me to a key. "How are we going to get through this door?"

Nora knelt beside me. "It's easy to open if you know how to pick a lock." She pulled a pin from her hair and glanced up. "There's a sign above that says *Keep Out*."

"That's never stopped me before."

Nora grinned. "Well then, watch and learn." She stuck the pin into the keyhole, fiddling with the lock.

"Noralei!" a voice behind us called. "I've been searching all over for you." Mr. Moore came storming up behind us. He was panting, sweat dripping off his forehead when he came to a stop in front of us.

Nora discreetly slipped the hairpin into my hand.

"My apologies, Ruby, but I need to steal Nora from you for a little while. It won't take long," Mr. Moore explained when he caught sight of my mortified expression.

"What now?" Nora whined.

"Your mother needs help with the kitchen clean-up. Mrs. Baker has suddenly fallen ill so she had to leave."

Once they were gone, I stuck the pin into the keyhole, fiddling with the stubborn lock until it clicked.

"Yes!" I fist-pumped, surprised by my lock-picking accomplishment. Nora would be proud. Taking one last cautious look behind me, I pushed the creaky door open and crossed through the entryway.

A cold gust hit my face. Darkness blinded me as I searched

the walls in search of any viable source of light. I located a switch and sconces along the walls roared to life, illuminated my surroundings, unveiling an enormous winding staircase in the middle of a rather drafty, empty room. Staring upwards, I followed the height of the staircase, but it faded into darkness the higher it ascended.

It made no logical sense, but the staircase had to end somewhere. I swore under my breath and grabbed hold of the handrail, ascending the monster one step at a time. By the time I reached the top, my teeth were chattering.

Clouds of mist spilled from my lips, swallowed by the darkness of the endless corridor ahead of me. Hazy light hovered over the corridor like fog over the sea. My breath hitched in my throat as I wrapped my arms around myself in an attempt to deter the chill. The air was thick… and it was quiet. Abnormally so.

I took a step forward, growing increasingly nervous as the foggy light blinked in and out of existence. The air chill increased the further I walked, until my whole body was shivering. The bird screeched from somewhere behind me, but it sounded miles away.

Without warning, I smacked into an invisible wall, hitting it so hard that my breath caught. I yelped, rubbing my sore nose. With stars in my vision, I stared ahead, but the path in front of me looked like miles of corridor. Absolutely nothing else was in front of me. Nothing but a dark tunnel.

Eyebrows furrowed, I walked forward, but again I was stopped by an invisible force.

Magic.

It must be.

I extended my fingers forward until they touched the invisible wall. White-gold shock waves streaked from the center of the invisible wall to either side of the corridor, like mini lightning bolts.

My suspicions were right. It was a magical barrier, like the one around Leavenfell Castle. Anyone looking at it would see nothing but miles of open ocean and a cliffside... no castle, no clock tower. Something important—or *dangerous*—had to be behind this barrier. Goose bumps danced along my spine. I wouldn't have found this place if not for Alden's note.

I brushed my fingertips against the barrier, fascinated by the bolts of light streaking from side to side with every touch.

"How do I get through this?" I pondered out loud. "There's gotta be something." I tried multiple approaches—pushing it, punching it, running into it again, only to end up with a headache. After many failed attempts, I sunk to the floor in defeat. There was no way Alden wasn't hiding something behind this barrier.

Exhausted, I stared at the wall again and grazed it with my fingers. My hands went still. When the shock waves rippled through the barrier, a keyhole came into focus. When the ripples disappeared, so did the keyhole. I swore under my breath, excited about my discovery and pissed off that I didn't bring the key with me.

Nora would be pleased to discover I found something, and that bird—the bird knew things. The creature's warning from before about following a bird... this must have been what it meant! That, or it was the friend Alden sent to help me. His note solidified my suspicions.

Sheer excitement coursed through me, my heart electric, as I turned on my heel and retraced my steps to the massive staircase, running as fast as my legs would carry me. I was certain the key would unlock the magic barrier. Whatever Alden wanted me to find had to be hidden behind it.

"Find anything interesting behind that door?" Nora asked, snapping her book shut when I entered the room with trembling limbs and the dire need for rest. I crashed onto my bed.

"A staircase that led to a very long corridor." The words spilled from my lips with excitement.

"Did you find any interesting trinkets?" she asked.

"You won't believe this, but I ran into some kind of magic barrier." I pointed at my forming bruise, as if that was all the proof she needed. "I couldn't get through it to the other side, but I think I might have figured it out. The key that bird led me to. It looks like it'd be a perfect fit."

I yawned. Magic, in any form, was draining to all mortals—a hard lesson I'd learned from Sullivan.

"That sounds crazy," Nora said, but her tone had shifted from boredom to interest. "But I believe you, so promise me you'll take me with you next time. I want to see it for myself."

"Promise," I said, a hundred thoughts racing through my mind. How did Alden keep this castle running with so much magic? He couldn't be a normal wizard.

Multiple raps sounded at the door. Nora opened it and the mechanical bird with emerald eyes flew inside, landing by my bedside. It dropped a small piece of parchment tied to a small white gem on my nightstand, its brilliant eyes watching me. With a content click, it folded its delicate, metal legs in half and lowered itself down to rest.

My eyes widened as I forced my tired body to sit up. I leaned over my bedside and grabbed the note and the gem, staring at the gem first. My mouth fell open. It was an *exact* replica of the gem Shay had fastened around her neck. I picked up the note and read it.

The key might lead to answers.

There was no signature on the small piece of parchment. I skimmed the writing a couple times before stuffing the note into my nightstand. *Did Alden send this?*

"Where did you get these?" I asked the bird. It chirped happily in response.

Nora sat on the bed beside me. "What is that?"

"I saw this gem in a dream," I answered.

Nora gaped at me. "You did not."

I handed her the gem. "I swear."

She turned it over in her palm, examining it. "How's that possible?"

"I don't know, but it has to mean something." I took the gem back from Nora and placed it inside my nightstand drawer. Determination built inside of me. I was going to find out what that note meant and what the gem was all about.

My thoughts shifted to that heated gaze Alden and I had shared in the great hall. I suspected the note and gem were tied to the prophecy. His expression also made me wonder if I was involved with the prophecy.

"Maybe we can go after class tomorrow," she suggested, returning to her own bed. "Do you really think we'll get answers for all this?"

"Maybe, especially if Alden's behind it. What if he's trying to tell me something?" I stared at the mechanical bird, who had fallen into slumber.

"If one of his birds is bringing you things, then he must be involved, but promise me you'll include me. I'm too curious now," Nora said, her eyes glued to her book as she spoke.

"Promise," I replied.

I watched the little bird until I fell asleep.

CHAPTER 10

BLACKOUT

THE GEM LAY COLD IN MY HAND AS I OBSERVED IT FROM EVERY angle, willing the damn thing to do something. It hummed softly, a faint echo of a whisper, but that was the extent of it. Frustrated, I placed the gem back into the drawer of my nightstand, deciding that I'd revisit it later.

The mechanical bird was still there when I woke up. It preened its creaking copper wings and ignored me until I greeted it. There were a few screws and scraps of metal underneath the bird that I hadn't noticed before. A nest of sorts. I glanced at my dresser drawers. Some screws were missing. *That little shit…*

A smile tugged at my lips. "You're a funny little thing, but I'd appreciate it if you didn't destroy my things," I said. "I think I'll call you Puko. Is that okay with you?"

The mechanical bird chirped in response, utterly delighted.

When we made it to the great hall, we were greeted by the savory smell of roasted beef. I headed in the direction of the buffet when my scar burned, the pull drawing me in the opposite direction. I followed the direction of the pull and found Lance waving us over from another table. *Of course.* This confirmed the pull was coming from him.

"Rue! Nora! Over here." He gestured at the extra plates on the table, already filled with delicious food, thanks to the tireless farm workers who worked in the greenhouse and barn, both attached to the back of the castle. I hadn't seen them in person yet, but I'd heard a few residents speaking of it while passing by one morning. One man had mentioned that Alden had a few wizards working the greenhouse to ensure the crops grew faster using magic, since snowfall was a common occurrence in Fennra.

A cautious smile stretched across Lance's angular face as we walked over, his eyes crinkling at the corners.

"How was your day?" I asked, getting as close as the pull would allow me.

"Not too bad," Lance replied. "I helped my mom get a lot done in the kitchen today. Figured I could grab you both a plate before I left."

"That's really nice of you," Nora said in between bites of food.

"Thank you! And thank your mom too. I'm sure she works hard," I replied. I dug in right away, savoring every bite of the perfectly spiced meat. I hated that I was enjoying food this delicious without Fang. He would have devoured this, especially after the nasty food we'd eaten at the Helm.

"Not a problem," Lance replied.

Throughout dinner, the pull ebbed and flowed with Lance's movements, and I winced when it got too intense. Lance kept a guarded smile while we spoke, and Peter was shockingly quiet, too busy shoveling food into his mouth like it was the last meal he was ever going to eat. I stared at him, both impressed and disgusted.

"Ignore him," Lance said when he caught me gawking at Peter. "He doesn't know what table manners are."

A smile tugged at my lips. "He's not bothering me."

Nora giggled. "Ruby used to slurp her food right off a plate until I taught her how to use a fork. It's like she was raised by wolves."

"Rue," I corrected her sheepishly, rubbing my burning left shoulder. The scar erupted with heat.

"Pretty name," Lance complimented, his blue-green eyes accentuated by his dark green trench coat.

"Thanks," I muttered. I stopped liking my full name after a particularly painful punishment from Sullivan. He'd always called me Ruby whenever he yelled at me. Ever since then, I told Arthur and Fang to call me Rue.

When I finished eating, I picked up my plate with the intention of returning it to the kitchen, but something inside me shifted and I plopped back down, sensing an oncoming attack. Within seconds, my body stiffened and I doubled over, resisting the urge to throw up and clenching my fists against my aching legs. I was hot and cold all at once, sweating and shivering as I folded in on myself. My scar burned with greater intensity.

"Everything okay?" Nora asked.

When her fingers brushed my skin, I trembled, shaking my head. Sweat dotted my forehead as pain spread across my limbs.

"What's going on?" Nora whispered, leaning her head towards me. "Effects from the magic barrier?"

"I need to lie down," I told her through gritted teeth, my jaw clenched as I remained as calm as possible. Every nerve was on fire, the pain so intense I was on the brink of passing out. *Voling's ass... not now.*

"Arthur? Where's Arthur?" Nora asked, her tone alarmed. She stood, but I caught her arm.

"Don't bother him. It'll pass." I drew in another deep breath, convincing myself I'd be okay. "It always passes." I'd been through this before many times, but this was on a whole other level—so much more intense. I was scared. Scared that the scar on my shoulder meant something. I'd been trying to avoid that thought for a long time. Maybe these damned symptoms were linked to the bite scar. *Exactly what kind of Voling had bitten me?*

Nora placed her hand on my back. "Let's go back to our room. Sleep it off if you can."

I gave her a stiff nod, hoping sleep would help.

By this point, everyone at the table was gawking at us. Olivia stared at me, her expression a mixture of fear and shock, her bronze skin taking on an abnormal pallor. She opened her mouth but promptly shut it again. A buzz of whispers reached my ears.

"Everything okay?" Lance asked. I couldn't look him in the eyes.

"Rue's not feeling well, so we're going to call it a night." Nora grabbed my arm and helped me up. I thanked the gods for her. If she hadn't helped me, my face would have made introductions with the floor.

Peter pushed his plate of food away, sticking his tongue out. "Don't tell me it's the food. Because I'm doomed if it is."

"It's not the food," Olivia snapped. "Stop being dumb, Peter."

I glanced at Olivia, who was staring at me in horror, as though she feared me. Another wave of pain hit, and realization slowly dawned on me that the battle to make it back to my room was going to be difficult. I lost my balance and fell, dragging

Nora to the floor with me. Lance helped me up, putting his arm underneath mine to support me. I moaned in pain, my bones cracking and splitting, rendering me into pieces.

"Just show me to your room," Lance told Nora. "Peter, go find the healer."

I stumbled, but Lance's grip around me tightened.

"It's a walk, so be prepared," Nora warned.

I quivered. Another bone cracked, but no one seemed to hear it. Stars dotted my vision, and shooting pain dashed down the back of both of my legs. My back arched and stiffened.

"I've got you," Lance said, but his voice was muffled, as if he was talking underwater.

My head swam and we were no longer moving forward. Everything around me froze in place, my vision blurring in and out of focus.

Alden appeared in my peripheral vision, swiftly approaching me with his great staff held out in front of him and a terrifying expression on his face. He mumbled something unheard as he locked eyes with me.

Darkness welcomed me into its arms.

Arthur was at my bedside pressing a cool washcloth against my forehead. I opened my eyes, my surroundings blurry and sounds muffled as I came to. My skin burned, but the shattering feeling was gone.

"You have an awful fever," he told me, face pinched with worry. He was dressed in his armor, the padding pressing against my legs. "You're lucky that your friends came to get me after you passed out."

I forced myself up, fighting the weakness in my limbs and completely mortified that I *had* passed out—in front of the *entire* great hall. "You're kidding?"

"You're sick. It's not your fault." Arthur cast a glance at the door behind him, sighing. "Your friends were quite worried, especially Nora. I told her to stay with her family tonight. I didn't want her to catch any sickness you might have. Oh, and..." His eyes fell to my lap. I followed his gaze, spotting the white gem.

How did he get this? Did Puko retrieve it for him?

"That gem is a talisman. It stopped the symptoms you were experiencing," Arthur stated. "Very curious object. Your little bird friend dropped it on my lap as soon as I arrived."

Aha. Of course it was the bird.

Arthur stared off, miles away. "Very curious." He shifted until he was comfortable and met my eyes again. "When the bird—"

"Puko," I corrected him.

Arthur cracked a smile. "When Puko dropped it onto my lap, I felt its magic, but again, how?" Arthur studied me, his expression hardening. "How did you get this to begin with?"

I looked at the bird, who was busy adding string to his nest, then returned my gaze to Arthur. His eyes shifted to the bird, bright with curiosity. Arthur said nothing else. He was lost in the confines of his own thoughts while I racked my brain trying to understand what had happened. I debated telling Arthur about my dream with Shay and the late-night encounter with what I assumed was a Voling outside my window.

The fact that I saw the gem in a dream and now had an exact

replica, given to me by a mechanical bird, baffled me. Arthur would laugh at me if I told him that story. Then again, stranger things have happened.

Arthur raised an eyebrow at me and picked up the gem, turning it over in his hand. "Regardless of how you got this, you should hold onto it. In case what happened tonight happens again." Arthur placed the gem back into my hand, his expression resolved.

I closed my fist around the gem. Now was as good a time as any to explain what had been going on with me.

"Arthur, I've been feeling off lately, even more than normal."

"I know," Arthur said, shadows crossing his face.

"There's something else," I continued. "My scar has been burning whenever I'm around this guy I met in class. And there's this strange pull. I can't describe it, but it won't go away." *Might as well tell him everything.* "I was hoping you could tell me what it is."

Arthur's face paled.

"What?!" I asked, my voice rising as I took in his alarming demeanor.

"Nothing." Arthur stood, as though in a sudden hurry. He never liked discussing my symptoms. "I need to go." He was at the door before I could blink. "I'm late for my next shift."

"Arthur, wait!" I called, my hands shaking.

"We'll catch up later. I'm sorry."

And then he was gone, leaving me with more questions than answers.

CHAPTER 11

THE PASSAGEWAY WITH CLOCK FACE DOORS

I WISHED I COULD DISAPPEAR FOR A DAY. OR A MONTH. However long it took to get over my embarrassment. Nora returned to our bedroom following class, sitting down beside me while I organized my clothes and belongings, storing them in a wooden chest. She wore a frilly blue dress, the front revealing ample cleavage. Her red hair was braided into fishtails.

"Hey," I grumbled.

Nora sighed. "Cheer up. No more sulking allowed."

I crossed my arms. "I'm probably the laughingstock of Leavenfell Castle by now."

Nora narrowed her eyes. "That's not true. If anything, you gave us all a huge scare when you blacked out. You should've seen the look on Lance's face when you went limp in his arms."

I buried my face into my hands, cringing. I *would* black out in *his* arms of all people. "I could've gone the rest of my life without knowing that."

"You couldn't help it," Nora reassured. "It isn't a big deal, I promise you."

I hated showing weakness. I hated weakness, period. I wanted to be the one that took care of everyone else. That's how it'd always been with Fang and Arthur. We took care of each other, but I was always the first one to hear approaching footsteps, or the rustling of leaves at night when everyone else was sleeping. I was the one that alerted Arthur when it was time to move locations. Somehow, I could always sense danger before it was upon us, though Sullivan was an exception. During our travels, I caught the first scent of blood on the roads and knew which areas to avoid. I'd never passed out.

And now everyone saw me *slip*.

I let out a nervous laugh. "Even Alden saw me."

"Alden?" Nora's expression crunched with confusion. "I'm pretty sure he wasn't there."

"What? I definitely saw him."

"I'm telling you he *wasn't* there. You were probably hallucinating," Nora said.

My confusion deepened. "Yeah, maybe I did."

"Are you feeling better now?" Nora asked. "Enough fluids in your system?"

I straightened my back and tightened my fist around the gem. A burst of energy rushed through my veins. Shay had been right. The gem was useful for something. If I ever got the chance to meet her again, I'd ask her about it.

"If you're up to it, how about we go on an adventure? It'll take your mind off things," Nora suggested when I didn't respond.

I arched my brow. "I can't say no to a good adventure." I

retrieved the mysterious key from my nightstand and discreetly tucked the gem back into the drawer.

"Is this the key Puko led you to?" Nora asked.

I nodded and placed the key in her hands, alleviating her curiosity. "I think it'll unlock that barrier. The one behind that magic door we found before your dad whisked you away."

"I still can't get past the barrier—*inside* the castle of all places."

I let out an exasperated sigh. "Come on. It's better if I show you."

When Nora and I made it to our destination, the crack in the wall had disappeared. Instead, the short corridor with the tall arched door was there and the Keep Out sign was still posted.

"You know, I'm really not loving this," Nora admitted as we crossed into the room past the sign. "It's way too dark in here for my liking."

"This is nothing compared to what's upstairs."

"Is it too late to turn around?" Nora asked.

"Do you want to see the barrier or not? Better yet, what's behind it?" I asked. "Don't be a scaredy cat." There was Fang speaking through me again.

Nora pressed her lips together and side-eyed me but agreed to keep going. I flipped the switch up, flooding the room with dim lighting.

"What the hells is that?" Nora gasped, pointing at the giant staircase, her fingers trailing upwards as if she was calculating how far it ascended.

"Prepare for the climb of your life," I warned her. "Shall we?"

"Lead the way."

When we reached the pinnacle of the staircase, we stared ahead, unsure what to do next. Sconces dotted the walls, giving off enough light so we could see the miles of corridor that stretched endlessly in front of us, but the sconces hadn't been there before. This place was full of magic, so much so that I could feel the energy brushing against my skin, startling me.

"What is this? And why is it so drafty up here?" Nora asked nervously.

"Wait until you see what's ahead," I answered, my voice echoing. "Come on. The barrier is—"

"What's that noise?" Nora interrupted, falling behind me. She crept backwards until her back was pressed against the wall.

"What noise?" I listened but heard nothing.

All color drained from Nora's face. "That... that whispering. You don't hear it? It's seriously freaking me out. We should leave."

I listened again, more carefully this time, but I only heard Nora's sporadic breathing.

"I don't hear anything," I told her truthfully, but the unsettling look on her face scared me.

Nora slid to the floor with her hands covering her ears. She pressed her trembling knees together and gave me another frightened look. The magic of the endless corridor beckoned me, almost like a whisper brushing against my ears. After I took another step forward, I stilled. *That sound...*

What Nora heard wasn't a whisper. It was a heartbeat—a racing heartbeat that steadily grew louder. I swiveled, realizing the sound was coming from *Nora* herself. My mouth parted, and I inhaled the intoxicating scent rolling off her skin. The sound continued to amplify with each passing second, the beat echoing in my head, until it was all I could hear. My scar blazed as I took a step towards her. Nora's lips were moving, but whatever she said fell on deaf ears.

The bittersweet scent of blood hung in the air, permeating the space around us. A lump hitched in my throat as I took another heavy step towards her. Her eyes widened in horror, but she sat still as a statue. Thick beads of sweat dripped down her neck. The beat of her heart matched the pace of my breath, and I fell deeper into a trance.

"Nora, I—" My lips stopped moving as her scent overwhelmed my senses again, lighting every inch of me on fire.

"What the hells, Rue!?" she yelled, holding her hands out in front of her. "If this is your idea of a joke, I don't find it funny."

I heard her. I wanted to listen, but my body wouldn't comply. I lunged at her. *Something* was whispering into my ear, telling me to rip into her throat.

Drink, an eerie voice said.

No. Stop. I thought, but my body wouldn't listen.

Nora punched at me as I pinned her against the wall, my throat dry as a bone. My lips parted, my breathing shallow. My lips grazed her soft, pulsing neck. Nora screamed and her balled fist contacted the side of my face. *Hard.*

I blinked back tears, my cheek stinging. I broke free of the trance, the scent of her blood dissipating and the sound of her heart slowing. I fell backwards and clutched at my aching throat, coughing hard.

"What the hells is wrong with you?" Nora cried, using her legs to scoot herself as far away from me as possible.

The haziness in my mind cleared as blood rushed to my head, my skin heating as I crawled forward. "Nora! I'm so sorry. I don't know what came over me." I reached for her, but she recoiled, adding more distance between us.

"Don't touch me!" she yelled, crossing her arms over her chest, as if warding off a monster. Tears streamed down her face.

"Something else was controlling me. I wasn't myself," I explained, my voice breaking. "I would never hurt you. I'm so sorry." My heart hammered against my chest. I searched her face, hoping she believed me. "Please say something," I begged.

Nora stood, her body tense as she straightened her back. "This corridor is cursed or—I don't know. Something isn't right about this place. That barrier is up for a good reason, Rue. It's not safe." Nora cast another hesitant glance my way, her lips parted like she was going to say something else, but then she turned, face pale, and raced towards the stairs.

"Nora, please wait!" I yelled after her, but she continued, her footsteps fading.

Biting my bottom lip, I listened until I heard nothing but the discomforting silence again. Nora was gone, and I didn't want to worsen the situation by chasing her down. Instead, I sank to the floor, my arms encircling my legs as I drew my knees to my chest. Nora was right. Maybe the corridor was bewitched after all. Although I was in control again, I still felt so… *off*.

Sighing, I rested my head against the barrier and brushed my fingertips against it, once again enraptured by the invisible keyhole flashing into view. I had to see what was on the other side, even if it was alone, and even if I was scared. I had to know. I retrieved the skeleton key from my pocket, brought myself to my knees, and shakily inserted it into the keyhole. When the magic barrier dissipated, a blinding light flooded the hallway, and an excruciating pressure struck me with such brute force that the back of my head crashed against the floor.

"Rue! Gods—what happened?" Lance sat before me, shaking my shoulders until my eyes snapped open. When I was alert, he helped me into a sitting position.

My hand darted into my pocket, finding it empty. *Dammit!* I'd forgotten the talisman. My body was trembling and weak from the expulsion of magic the corridor had flung at my face. I'd crossed a magical line and received my punishment. Deserved after what I'd done to Nora.

"Are you okay?" Lance asked.

I rolled my head back to look at him. "Never mind that. How did you find this place?" The pull hovered between us, and I winced when my scar twinged with pain.

"Nora told me where to find you," he replied. "Why were you unconscious? What happened?"

"I'm fine. I'm guessing she told you what happened," I said, despair pooling into me at the mention of Nora's name.

"She told me that you both came up here, but she got scared and left. She was worried when you didn't follow her. You know this corridor is off limits. Why are you up here?" Lance gave me a stern look that said I should know better than to break the rules. "There's a cracked Keep Out sign posted." He berated me the way he did with Peter. It was endearing in a way.

I pursed my lips. "I wanted to see what was up here."

Lance sighed and pinched the bridge of his nose. "It doesn't matter. I'm taking you back. You have a nasty bruise forming on your head that should get looked at and—"

"There was a barrier," I blurted, not wanting to leave. "It's gone now, though. And I had a key. The key! Where's the key?" I asked in panic, scanning the floor in a desperate attempt to find it.

"It's okay. I got it right here." Lance handed it to me, his hand lingering on mine. "I found it on the floor beside you." He pulled his hand back like I'd stung him. "What is this place?"

As if the corridor heard us, the candle sconces blazed brighter, illuminating our surroundings. A faint but eerie breath darted past us. Startled, I jumped to my feet and stepped backwards until I stumbled against Lance's chest. The barrier was gone, revealing a narrow corridor hiding something that I would've never believed if I hadn't witnessed it myself.

Five massive, round clock faces, attached to either side of the passageway, stood ahead. Two on the left, two on the right, and one at the end of the corridor. The one at the end of the corridor was hanging off the hinges and completely rusted. It was also missing an arm. The other four looked perfectly fine. If someone needed convincing that Alden was obsessed with clocks, this corridor would certainly do it.

"What in the..." Lance murmured. "I don't think we should be here."

"They're only clocks," I said, my gaze flickering towards him. "What are they going to do? Tick tock us to death?"

Lance's lips twitched. "I still don't think we should be here," he repeated. "It doesn't feel safe."

"Then leave," I instructed, but he didn't budge. Instead, he moved forward alongside me to examine the clocks.

The craftsmanship alone was impressive. The clock faces, made from solid marble and embedded with numerous tiny diamonds, gave off a glittery appearance. Black Roman numerals were deeply engraved onto the faces, and a knobby handle was connected to the middle of them. Almost like a doorknob. The hands of the clock face in front of me were both sitting on the Roman numeral twelve.

"This is amazing," I said, pressing my palms against the cool marble of the clock. "I wonder if they'll open." I grabbed the knob and twisted, but the clock door didn't budge.

"Huh. Maybe they're not doors," I said.

"Maybe they're just clocks," he suggested with a grin. "You know how Alden is."

"You're probably right," I giggled, thinking about the crazy old wizard, but if his note meant anything, then something had to be here. "Still—there's gotta be more to this." I strode to the first clock on the left side of the corridor and pulled at the handle weakly, not expecting anything—but the door rushed forward so hard and fast that I was thrust inside its depths without warning, Lance screaming my name behind me.

CHAPTER 12

THE CLOCKMAKER'S SON

THERE WAS A TERRIFYING MOMENT WHERE I WAS SUSPENDED in absolute nothingness, somewhere between time and space, before slamming face first onto a hard floor. Groaning in pain, I pushed myself up with my elbows, tasting blood on my tongue. *Shit.*

Arthur was going to kill me if he found out. Lecture me first, then kill me. I swiveled, taking in my surroundings. This had to be the strangest room I'd ever seen. The wood-paneled walls were adorned with all sorts of ticking clocks. Round clocks, square clocks, cuckoo clocks, owl clocks, grandfather clocks... every sort imaginable. Fatigue rolled through me, and my skin tingled, an indicator that this room was full of magic. *Great. Take all my energy, room. Damn you!*

Several mechanical birds, similar to Puko, flitted nearby before landing on a crooked, whimsical perch, their beaks clicking, as though in conversation amongst themselves. Their metal eyes, much different than Puko's emerald eyes, blinked rapidly as they observed me. It was clear by the way their wings flitted aggressively that they were not happy. Regardless, I found myself fascinated with the gears and parts that pieced them together.

Documents flew across the room, landing in a neat stack on a desk in a rounded corner. Hundreds of sheets littered the floor, sketches on each of them, most marked with blueprints resembling odd machinery. I snatched a few of the sheets, hoping to find clues about the prophecy, when a voice greeted me from the shadows.

"Who the hells are you?"

I whipped my head towards the voice, scattering the sheets across the floor. In the far corner of the room stood a boy who couldn't have been much older than me. The boy was fair-skinned, with medium-length, light brown hair that was layered and tucked behind his ears in a disheveled manner. His eyes were like burnished gold. Now that I thought about it, he must've been the boy I'd spotted entering Alden's office a week or so ago.

"Are you deaf?" the boy asked coldly, a scowl set across his face. "I asked for your name." He set a cup full of steaming tea down with more attitude than necessary.

"I heard you the first time you asked," I snapped, taken aback by the boy's demeanor. "The name's Rue."

The boy arched an eyebrow and gave me a sour look, the line of his jaw hardening. "Nice to make your acquaintance, Rue. Now leave." He pointed towards the door, glaring at me like I was his mortal enemy. His brows furrowed when I didn't get off my ass, but I had no intention of going yet, even if I was intruding on his space.

Instead, I crossed my legs and studied him, trying to memorize his face. He wore brown, clean-pressed pants and a blouse with half rolled-up sleeves. A gold pocket watch hung from his pants pocket, and a large diagram of a strange container holding a heart sat on an easel behind him. His hands were covered in ink, and he must've caught my notice, because he hid his hands behind his back.

I was struck with a sudden desire to know who he was and why he was hiding behind a strange clock door.

His lips were pressed together so tightly they were nearly white. "Am I going to have to throw you out of here?"

I uncrossed my legs and scowled at him. "You haven't told me your name."

The boy turned his back to me and picked up his cup, bringing it to his lips. "I don't see how that matters. I have no interest in knowing anything about you."

My mouth gaped. Never in my life had I been spoken to in such a way by a stranger. "It's only fair if you tell me yours, so if you wouldn't mind—"

"I do mind!" His tone carried a rigid sharpness, but as he cast a glance over his shoulder, there was something off about him. There was a hint of either vulnerability or uncertainty behind his gaze. I couldn't tell which.

I paused, unsettled by his attitude. "There was a note… I'm searching for something," I explained, hoping to appease him.

"Why would a note lead you here? Get out!"

I let out an exasperated sigh and forced myself towards the door. I turned back for a moment, taking him in one more time. His expression softened like he might have changed his mind, but only for a moment. That moment came and went, and he was back to glaring at me again. My shoulders tensed. What a complete waste of my time.

"I hope I don't run into you again," I said half-heartedly.

The boy paused, giving me a hesitant glance as he fully faced me. He laughed, but it wasn't friendly in the least bit.

"Likewise," he said.

The nerve of this guy!

Cursing under my breath, I thrust open the door, walked into the darkness, and stumbled right into Lance's arms. The clock door slammed shut behind me with a locking sound.

"You're still here?" I asked in disbelief.

"You were only gone for two seconds," Lance said, his chin dipping towards my face.

"I was gone longer than that," I corrected him. I'd been inside that room for at least five minutes.

Lance stared at me. "What was in there? I couldn't get the door to open."

"An asshole," I deadpanned, wanting to erase the boy's attitude from my memory.

"Who?"

"I don't know. He wouldn't tell me his name," I seethed. My blood was boiling, but I tried to think of it from the boy's perspective. I'd invaded his space, probably his room. I would likely be disturbed if something like that had happened to me. But it wasn't like I intended to encroach on his space. Still—his reaction was strange. I wished he'd at least told me his name. Regardless, Alden's note remained a mystery.

"Let's get out of here," Lance suggested, grabbing my hand. "It should be obvious by now why this place is off limits."

"No kidding. I'm right behind you."

When we made it back to my tower, we bumped into Arthur.

"Rue, there you are. I left something on your bed for..." Arthur stopped mid-sentence. My reflection caught my eye, revealing the disheveled mess I was. Arthur's arms tightened around his body as he bit his bottom lip, his eyes roaming from my clothes to our entwined hands.

"We were only exploring the castle." The words left my mouth in a rush. "Nothing else." Leave it to Arthur to suspect that I was off doing naughty things with a cute, older boy.

"Did something happen? Why are you such a mess?" Arthur asked suspiciously.

Did something happen? The most interesting thing since moving to this castle happened, but I sure wasn't going to tell him that. He'd blame Alden's note as soon as the words left my mouth.

Lance shot Arthur a nervous glance, releasing my hand. "I should get going."

"Smart boy," Arthur growled. "Don't let me catch you up here again."

Lance darted down the staircase, not daring to look behind him. He bolted like a bat out of Vol across the bridge and disappeared under the curtain of heavy snowfall.

"Arthur," I scolded, my skin heating. "He's only a friend."

"I'll ask you again. What happened?" Arthur enunciated every word slowly, giving me an odd look.

I almost attacked my new friend, found an enchanted corridor with clocks for doors. I discovered a mental, deranged boy. I wanted to tell Arthur but held my tongue.

"I'm fine, but you shouldn't be so mean to Lance. He didn't do anything wrong."

"I'm only concerned about you," Arthur said.

"I know you are."

Arthur placed a hand on my shoulder. "Never mind. Get some rest. You look like you need it."

He had no idea.

After we parted, I let out a strangled breath and went inside my room, my stomach full of frantic butterflies as I readied myself to confront Nora. The sound of running water greeted me behind the washroom door. I considered knocking and apologizing for what happened earlier, but I stopped myself, thinking about how I should explain everything to her. Maybe there were enchantments put in place that affected us, causing hallucinations. That would clear some things up, but the guilt pressed down harder than any spell.

Defeated, I flopped onto my bed, my arm hitting something hard. I glanced down, finding a small package on the edge of my bed with an old photograph atop it. I picked up the faded photo. It showed a man with tousled brown hair and glasses sitting at the tip of his nose. He had one arm wrapped around a woman with long black hair and light blue eyes. In his other arm, he held a small child. She looked about three or four years old, and her dimpled face had big eyes framed by chestnut waves. In one arm, she clutched an old, ragged teddy bear. I grabbed the package and opened it. Inside was the same teddy bear that the little girl was holding.

The note attached to it read: *I found this back at the Helm. Figured I should return it to you. — Arthur*

Clutching the bear, I dragged my eyes back to the photograph. I'd almost forgotten what my parents looked like. My father had gray eyes, very much like mine. *We looked so alike.* Seeing him again brought back a memory of the time we'd sneaked into a castle's kitchen in the middle of the night for a piece of strawberry cake. I'd been so young at the time, but the image of my father sharing the cake with me, his own face covered in red frosting, was something I'd never forget. It was the only memory that stuck with me before everything fell apart.

"Are they your parents?" Nora asked, hopping onto the mattress beside me.

"Yes," I replied, not taking my eyes off the photo.

"You look a lot like your father," she commented, a small smile painting her features. "You can tell they really loved you." There was a hint of jealousy in her tone that made me feel bad for her.

I set the picture on my nightstand and studied my reflection in the window, seeing the features on myself that resembled my father. Besides the green in my hair, there was no denying the similarities. A hard lump caught in my throat as I shifted away from Nora, wiping tears from my eyes. I'd barely spent a fraction of my life with my parents, yet I missed them all the same. They were always in the back of my mind, only brought to the surface when Arthur spoke fondly of them. Arthur had told me that my father used to work with an organization that fought against the Volings, which made me wonder if that was the reason behind my parents' deaths. But I didn't know that for sure, and Arthur always said it was best if I didn't know the details.

"You okay?" Nora lightly touched my arm.

"I'm fine," I answered, turning to face her. "I should be the one asking you if you're okay." I hung my head, afraid of how she would respond. When her eyes met mine, I flinched, half expecting her to yell at me again.

But Nora only smiled. "I'm great, although my head feels a little fuzzy." Her confused expression was a dead giveaway. She didn't remember a damned thing.

Dammit, Arthur. She probably let it slip to him about what had happened, which resulted in him using a memory charm. I made a mental note to ask him about it later.

A knock sounded, drawing our attention to the door.

"Who could that be at this hour?" I asked, glancing at the clock.

Nora strutted to the door, cracking it open and revealing a distraught Lance. His posture was stiff, as if he didn't know why he was here. The pull slammed into me full force and I bit down on my tongue, mystified by what it meant.

"Do you realize how late it is?" Nora snapped. "We're about to go to bed."

"I wanted to check on Rue." Lance rubbed the back of his head and slipped past her. I tensed as he knelt by my bedside, resting his elbows on the edge of my mattress. "I'm sorry for bolting earlier. I thought that man was about to end my life." Lance let out a small laugh.

"I promise Arthur doesn't bite. He's only being protective of me," I explained, gently setting the teddy bear by the unlit candlestick on my nightstand next to a sleeping Puko. Wind rattled the tower as sleet relentlessly pelted the glass windows. I peered outside, taking in the dark skies and the clouds, which were hanging lower than usual, black and unsettling. The cold seeped through the glass like lingering guilt, matching my current mood.

Lance touched my hand and the pull subsided. *That was weird.* "Are you okay?" He asked.

I glanced over my shoulder at him, taking note of the redness on his cheeks. "Sorry," I apologized. "I'm not ignoring you. I'm exhausted and have a lot on my mind right now." I grabbed his hand, and the magnetic connection diminished again, surprising me. *Huh.*

His cheeks flushed and he withdrew his hand.

"This whole day has been weird," I said, drawing my knees to my chest.

Nora yawned, stretching her arms over her head, "Well, I'm going to bed. I'm tired, so goodnight." She tucked herself under her blanket and went quiet. I gawked at her, concerned that she hadn't acknowledged what had happened in the hidden corridor, which further solidified my suspicions that Arthur was involved with her memory loss.

"I can go if you want me to," Lance said. He pushed himself up to go, his hesitance obvious, but I grabbed his hand, tightening my fingers around his palm. The pain in my scar melted away.

"I'm not telling you to leave."

"Really?" he asked, his free hand fiddling with the sleeve of his gray shirt.

I patted the spot next to me. Better the bed than the floor I supposed. When he was tucked in, I rested my head on the pillow beside him and closed my eyes, trying to ignore the way the pull lessened as he closed the distance between us. I had no idea what that meant. I draped my arm over his, melting in the warmth his presence provided. In a way, I was glad Lance was here. Fang had always slept in the same bed as me, and despite his obnoxious snoring and large size, his being there was more a comfort than anything.

My eyes grew heavy as I slipped underneath my thick comforter. Lance stretched his legs outward and laid his head on the pillow, so close to me that our noses barely touched. His eyes caught mine, and I could almost see the thoughts spinning behind his eyes. He was confused—that much was obvious, though I had no idea what about.

"Goodnight, Rue."

"Sleep well, Lance."

When fatigue took over, my last thought was not of Lance, but of the cold-hearted boy in the hidden corridor.

CHAPTER 13

—————

HARD TRUTH

NORA LAUNCHED HERSELF ONTO MY BED MUCH TOO EARLY IN the morning, earning a string of swear words from me as she pelted me with her pillow. Concern that she hadn't acknowledged what had happened yet lingered in the back of my mind.

"So… how did it go last night with Lance?" she asked, her tone amused. "I was surprised to find him still in your bed when I got up to use the washroom in the middle of the night."

In response, I threw a pillow at her head, which made her erupt into laughter.

I slung my arm around her shoulder. "Nothing happened. I was out like a light and when I woke up, he was gone."

Nora waggled her eyebrows. "You must like him though, don't you?"

"Not like that," I told her, though I wasn't fully certain what I felt. Besides the pull that drew me to Lance, I had more interest in the asshole behind the clock door. When I'd caught that flicker of vulnerability behind his eyes, I knew there had to be more to him than a cold exterior.

"Well, it's obvious he likes you," Nora said. "He's always watching you."

"I don't think I like him in a romantic sense."

"Sure." Nora rolled her eyes. "Whatever you say."

I nestled under the comforter, stretching my legs out in front of me, silently replaying the events of last night. My thoughts shifted to that boy. I wanted to know his name. What he liked. What kind of tea he was drinking. Why I hadn't seen him around the castle…

His image spilled into my mind with such vividness that it stole my breath. His golden eyes, half-hidden by light brown hair, glowed like molten honey under the flickering candlelight. The elegant cut of his outfit accentuated his lean frame. His jawline was sharp enough to cut through steel. The boy behind the clock door was the most intriguing boy I'd ever laid eyes on.

We helped Peter and Lance with kitchen cleanup, catching glimpses of an older woman with black and gray hair hanging posters on the walls, showcasing Leavenfell's ballroom. Nora and I exchanged confused glances, wondering what that could be about.

After chores were done, I found Arthur in the west wing of the castle alongside Alden, deep in conversation.

"She must get involved with the prophecy. There's *no* other option," Alden said, tension evident in his tone.

My scar flared at the mention of the prophecy, but Alden snapped his mouth shut when he saw me approaching

"Arthur!" I ran over to him and held up the photograph, waving it in front of his face. "Where did you find this photo?"

"We'll continue this conversation later, Arthur," Alden said, his robe swishing as he turned.

Arthur glanced at Alden, deep lines engraving his skin as his eyes dropped to the ground. "Of course."

Once Alden was gone, Arthur took the picture from me and studied it, fondness painting his features. "I had a feeling you'd search me out this morning."

"What did you suspect would happen when you leave stuff like this on my bed?"

"Alright, alright." Arthur held up his hands in a gesture of surrender. "I found it back at the Helm, before the attack. Slipped them into my bag and forgot about them until I unpacked my stuff." He returned the photo to me. "It was in Sullivan's quarters. I'd gone in there to grab something for him, and that's when I found it." He stared at the ceiling as though he was trying to recall every detail.

"Well, thank you for finding this." I slipped the photo into my pocket, my heart aching. I hardly remembered my parents, but my dad was supposedly an important person. With what exactly, Arthur wouldn't say, besides the fact that he worked against the Volings. He kept everything else on a *need-to-know* basis.

"I would've given it to you sooner, but I was preoccupied with guard duty and Fang."

"Any updates regarding Fang's whereabouts?"

"No, but I'm sure Rorik will send word once he knows something."

I frowned, disappointed that there hadn't been any developments. "By the way, what's this about the prophecy? Who needs to get involved? I heard Alden mention it."

Arthur went still. "It doesn't concern you, so don't fret over it."

"Why do you always keep secrets from me?" I was growing increasingly nervous over talks about the prophecy. Alden had said that *she* needed to get involved, but I hadn't the slightest idea who *she* was. Arthur didn't have any lady friends. None that I'd known of.

And if there was a prophecy out there telling us how to close Vol off from the other realms, I wanted to know about it.

"There are some secrets you don't need to be involved in, especially concerning dangerous prophecies."

Here we go again.

He paused, drawing a long breath. "Your safety is my number one priority. I want you to understand that." Arthur took a step forward, his armor creaking. "Now it's my turn to ask questions. Where were you last night with that boy?"

"His name is Lance," I corrected him. "And if you really need to know, I explored the castle and found a bunch of weird clock doors in a strange corridor."

Arthur's jaw went slack and it took him a few moments to respond. "Rue, it's forbidden to go there. That's why there's a sign posted. It's for a damned good reason," he snapped.

Gods, everyone knows about the damned sign. It was surprising to me that Arthur even knew about the clock doors.

"I don't give you many damned rules, but I want you to stay away from that corridor. Understood?" Arthur hardly ever swore, but when he did, he meant business.

"Understood," I half-heartedly replied, wanting to appease his temper. Angry Arthur scared me.

"Tell me, why did you go there to begin with?" Arthur demanded, his face reddening.

"I was only curious," I snapped. "And Puko practically led me there. That bird knows things." I was certain that Puko was the friend Alden spoke of in his note, and if Arthur wouldn't tell me anything, then I'd have to rely on Puko to give me clues.

"You mustn't go there again. I don't care if the bird takes you over the rainbow. Don't blindly follow it."

My lips parted. I suspected Arthur was concealing the truth about the prophecy, meaning I *had* to be involved with it somehow. Why else would Alden invite us to live in his castle?

"What's wrong with the bird?" I asked.

"I don't trust Alden's intentions, so don't follow it."

"Exactly how powerful is Alden? Puko seems sentient, but Alden's only a wizard. Usually, they have a limit on the magic they can use." Rorik always mentioned when he was at his limit. His magic drained him if he used too much of it at once. But Alden... he was different.

Arthur sighed, pressing his back against the wall. "Alden's very powerful, much more so than most wizards. His family is multi-gifted in many aspects, which is why he's so well-respected and looked up to."

So he's powerful and he knows things about the prophecy. I'd have to find a way to get that information out of him. Maybe I could catch him talking about it again while keeping myself out of sight.

My bite scar burned, lighting up my shoulder in pain. I took a step away from Arthur, sensing the burning return of symptoms I wanted nothing to do with. I quickly brushed my fingers against the talisman in my pocket and the symptoms dissipated.

Thank the gods.

Arthur's expression shifted from anger to concern. "You look unwell. What's wrong?"

"Nothing," I lied.

Arthur stared at me with annoyance before shaking his head and pushing past me.

"Arthur!" I called out.

But he was already gone.

I kicked the wall, cursing under my breath. Frustration burned in my chest, and I arched against the wall, sinking to the floor and tucking my head against my knees.

"Hey." Lance approached me, each step nearer intensifying the pull that roared between us. "Class starts soon. You coming?"

"Are you following me?"

A boyish smile broke across his face. "I'm not following you. Promise. But Nora did tip me off that you were looking for Arthur. Also, I wanted to apologize on behalf of Peter."

"What's he done now?" Where Peter was concerned, it was always something.

"He might be eating the rest of your breakfast as we speak. I can get more food if you want."

"Thanks, but I'm not hungry," I said with a groan. "And does your brother ever stop eating?"

"I don't know where he puts all of it to be honest."

I grumbled and averted my eyes.

"Are you okay? What's wrong?" Lance asked.

"It's nothing important." I bit the inside of my cheek.

Lance gently touched my hand, the contact of his skin sending an electric shock through my body. The magnetic pull dulled, ebbing and flowing like a gentle wave, but it was more of a gentle tug than a pain.

"You know you can tell me anything, right?" Lance whispered, tilting his head towards mine. "We're friends, and I care about you."

My skin heated. I'd rather be telling all my troubles to Fang, but here was Lance… offering his friendship.

"There's so much going on that I don't know where to start," I admitted after a tense moment. My gaze drifted to Lance's long blonde hair. He could never keep those few stray strands out of his face.

Lance squeezed my hand. "I'm not here to judge."

I stared at the floor, tapping my heel against the shiny wood. "I don't know. I can't shake the feeling that Leavenfell's not as safe as Alden makes it out to be." My mind drifted back to the clock doors. What could possibly be behind the other four, and why the hells would Puko lead me to a door hiding the magic barrier and clock doors? Was there any chance the prophecy was tied to them?

"There's more, but I'm not ready to talk about it yet," I admitted, dismissing my frustration with Arthur while everything else bubbled to the surface, sending tears to my eyes.

Fang.

My scar.

The hot asshole in the hidden corridor.

The prophecy.

Alden and Shay.

All things I wasn't ready to talk about, at least not to Lance.

Lance rested the back of his head against the wall. "You're

not alone in that feeling. The fact that I've lived here longer than you and have never seen those clock doors is something else."

"You should have seen how Nora and I discovered that place to begin with." I recounted our adventure to him, including everything about the bird, the crack in the wall that changed into a corridor, and the tall door I'd lockpicked with Nora's hairpin, only leaving out the part where I was compelled to attack Nora in the corridor.

Lance released a nervous laugh. "This castle gets stranger by the day."

We stayed there awhile, not paying attention to how much time had passed or caring about what was going on with the rest of the castle. When his hand reached for mine again, I didn't pull away, instead embracing his warmth.

"Ahem," a voice interrupted.

"Well, if it isn't the food thief," I joked, narrowing my eyes at the suspect. "Come to apologize?"

Peter stood in front of us with a plate of what I could only assume was the remainder of my breakfast. In response, he took another bite of *my* food, his lips twitching into a taunting smile.

After he was finished chewing, he said, "With how cozy you two look, I'd tell you to get a room, but class is about to start and apparently, there's going to be some sort of announcement." He grinned at us and stalked away, whistling happily and shoveling the rest of my food into his mouth.

Glitch, my nickname for the steambot, announced in class that there would be a Solstice Banquet in about a couple months, and that we'd all be expected to attend.

With partners.

So that's what the posters were about. My stomach fluttered at the thought of dancing with anyone. It wasn't that I didn't want to, but Fang used to tell me that I had two left feet. His bruised toes were proof enough that he wasn't lying to me. I haven't attempted dancing since.

According to Glitch, the Solstice Banquet was a longtime tradition of Leavenfell Castle that took place every Winter Solstice. For one night, we'd be expected to pretend we were free of the Voling threat and dance the night away under the two moons. Peter mentioned that the residents also tended to grovel at Alden's feet that night, but with dancing and food included, it was an escape of sorts.

I understood.

I really did.

But I wouldn't be letting down my guard, even for one night. I cast a glance over my shoulder at Nora, who was whispering excitedly to another girl with curly brown hair. She caught my eye and winked at me.

Oh yeah. I'd be hearing about her dance prospects later. Specifically, a guy whose name rhymed with *pin.*

Peter tilted his head backward, his eyes snapping towards Nora's displayed chest. I stalked over to where Nora was seated and pulled up the collar of her pink shirt, covering her boobs while adding a smack to the back of Peter's head. Nora and the other girl cackled.

Later that evening, Puko perched on my shoulder, chirping happily as I sat on my bed, recalling my conversation with

Arthur. There was no way in hells I was staying away from the hidden corridor. But to avoid suspicion from Arthur, I'd wait awhile before returning.

I patted Puko's copper head, deep in thought. Sneaking around the castle to catch Alden in a conversation about the prophecy wasn't the smartest idea. If I could find a way to get closer to the boy behind the clock door, maybe I'd find *something*, after I got on his good side… if that was possible.

Still, I'd been upset when Arthur scolded me for my curiosity. It was something he should've gotten used to after practically raising me and Fang. The hard truth about Arthur was that he was never going to share information with me that he thought would hurt me. The fact that he was keeping the prophecy a secret meant that the details of the prophecy could potentially hurt me, which kinda scared me, but if there was a chance I was involved, then I was *way* more determined to find out more about it. Even if that meant betraying one of the people I cared most about.

Chapter 14

Lessons of Defense

A vague letter from Rorik arrived a couple of weeks later, stating that he hadn't found any signs of Fang yet but would continue his tireless search. I stuffed the letter into my brown pants pocket and released a frustrated exhale. It'd been a heck of a day already.

I wiped the sweat from my forehead as I continued sweeping the kitchen quarters with Lance's mom, weaving around long counters stuffed with raw meat and chopped vegetables, and knocking my head against the low-hanging pots and pans. The smell of spices and freshly baked bread hung in the air. Taking a short break, I set the broom down and rested against the wood-paneled wall when a hushed voice caught my attention.

"Alden better get on it sooner rather than later if he wants to prevent the Volings from overrunning his castle," a male voice said.

The hair on the back of my neck stood up. I craned my head, inching closer towards the kitchen exit.

"What were you saying about the prophecy?" a woman asked.

"This so-called prophecy says Vol can be closed. I wonder if the girl is directly involved with it," the man said.

My blood ran cold. *What girl?*

"Now where did you hear that?" the woman asked.

"Read about it in an old book."

When the woman didn't respond, the man said, "Baaa… you'll see. Mark my words."

"Should we leave the castle? Is it not safe?"

"It's not safe anywhere," the man said. "Best to stay put until Vol is closed."

A crashing sound brought my attention back to where Mrs. Baker was bent over, picking up a platter of thickly cut sandwiches. I scurried to her side, bending down to help pick up the mess.

She wiped the sweat from her brow. "Thanks, hon," she said. "I think we're done here."

"Great," I answered, removing my apron and handing it back to her. "Thanks."

Following my search minutes later, I found Nora in the chapel. Her father gave me a dirty look when I sat down beside her, and her mother's hands were clasped together in prayer. Benny mimicked his mother's movements, watching her carefully.

"How did cleaning go?" Nora whispered.

"It was fine." I mentioned what I'd heard about the prophecy, but she brushed me off and changed the subject to the upcoming Solstice Banquet, which was just over a month away.

"Has anyone asked you to the banquet? I haven't had any offers." Her ears drooped at her admission.

"No one's asked me, but we can always go together," I offered.

"Goodness, Rue, are you asking me? I accept!" she exclaimed, her back arching as she stretched her arms over her head, all while beaming at me like going to the banquet together was the greatest idea ever. Her father gave her a death glare and told her to quiet down.

We left the chapel, reminiscing about the past couple of weeks. We'd spent a lot of time with Lance and Peter, getting to know each other and sneaking around the castle, chasing Puko down corridors and drinking the liquor Peter had snuck from the wine cellar. It was a good distraction from what I really wanted to do, but I knew it couldn't last forever.

During lunch hour, Lance sat beside me at the table, sketching on a piece of parchment. One of the few things I'd learned about him recently was that he loved drawing. I'd caught him on more than one occasion sketching during his free time or doodling in class during particularly boring lessons about Fennra.

Peter arrived, sitting down beside Lance with a bored expression on his face. "I don't understand why none of these girls want to go to the banquet with me." He ruffled his already messy hair. "Am I not cute enough for them?"

Nora, who was sitting beside him, snorted. "Hmm. I don't know, Peter. Maybe if you hadn't asked every single girl our age in the castle, you'd have more luck. Everyone knows you can't commit to a single girl."

"I would if they'd pay attention to me," argued Peter.

Nora flicked his forehead. "You're missing the point, dumb-ass. A girl wants to feel like she's the only one a boy has eyes for. You have no restraint and flirt with everyone. You would date a girl bogfrog if you had the chance."

"Only if she was pretty. I like my bogfrogs perfectly spotted."

Nora let out an exasperated sigh. "See? You're hopeless. Also, there's nothing wrong with the way you look and you know it, so hush."

Peter blushed at her admission. "You're not so bad yourself. If you wouldn't mind—"

"Peter Baker!" Mrs. Baker emerged from the kitchen quarters and stomped over to our table, a cross expression on her wrinkled face. Her blonde-gray hair was covered in flour, as was her apron and black dress underneath. She stopped in front of Peter and grabbed him by the ear. "What did I bloody tell you about washing the dishes thoroughly before putting them away? Goodness, the mess you've made!" She yanked him up by the ear and dragged him away.

Lance shook his head, suppressing a laugh. "He never learns."

Nora and I snickered, watching as Peter grumbled all the way back to the kitchen.

Alden finally announced that the day had arrived for our first defense lesson, and that it would be occurring tonight. Excitement bubbled inside me. I couldn't wait to put my hands on a weapon again. I glanced towards the back of the hall where tables of weapons were being set up. I eyed the archery equipment, hoping to get the chance to learn how to use them. Maybe I could rival Lance's skill.

"You'd think they'd have put these classes together faster considering there are Volings about in the realms trying to kill us," I said to Lance, his eyes lingering on me as he smiled.

Nora angled her chair towards the back of the hall, searching for Finn, who'd returned from Talem, but quickly looked away when Liessa joined him, hanging off his arm like a rotleech. Finn and Liessa were rumored to be a *couple* now, although none of us knew how and when that happened, especially since he'd been away. Nora's gloomy face and droopy ears told me it was eating her alive.

After we finished eating, we gave our plates to Lance's mom and made our way to the back. Finn greeted us at the podium and held out the parchment. It looked like everyone that signed was approved, but not many people had shown up.

"Due to low attendance, Alden lowered the age of requirement to fourteen, so we should get some younger folk soon." He glanced at everyone as he spoke, including Nora, who gave him a shy smile. Liessa shot Nora a dirty look.

"Since we have such a small group tonight, I will only be presenting a short history about a couple common races of Volings, paired with sword demonstrations." Finn announced. There was a simultaneous groan, the excitement fizzling out as everyone exchanged weary glances.

"How about we skip that part and learn how to kick Voling ass!" Peter shouted. Oliver cackled, as he often did at Peter's obnoxious behavior.

Lance gave Peter a stern look. "Will you shut up for once," he scolded, eliciting a grin from both me and Peter.

"I assure you that we will get to that on Thursday," replied Finn, unfazed by Peter's outburst. "But for today, it is important to learn about the Volings. Why don't we all take a seat over there?" Finn pointed to a long, rectangular table in front of the stage.

Once everyone was seated, Finn began his lesson. "Volings include many races, including the commonly known hyena-hybrids, vampires, and werewolves.

Finn pulled a wooden stake from the cloth. "Even though vampires are fast and lethal, they're fairly easy to kill if you know what you're doing, but you have to be quick about it."

"How do you kill one of them?" Oliver asked, his hand brushing against Willow's thigh, and I caught myself longing for physical touch from a partner of my own.

Finn clapped his hands together, snapping my attention back to the lesson. "The only way to kill a vampire is to stake its heart or decapitate it. I will be teaching you how to stake on Thursday."

Mostly everyone seemed interested in the lesson, except Peter, whose eyes were glazed over as he stared out the central window, his mouth gaping open. Finn tossed the stake to Peter, who was caught off guard and almost dropped it.

"As I mentioned before, one way to kill a vampire is to stake it through its heart. Please pass the stake around. Get a feel for it so you will be somewhat prepared for Thursday," Finn instructed.

Peter swung the stake around in the air, pretending to strike invisible enemies and almost stabbing Oliver. Oliver smacked Peter's arm hard, causing Peter to drop the stake. It hit the ground with a clack. Lance snatched the stake off the ground and apologized to Finn for his behavior, but Finn dismissed him. Everyone else examined the stake when they got their turn, turning it over in their hands and getting used to the weight of it. After I was done examining it, I handed it back to Finn.

"Now back to werewolves," Finn began, putting the stake away. "We don't know much about them, only that they escaped from one of the shadow realms within Vol called Svalrock." It was common knowledge that Vol had realms within it, but it was odd considering Vol was a realm too. Realms within a realm were typically unheard of, but Arthur had no other way of describing it when I'd brought it up previously.

Svalrock. An image flashed through my mind: a vast but dark realm with many cragged cliffs and caves, dark streams, and dead trees. The scene was so vivid that it felt like I'd been there before.

Finn continued, "Werewolves have the potential to change mortals into their kind with a single bite. However, not all mortals that have been bitten have changed, so it's suspected that the wolves choose who they want to change and selectively release venom into their bite. But this is only speculation. Regardless, they are extremely dangerous and tend to hunt in packs rather than alone." Finn paused to take a breath, then asked, "Can I have a volunteer?"

Nora's hand shot up. My eyes roamed over her, falling to her chest, which was suspiciously larger. I stifled a laugh. Of all the things Nora would shift, it would be *that*, in front of the guy she fancied. Finn motioned for her to step forward. He withdrew a long sword from its sheath and showed it to everyone before facing Nora.

"Take it," he said, offering it to her. Nora grabbed the handle.

"This sword," said Finn, "is made of silver. Silver, whether it be a bullet, arrow, or sword, is the only thing that can kill a werewolf. And I want to stress... the *only* thing that will kill a werewolf."

"So you're saying that if I stabbed a werewolf through its heart with a regular sword, it wouldn't die?" Peter asked.

"Slow it down, maybe, but unfortunately not. The wound would begin to heal and the werewolf would fully regenerate in a matter of seconds. And you'd better hope you're not in its vicinity when it regenerates."

Peter's face drained of color as he sunk back into his chair.

"Nora, please allow me to show you a basic technique." Finn walked up beside her and put his hands on hers, causing her face to redden. He guided Nora's stance, then moved her hands into a thrusting motion with the sword. "If you're aiming for its head, you want to thrust the sword forward and up, running it straight through its skull. Fastest and most effective way to kill it with a silver sword, but you must be faster than they are. Easier said than done."

Admiration was evident through Nora's expression, though Finn took no notice of it. Finn released her and took the sword, demonstrating a couple attack moves. His movements were calculated. Precise. He handled the weapon with such grace, almost like it was another limb.

"And that is how it's done," Finn concluded. "We'll practice some of these moves on Thursday." Finn slipped the sword back into its sheath. "Thank you for volunteering, Nora. You may take a seat."

Nora pranced off the stage and rejoined me, a satisfied grin on her face. Finn went on for a while longer, discussing the hyena Volings, which he called *hyelings*, and describing the manner of their hunting. They were the most feared by the residents of Leavenfell Castle, since they were the most numerous race of Volings, and the manner of their kills was extraordinarily brutal.

"I urge you to come back for another lesson on Thursday. Goodnight," Finn concluded.

On our way out of the great hall, Lance caught up with Nora and me. "Short lesson, but I figured it would've been much more boring than it was." He squeezed himself between us and draped an arm over my shoulder. "What did you think?"

"It was boring, but informative too. I can't wait 'til Thursday," Nora answered.

"It wasn't bad," I agreed with a half-smile, "but I would've liked some action with the weapons, so I'm siding with Peter on this one." I smirked, knowing I was treading dangerous territory.

Nora gasped, feigning shock while holding a hand over her mouth. "You *wouldn't.*"

"What? He had a point," I said.

"Don't tell Peter you said that," Lance said, his lips twitching.

"Said what?" Peter asked as he caught up to my side.

"Nothing," Lance and I said simultaneously.

"At least we know some of what we're up against," Nora remarked.

"Seems like most people are scared of the hyena Volings the most," Peter said, shuddering.

"Finn called them hyelings. I like that term better," I admitted.

"Hyena-hybrids… hyelings. It's all the same to me. I try not to think about them." Nora's shoulders tensed as she slowed her pace.

Lance shifted away from me, shoving his hands into his

pockets. "I should get going. I'm sure my mom needs help finishing kitchen clean-up after all that sticky glaze she made for the pork. One of us has to do it." He pointedly looked at Peter. "I'll see you later."

"See you later." I waved as he ran off. Peter rolled his eyes and begrudgingly followed his brother, muttering something about not wanting to do dish duty again.

Nora linked her arm with mine as we made our way back to our bedroom for the night. "Lance can't keep his hands off of you."

"We're only friends," I clarified with an eye roll.

"You are the most oblivious person I've ever met." Nora snorted. "He's crushing on you hard. Why else would he put his hands all over you?"

I shrugged, not answering her, but my mind went back to the boy in the clock room. I couldn't keep him out of my thoughts. *That damned scowl...*

After crossing the bridge under blizzard-like conditions, we arrived at our room and found a letter taped to the front of the door.

My name was written on the front in big, block letters.

CHAPTER 15

THE ROOM OF MEMORIES

Rue,

You have my permission to go to the hidden corridor. Stop at the first clock on the right side. The time is six. Good luck.

— Arthur

I read the letter repeatedly, trying to make sense of it. Nora peeked over my shoulder, and I held the letter up, allowing her to read it. The clock chimed ten times, warning us of the late hour. I folded the letter in half and slipped it into my pocket, a sliver of dread seeping into my thoughts.

"I don't know if you should go there again," said Nora as she changed into a pair of white thermal pajamas. She gave me a hesitant glance, and I didn't miss the tremble of her hands. "I don't like that Arthur's encouraging it, either. I thought he was against it."

I shrugged. Arthur had been acting strange since we arrived at Leavenfell, putting distance between us and keeping more secrets than normal, so receiving this letter from him was odd. I patted my pocket, the paper crinkling as my hand grazed the fabric of my pants. *What did Arthur mean by the time is six?*

As much as I appreciated the letter, I wished he would've told me his thoughts in person and stopped being so damned cryptic, but at least I didn't have to sneak back to the hidden corridor. Maybe now, I would find clues to the prophecy Arthur was so determined to keep from me, or more information about Shay.

"You have to admit you're at least a little bit curious," I told Nora, who'd gone silent.

She stiffened but said nothing, rubbing her head as though she was trying to remember something. Her lips curled and she swallowed hard. "I don't know, Rue. I don't want you to get hurt. I'm worried something will happen if you go back." Her voice rose as she spoke, "That corridor is off-limits. I don't think Alden would be happy if he found out we'd been up there."

"If Arthur doesn't seem concerned, then it'll be okay," I reassured her, although I wasn't entirely convinced myself. The goosebumps on my arms weren't helping. "I don't think Alden really cares what we do outside of chores and class," I added. His note had been proof of that.

"I'm not going to argue with you. Just promise you'll be careful."

"I'll be back before the sun rises," I promised her. I grabbed the key from my nightstand and rushed out the door.

I stopped in front of the barrier and inserted the key, watching the barrier melt away. Pulling the letter from my pocket, I read it again: *First clock on the right... the time is six.*

What the—? I stared at the clock in front of me, contemplating the instructions as I touched the large clock face, the marble cool underneath my fingers.

Time is six...

My eyes widened. Arthur was a damned genius.

I grabbed the hands of the clock and guided the long hand to twelve and the other hand to six. A loud click, followed by a harmonious chime, echoed off the walls. All five clocks began to tick in unison, but another sound, apart from the ticking, caught my attention. I swiveled, sensing a presence behind me, my heart hammering against my chest. There stood the tall boy I'd been hoping to see again, but the smile quickly dropped from my face when I was greeted with narrow eyes and a pinched expression.

"What in the hells are you doing here?" He asked sharply, cocking his head to the side.

My breath caught as I fumbled for a response. Despite his sour attitude, I couldn't help but admire him. Brown hair fell across his golden eyes, and the dark circles underneath somehow suited him, adding a mysterious touch of darkness to his features. He smelled like spiced cinnamon and wore brown trousers paired with a beige blouse, the sleeves rolled up to his elbows.

"What are you doing?" he asked with furrowed brows. He crossed his arms over his chest, his scowl deepening.

"You've already seen what I'm doing," I snapped back, attempting to match his hostile tone. "Idiot," I muttered. *Hot* idiot, but still.

"Tsk." He loomed over me. "I only see one idiot here and it's not me."

Heat flooded me and I resisted the urge to argue with him.

Instead, I waved the letter in front of his face. "I got instructions this time. Otherwise, I'd be tucked safely into my bed like the law-abiding resident I am."

The boy tried to snatch the letter out of my hand, but I held it out of reach.

"Who gave that to you?"

"I don't see how that's relevant," I said, mimicking his previous words to me.

"For the record, you don't give me law-abiding vibes," the boy said through gritted teeth, his jaw clenching.

"You're one to talk." I turned back towards the clock face and pulled on the knob, but the door wouldn't budge.

"It's not going to work if you don't insert the key."

"Oh, so you're going to help me now," I grunted. "Never thought I'd see the day."

"Whatever it takes to get you out of my sight," he snapped back.

I bit my bottom lip as I lowered my head, my chin traitorously trembling. His comment stung more than it should have. Shaking my head, I retrieved the skeleton key from my pocket and slipped it into the keyhole, located at the center of the clock face. The clock door shuddered and swung forward.

Darkness swirled behind the doorway, and a shiver ran down my spine as I tightened my fists. I flipped my hair over my shoulder and cleared my throat, but I couldn't move forward. *This is what you came here for. Answers. Move, dammit.*

"Are you coming with me?" I asked, hoping he would entertain the idea so I wouldn't have to enter the darkness alone. I didn't know what awaited me inside, but going alone terrified me.

The boy took a deliberate step back, his hands clasped

against his chest. "No." The word came out like a weapon, poison tainting his voice.

I gawked at him. This guy could give Fang a run for his gold with that attitude of his.

"Well, go on then." He moved towards me and shoved my back.

I fell into the dark room, throwing my fists at him, but unable to fight back because the clock door slammed shut in my face.

A thick, foggy haze swallowed me. I frantically turned back, but the door had already locked itself. Just when I started to think that this was a terrible idea, the fog disappeared, and I found myself hovering above the center of an ancient, dilapidated library. I floated downward, my body weightless as I took in countless bookshelves stretching miles into the open night sky. Loads of pristine books were placed neatly on the sparkling shelves, as if they had been tended to daily.

When my feet hit the floor, I gasped. Kneeling, I reached my fingers towards the stars. The circular floor was see-through, a gaping void saturated with bright stars and swirling galaxies underneath my feet, illuminating the darkness. My pulse raced as I scurried to the rounded edge of the library, keeping my back to the walls, afraid I would fall into the void of stars. I clenched my fists, overcome with wanting to punch that boy in the face for pushing me in here. He wouldn't hear the end of it next time I met up with him.

I drew in a deep breath, my nerves settling as I planted my

feet onto the glass floor and moved forward, stopping in front of a shelf holding books bound with gems. I grabbed a book and flipped through the pages, unable to understand the language written inside. Sighing, I placed the book back on the shelf when an ice-cold hand grabbed my arm. I startled, swiveling towards a very strange man. He wore thick, round spectacles and had so many wrinkles, it was a wonder he could see me. He flickered like a ghost as he regarded me. I briefly worried that he would beat me with his cane for intruding in his library.

"I knew you would come one day, Ruby Watson," he said with a quivering voice. "I've been waiting for your arrival for a very long time." The man turned his back on me and floated towards a spindly glass cabinet that sat atop an oval, iron-wrought table in between the bookshelves. He opened a little door on the side of the cabinet, reached in, and withdrew a translucent teardrop-shaped vial filled with tiny, luminescent stars.

"I'm sorry, b-but who are y-you?" I stuttered, my gaze darting across the library, searching for an exit. To my dismay, the clock door had disappeared completely.

The man faced me, vial in hand, his expression warm but apologetic. "I apologize for frightening you. My name is Wilbur Watson. I am your great, great-grandfather."

"That's impossible." Though I shook my head in disbelief, my scar flared at his words.

His gray eyes were the same stormy shade as mine, invoking a sense of unrequited longing inside of me. The wish for something impossible, like my own father being here instead of him. Even if this man was related to me, what the hells was he doing in a realm inside Alden's castle? The fact that this realm even existed inside Alden's castle didn't make any sense.

I scanned the galaxy below the glass, my heart thumping hard enough to crack a rib. This couldn't be real. Maybe I'd been knocked out after the boy pushed me and this was all a dream.

"I assure you this isn't a dream. I'm a memory engraved into the confines of this cursed realm, sent here to prepare for the day you would arrive. I'm sure you know why you came here, don't you, Ms. Watson? You must know your purpose by now."

Alden's note had mentioned something about my purpose, whatever that was. I shook my head, hungry to learn more about this *purpose*. I'd drawn in a settling breath when something spoke inside my head.

Not all memories are safe, the whispers said. *But all memories lead to purpose. Memories can lead to one's dark fate.* The voices faded away. My heart pounded.

"You came for answers." The man handed me the vial of stars. "Someone sent you."

Arthur.

I grasped the vial, wrapping my fingers around the smooth glass, afraid it would slip through my fingers and shatter against the floor.

"You know what to do. A single star will suffice," he instructed. "Your father prepared this vial for you."

"My father?" I asked, my eyebrows raised as I stared at the bottle. "My father made this?"

"He was quite the alchemist," the man said.

I'd known that Arthur was an alchemist, but he'd never mentioned my father being one. I glanced at the vial, the glass slick with my sweat, contemplating whether I should trust this old man. When I hesitated, those whispers came back to me.

Memories can lead to one's dark fate.

Was I cursed to fulfill the prophecy? Every time I thought

about it, my scar blazed, like the edge of a dagger being forged against my skin. *Damn it all.* I hesitated, then tipped the vial into my mouth and swallowed one of the slippery stars, grimacing when the substance hit my tongue. It tasted like nothing and everything all at once, like the sweetest dessert dulled by time and magic. The library fell away piece by piece, and the man disappeared. Like puzzle pieces being scattered, the glass floor disintegrated, and I fell into the stars.

I screamed, thrashing my arms and legs around like a fish flopping on land, trying desperately to grab hold of something. I squeezed my eyes shut, expecting imminent death, but the falling sensation stopped, replaced with a gentle landing on soft ground.

I peeled my eyes open. A grassy moor, full of lush greenery, flowers of all sorts and colors, and warm sunlight, greeted me. The scenery reminded me of Fleurya, my hometown, full of flowery trees and open moors as far as the eye could see. The earthy grass smelled like home.

A little girl, no older than three or four years old, sat in a patch of grass barely ten feet in front of me. She was *me,* or rather a younger version of myself. My parents were nearby, in a conversation of their own, but carefully keeping their eyes on the girl. A familiar ache bloomed in my chest. I desperately wanted to reach out to them, but I was rooted in place, my feet frozen.

"Ruby, come here," my father called. He scooted his glasses back to his eyes, but they slipped back down to the tip of his nose shortly after. He had to know that was a battle he'd never win. My younger self sprinted over to him, and my mother gathered a small cake from the straw basket she had at her side.

"Happy birthday, sweetheart," my father beamed, scooping the girl into his arms.

"Four years old, and on a beautiful day too," my mother said, admiring the cloudless sky, her face lifted towards the sun.

Their smiles were short-lived. My father's expression shifted to a grimace as he set the little girl down. "It's beautiful, but we can't stay long," he reminded her. "It was risky coming out here without Sully's approval."

Sully. Or as I'd known him, Sullivan. I couldn't believe my father associated with him, much less called him by a silly nickname.

My mother stilled. "We needed to get out. Feel the sun against our skin. It's been so long." The way the shaky words left her lips made me wonder if they were prisoners of Sullivan, much like me and Fang had been. The thought of that angered me.

My father squeezed her shoulder. "I know," he whispered. "Just this once."

The Volings spilled through the crack. They shouldn't be where the Volings can find them. The voices from the library whispered in my head. A heavy sadness spilled through the strange voices. *They cursed the girl.*

I held my breath, my heart hammering against my chest as their words sunk in. I glanced at my shoulder, wondering if I was cursed.

"Who opened the realm?" I asked the voices, my gaze trailing back over to my parents. The silhouette of them froze as the voices spoke.

One word returned, sending chills down my spine as I held back the urge to vomit.

Sullivan.

Sullivan had opened Vol, a massive realm, somewhere between the southern borders of Calzour and Solendia—

resulting in the end of numerous mortal, but innocent lives. This all but confirmed that I was tied to the prophecy, and maybe, just maybe, this is what Alden wanted me to find out.

An impending sense of doom flooded me as my gaze turned back to my parents, trying to figure out which memory this was. The memory shifted, the sky filling with swirling, gray clouds, draining the environment of all its warmth. My father drew his sword, fear stretching across his features as he pushed his glasses up his nose and squinted in the direction of the dense forest's edge.

"What is it?" My mother's eyes widened with fear. She picked me up and hugged me to her chest, her arms trembling.

"Wolves from Svalrock. A whole pack, inside the tree line just over there. They're watching us," my father whispered. "Try to not make any sudden moves."

Fear radiated through me, growing until it hit a crescendo, like tumultuous waves crashing against a rocky shoreline.

"Go!" I yelled, but they couldn't hear me. Of course they couldn't. Everything that was about to happen had already come to pass.

"Can we make it back?" my mother said, her tone rising.

My father withdrew a small glass bottle from his trouser pockets and handed it to her. "Find Arthur and give this to him. He should be waiting by the wagon. I'll distract them. Whatever you might hear, don't turn back," my father ordered. "Go now." He kissed me on the cheek and threw his arms around us. "I love you both."

With a whimper, I reached my little hands towards my father, but my mother held me close and ran for the hills. I screamed out in terror as the wolves descended upon my father, my heart leaping out of my chest as I called for him, but the memory disintegrated.

"Fuck!" I yelled, my breath coming in heavy pants. Before I could process what had happened, a new memory came in its place. I forced my eyes open, pinning my shaking hands to my sides.

My small, four-year-old self was unconscious in the arms of a familiar man. *Arthur.* There was blood. A lot of blood coming from my small broken body. My skin was sliced into shreds, raked through by claws too sharp for such fragile skin.

I stared in horror at the single bite mark on my younger self's shoulder. I glanced down at my own shoulder. My scar roared to life, burning with such unbearable intensity that I flinched.

Monster, the voices said.

"I'm not a monster!" I yelled into the void, clasping a hand over my bite mark, but the voices ignored me.

Arthur paced the side of the overpass, the channel of water separating him from Leavenfell Castle. After a moment, the bridge lowered and Arthur sprinted across, holding my unmoving body against his chest. The clouds separated, revealing the bright sky above. The sun was unforgiving, like an omen that told of monsters that could attack in broad daylight.

Sullivan met him at the gate, his expression infuriatingly smug as his lips curled upward. His onyx eyes brightened, as if he'd known that Arthur would be coming.

"Arthur," he acknowledged. "You were wrong to bring her back here." He slicked his graying hair back, his eyes dropping to my unconscious body while his hands fiddled with something in his heavy coat pocket.

"She needs a healer," Arthur said. "Let us through."

"You know I can't allow that," Sullivan said, his expression darkening. He stood tall, dwarfing Arthur, as most shifters did, his stiff arms crossed over his chest.

"Please," Arthur cried, tears covering his face. "I'm begging you."

Arthur… My heart tugged, seeing him so broken.

Sullivan pulled a small pocket watch from his coat pocket and touched the clock's face. For a moment, nothing happened. Then the barrier dropped, and Arthur tumbled forward.

I gasped, my eyes darting back to Sullivan. He'd used the pocket watch to erase the protective barrier around the castle. Horror emptied into the pit of my stomach as it dawned on me that Alden had that *same* pocket watch. He carried it on his person every day, constantly fiddling with the thing. How did Sullivan acquire it from Alden?

I doubted that Leavenfell was as safe as Alden and Arthur swore it was. Sweat pooled onto my skin as I stared into the memory.

"Thank you," Arthur panted, sweat pouring off of his forehead.

Sullivan pocketed the watch. "You can stay here, but she cannot. She's been bitten by the monsters." He unsheathed a dagger and aimed it at my neck. "I'm sorry, Arthur."

Arthur shielded me with his body. "She's only a child!"

"Be that as it may, she'll become one of them. I cannot allow that in the castle."

"Please. I'm begging you—give her a chance. She won't change. Not everyone who's been bitten changes!" Arthur's desperation made me sick to my stomach. I hadn't known the extent of what he'd gone through. My parents' deaths were fresh in his memory, yet he'd still tried to save me from Sullivan.

Sullivan studied my little body, time passing slowly as his eyes grazed every open wound, specifically the bite on my shoulder. "Has she shown any signs of changing?"

"Nothing," Arthur answered.

Sullivan nodded after a tense moment. "Bring her in." He slipped his hand into his pocket, withdrawing the pocket watch. Once he touched its face, the barrier returned, encompassing the castle. "The healers will tend to her wounds, but if she shows any signs of changing, you know what needs to be done."

Arthur nodded, his face pale. "I understand."

"Theodore and Rowan?" Sullivan inquired as they entered the castle through the main entrance.

My parents' names.

Arthur's lips quivered. "Dead. Ruby came running to me while the wolves were distracted with..." He trailed off, his eyes widening as though he was recalling the horrific scene. "There was nothing I could do. I couldn't save them."

Sullivan showed no empathy. "A shame that their choices led to this." His lips twitched, so subtle that I nearly missed it. He *knew*. He knew. Either that or he set them up to die. "I warned them not to leave the castle. This could have been avoided."

Arthur hung his head.

"Be that as it may, we did learn one thing from this." Sullivan heaved a great sigh. "Fennra is no longer safe."

Arthur lifted his head and met Sullivan's gaze. "The realms are in disrepair. They have been since—"

"I know," Sullivan admitted. "And it will only get worse." They took me inside the castle. "We need to discuss what can be done. Come. Let's get a healer for the girl."

The memory disintegrated, but it hadn't been enough. I needed to know how Sullivan had gained access to Leavenfell, and if me and Arthur really lived at the castle years ago. I needed to know Sullivan's reason behind setting up my parents.

What was that bottle my father handed to my mother? More questions raced through my mind, but before I could fully absorb what I'd witnessed, another memory took its place, grounding me in a new environment.

I was a bit older, maybe seven or eight years, and my hair was no longer just brown. The brown melted into green at the ends. I was standing inside Alden Hall's present office, but Sullivan was the one scolding me.

"You do not bite people. Do you understand me?" He'd knelt on one knee so that he was eye level with me, his sharp eyes narrowed. He grabbed a green piece of my hair, pinching it while I trembled, tears staining my face.

"We were just playing," I sobbed. "It was an accident."

"No excuses, young lady. Now get out of my sight," Sullivan snarled, releasing my hair and waving a hand at me in dismissal.

I ran out of the room, crashing into Arthur's legs.

"I've been looking all over for you." Arthur knelt and took my face in his hand, rubbing the tears from my cheeks with a handkerchief. Fang peeked at me from over his shoulder, a welcome presence. A few of my own tears slipped from my misty eyes at the image of us together.

Sullivan stormed out of the office. "She's supposed to be under your strict watch, Arthur. I have no choice but to move her room to the dungeon."

"Don't you think you're being harsh?" argued Arthur. "She didn't mean any harm."

"She's a danger to others," Sullivan replied, his eyes pinned.

"Use your gift wisely, Arthur. I don't want her to have any memory of the bite. It keeps the curse dormant."

Monster, the voices repeated, louder this time.

"Shut up!" I screeched, covering my ears.

"For how long do I need to keep this up?" Arthur demanded.

"Until she dies. You will continue to look after her and you will be responsible for her actions. One slip up and I swear—she'll be executed on the spot." He let the threat hang in the air for a moment. "There will be no more warnings. This is the last one, Arthur." Sullivan gave him a hard nod. He stormed back into his office, slamming the door behind him and leaving Arthur and my younger self stunned. Fang began to cry, his wailing catching the attention of the kitchen staff.

Arthur peered down at our scared faces and squeezed my hand. "Everything will be okay. Don't worry. We only need to lie low for a while. Alden will be back soon, and he'll fix this." He patted both of our little heads. "And Ruby, we'll need to cut the green strands off again. You know it bothers him."

I squeezed his hand back, letting him know I understood, and wiped the tears from Fang's eyes.

"It's going to be okay," little me told him. "I'll protect you."

Fang slung his arm around my shoulder and smiled at me. Even through the worst of it, he'd smile. My own smile faded as reality set in. Fang was gone, lost to Helm Castle, but I couldn't let him go. I couldn't accept that he might not be coming back. An unbearable pain welled up inside of me, burying into my stomach. Seeing him—seeing us as children again brought back fond memories of how close we were and how he was such a constant part of my life.

Until Helm Castle.

Tears stung at my eyes, and I squeezed them shut, willing the pain to go away, but to no avail.

Monster. Monster. MONSTER! The voices screamed in my head.

"Go away!" I screamed, bringing my hands to my ears. "Leave me alone!"

"No," a voice responded, and the memory disintegrated.

My eyes snapped open. The boy was in front of me, the back of his hand pressed against my forehead. He tore his hand away the second my eyes found him. Startled, I shifted away from him, stunned to find myself back in the library where I'd started. The clock door reappeared and was calling to me, its magic reaching out, faintly brushing against my skin. Disoriented and weakened from the magic, I drew my knees to my chest, placing my head in between them.

"Go away," I told the boy.

When he didn't budge, I closed my eyes, blocking him out, attempting to process everything I'd seen. Arthur had been deep in his own grief, but he'd done everything he could to protect me, more than I'd given him credit for. A shiver ran through me. Sullivan had been a threat to my life, not only when I was a child, but at Helm Castle as well. He must've had a reason for keeping me alive. But I wasn't so sure…

And *Fang.* My breath hitched and suddenly, I couldn't breathe. My fists found their way to my head, and I cried. I missed him, so damned much that his absence left a gaping hole inside me. I remained in that dark place, losing a piece of myself as I sat in the haunted shell of the library. I stayed there for a long time, until the asshole boy shook my shoulders. I ignored him, staring at the stars beneath my feet instead.

When I finally lifted my head, the boy was by my side, his

legs crossed and his face pale. He watched me with an unfamiliar softness and extended his arm. An invitation. I scooted closer, hiding my tears behind a curtain of hair. Slowly, I peeked at him, catching his lingering gaze. He looked as though he wanted to say something, but pressed his lips together instead, a faint blush coloring his cheeks. A subtle humming sound caught my ears, but I couldn't tell where it was coming from. Likely another mystery of the library realm.

My scar throbbed. The hole inside me deepened, like a crater expanding across my chest, threatening to drag me under the numb waters contained within. Needing more comfort, I reached my hand towards the boy, letting my fingers brush against his warm skin. The boy jolted, grabbing my hand and slamming it to the floor.

"Don't touch me," he snapped.

"I was making sure you're real," I lied, embarrassed with myself.

The boy scowled. "Of course I'm real. What kind of idiotic statement is that?"

There went that fleeting sweetness.

"I should get some sleep." I stood and walked towards the clock door.

"Best idea you've had all night."

Ignoring his comment, I grabbed the knob and turned. The door clicked and swung forward. *Thank the gods.* I cast a glance over my shoulder, but the boy was gone.

The boy's absence left a strange ache inside me. He'd been cold before I'd entered that library, but something had changed between us after the memories washed away. At least for a few moments.

His presence had been comforting, at least while it lasted. It was like being thrust into a warm bath after swimming in the iciness of Dagger Sea. He couldn't be the cold person he'd made himself out to be.

Nora hopped into bed beside me, and I wrapped myself around her, needing the comfort of physical contact and missing Fang's bear hugs.

"I'm so glad you're back in one piece," she said, her arms tightening around me. "What happened up there?

I lifted my head from her chest, the hairs on the back of my neck standing up. Even though my encounter with the boy was something I took an odd comfort in, there was still the issue of the castle, and the magic held within.

"There are more secrets to this castle than we thought."

Nora tensed. "What do you mean?"

I sat up and drew in a deep breath, meeting her eyes, "I'm scared the castle is in danger."

CHAPTER 16

EVERETT FANG

I WOKE EARLY, ANNOYED THAT THE MYSTERIOUS BOY'S SCOWL haunted me in my dreams. I couldn't escape him, not even in slumber. After getting ready, I dressed in a pair of tight black trousers and a green blouse, then rushed to the great hall.

Relief flooded through me when I spotted Arthur, but I hesitated, unsure of how to bring up the events of last night. I didn't know if he wanted to relive those days. Tears stung my eyes as my grief came rushing back. I sucked in a long breath and tapped my cheeks, trying to settle my nerves.

"Arthur." His name came out as a whisper.

"Rue, I'm so glad you're here," Arthur said cheerily. "I was about to come get you."

My feet rooted to the spot, unable to move as Arthur deliberately stepped aside. Someone stood behind him, deep in conversation with Rorik, that familiar black hair longer than I remembered.

"Fang?" I stared at him in disbelief and rubbed my eyes,

hoping to the gods this was real. Time slowed as I searched for words. Fang was *alive*. My heart buzzed with electricity as I took a heavy step forward, that empty piece of me finally whole.

Fang stopped mid-sentence and faced me, a wide lopsided smile lighting up his face. Unable to contain my emotions, I flung myself into his arms. "Fang! Gods… what are you—" My voice broke as I sobbed in his arms, his shirt soaking at an alarming rate, but I couldn't stop myself.

"How did you—"

Fang deepened the embrace, nuzzling his head into my neck. "Hey, stranger," he greeted me in a raspy, tired voice. Dirt caked his black pants and gray shirt, his black locks tangled more than the bramble of wood outside the Helm, and he smelled like he'd been trudging through pig shit, but I didn't care. He was here, his heart still beating, and he was in my arms again. I hugged him until my arms ached.

"I've missed you so much." I cried into his shoulder, wiping my tears against his torn sleeve. "Where the hells have you been?" I craned my head to look up at him.

"Wondering where the hells you've been," Fang replied, his eyes twinkling with that mischievous glint of his. *Yup… same old Fang.*

"I thought you were really gone."

"So did I, but I'm here. Thanks to Rorik," Fang said, nodding in Rorik's direction. Rorik was just as dirty as Fang, except his mushroom blonde hair, which was always flowy and combed to perfection. I needed to offer him my endless gratitude later. Perhaps Lance could sneak extra food from the kitchen for me to give to him.

Arthur stepped between us, interrupting our reunion. "Rue, I hate to cut this short, but Alden has requested our immediate attention. He says it's very important and unfortunately, it can't wait."

"Right this second?" I whined. "Fang just got here." Instead of obeying Arthur, I grabbed Fang's shirt, clinging to the weather-torn fabric as tightly as I could.

"It's fine. I'm not going anywhere." Fang patted my back, gently releasing me from his arms. "The matter with Alden sounds important."

I wanted to argue with him, but Alden appeared from around the corner with a frightening scowl on his face. One of his mechanical birds poked out of his beard and squawked an unintelligible order at us. He gestured for us to follow him.

Rolling my eyes, I followed after Alden, tugging Fang along with me, not ready to let him out of my sight.

"Fang, please wait outside. You'll have plenty of time to catch up later," Alden told him. "And I'll need to talk to you afterwards, so don't stray."

Fang nodded and took a seat at one of the tables in the great hall. Mrs. Baker, covered in the usual mixture of flour and spices, rushed to the table and offered him a plate of meat and potatoes, which he graciously accepted. I thanked her for bringing it to him. Glancing back at Fang, I couldn't help but notice that he'd dropped a few pounds.

"I'll be right back," I told him, squeezing his shoulder, which was bonier than the last time I'd had my hands on him, confirming that he'd lost weight.

"And I'll be right here," Fang replied. His eyes quickly shifted to his plate of food, and he took a bite of the roast. He moaned his approval the moment the food passed his lips. I wondered how long he'd gone without a proper meal.

Arthur tapped my shoulder and nodded towards the tower

office. I grimaced and followed him through the doorway. Upon entering, I plopped down, crossing and uncrossing my legs, wondering what the hells could be so important that Alden needed to see us right now and hating that I had to leave Fang alone. I wrinkled my nose. Alden's office smelled like old musty books and smoke.

Alden straightened his posture, and his mechanical bird flew to a nearby perch attached to the wall close by. Puko, to my surprise, sat beside the other bird and snapped his beak at it, as if angry about having to share the spot. I bit back a laugh.

The eggshell-colored walls were stacked with crammed bookshelves. Documents and sketches were scattered all over his desk and the wooden floor below. I didn't know how Alden could breathe in this cramped office, much less get any work done. The only salvation was the towering ceiling that seemed to extend into the morning sky, illuminating the office with light.

Alden handed us a plate of food, fresh out of the kitchen, then clasped his hands in front of him. "Now that I have you both here, I'm going to come out with it. First order of business —no more secrets. Too much is at stake." Alden gave Arthur a stern look, his eyes narrowing underneath his wrinkles, before sliding his gaze to me. "We'll start with your whereabouts last night, Rue."

I folded my hands in my lap and released a breath. There was no point in lying, so I confessed where I'd gone. Not that he should care. Alden all but encouraged me to search the castle.

Arthur glanced at me, his eyes widened with concern. The mechanical bird clicked its beak, but it sounded like a groan. These odd birds were good at mimicking Alden's moods. All besides Puko, who only cooed when I glanced at him. Puko being here was all the confirmation I needed that he was the friend Alden had sent to help me.

"And what did you find there?" Alden asked, his eyes twinkling. I gaped at him. He knew exactly what he was doing.

"Well, for starters, I found out that I was bitten by a werewolf," I said, heat rushing to my face. All my symptoms now made sense, though strange, but at least I'd found out where the bite was from. A damned *werewolf.*

I shot a heated look at Arthur. "You never once mentioned anything about the bite. You knew I was bothered by it. This whole time —"

Alden held up his hand. "Now is not the time —"

I cut him off, my temper rising. "Stop! You've kept so much from me and allowed me to feel like an idiot while dealing with these symptoms. My scar has been burning like mad since we've arrived. But you couldn't tell me why, could you?"

Arthur didn't deserve my anger, but the fact that he kept the source of the *bite* from me... only angered me at that moment. I could hardly look at him. Alden's eyes widened, his mouth hanging open as though he hadn't expected my outburst.

Arthur's expression filled with remorse. "I didn't feel that it was necessary to tell you, because in all the years that I have cared for you, you've never once changed. I kept it a secret to protect you. That's always been my first duty."

I shook my head and exhaled. "I don't need to be protected. In case you forgot, I was *always* the one that looked out for you and Fang. Always. You can thank my heightened hearing for that." I shivered, trying not to think about the bite and what it could mean if my symptoms came to a crescendo, forcing me to shift into one of *them.* Hopefully it never came to that.

The voices from last night came back to me.

Monster.

But I refused to listen. I wasn't one of them.

"And you've done a great job, but please listen to me. The only thing that changed after you were bitten was your hair." Arthur grabbed the ends of my hair, rubbing the strands between his fingers. "The green was never there prior to the bite." He exhaled, his wrinkled face pale.

"About that… why are my ends green?" I asked, snatching my hair back.

"When werewolves shift to human form, their hair matches their magic affinity," Alden answered. "You have an affinity to the woodlands… the forest."

Arthur held up his hands, giving Alden a warning look, "But that's all. I'm sorry I didn't tell you sooner." He hung his head. "And I'm sorry I didn't say anything about Sullivan sending the wolves after you and your parents. I didn't want to add trauma to the fire."

My parents were dead because of Sullivan, who'd let me live only to torture me later with dark magic. His magic had been a terrifying tool that aided his corruption, and it only got worse as time went on. Of course, Arthur had wanted to protect us against that.

My eyes fell to the floor as I hung my head, frustrated with myself for being such a damned coward when it came to Sullivan. I should've done more to shield Fang from the dark magic, but I'd been powerless at the time. My symptoms were another issue. My raging scar, the shattering feeling in my bones, the coldness in my skin, the nausea and disorientation. Everything fell into place. The curse was there, slowly manifesting into something I wanted *no* part of.

"You knew the bite affected me, but you dismissed everything." I slumped into my chair, defeated. "And by the way, thanks for erasing Nora's memory. I know you were behind that. While I'm grateful she doesn't remember, I wish you'd let me fight my own battles, Arthur. I'm not helpless."

Arthur's mouth snapped shut and he averted eye contact. Redness tinted his skin, giving away his shame. He *had* altered her memory of the incident. Days like this were reminders of how much I loathed Arthur's gift.

"Sullivan said I bit somebody," I deadpanned.

"You were only playing with another child. It was accidental. There haven't been any incidents since then and the victim is fine," Alden cut in. "There's no need to push the issue any further."

I side-eyed Alden, knowing damned well that the memories wouldn't have shown me that tidbit if it didn't mean something. "How do you know the boy is fine? If I remember correctly, you weren't even there. Sullivan was in charge of your castle for some gods-damned reason."

Alden crossed his arms. "I know because the boy's name is Lance, and he attends class with you. As you can see, there is nothing wrong with him. That should clarify that you're not a danger."

I stuffed a bread roll into my mouth, chewing violently as I shot Alden a scowl.

"Arthur," I said after swallowing the roll. "When did we leave Leavenfell and why don't I remember Lance and Peter?" Peter was someone I would never forget. His antics alone were unforgettable.

"We resided at Leavenfell for six years after you were bitten. Though we briefly left during our time here to visit your hometown. We found Fang along the way."

I remembered finding Fang, but I didn't recall returning to Leavenfell. "Six years? I don't remember being here even one year!" I exclaimed.

"You, Fang, Peter, and Lance all had your memories tampered with before we left. Sullivan wanted to leave no recollection of anything. His parting gift... out of spite. You were all very close, the four of you." Arthur stared up at the towering ceiling, his eyes lost as if he were reminiscing.

I held my breath, so many thoughts racing through my head at once. The pull that tugged on me when I was around Lance... it had to be some kind of wolfish bond.

I leaned forward, placing my chin into my palms, the ache in my head matching the ache in my chest. Fang was still in the great hall waiting for me. I needed to wrap this up sooner rather than later.

"Lance doesn't remember the bite?" I asked, raising my head.

"His memory was erased, just the same as you, once Sullivan demanded it of me. Please, if I hadn't done what I did, Sullivan would have had you killed." Arthur released a strangled breath, shifting uncomfortably in his seat.

I let out a sigh, my mind reeling. I hadn't remembered Sullivan during our time at Leavenfell, other than what the memory showed me. My memory was hazy. I tried to recollect all the various places we'd traveled throughout the years. Fleurya. Talem. Ju...

When we ended up at Helm Castle in Calzour two years ago, we ran into Sullivan. He was welcoming at first, but that changed over time, ensuring that every day there was misery. He was a thousand times worse than he was in my limited memory of Leavenfell Castle.

"What is Sullivan's tie to us, Arthur?" I asked, rubbing the sides of my head with extended fingers.

Arthur hesitated, tapping his foot nervously. "Sullivan was once a kind and wonderful person, Rue. It's hard for me to talk about." Arthur's eyes glistened, but he never once averted his gaze.

"No more secrets," I reminded him.

Arthur closed his eyes and swallowed hard, sweat beads dripping off his forehead. "He wanted you dead. He wanted your whole family dead," Arthur began. "Because of your father. Your father worked as an alchemist, but he also joined an organization that was involved in highly dangerous jobs of keeping the realms under control and protecting humanity from the dangers that lurked inside Vol. Sullivan knew of this, and I'd bet my ass he was a part of the reason why Vol opened. One year before your parents died, Sullivan grew close with your father and got involved with the organization. Somewhere along the way, Sullivan changed…" Arthur drew in a deep breath, hesitating, and I could see in his eyes that he was struggling to find the words to say. "He changed," Arthur repeated, his voice hollow, "and none of us saw it coming." The grief behind Arthur's eyes startled me. He must've cared so much about Sullivan before he'd taken a darker path.

"Why?" I asked. "Why do you think Sullivan is tied to the opening of Vol?"

Arthur leaned towards me, placing a firm hand on mine. A pulse of light exploded behind my eyelids, and the realm fell away.

CHAPTER 17

ARTHUR'S REVELATION

ARTHUR'S EYES WERE A GLASS WINDOW INTO HIS PAST LIFE, the curtains drawn aside, allowing me entry, as I rooted myself inside him. He stood inside the heart of a gothic castle, the earth-toned walls adorned with old paintings and iron sconces. Heavy burgundy curtains blocked out sunlight, and gold trim lined the walls and vaulted ceiling. Arthur neared the back of the chamber, where figures dressed in burgundy hooded robes stood beside a massive statue of a hyeling.

The ivory hyeling pinned a human to the ground, its jaws open wide, ready to consume its victim. The statue was detailed, the expression on the man's terrified face captured with perfection, his scream frozen in time. The hyeling's eyes gleamed as Arthur observed it.

"This isn't right," a man snapped, pacing in front of the statue, staring up at it with disdain. "An abomination." The man's hood dropped, revealing my dad's gray eyes and tense expression. One of the lenses on his glasses was cracked.

Another hood dropped, revealing Sullivan's face.

"Power. That is what Alester is offering. Power and immortality. I will not turn that down. Neither should you," Sullivan argued. His features were young but sharp, and there was no scar across his left eye.

"He's right," Arthur said to Sullivan. "We can't accept it. It'll throw the realms into disarray."

Sullivan scoffed at him. "It'll weed out the less powerful. It will give us better control of the realms. It wouldn't hurt to get rid of the mortals and free up land," Sullivan pleaded his case. I felt Arthur's nausea. He knew Sullivan wouldn't comply.

My father grabbed the front of Sullivan's robes. "You are my dearest friend, Sully. How can you blindly accept Alester's offer, knowing what it will cause? What about m-my child? My wife? What will happen to the people of Fleurya?" His voice broke.

Sullivan shoved my father's hands away, a look of disgust crossing his face. "Only the strong will survive, but I promise that I will protect your wife and daughter. You have my word."

"Is there someone influencing Alester?" my father asked. "Don't tell me Vaddeus is behind this? If he is, then you might as well be working alongside the monsters of Vol."

"I'm not working alongside them. You should know this," Sullivan argued, but the way his eyes flicked to the side had me questioning him.

My father took a step back, his skin paling. He held a hand to his chest. "Sullivan. I beg you. Please think this over."

"I've already made up my mind. You're either with me or you're against me. Choose," Sullivan snapped, darkness swirling behind his eyes.

"Please don't make me choose," my father begged, but Sullivan strode away without a backwards glance.

The curtains snapped shut.

I gasped, my eyes stinging as they rolled back into place. I'd returned to Alden's office, thankful my body was my own once again, though my head throbbed. I hadn't known Arthur could show memories through his own eyes.

"He's immortal," I stated, my heart sinking.

Arthur nodded.

"This offer he accepted. Was it to assist with releasing the Volings into Fogstone?"

"Yes, a wicked plan Sullivan aided, exchanging his humanity for power and immortality," Arthur confirmed.

"He set my parents up to die because they didn't agree with him." I realized.

"I believe so, but it didn't become clear to me until Helm Castle that Sullivan was involved in their deaths. I'd thought Alester was behind it."

I shook my head, gazing at a random drawing of a machine on Alden's desk. It all made sense. Sullivan's insane strength and his growing magic, not only from drawing on me and Fang's energy, but from taking countless mortal lives.

"Who is Alester? And Vaddeus?" I asked, desperate for all the information I could get.

Alden answered, "Alester was an old friend of mine. One who was corrupted by magic, along with Sullivan later on. He got to Sullivan after his failed attempts with me. As for Vaddeus..." Alden drifted off, staring somewhere far away. "He is a necromancer capable of many terrible things. A god of sorts. We don't speak of him," Alden said, his tone stern.

Arthur leaned forward, fiddling with one of the feathery quills on top of Alden's desk. "In Calzour, Sullivan swore he wasn't working with those monsters. I believed him because I was blinded by the illusion that he was his old self again."

"He never was," I said.

"I know that now, but then, I doubted myself for thinking he'd been involved in your parents' deaths. I was wrong. A fool to believe his act for even a second, and an even bigger fool to endanger you and Fang."

I took a deep breath. Sullivan had been responsible for my parents' deaths, and I was certain he had it out for me too.

"The prophecy…" Arthur continued. "Sullivan believes that you're tied to the prophecy."

"She is," Alden cut in. Arthur shot him a dirty look.

"You don't know that for sure," Arthur spat before turning back to me. "It speaks of a gifted girl who is responsible for the closing of Vol. He was aware that you were born without gifts, but he still suspected, and for that reason alone, he wanted to *prevent* you from fulfilling that prophecy, especially since he's working with the Volings. If Vaddeus is pulling the strings—"

"That's enough," Alden interrupted.

Arthur hung his head. "I believe he treated you that way to elicit a reaction, to see if you had a hidden gift, but you never showed any signs. Rue, you're alive because you have no gifts."

Alden tapped his staff against his desk, a grunt escaping him. "The prophecy spoke of a cursed girl, not a gifted one," He clarified. "It's her."

I trembled, struggling to form a response to that, but Arthur smacked his hand against the desk.

"She's not involved with it!" Arthur yelled, his cheeks reddening.

Alden shot out of his seat. "You need to accept the inevitable. It's already been set in motion. Her symptoms are proof enough."

A chill ran down my spine. Tears welled in my eyes, and I caught myself longing for that boy's comfort, even though Fang was right outside.

Arthur paused. "When Helm Castle fell to the Volings, that confirmed to me that Sullivan was working with them." He stared at the wall behind Alden, his eyes distant, his shoulders trembling.

I winced at the memory of torn apart bodies littering Helm Castle's grounds. *There'd been so many.* "And the prophecy? The one that supposedly closes off Vol from Fogstone? Why do you think I'm not involved? I *am* cursed, in case you've forgotten," I said, my voice shaking. "Alden seems to think so."

"I'm not saying anything more."

Puko descended from his perch to my right shoulder, clicking comforting coos in my ear.

"Why didn't you tell me about the prophecy?" I asked.

Arthur's face fell into his hands. "I didn't want you to fall into your father's footsteps and put yourself in danger over a prophecy that may or may not exist. There's supposed to be a record of it somewhere, but we don't even know where to find the cursed thing."

"But we should look. The prophecy could save everyone," I said, desperation rising inside of me. "If the girl from the prophecy *is* me, I would gladly close off that realm!" My heart leapt at the notion of a kingdom without monsters. A kingdom where no one would have to watch their backs. No one would have to hide anymore.

"We could save so many people. Not only us, but so many other races that are in danger." I leaned forward, placing my hands firmly on the desk. "We can close Vol, Arthur. This nightmare can finally be over."

A look of shock crossed Arthur's face. "You are *not* getting involved," he snapped, "It's too dangerous, especially with Sullivan still out there."

I shut my mouth, not daring to argue with him when his tone got that heated.

"Unfortunately, I've been unable to locate Sullivan since the Helm fell," Alden admitted, tightening his grip on his staff. "But I assure you that once he is found, he will be captured and *taken care of.*"

"How do you even know Sullivan?" I growled.

"Sullivan was an old friend. Like Arthur mentioned earlier, he wasn't always a terrible person. He was kind. Caring. Magic can corrupt even the best of people, and as with Alester, the same unfortunately happened to Sullivan. I'm sorry you had to be a victim of it."

Corruption or not, I hated Sullivan. I hated everything he'd done to me and to those I loved.

Alden let out a sigh. "Arthur, I trust you'll make an effort henceforth. No more secrets and stop disclaiming the prophecy."

"Fine."

Alden tapped his staff on the floor. "Very well. Please leave us for a moment. I need to speak with Rue alone."

Arthur stood up and rested his hand on my shoulder. "I'm sorry for not telling you about your parents. I thought it was something you wouldn't want to know."

I gave a stiff nod, not sure how to respond since I was still processing my feelings. After a tense moment, Arthur left the room, flustered and pale.

Alden studied me with curiosity blazing in his eyes. I waited for him to speak, my arms crossed over my chest as I tapped my foot against the floor.

"I presume you know why you're still here, Ms. Watson." It wasn't a question. Alden folded his hands and placed them on the desk. "I'm aware that you've been through a lot today and I'm sure you want to be with Everett Fang right now, but there are private matters we still need to discuss."

That note for one.

"Did I find what I'm supposedly looking for?" I asked him, eyebrows raised.

Alden smiled, gesturing at Puko, who was still perched on my shoulder, content as can be. "I'm glad my friend helped you, but you need to be careful with how you move forward. You lose a bit of yourself the more you visit those doors."

Lose a bit of yourself? Is that why I'd attacked Nora?

I crossed my arms, hoping my face wasn't displaying the multitude of emotions raging inside me. The presence of magic always took its toll, but Alden made it sound like the rooms behind the clock doors drained more energy than normal with its magic. But he was wrong. Leavenfell Castle's magic was waning.

"So all along, you intended for the key to fall into my hands, because of the prophecy. That's why you sent Puko to help me," I said. "And you knew damned well that Arthur wouldn't tell me anything, and since he was watching you, you made Puko lead me to it."

A small smile pierced through Alden's mask. "I'm sorry for the way I went about it. Regardless, the purpose of this meeting with Arthur was to allow you to take the next step forward, without him hindering you."

"And the key?" I asked. "Will it lead me to the prophecy?"

"Perhaps. However, use caution with the key. Those clock doors are not merely rooms. They change... sometimes into realms, which can be very dangerous."

"How in the hells did you manage to fit realms into your castle?" I snapped. "Behind weird-ass clock doors. Who does that?"

Alden hid his face behind his hand, and I suspected he was hiding a smile.

"I created the clock doors, but not the realms. The doors choose what to show the person who enters, on their own."

My lips parted. His magic was out of control. *Great.*

"To a normal person, the doors would reveal a small storage closet, but you... you confirmed everything I suspected, because those doors showed you something entirely different. This confirms that you *are* tied to the prophecy, like it or not."

"*You* wrote that letter." My words came out as an accusation. "Why?" I demanded, slamming my hands against his desk so hard that Puko screeched and flew across the room.

"You needed a push, hence why I gave you that note." Alden stated. "To help find the prophecy. The doors could lead you to it."

"You really believe that the prophecy could be hidden behind one of those doors," I said through gritted teeth.

Alden studied me, scrutinizing my every movement and facial expression. The room was silent besides the ticking of the many clocks that hung on his study wall, on every free space where there wasn't a bookshelf.

Alden sank back into his leather chair, his expression thoughtful. "Yes."

"Why can't you find it?"

"I've tried. The doors won't show me anything because I'm not tied to the prophecy," Alden answered.

"What's my purpose in all of this?" I asked, flinging my hand outward with annoyance. "That was in your note, remember?"

"To find the record of the prophecy," Alden said. "You already wanted to, but I fueled your curiosity with that note."

The nerve of this wizard. It felt like we were talking in circles.

"We're done here." I started to get up, but Alden smacked his staff against his desk. A few angry screeches came from behind his beard.

"What?" I snapped, sitting back down.

"Before you go, I'd like to ask you one question."

"Make it quick," I snapped.

"Brilliant as you are, Ruby, and you are one of the brightest of your age group—tell me this. Have you managed to figure out the secret of time?"

I stilled, the question catching me off guard. I took a moment to deeply think about the intent behind his question before answering. That pocket watch came to mind.

I cocked my head to the side, then it hit me. "Let's say the clocks stop ticking." My eyes came to a rest on the pocket watch that so openly hung from his robe pockets.

Alden gave me a curious look.

"When that watch stops, what happens to us? Are we still safe?" I replied, believing I was on the verge of something massive. "It seems to me like you're carrying the secret of time in your robe pockets." I gestured to his pocket watch. "And your magic is failing."

"It's not failing," Alden growled.

"But it is. I felt it in that library realm. The magic shifted," I told him. "It became weaker, and as far as I'm concerned, that's not normal."

Alden regarded me with fascination and a bit of horror, as though he was impressed by my findings. "That happened in the realm, not the castle."

"The realm is inside your castle in case you've forgotten," I pointed out. I stood up to leave, but Alden grabbed my arm, his grip strong for an old man.

"Before you go, Ms. Watson. Another word of advice," Alden said, his voice low. "Be careful around Everett Fang."

My head whipped towards him. "Why would I be careful around my best friend? I've known Fang my whole life."

Alden raised a bushy eyebrow. "Be careful." He didn't say anything more on the subject. "Send him in after you leave. I'll catch up with you shortly. This conversation isn't over."

I opened the door leading into the great hall, relieved to see that Fang hadn't moved from the spot I left him. His plate was empty, but his eyes roamed over the kitchen, where Mrs. Baker was hard at work on breakfast. I'd have to grab him another plate before we went to my room.

"Alden's asking to see you now," I told him, wrapping my arms around his neck. "But don't be too long because I missed the shit out of you."

That familiar wolfish grin of his spread across his face, but his eyes were distant, as though he were miles away.

"Don't worry, Ruby. I'll be quick," he reassured me, squeezing my arm. The office door shut behind him. I faced the now closed door, unable to process that Fang had called me by my full name.

He hadn't called me that in a long time.

CHAPTER 18

THE ORIGIN OF ALDEN

FANG CHANGED INTO A CLEAN SET OF CLOTHES GIVEN TO HIM by Alden and then followed me out onto the bridge that led to my tower room. We didn't make it far when Alden caught up with us. He moved surprisingly fast for an ancient wizard with a staff carved from an ancient tree.

"How did you know?" Alden came to a stop in front of me and rested his elbow on one of the branches of his staff.

I stiffened. "Know what?" The chill of wet snowflakes against my skin made me shiver.

"You can go ahead," Alden directed Fang, gesturing at the door ahead of us. Fang side-eyed me. I slumped my shoulders, already dreading his absence. Alden had said that our conversation wasn't over, but I didn't think he'd seek me out this fast.

"I'll catch up soon. My room is at the top of my steps," I told him. He gave me a quick hug before darting across the bridge and disappearing under the heavy snow.

"Fyrendio," Alden muttered the incantation, and a gust of warmth surrounded me, nearly searing the hair off my arms.

"The pocket watch. Explain," Alden ordered.

Heavy snow pelted us, but it melted against my heated skin, the cyclone of warmth from his spell swirling around us.

"In one of the memories, Sullivan tinkered with a small pocket watch. One *exactly* like yours." I snapped, letting the implication hang. "When he touched the center of it, the barrier vanished, and Arthur was able to enter the castle grounds. When he touched the same spot later, the barrier returned."

Alden gave a small nod. "I'm surprised you noticed such a tiny detail in the confines of your memory."

"Why did he have your pocket watch? Where were you at the time?"

"I'd taken a reprieve from the castle and left it in the hands of my friend," Alden said plainly. "Nothing more, nothing less."

I regarded him with skepticism. This man must've thought me stupid. Why would he stay friends with a man who'd unleashed chaos into Fogstone? A lot of people had died because of Sullivan.

I took a step towards him. "I should ask you — what are you playing at?"

"I can assure you that I'm not playing any games, Ms. Watson."

"What happens to all of us, here in Leavenfell Castle, when that pocket watch of yours stops ticking?" I asked heatedly. "You know exactly what I'm implying, so don't treat me like I'm stupid."

Alden bent down towards me until he was right by my ear, the pocket watch gripped securely between his fingertips. "This watch is a very powerful talisman, Miss Watson. One that I created myself and that I have complete faith in. You needn't worry."

I stepped back. "If that barrier fails —"

"It won't," Alden interrupted. "It will *not* fail."

I gawked at him, rendered speechless. He had such faith in that pocket watch, but if I knew one thing about magic — it wasn't reliable or permanent. The chill of the heavy, wet snow against my skin meant that his incantation spell had already burnt out. Spells didn't last.

"If it did, though," I pressed. "Is there a back up to your grand plan?"

"Let me give you some history… to help you better understand," Alden said, pocketing the watch deep into the folds of his gray robe.

Of course. There's always a damned story…

"You must think I have all the time in the world to listen to your stories," I snapped. "I need to go. My best friend is finally back, and I'd like to spend my time catching up with him. Alone."

"If you're worried about time, I'll put a stop to it."

Alden struck his staff against the bridge planks. The magic from the force of his staff slammed into me and I squeezed my eyes shut, temporarily stunned. When I opened my eyes again, snowflakes hung motionless midair. The wind had stopped, and the trees were no longer rustling. I glanced at Dagger Sea in the distance. Even the choppy waves had gone still. It was an unsettling sight.

"Humor me for a moment. It's not a request."

"What are you exactly?" I asked.

"Far beyond a wizard," he admitted, his voice dripping with power so paralyzing, I took a step backward, swallowing hard.

"A long time ago, Sullivan and myself met a necromancer called Alester, who agreed to take us on as his apprentices. Alongside him, we worked hard to hone our magic, improving our potential beyond anyone's imagination." Alden paced back and forth as he spoke, the wooden bridge creaking underneath his wool-clad boots. "Years later, we learned that combining a bit of forbidden magic with elements of nature created a new source of magic. One we called our own."

"Your own magic?"

"Yes. We called it the *Netherros*."

"The Netherros," I repeated, the word vibrating off my tongue.

Alden nodded. "The Netherros, although dangerous, allowed me to accomplish feats I never thought possible. I forced a fragment of the Netherros's magic into my old pocket watch and created this." He dangled his pocket watch in front of my face, his eyes maddened, like its power consumed him. "As you know, there's much more I can do with this watch besides creating protective barriers." He gestured at the dangling snowflakes, still unmoving.

"But why a pocket watch? What's the significance?"

"I was born with the gift of controlling time, as well as many other gifts I won't go into detail about," Alden said. "Bend it, stop it, control it, even reverse it." Alden's eyes glowed with an unnerving whiteness, the shape of twisted branches threaded across his pupils, and I took another hesitant step backward, putting some distance between us.

"If you can reverse it, then why didn't you save my parents?" I asked.

"There are rules with time, Ms. Watson. Rules that don't allow anyone to play with death lightly."

An icy chill seeped into my veins. I was scared. Not only for myself, but for everyone that I'd grown to care about in Leavenfell. Alden held everyone's lives in the pockets of his robes, in that old *pocket watch*, and no one knew about it but me. If Alden's magic was unstable and potentially dangerous, then it was only a matter of time before the barrier around the castle gave way. I glanced at the castle, imagining a broken shell instead of a grand structure. The imagery made me swallow hard.

"After I separated from Alester, I traveled here and became enamored with the cliffs of Fennra. Naturally, I built a castle on the grounds near Dagger Sea and named it Leavenfell. About twenty-five years ago, I fell in love with a mortal woman. Her golden eyes were a sight to behold," he said fondly, sounding almost human again.

Golden eyes. The boy from the clock room had golden eyes.

"We ran away together, embarking on the great adventure of life. Nothing was impossible with the magic I carried, so we left the castle in the hands of my former childhood friend, Sullivan, like I'd done many other times before. I also left him with my pocket watch—to protect the castle while I was gone." The way his voice softened told me his story wouldn't end well.

"What happened after?" I asked.

Alden hung his head, and I saw the grief in his eyes, something I was familiar with myself. He didn't have to say anything.

"You only need to know that I'm home now and I'm keeping the castle safe. Keeping your family safe."

"You brought us here because you suspected I was tied to the prophecy, much like Sullivan believed," I deadpanned.

Alden lifted his chin. "You're not wrong."

I exhaled. "I can't hate you for that. Even if I hadn't met you, I would've searched for the prophecy myself after learning about it, especially if that meant saving the realms from those monsters."

"That's why I respect you, Rue. You're not afraid to get involved." Alden tapped his staff against the bridge, and everything returned to the way it was. The snow descended as if nothing had happened to begin with. I wondered how many moments he'd stolen like this.

Alden's eyes returned to normal, and he stared at the sea, lost in his own thoughts.

"How old are you?" I'd been curious about his age since meeting him.

"Seven hundred and twenty-four," Alden replied, lifting his head towards the cloudy sky above.

"And the boy with the brown hair and golden eyes?" I needed to confirm my suspicions.

"Ah, you found him, did you? That would be my son, Thomassen. He has his mother's eyes."

A name, finally.

"Why haven't I seen him around the castle with everyone else?"

"He comes around when everyone else has gone off to bed. Shy one, that boy," Alden explained. "Prefers to keep to himself."

A thought hit me. "Your clock door took me to his room. Why? Is Thomassen involved in the prophecy?"

Alden gave me a dark look. The weight of my question hung between us, and I swore I saw the darkness swirling behind his eyes, as though the Netherros's dark magic was concealed within him.

"Ask him that *next* time you see him," Alden said after a tense moment. The darkness faded.

If I could get him to talk to me at all.

"And what of Alester?" I asked.

"Lost somewhere, likely a shell of who he once was. You see, the Netherros can corrupt its users. Before Alester disappeared, he often called on the dark magic of the Netherros, so much so that… well, you can guess the rest. Sullivan was a victim of its corruption too, unfortunately," Alden said.

Arthur's story about Sullivan not always being the bad guy was becoming believable, especially if the Netherros had a hand in corrupting him. Still, nothing would justify what Sullivan had done to me or my family, even if there was a sliver of humanity left inside him.

"I suggest putting him out of your mind for now. The answers will come to us when they're ready." Alden turned, his robe swishing. "I'm taking my leave. I've held you up from your friend long enough." He cast a glance over his shoulder, "Feel free to visit Thomassen. He does get quite lonely."

Chapter 19

Betrayal

I found Fang on my bed, nuzzled against the warmth of my comforter, sleeping like the dead. I laid beside him and wrapped my arm around his waist, not wanting to wake him but also needing contact, a way of reassuring myself that his presence was real. While he slept, I debated taking him to the hidden corridor with me, then thought better of it. Knowing my luck, I'd run into that grumpy boy again, Thomassen. He'd say something mean like he always did, which would result in Fang's fist in his face. *Yeah... never mind about that.*

I scooted off the bed to use the washroom when Fang's eyes snapped open. He jolted upright, his hands held out in front of him as though defending himself from something unseen. His hand twitched towards me, but he stopped himself.

My heart raced. "It's okay. It's just me." I hopped back onto the bed and wrapped him in a hug. My bladder would have to wait.

"How long was I out?" Fang yawned.

"About an hour. You can sleep more if you need to."

Fang yawned, stretching his arms over his head. "Nah. I'd like to go to class. Need some structure today."

I groaned but didn't want to upset him. "Class is supposed to be starting now."

Fang planted his feet on the carpet, snatching his black boots from the side of the bed and sliding them on.

"Ready," he announced, smoothing his hair out of his face.

"Shouldn't you shower first?" I asked, holding my hand over my nose.

Fang cracked a smile. "I used the balm from your nightstand. I hope you don't mind."

I looked at the bottle beside the candlestick. Nora had given me that balm. It smelled like freshly washed laundry and a hint of vanilla. I sniffed the air. Fang smelled like pig shit doused in vanilla.

"You're showering after class," I told him, crossing my arms. A part of loving Fang was looking out for him, even if that meant tough love.

"Fine," Fang agreed.

After we arrived at the classroom, Fang went inside, earning a bunch of curious stares. I left him there and went to the washroom, only to return to find Liessa and a girl with black hair fawning over him. Fang kicked his legs out in front of him, his hands behind his head as he gave them a dashing smile. *Gods above…*

I took a seat beside him, rolling my eyes. It was totally like Fang to have women swooning after him, with no added effort on his part. His black locks, deep blue eyes, and dimpled smile were all he needed. After a few minutes of listening to the girls flirting with him, I shooed them away.

"*Please* tell me you don't fancy them," I whispered, my tone coming across sharper than I meant it.

Peter craned his neck to look at us, a smile ghosting his lips, and I already knew what he was about to say. He turned, resting his arms on my desk, and made that stupid look that told me I should probably walk away before I got the urge to smack him.

"Who wouldn't like those two?" Peter said, ogling the girls as they exited the room. "Did you see the way Liessa's rump swished when she—"

"Gods, Peter! You're disgusting." I shoved his arms off my desk, giving him a dirty look. It wasn't even noon, and I was already fed up with him.

Fang laughed, catching my eyes. "I didn't notice."

Peter snickered. "Take a better look next time. It's worth it."

Nora walked by his desk and lightly smacked the side of Peter's head with her history book. "If I hear you mention Liessa's ass one more time, I might throw up."

Peter shook his head at Fang, but Nora lifted her leg and placed it on his desk, blocking his view. I thanked the gods she was wearing pants, but Peter peeked up at Nora with anything but an innocent smile.

Nora snorted. "Don't even say it, Peter. The only time you'll ever get a view of my panties is if I'm dead."

I bit back a laugh.

Peter's face reddened, and he faced the front of the classroom, taking a sudden interest in fiddling with the buttons on his jacket sleeve.

Fang stared at Nora, smiling so big that his dimples made an appearance. "You're incredible."

Nora blushed, but her ears perked right up. "Someone's gotta keep Peter in line when Lance isn't around."

Peter swiveled, the tops of his ears reddening. "I'm behaving," he whined.

She dipped her face in front of him, flicking his nose. "Then stop talking about Liessa's rounded rump. I'm sick of it. So is Rue."

"I'm sorry," Peter said earnestly.

Glitch entered the classroom and directed everyone to open their books, but Fang had my full attention. His eyes followed the steambot's movements, his mouth parting. He spared me a glance, his lips downturned and arms crossed.

I leaned towards him. "Are you okay? Arthur and I—we were both so worried about you. We thought we'd lost you."

"Let's talk about it later," Fang whispered. His narrow eyes dropped to his desk, wandering across it rapidly, as though he were remembering some horror. My pulse quickened.

Before I could respond, the steambot bumped into my desk.

"You're late," it said.

"I was here before you," I argued, raising my upturned palms in confusion.

Glitch observed me with contempt, the sides of its metal face folding downward. "Friends can catch you up on today's lessons," it said, walking back to its desk.

I turned to Nora, whose expression mirrored my own hesitation. "What lesson?"

Peter made a face. "This class is pointless," he said. "We never learn anything, and Alden won't fix the bot."

"It's not like this every day, is it?" asked Fang, leaning forward and resting his elbows on his desk.

"We can ditch if you want," I told him.

Fang's crooked smile made an appearance. "I can't say no to that."

We slipped out of the room after I told Nora I'd catch up with her later, and headed towards the back entrance of the castle, past the farm and greenhouse, only stopping when we reached the edge of the rocky cliff. I swung my feet over the ledge, and Fang followed suit.

"Peter is wild," Fang said with a grin, his gaze set forward on the sea.

"That's one way to put it," I said.

"Is he always like that?"

"Unfortunately," I sighed. "But he can be funny sometimes."

Fang rested his back against the ground, his legs dangling over the edge of the cliff. He interlocked his hands behind his head, cushioning himself against the hard rock underneath. I laid on my side beside him, happy to be with him again, like old times.

"What happened out there?" I asked.

Fang peeked an eye open, his expression darkening. "I don't want to talk about it."

I nodded. He wasn't ready to open up and that was fine. I wouldn't push him. We remained side by side for the next couple of hours, listening to the sound of the crashing waves and breathing in the salty mist of the sea. Fang was so quiet I figured he'd fallen asleep, but he peeked one eye open every once in a while to check on me.

"Don't ever go missing on me again," I whispered.

Fang gave me a sad smile.

When our stomachs started growling, we decided it was time to go, so we headed back into the castle. I bumped into Olivia on our way to the great hall. I apologized, but she sighed with annoyance, looking me up and down with scrutiny.

"You might want to go find your friend, the red-headed girl," she said coolly. "Novalein."

"It's Noralei," I corrected her.

"How've you been since passing out?" A tone of suspicion rattled her voice.

"I'm fine. Why?" I asked.

"Only curious. When you find Noralei, tell her to stop blubbering over a guy who has no interest in her," Olivia snapped. "You should also watch your own back where boys are concerned."

I rolled my eyes at her. Was she that upset over my friendship with Lance? I'd caught her staring at him during meal hours, her eyes burning with intensity as though she had some claim over him.

"There's nothing going on with Lance," I explained. "He's my friend. That's all."

"Isn't fighting over boys a bit amateur?" Fang asked her.

Olivia ignored him, pinning a glare at me. "I never said this was about Lance." She turned heel and walked away, flipping her long black hair over her shoulder.

Sheesh. Fang stared after Olivia, shaking his head.

"Come with me to find Nora?" I asked him.

"Sure. Everything okay with—?"

"Olivia, and don't worry about it. It's not worth discussing," I said.

We found Nora in the tower sitting on the floor, looking about as flustered as I'd been after my brief conversation with Olivia. I sat beside her and wrapped my arm around her. She vented to me while Fang took a much needed shower. After a few minutes, Nora pulled away, brushing her hair out of her eyes. Her skin was blotchy from crying and her ears hung lower than I'd ever seen them.

She rubbed the wrinkles out of her skirt. "You should've them during lunch. Liessa was all over him. It was so awkward that even Peter screamed at them to get a room." She flopped onto her bed. "Stupid Peter," she muttered with a smile.

"Leave it to Peter to make a comment like that."

"He's a dumbass," Nora grunted.

Fang emerged, his hair still wet from his shower, but at least he was dressed. Back at the Helm, he'd come out of the shower butt naked. It didn't matter who was in the room. Fang simply didn't give a damn.

"What's this about Peter?" Fang asked, towel drying his hair. "Is he worried I'm going to steal all the attention from him?"

"I'm sure he's worried he has competition now," I said. "I mean look at you." I gestured at Fang, and he laughed.

He turned in a circle with his palms outstretched. "You're right. I mean look at this chiseled figure."

"Don't be cocky," I joked, earning a dimple from him.

Fang feigned shock. "Ruby, I'm hurt." He clenched his hand over his heart, but I couldn't move past him using my full name again. I recalled my conversation with Alden, and I couldn't help but remember his warning.

Be careful around Fang.

The room filled with the sound of Nora and Fang's laughter, but it was hard to stay present. There was so much going on in my head that I could hardly compartmentalize any of it. I should've been over the two moons that Fang was back, but I couldn't shake my worry over the werewolf bite and the knowledge that the barrier was being controlled by Alden's pocket watch. If that secret got out and backfired on me for not telling anyone, I worried I'd lose my friends.

It was insanity that no one else had noticed. Were the people of Leavenfell so blinded by the mask of safety that they couldn't pick up on such an important detail? One that Alden carried with him everywhere. Someone had to have seen *something*. I shook my head. There was the matter of the prophecy as well. Alden had been right. His note had fueled the curiosity inside me. I needed to find the prophecy, even if that meant risking my own safety.

Nora tugged on my shirt, her eyes bright as she tossed her long red hair over her shoulder. "Ready to eat?"

"Dinner already?" Fang asked in disbelief. We never had meals this often at the Helm.

Nora nodded, but her cheeks reddened. "It is a bit early, but for reasons I can't explain, I'm missing Peter's presence, so let's go."

Lance waited for me at the bottom of the staircase, leering at Fang, his lips pursed. I imagined it looked bad that Fang had come from the direction of my bedroom, but Lance's expression softened when Nora caught up with us.

Lance held my hand as we entered the great hall, and Peter whistled in our direction, his eyebrows waggling.

Heat rose to my cheeks and I yanked my hand out of Lance's. "Peter—I swear to the gods—don't start."

Peter cackled and started making loud kissing sounds, earning himself a smack on the back of his head from Lance. I took a seat next to Nora, ignoring Peter's ongoing comments about my relationship with Lance.

"You know what's funny," I said to Nora, ignoring Olivia's pointed glares. "They say when you ignore a dog's bad behavior, the dog stops doing that behavior. But with Peter, he gets worse."

Nora gave a half-hearted laugh at my joke, her mind elsewhere. She glanced over at Finn and Liessa, who were eating dinner together, but Liessa kept stealing glances at Fang, who paid her no mind. I wondered if he was still held up on Myrabell.

"Ignore them and eat," I told Nora, wishing she'd move on from him. She deserved someone who was interested in her, and Finn was too old for her anyhow.

"I'm not hungry," Nora complained, but her growling stomach said otherwise.

"Eat," I reprimanded her, handing her a fork.

Nora smiled weakly and took the fork from me, while Peter stood and retrieved a blue droughtfly from his coat pocket.

"What the hells, Peter? Sit down *now*," Lance scolded.

"Relax. I'm trying to get a date for the banquet," Peter argued.

"Out of all the flowers in the garden, you chose a *weed*?" Oliver's face was beet red from laughter.

"It's a *droughtfly*," Peter corrected him.

"A droughtfly *is* a weed, dumbass," Olivia snapped. Her gaze slid to Oliver's with such focus that they must've been communicating telepathically amongst themselves. Oliver went quiet, his shoulders tensing.

"I snuck out earlier to grab it. The effort should count for something," Peter said.

"We're not supposed to go out there," Olivia sternly informed Peter. "Alden said so."

Peter twirled the droughtfly around in his hands, ignoring her.

"Peter, I swear to gods," Lance threatened.

Everyone in the great hall was staring at Peter with interest by this point. Peter took a deep breath and strutted over to the pretty girl with long black hair and hazel eyes.

"That's Isobela," said Nora when I looked to her for help. She was one of the girls flirting with Fang earlier.

Once Peter reached their table, he handed the droughtfly to Isobela. Without hesitation, she swatted it away with a mortified expression on her face. She shook her head and mouthed the word *no*. Peter returned to our table and plopped into his seat with a disappointed expression across his face.

Fang patted his back, trying to stifle a smile. "We *really* need to work on your flirting skills."

Peter lifted his head and said the most serious thing I'd ever heard Peter say. "I'm not good at this sort of thing."

Catching the defeated expression on his face, my heart squeezed. "You only need to go about things in a better way. Commit yourself to one girl. It shouldn't be that hard," I said.

"And stop staring at rumps," Nora added, pointing her fork at him. Peter cracked a smile.

"I appreciate you being so honest with him," Lance said to me. "He needs to hear it from others."

"Yeah, well… we should all be more like you and tell him the truth," I said. "It's an admirable trait to have."

Lance blushed and released a small laugh. "You're amazing, Rue." He leaned forward, pressing his lips against mine. It happened so suddenly that I froze, unable to form any words or think any coherent thoughts.

My skin heated as I broke away from him.

"Um, I— W-what was—?" I stuttered, shifting further away as I brought my fingers to my tingling lips. My scar flared to life, burning against the pull. *What the hells.*

"At least someone is getting action tonight," Peter said. I shot him a look that threatened strangulation.

"You kissed me," I said, my body tense. When I dared to look at Lance again, his expression softened.

"I did," Lance confirmed.

My scar blazed hotter, and I released an unintentional groan. Lance's soft expression shifted to concern as he brushed his hand against my forehead. I flinched at the contact.

"You're burning up," he stated. "Are you feeling alright? You just went really pale." His brows furrowed as he searched my face.

"Again, you *kissed* me. My body probably reacted."

Olivia scowled at me before sharing a heated glance with Oliver, then departed the table. I glanced at Fang, whose eyes had gone dark and his posture stiff. Worried that he wasn't acknowledging me, I reached underneath the table and grabbed his hand. He slowly faced me, eyes distant, his hand twitching. Something was very wrong.

Every source of light in the great hall flickered and went out. Chaos erupted as everyone jumped from their seats, screams echoing throughout the vast room. Chairs loudly scraped against the floor as people darted towards the exit. Shattered plates and half-eaten food littered the ground, and some people tripped over each other trying to escape. The great hall had turned into a scene from a nightmare.

A strange noise drew my attention towards the windows and the dark sky outside. The hair on the back of my neck stood up. Shadowy figures stood outside, their bony fingers scratching and tapping the windows, a harrowing sound, like nails cutting through glass. There were at least twenty of them, maybe more. Volings.

But they looked like skeletal ghosts… a race I'd never seen before. My heart hammered against my chest as I pulled on Fang's arm. Peter tripped over a chair and fell face first to the floor. Nora raced towards Alden's tower, Lance and Olivia following directly behind her.

A shrill scream sounded, and the grand arched windows shattered. Glass flew everywhere, scattering across the hall. A shard of soaring glass sliced my cheek, and warm blood drizzled down my face. My breath went still, clouding my lungs.

Amid the unmoving monsters stood *Sullivan*. My eyes locked with his against my will, a strong force gripping my chin, like he was compelling me to look at him. A strange language escaped his lips, rooting into me with staggering force while my energy slid from my body, coating the ground before slithering into his extended palm. I tried to scream, tried to run, but I was frozen in place, Fang unconscious at my side, his hand tightly interlocked with mine.

"Fang, wake up!" I yelled, desperation coiling inside my chest. My scar blazed too hot, and I screamed in pain.

Sullivan placed a large hand on the windowsill, a frightening smile painting his wrinkled face, the scar over his left eye bleeding black. I opened my mouth and closed it, trying to force a sound out of my throat.

The spell broke. I turned towards Fang, finally able to move, and shook his shoulders with as much strength as I could muster. Fang opened his eyes. The candles along the walls flared back to life. I returned my gaze to the windows, but the figures and Sullivan were gone, the windows still intact.

My eyes widened in disbelief. Everyone was still seated, chattering with their family and friends as though nothing had happened. There was no screaming, no panic, no shattered dishes on the floor. A tear slid down my face as I brought my hand up to my cheek, but no cut was there. Beside me, Fang brought his hand to his head, groaning as though he had a brewing headache.

"What just happened? Did you see them?" I faced Peter and Nora, who were still eating. From how hard my heart was racing, I expected it to explode out of my chest at any second.

"See who?" Lance asked, his cheeks flushing as he touched my hand. His brows stitched together with worry.

That terrible bone-breaking feeling crept up on me, and I trembled.

"Are you sure you're okay?" Lance asked.

"I have to go." I rushed out of the great hall without an explanation, but not before Peter called, "You must be a terrible kisser, Lance."

"What's going on?" Fang asked, catching my arm. He was sweating profusely, his eyes widening when he met my gaze.

"I saw Sullivan," I explained, voice shaking as goosebumps trailed over my skin. "He's here."

Fang paled. "Look, I know you're scared, but there's no possible way Sullivan can be here. Leavenfell is heavily guarded by magic. Alden said—"

"I don't give a damn what Alden said. He's not reliable," I fumed. "I saw him. Somehow, I *saw* him." I drew in a shuddering breath. "I'm scared, Fang. I'm scared he'll find us again and hurt you. What if he followed you? What happened out there?"

Fang lowered his head, his eyes darkening. "Being out there, Rue, it was horrifying. When I realized we couldn't win against the Volings at the Helm, I blinked myself and Myrabell out of there, but they caught up to us. They— they tortured Myrabell. They killed her in front of me. I—" Fang stopped, his voice breaking. I pulled him into a hug, my heart aching along with him. I hardly knew Myrabell, but she hadn't deserved a fate so cruel.

"I'm so sorry, Fang." I hardly knew Myrabell, but she meant a great deal to Fang, and for that, my heart clenched with pain.

"That's not all. Sullivan tortured me. Cursed me with his dark magic. I couldn't do anything, but I felt... I felt *everything*." Fang slumped against me, his arms tightening around my shoulders. "I felt them consume her."

A sharp chill ran through me, paralyzing me. *I'll kill Sullivan for what's he's done.*

"You should stay with me tonight. Every night from now on," I said, talking into his shoulder. "Please." If Sullivan was around, getting into our heads somehow, then I wanted Fang and I to be together. I needed him to be safe.

"Of course," Fang said.

"I'll stay with my parents tonight," Nora announced from behind us. "It seems you both need time to catch up."

"You don't have to," I told Nora, peeking at her over Fang's shoulder.

"It's fine," Nora said as we shared an awkward stare. "By the way, Lance looked pretty upset after you ran off. Should I tell him anything for you?"

"No. He shouldn't have kissed me. I didn't ask him to," I said. "It made me uncomfortable."

Nora's gaze dropped. "I expected something like that out of Peter, not him."

Although the kiss had flustered me, it did confirm something. I wasn't attracted to Lance. At least not in *that* way. Kissing him was like kissing Arthur. A friendly kiss shared between family, not one of passion. The kiss didn't give me any butterflies. My knees hadn't gone weak.

Nora offered a small smile. "Talk tomorrow?"

I nodded, holding onto Fang tight. "See you then."

When Fang and I got to the bedroom, he made himself comfortable on my bed, stretching his legs out in front of him.

"You're going to have to scoot over," I insisted.

Fang obliged and I took the spot next to him.

Puko flew above our heads, clicking its beak in disapproval. Clearly, Fang was not allowed in my bed. I shooed the bird away, but he landed on the nightstand and began pecking the wood in exasperation.

"What's gotten into you, Puko?" I asked. Puko responded with an angry squawk. I ignored him and turned towards Fang.

"Tell me what else happened out there," I pressed, side-eyeing Puko as he carried on with his tantrum. "Where did Sullivan go? Is there any chance he followed you and Rorik?"

Fang visibly shuddered at the mention of Sullivan's name, and I wanted to pinch myself for asking.

"I-I don't kn-know," he stuttered, his black locks curtaining his eyes. "I swear. After Myrabell died, everything was a blur."

I wanted to pinch myself for asking. Instead, I pulled him into a hug. "I love you, Fang, and I'm so sorry about Myrabell."

Fang flinched, his arms dropping by his side as he released me. "Don't talk about her," he snapped.

I was caught off guard. Fang's actions made me wonder about the extent of Sullivan's abuse. I didn't know how else to respond, so I hugged him again, trying to ignore the way his body stiffened against mine. Tears stung my eyes. I missed my friend. He was here, but he wasn't the same, and I hated that feeling.

"I love you forever," I told him again, repeating the words until they stuck with him.

Fang eventually relaxed into the hug, a piece of his old self coming through. "Forever."

There was a large wolf hunting in a wooded hollow. She approached a dying boy, curious about him, but was surprised when the boy stood, showing no trace of fear...

... and he looked so familiar. Light brown hair and golden eyes. He held a knife stained in dark blood.

"Rue, wake up! You must wake up," he ordered, terror flashing behind those eyes.

The boy dropped the knife, grabbing his neck, choking and —

I awoke suddenly, gasping for air. Cold, sharp metal pressed against my skin. I smelled the blood before I felt the searing pain on my neck. Fang pinned me to the bed, holding a dagger to my throat.

I choked, unable to speak. His full weight bore down on me, so heavy I couldn't struggle. His eyes locked onto mine, nothing in them but sadness, confusion, and rage. A rage I'd never seen in him before.

Why? Why are you doing this? I bucked against him, attempting to force him off me, but he was unbelievably strong.

His breath came in heavy pants, his dark hair slick with sweat. "Why can't you do this?" he cried, his voice edged with panic. "Just do it."

"Fang!" I managed to scream. "S-stop!" I choked when his other hand pressed against my clavicle, the knife digging deeper. Warmth drizzled down my shoulder blade.

His eyes widened in horror. He released the knife, but he continued to pin me down. "I'm sorry," he cried. "I'm sorry, Rue." His free hand lifted to his head, cradling the left side of his skull, and he yelped in pain.

Tears stung my eyes as I fought for another breath. "Why?!"

"They'll kill me." His voice broke and he screamed again, his hand glued to his head.

Who will kill you? But the words never left my lips.

"I have to stop this." Fang's grip tightened around my throat, leaving me unable to talk. "I can't take it anymore."

I was certain that I was going to die. My vision darkened as I struggled to breathe. Gasping, I blindly clawed at his face, my attempts weak.

Fang caught my hand, bringing his other fist down to the side of my head.

CHAPTER 20

AN UNWELCOME PARTING

A HAUNTING SOB ESCAPED MY LIPS.

The waves of the sea crashed against the jagged cliffside in a melodic, sleepy whoosh. The spray of water splashing against me was cold, but I didn't care. A hollowness seeped into my skin as I pulled my knees to my chest, rotting me from the inside out until I sensed a calming presence beside me. *Fang*. I looked up at him through glassy eyes. My tears ceased.

Fang stared at the sea, the wind tussling his curly hair, his eyes sad and full of longing. "This view never gets old," he breathlessly whispered. "That's why I keep coming back to this."

A painful lump formed in my throat. "You've been here before?"

Fang's expression changed. He balled his fists against his sides. "We both have. At the Helm. The cliffs there were... mesmerizing."

I stared up at him, watching fearfully as he paced the edge of the cliff. Fang had blinked us to many places before, but for some reason, I couldn't remember the location he was speaking of. Not at the Helm. Not where Sullivan would have found us.

Fang's eyes were distant. "Maybe we're really here and this isn't a dream."

"I have to go soon," I told Fang, my body trembling against a heavy pull determined to drag me away, despite my nails clawing into the dirt.

"I didn't mean it," Fang said. "I would never knowingly hurt you." Fang bent down and kissed the top of my head.

The ground underneath me rumbled, a warning. "I have to go. I can't stop it."

"The other night, you told me *I love you forever*. I won't forget that," Fang said.

My eyes widened. "You're my brother, Fang... I'll always love you."

The vision started cracking at the seams.

My fingers began to slip through the ground below me, like rain descending from a cloud. "Fang!" I cried, terrified that I was about to lose him forever. He was slipping away, and I wasn't certain if he'd ever return.

Fang knelt beside me, a hint of clarity behind his eyes. "Rue, it's not safe there anymore. Leavenfell is not safe."

I began to drift away, neither here nor there, but I was desperate to reach out to Fang and tell him I needed him by my side.

"I need you to know what happened in your bedroom—it wasn't me," Fang said, and then he was in my arms. "It was never me." His voice echoed in the wind.

I extended my hand, meaning to caress his cheeks, meaning to tell him that I understood, but the cliffside, along with Fang, fell away.

I wanted to let the darkness claim me. Let it swallow me whole until there was no chance of returning, but I couldn't. The darkness warned it wasn't time yet, so it spit me back out into an agonizing reality where I couldn't bring myself to get out of bed.

Outside my window, snowflakes lazily descended from gray clouds onto the wet earth, covering the cliffs in a blanket of snow. I was half amazed by the never-ending snow and terrified that Fang was out there somewhere, freezing and alone.

A knock sounded at my door. *Alden. Arthur.* I'd known they would come, though seeing Rorik was a surprise. The mechanical bird perched on Alden's shoulder, clicking its beak in a manner that made it appear to be in conversation with Alden.

"Yes, yes. I know," Alden whispered to the bird.

Arthur strode in and sat on the edge of my bed, while Alden and Rorik kept back. Rorik wore the same armor as Arthur, and both of them looked melancholier than I'd ever seen them.

"I know what you want to say," I told them without looking at them. It was hard to look anyone in the eye after what happened.

When the healer spread word about my neck wound, Arthur had rushed to my side, his special concoction in hand and a million questions spilling from his lips. I spent the rest of the night bawling in his arms, until my eyes had dried up.

Alden stepped forward, staff in hand. "I warned you to be careful around him."

Unbelievable. Of all the things Alden was going to say, he had to start with that.

I clenched my fists, resisting the urge to scream at him. "You're here to gloat. Fantastic."

"No," Alden said. "I'm here to explain what happened. The blackout you experienced. Everything that happened last night. It was all related to Fang."

"You *knew*," I seethed. "You knew that Sullivan stood outside the castle with Volings by his side."

"Yes."

"Why didn't you come find me? Why didn't you tell the people of Leavenfell what had happened?" I demanded.

Alden sighed, wearing a weary expression. "What happened was something that only you and Fang experienced. It happened because Sullivan wanted you to see. He wasn't here, but he led you to believe he was... through Fang," Alden explained.

After Lance had kissed me, I'd grabbed Fang's hand when he'd been acting strangely. That was when everything dissolved into chaos. *Did Sullivan force Fang to do that?*

I snapped my gaze back to Alden. "If Sullivan wasn't physically here, then he must know we're at Leavenfell."

Alden's gaze dropped to the floor in confirmation, sending chills down my spine.

"We're not safe. We need to leave."

"I assure you, Ms. Watson. We are heavily guarded by the barrier. He can't get through."

"Where did Fang go? Does Sullivan have him? Can we bring him back?" I bit back tears.

Rorik came to my side and placed a hand on my shoulder. "To be frank with you, Rue, I'd given up on my search for Fang. I was returning to Leavenfell when I found him wandering outside, near the castle barrier. He was unable to get through, but it was as if he knew you were there."

Arthur grimaced but said nothing.

"I alerted Alden immediately. That's part of the reason why Alden took the two of you to his office, so Mrs. Baker and I could observe him," Rorik said. "But he seemed normal during that time."

"Can we bring him back?" I asked, growing impatient.

Rorik shook his head. "Last night's events confirmed what we suspected. He was under Sullivan's compulsion, and it sounds like Sullivan was able to show you that vision of him and the Volings through Fang. We can't bring Fang back without risking everyone's lives here in Leavenfell. Not until we come up with a plan."

"I'm sorry, Rue," Arthur said, his shoulders slumping in defeat. "I know how much this hurts to hear."

Alden seated himself at the edge of my bed beside Arthur, his gaze locked on Puko, who was perched comfortably on one of the pillows behind me. "I should've investigated further. I sensed something was off about him, but I didn't want to alarm you. I only wanted to warn you to take caution. Just know that whoever was in your room with you that night... that wasn't Fang."

"I know," I admitted. "He would never hurt me. But why would Sullivan compel him to kill me?"

Alden clicked his tongue. "You know why."

The prophecy.

"The compulsion he's under is very strong," Alden added. "If we were able to bring Fang back, it's not something that can be easily reversed."

"The only way to undo the compelling is to kill Sullivan. Unless Sullivan were to release him himself. But I don't foresee that happening. At least not anytime soon," Arthur said.

I groaned, rubbing my sore head. Even if we recovered Fang, there was still a chance he'd try to kill me. There was no way Sullivan would release him from the compulsion.

Arthur squeezed my hand, but I pulled away. I had no idea what to say. I stared up at my golden canopy, lost in the glittery stars as my heart crumpled again.

An idea hit me, one that left me feeling hopeful. Sullivan might use Fang to try to reach me again, and if I got my hands on Fang, then we could lock him up in the castle until we killed Sullivan. Fang would be safer in a cell than he was in Sullivan's hands.

I met Rorik's and Arthur's eyes, and they pulled me into a hug.

Until we meet again, Fang.

Chapter 21

A Secret Untold

IF THERE WAS ONE THING AS CONSTANT AS TIME, IT WAS THAT damned blonde boy with the old trench coat and warm smile. Lance always waited for me at the bottom of the staircase with his hand outstretched, paired with a smile so wide that my worry melted once our eyes met. His friendship was the distraction I needed right now. Between him, Nora, and Peter, company was the only thing that soothed my grief over Fang.

I stopped in front of him, shaking my head in disapproval. "You know you're allowed to come to my room, right? There's nothing stopping you from walking up those steps. Arthur isn't up there, I promise you."

Lance grinned, showing his teeth. "I'll work my way up there eventually. Let's go."

Nora sat at a table by the fireplace, her nose in a book as she waited for us to join her. Her hair had been shortened a couple of inches by her mom, the autumn layers now framing her face with a softness that made her even prettier. She wore a vintage gray corset that Willow had sewn for her, paired with ruffled, black trousers.

The change didn't go unnoticed. Peter made some comments about her appearance and how he was able to see how nice her figure was now that her hair was out of the way. This earned him a particularly hard smack to the back of his head from Lance.

"Typical Peter," she muttered into my ear, a big smile on her face.

"He should keep those kinds of thoughts to himself," I said.

"I know, but at least someone here fancies me," Nora admitted, a blush coloring her cheeks.

"Peter fancies every girl that gives him the time of day," I reminded her. Although Peter was funny, he was quite immature when it came to girls.

Defense lessons had been on hold since Finn was often whisked away on missions outside of Fennra, but following his recent return, everyone readied themselves for the evening's lesson. Back on the stage, I stole a glance at Olivia, who'd newly joined the class with Oliver, a result of the age limit being lowered. She had her arms crossed and a disinterested scowl on her face. She caught me looking at her, narrowed her eyes, and pointedly looked away.

There was something unsaid between us, the way she watched me during dinner, her eyes flickering to Oliver as though she was communicating telepathically. Whenever she did so, Oliver tensed, as if he didn't like what he was hearing, but he never stopped being friendly towards me. He and Willow always greeted me during breakfast.

As Finn took attendance, his gaze paused longer than usual on Nora, who was a bit curvier today thanks to her improving shapeshifting ability.

Finn cleared his throat. "Sorry for the delay in lessons, but we should be on track now. Tonight, we have a few dummies to practice on. One by one, I would like for you all to come up and show me how you would take a defensive stance when facing a Voling. I'll offer advice as needed."

I let my mind drift off while everyone took their turns, already as bored as Peter looked. Afterward, Finn moved onto fighting against werewolves, a subject that slightly unnerved me.

"We'll start with archery tonight," Finn said, equipping a bow and a silver-tipped arrow. "Since distance is the safest option when trying to kill a werewolf." He replaced the standing dummy with a dummy that resembled a very large wolf. It baffled me where they even got this equipment, although Nora's new motto was: *When in doubt, it's Alden. It's always Alden.*

The lesson carried on a while longer as Finn helped everyone learn how to hold and utilize the bow. Most were horrible at shooting, especially Liessa, who missed the dummy completely and shot the banner on the wall behind it.

When it was Lance's turn, he shot the dummy through its mouth with precision, proving he really was the pro he claimed to be, but when my turn came, I couldn't focus. Thomassen had been haunting my thoughts no matter how hard I tried to push him from my mind, and my symptoms kept flaring, which didn't help.

After multiple attempts, I managed to strike the dummy's side. Finn told me not to worry and that I'd get better with practice. It went on like that the following two weeks, time passing slowly as I struggled with missing Fang and a boy I hardly knew anything about, but I went to practice each Tuesday and Thursday evening, busying myself with archery practice until my fingers hurt.

The wind whistled, rattling the windows when I awoke with a start, sweat pouring off my skin and heart racing. I wrinkled my nose, smelling the salt dripping from my skin as I clenched my fists to my chest. The monster inside me wasn't easy to calm.

Please don't shift.

Each day was an uphill battle against the wolf. I kicked my feet out of the comforter and onto the floor, attempting to ground myself. When that didn't work, I yanked open my nightstand drawer and immediately sought the talisman. Relief rushed through me, my rigid body relaxing, and I settled back into bed, stretching my limbs and wondering if I should try to sleep a little longer.

When I made it downstairs later, I found Nora beside Peter. She snatched an orange slice from off his plate and plopped it into her mouth with a satisfied squeal.

"You're pretty bold to be stealing food right off my plate," Peter said, fork ready to stab her hand.

"You could've stopped me if you wanted to," Nora shot back with a smile, taking another slice from him.

"Fine. You can have my food *if* you let me take you on a date."

I expected Nora to snort with laughter, but she nearly choked on her food, her pointed ears reddening. "O-okay," she answered after swallowing her food.

The table went silent, but if anyone was more surprised, it was Peter himself.

"You're serious?" Peter raised an eyebrow at her, angling his body towards her.

Nora slumped forward and rested her chin in the palm of her hand. "Maybe I am."

Peter's face lit up while Lance and I exchanged disbelieving glances.

"Only as friends, though, so don't go getting any ideas," she added. "Name the time and place."

I'd never seen Peter smile so big.

After we'd eaten, the news about Nora agreeing to go on a date with Peter spread like wildfire in our classroom. Liessa and Isobela had a laugh about it when they found out, making a point to make fun of Nora when they bumped into her in class.

"You're both jealous you haven't gotten your own dates," Nora snapped back at them. They sauntered back to their seats, whispering amongst themselves.

Nora exhaled. "They're ridiculous, aren't they?"

"They could be friendlier, considering we could all die at any moment," I replied cheerfully. Peter laughed.

"Are you ready for the test?" Nora asked, flipping through her textbook.

"What test?" I was not aware of any test, much less prepared for one.

"The test on werewolves? We were told about this a couple weeks ago," Nora said. "Glitch mentioned it like three times."

Right. Just after Fang disappeared.

Olivia's shoulders tensed and she shot me a wary look. *What was her problem?* I shook my head at Nora, my brows furrowing as I tried to ignore Olivia's tension. I'd completely forgotten about the test today. By the look on Peter's face, I wasn't the only one.

"You too, huh?" I asked him.

"Oh, I knew about it, but I hate studying," said Peter.

"You two." Nora rolled her eyes. "Here. Take my book and study the underlined notes," she offered, but it was too late. Glitch was handing out the parchments. Peter and I exchanged *oh shit* glances.

When Glitch reached my desk, Olivia raised her hand.

"Y-y-yes?" Glitch asked.

Olivia straightened her back. "Isn't it considered cheating to take this quiz if someone has experience with being a werewolf?"

The hair on my neck stood up, but I didn't dare steal a glance at her.

"P-pardon?" Glitch asked, its eyes clicking. Steam pumped out of its barrel, smacking Peter in the face. Peter turned around and coughed, waving a hand in front of his face to dissipate the steam cloud.

"Rue is part werewolf, isn't she? She was bitten by one, so wouldn't it be considered cheating, since she knows more about werewolves than any of us?" Olivia asked, making sure to speak loudly enough so that everyone could hear her. She turned ever so slightly in her chair, enough so that I could see her profile. A smirk crossed her lips.

I gripped my quill until my fingers turned white. "What are you on about?" I asked, careful to keep my tone calm. There was no way she'd know about the werewolf bite, not unless she eavesdropped on me when I was in Alden's office. *Fuck.*

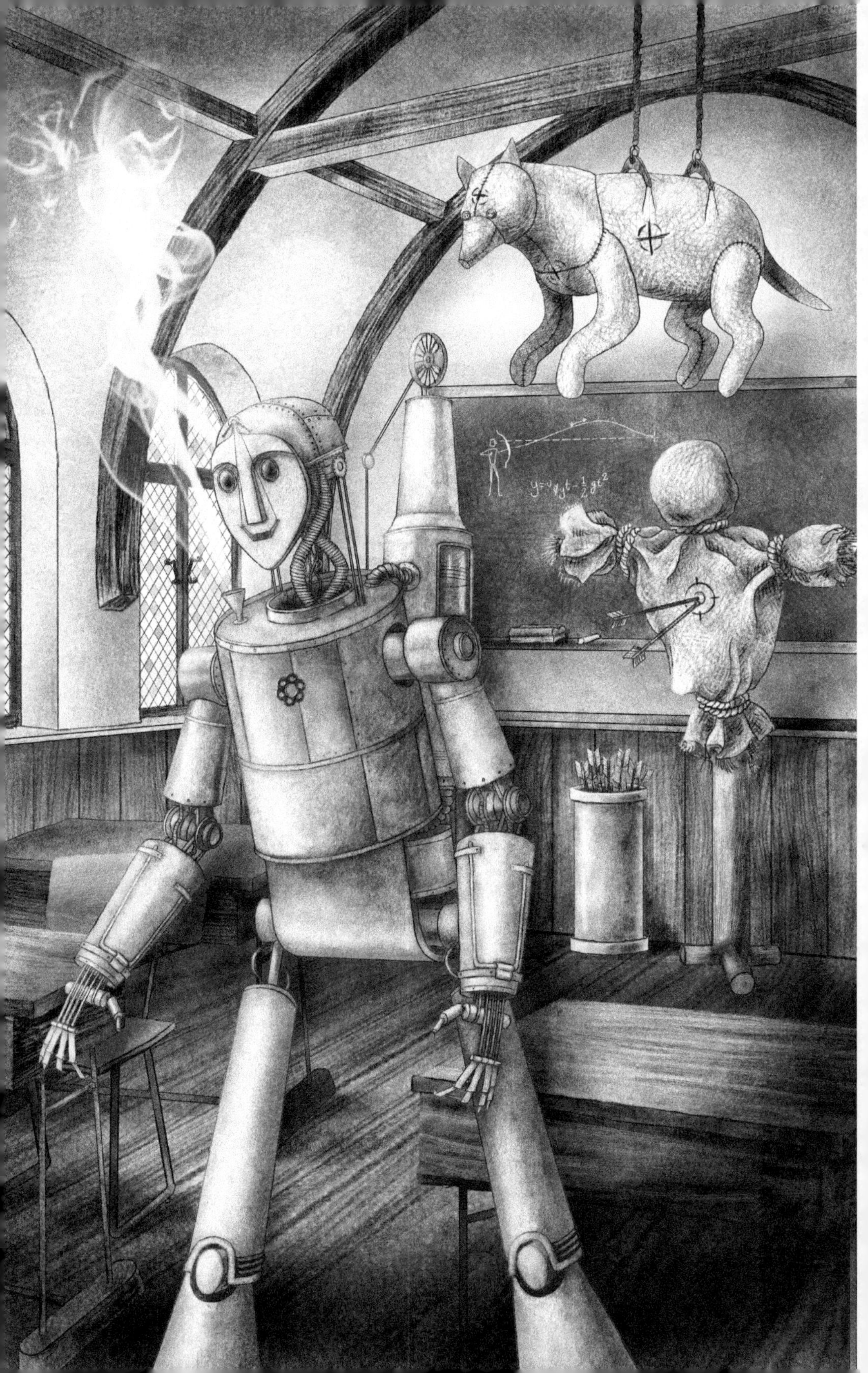

$y = v_{0y}t - \frac{1}{2}gt^2$

Oliver stared at his twin, focused on the back of her head.

"I'm being completely serious," Olivia responded sharply before facing her brother, who I assumed was communicating with her via their shared gift.

The room's silence crushed me. Spreading this around could get me killed if any single person believed her.

Olivia's lips curved into a smile. "Tell them, Rue."

"There's nothing to tell," I snapped, my palms sweating.

"You're lying," Olivia croaked. "You're a danger to everyone in this castle." She jabbed a finger into my chest, hurting me more than it should've.

Everyone's eyes fell on me as the question hung in the room, weighing me down. I was trapped, my head underwater with no way to the surface.

"Why are you making these accusations? You're trying to ruin my life over something that isn't true." I stood, my palms firmly planted on her desk as I hunched over her.

"What the hells, Olivia? Why are you doing this?" Nora added in my defense.

Lance scowled at her. "Seriously. Back off."

Olivia's smirk faltered slightly, but she held firm. "Tell them, Rue."

"Of course it's not true. Do you think Alden would let a werewolf into this castle? He wouldn't put anyone at risk like that," I stammered. I sunk back into my chair and slipped my hands into the pockets of my pants, needing for them to go somewhere that wouldn't end up around Olivia's throat.

"Olivia, please leave the room and go to Alden's office at once," Glitch ordered.

"I don't need to go. She does," Olivia argued.

"Now," Glitch said, steam rolling out of his barrel, and for a moment, I swore I heard Alden's voice instead of Glitch's.

My skin heated as I glanced around the room at everyone, trying to weigh their reactions. Nora's eyes darted back and forth between me and Glitch, her expression stunned.

Olivia bent down beside me on her way out. "I know what you're hiding. You're a filthy Voling like the rest of them," she whispered through gritted teeth. "And you're not going to get away with it."

I stared up at her, my mind reeling with multiple possibilities. I'd no idea how she even found that information out. What mattered now was the fact that everyone heard her accusation, and now everyone was probably wondering if it was true. I stared after her as she stormed out of the room, slamming the door behind her.

All eyes landed on me, in a way that felt entirely suffocating, and I did what my instincts told me to. I bolted from the room as fast as I could, not daring to look behind me.

CHAPTER 22

THE WOLF AND THE BOY

THE HIDDEN CORRIDOR WAS THE PERFECT PLACE TO HIDE. I unlocked the barrier, my hands shaking as I clumsily shoved the key back into my pocket and scooted myself up against the wall on the other side. I held my breath as the barrier extended from the creases of the paneled walls and met in the middle, locking in place and making me invisible to anyone looking down the hallway.

Safe. I'm safe, I thought, willing myself to calm down. Hot tears stung my eyes, burning streaks down my face. I didn't know why I was hiding where no one could possibly find me, crying over a girl that had no good reason to expose me.

My secret had been well kept—

"Tch," I muttered, wiping the tears from my face. My scar flared, and I fought back the symptoms of my curse, angry at myself for forgetting the talisman.

Dammit. My curse presented itself every time I was upset, a trend I'd picked up on. I couldn't risk letting my emotions get the best of me, for fear that I would turn. Shifting in front of everyone in the castle, *especially* Olivia, would be horrifying.

"Why are you crying?" Thomassen emerged from the darkness, looming over me, wearing black pants and a white button-down shirt, the sleeves neatly folded up to his elbows. Despite being well-dressed, there were shadows underneath his eyes hinting at his lack of sleep.

"What could you possibly want?" I asked.

Thomassen knelt beside me. "It seems like every time we meet, you're upset over something."

"I don't see why you should concern yourself over my feelings," I snapped. It wasn't the polite thing to say to him, but at that moment, I didn't care. I rested my head against the wall, ignoring how close he was and gritting my teeth as my bones ached. Thomassen placed a hand on my shoulder, his touch relieving my symptoms.

"You're not a monster," he said. "But if you keep this up, you're going to shift."

"You're a mind reader now? Fantastic. What else have you got up your sleeves?" I quipped, cocking my head to the side as I scowled at him.

Thomassen sank to the floor beside me. "You're something else, you know that? Not a monster. But something."

"Hilarious," I scoffed, arms crossed over my chest.

Silence fell between us as we sat side by side in the darkness. Tension rose from Thomassen like an impending thunderstorm, and I scooted away, putting a few inches between us. The clock doors stood in the distance, ticking in eerie unison, reminding me that I needed to move forward and look for the damned prophecy.

"I don't need you to babysit me, you know," I said. "I can take care of myself."

With an annoyed huff, Thomassen stood, grabbed my arm, and yanked me upwards. He dragged me down the corridor and through the first door on the left. As we walked inside, the scenery in the room changed to a grassy hill sprawled underneath a starlit sky.

"What the—" I inhaled, slowly taking in the sight. My brain wasn't registering the view before me.

"My room changes into whatever I want it to. It's one of the gifts I was born with. Illusions," Thomassen explained. "If it was always the same, it'd be boring, don't you think?" He grabbed a cup of steaming tea and sat down on a soft patch of grass, staring up at the breath-taking sky, his eyes resting on it in a way that made him seem worlds away.

"Don't the clock doors lead to somewhere different each time?" I asked, remembering my conversation with Alden.

"Only my room is behind that door. The others... yes."

"Do you think the prophecy is inside one of them?" I asked, testing my luck.

"Who knows." Thomassen didn't say anything more on the subject.

Instead of gazing at the stars, I watched him in awe. "You are the strangest boy I've ever met."

Thomassen laughed, a sound I never expected to hear from him. My face heated. His laugh was warm and inviting, nothing at all like what I'd expected.

"And you think you aren't the strangest girl I've ever met?"

"Why did you bring me here?" I asked.

"Because you looked like you needed a break from *whatever* was going on back there."

Releasing a sigh, I sat down beside him, setting my gaze upwards at the illusion of the night sky. It felt intimate sitting here with him under stars that pulsed with magic.

"Don't you get lonely being by yourself all the time?" I asked.

"I prefer solitude," Thomassen said, taking a sip of his tea. It smelled like him… comforting with hints of cinnamon and honey.

A strange noise pulled me away from my thoughts. I strained my ears, picking up something resembling a subtle humming sound.

"That noise. Where's it coming from?" I asked.

"What noise?"

"That repetitive humming. I've heard it before, in the library realm." I carefully surveyed the area, trying to find the source of it.

"Oh, that. It's coming from here." Thomassen pointed to the middle of his chest.

"Excuse me?"

"Shut up and listen." He set his cup down and pulled my head against his chest so I could hear the sound better. Or rather —it was more of a barely-audible ticking sound accompanied by humming and whirring.

I yanked my head away. "How?" Last I remembered, hearts didn't sound like that. I touched my hand to my own chest, as if unconsciously reminding myself.

Thomassen's cheeks flushed. "It's not *just* a heart exactly."

"What do you mean?" I held my breath.

He looked back up at the stars. "When I was very young, I was dying. I don't know why it was happening. It just was. My father couldn't stand to lose me after my mother had passed, so he requested the help of one of his lousy wizard friends."

Poison tainted his tone, the words spilling out of him like sharpened daggers. "This friend helped him create a bizarre new magic," he continued. "My father made me absorb it, using a spell he'd created. Tendrils from the magic spread inside me and wrapped around my heart. It was placed there with the intent to keep me alive," Thomassen confessed. "It's technically forbidden magic."

The Netherros. Knowing what I knew about the Netherros, I wondered if the corrupt magic affected Thomassen, considering he was usually mean. If the Netherros had been able to corrupt Sullivan and Alester by using it, then what could it do to someone it was inside of. Still, Thomassen was alive because of it, so maybe it wasn't a bad thing after all. At least for him.

"That's amazing. To be kept alive by magic, I mean."

Thomassen picked up his tea, bringing it to his lips. "Not entirely. The magic could stop at any moment, and I would die."

"Or you could live forever," I suggested. "Immortal."

"That would be a tragedy." Thomassen averted his eyes, shifting away from me.

"Thanks for telling me."

Thomassen's eyes crinkled when he looked at me. "If you think about it, I could be called as much of a monster as you are. But we're not really monsters. We're normal people."

"Point taken," I said, glad to know he was someone I could relate to.

"Misunderstood but normal," Thomassen added, finishing his tea. His cheeks colored like the warm glow of a candle. The blush was subtle, but I hadn't missed it, and somehow, it made my stomach flutter with butterflies.

"Okay, okay. I get it." I laughed. "We're normal people." I made air quotations with my fingers.

Thomassen fell backwards onto the soft grass, yawning. We laid there for a long time, comfortable in our silence. I put the thought of the Netherros's corruption in the back of my mind.

After some time passed, Thomassen changed his room into a rocky cliff overhanging the sea. I tilted my head back, enjoying the wind on my face and the salty mist from the thrashing waves on my skin. It reminded me of the time I'd spent with Fang behind Leavenfell Castle. Although it'd been a short excursion, only a breath away from the castle, we'd had enough space from the castle walls to clear our heads and enjoy each other's presence. It was a shared moment that was now gone, leaving me with a bittersweet memory and an aching hole in my chest.

My pulse raced and I swallowed hard, turning my head towards Thomassen, who made my heart treacherously skip a beat. Being with him was different than when I was with Fang. Thomassen both terrified and excited me, and I wasn't so sure if it was because he comforted me or if there were feelings there. The latter made me question my sanity.

Thomassen leaned backward, propping himself up using his elbows. His neck arched back as the ocean breeze lifted soft strands of his hair, and he tilted his head towards me, his eyes closed. The wind picked up, roaring around us, and I extended my fingers towards him, wanting to touch him, even just to hold his hand. My hand trembled with uncertainty, and I paused, biting my bottom lip. *What am I doing?*

Thomassen's eyes snapped open, meeting mine, and his face paled. He stood with sudden abruptness, brushing off his clothes. "It's time for you to leave."

"What?" I asked, shoving wind-swept hair out of my eyes.

Thomassen changed his room back into… well, his room, and led me to the door.

"Did I do something wrong?" I wasn't ready to leave. Not like this. "I thought we were getting along."

"Please go." Thomassen's lips twisted downward into a sullen frown.

I held up my hands. "Fine, but first—" I flung myself into his arms, giving him a quick hug and then retreating before he could push me away. The brief touch was enough to send shockwaves down my spine.

"Thanks for bringing me here." *And for comforting me and telling me one of your secrets.* The fact that he told me anything about himself was monumental in itself.

Thomassen's face flushed, and he rubbed the back of his neck. "Stop hiding in the corridor, then I won't need to come get you."

There was that cold side of him again. Whatever problem he had with me was still bothering him.

I crossed my arms, aggravated by his response. "I never told you to come get me, you know. You did that on your own."

"I won't bother next time," Thomassen said.

I winced, hurt by his sudden change in attitude. I couldn't help but wonder if the Netherros's magic made him push people away. *Right when I thought I was getting somewhere.*

"Why don't you come join the rest of us in the lower levels of the castle. I know you're not a people person, but it'd be nice to have you around."

He let out a low laugh. "Thanks, but I'll pass."

"Then we can hang out alone," I suggested. "You're welcome to visit my room."

"I wouldn't consider us close, so again... no," Thomassen growled, his eyes lingering on mine.

"And here I was… beginning to think you liked me," I admitted before I could stop the words from leaving my mouth.

"I never said I liked you," Thomassen said, shoving me out of his room, but I swore I caught a small smile on his face before the door closed.

CHAPTER 23

ACCEPTANCE

"Where have you been? We've been so worried about you!" Nora flung her arms around me, sending us crashing against the wall while she sobbed into my shoulder. Puko flew over and landed on top of my head, his copper wings brushing against my scalp. He preened my hair at a faster pace than normal.

Lance sat on my bed, his hands fidgeting in his lap. "I tried following you, but you were gone so fast," he said, his expression pained. "Didn't you hear me calling out to you?"

I didn't. I'd been so wrapped up in my rage that I hadn't paid any attention to anything that happened until Thomassen met up with me.

"I'm sorry. I wanted to be alone to process everything that happened," I replied, the guilt of worrying them weighing on me.

Lance crossed his arms and frowned at me. I'd never been on the receiving end of his scowls until now, and I didn't like it one bit.

"You shouldn't have run off," he said. "And forget Olivia. She's—"

"She wasn't wrong," I interrupted him, not taking my eyes off either of them.

Lance opened his mouth to respond, but I held up my hand, silencing him. I sat on the bed beside him, drawing in a deep breath, my mind made up. No more secrets, especially from two people I considered friends.

"I have my suspicions as to how she found out, but I'm sorry you both found out this way."

Lance and Nora processed my confession silently, but neither of them looked afraid.

"To be honest, I suspected something was different about you. You have these moments where you aren't yourself," Nora admitted, "if that makes sense."

I inhaled sharply, shocked by her confession, but at least my suspicions were confirmed. "I'd like to explain everything to you, so let's get comfortable."

The fire's warmth eased my nerves as we moved to sit by the fireplace. I told them everything about my parents, Arthur, and Sullivan. I went into detail about the wolf bite, how I'd grown up with Fang, Lance, and Peter, and how I'd bitten Lance as a child. Lance had no recollection of this thanks to Arthur's memory charm. When I brought it up, Lance examined his skin for any signs of faint bite scars.

"There'd be nothing there anymore. Arthur probably used his famous concoction to patch you up. That stuff does wonders," I mentioned, watching Lance feverishly lift up his sleeves and the bottom of his shirt, revealing his tan, toned stomach.

"His famous what?" asked Nora.

I waved a hand. "Never mind."

"How do I not remember you or Fang?' Lance asked. "Especially since we lived together *that* long."

"Arthur's gift is memory charms. He can give memories and take them away." I explained the permanency of his charms, and Lance nodded.

"Since the day we were reunited, I've felt a strange pull to you, Lance. I couldn't explain it, not even to Arthur, but it's always been there." I mentioned that my scar burned too.

"I've felt the same but was afraid to bring it up. It's hard to describe. I thought it was because I thought you were pretty."

I blushed, embarrassed by Lance's admission. Nora failed at hiding a smile behind her hand. I carried on talking about Fang and explained again what happened that night before he disappeared again, in more detail. I hesitantly brought up Thomassen, unsure what to say about him or how to describe him.

"I've known Thomassen for a long time. He keeps to himself," Lance said. "He's never been a friendly person."

No kidding.

As I finished my story, Nora grabbed my hand. Her eyes watered, but there was no sadness in them. She pulled me into a warm hug.

"This changes nothing. Like Arthur said, you haven't changed," she said, reassuring me that she wasn't leaving my side. "Also, Olivia sucks. She had no right saying that in front of the whole class."

"How did she find out?" Lance asked. "Where would she get that information from?"

"I discussed it in a meeting with Arthur and Alden, the day that Fang returned. If I had to guess, she was probably outside the office, eavesdropping," I said with a shudder. Now that I thought about it, I wondered if Olivia had been trailing me. Maybe she *wanted* dirt on me, for whatever reason.

Nora frowned, crossing her arms over her chest. "She could've gotten you in trouble with others. Lots of people at Leavenfell fear stuff like that. If it gets around…"

"I'll make sure it doesn't," said Lance firmly.

Nora and I gaped at him.

"How?" I asked.

"She likes me, so maybe I'll talk to her… try flirting with her. I don't know. I'll figure something out."

"Just don't get any pointers from Peter," I joked, eliciting a laugh from them both.

Lance had a point. Maybe he could use her feelings to his advantage to keep her quiet. Intentionally hurting Olivia to get her off my back was a dirty idea, one that didn't sit well in my stomach, but if it helped, then so be it.

Lance scooted over until he was by my side, his knee brushing against mine. "I'm with Nora on this. You're stuck with us," he said earnestly. "And even though our friendship started because of that bond we both felt, I really do care about you."

I dragged him against me, hugging him tightly with tears in my eyes. The pull between us settled into a comfortable wave, as though our acceptance of the bond calmed the rigid waters.

"You have no idea how relieved I am," I told Lance. A weight lifted from my shoulders, knowing that he liked me for me and not because of the wolf bond. "I can't thank either of you enough, not only for being my friend, but for sticking by me, knowing everything."

"We stick together. No matter what," Nora said.

Lance let out a contented sigh. "I can't imagine my life without either of you."

"Me either," I said, reaching for their hands.

"Alden knows as well. That means you should be safe under his care," Nora added.

I nodded, wondering if I should tell them what I'd known about Alden. A part of me wanted to, but I needed more information from him before I told anyone anything. Alden was so invested in his pocket watch and confident in its power, but I'd seen how the magic had consumed him on that bridge. He'd been unstable.

Thomassen might be able to shed more light on the situation if he was up to seeing me again, but the way he shot down talks of the prophecy earlier had me skeptical.

"So what of this boy in the corridor? Why hasn't he come to class?" Nora asked.

"He said he prefers being alone, but I wish he'd come to class with us," I admitted, missing his presence. "It'd be nice to get to know him more."

The flames in the fireplace dwindled into ash as Lance stood and straightened out his trench coat that'd wrinkled from sitting on the floor for so long.

"I should go. Otherwise, my mom will have my head, and Peter will assume I've been doing unspeakable things. Don't forget what I said, though." Lance knelt down and embraced me. "I'll see you tomorrow. Don't go hiding again."

"I won't, so go to bed and stop worrying. And tell Peter to mind his business," I said.

Lance beamed at the two of us and said goodnight once more, opening the door and disappearing under the night sky. Nora slid over, smoothing the wrinkles out of her brown skirt and taking Lance's spot as I reignited the fire. She warmed her hands and yawned, resting her back against my side.

"Something else has been on my mind today," I told her.

Nora tilted her head to look at me. "What?"

A smile tugged on my lips as I recalled her conversations before class. "Out of curiosity, what could have possibly possessed you to agree to go on a date with Peter?"

Nora flushed and drew her eyes away from my face, and I thought I'd offended her, but then she rolled her eyes and gave me a wolfish grin. "Come on. He's hot."

"That can't possibly be the only reason," I laughed.

Nora's skin reddened. "Peter's really funny, and I know he needs to grow up a bit," she said hesitantly. "But to be honest, I was hoping our date might make Finn jealous."

There it was.

"I knew it," I said. "I thought you were over him."

"I thought so too, but if it happens, it happens," Nora said, her ears turning sideways.

"I see you've gotten better with your shape-shifting gift," I gestured to Nora's chest.

"It's the little things," Nora said. "It may seem trivial, but every little detail counts."

"Small progress is still progress," I said with a grin, though I was internally cringing at the image of Nora and Finn together. Somehow, Peter seemed like he'd be a better match for her. Behind his mischievous facade was a guy that hid his pain with humor and kept his walls up, and if anyone could bring down those walls, that person would be Nora.

CHAPTER 24

THE LEGEND OF BLACKWOOD BOG

ALDEN'S FACE APPEARED IN A WISPY CLOUD. HE WAVED HIS hand over his head, commanding everyone's attention, as though the strange cloud hadn't done that already.

"With the Solstice Banquet approaching, the ballroom is undergoing construction to get ready for the festivities," Alden announced, his face appearing in the odd wispy cloud, commanding everyone's attention.

Collective excitement resounded through the hall. As I finished my food, I caught Lance watching me, suspecting he was about to ask me to go with him.

"Will you be my dance partner at the Solstice Banquet?"

There it was. Though I'd been expecting it, my shoulders tensed. With Thomassen's fleeting warmth echoing in the back of my mind, I wasn't sure how to answer, but Olivia beat me to the punch.

"Why would you want to take a dog to the dance?" She'd recently arrived at the table with Oliver by her side. Oliver squinted his eyes, mouthing an apology to me as he pushed past his twin.

I twisted in my seat, heat rising to my cheeks as I bit back a snarky response.

"Please stop spreading that rumor," Lance said, his tone more patient than I could have ever been.

"Why would I do that?" Olivia asked.

Lance cocked his head to the side. "For starters, it's not true. Also, I'd been thinking of sharing a dance with you at the banquet, but you've been rude to my friend, so—"

Olivia turned red in the face. "I… I'm sorry. It won't happen again."

I gaped at Lance, taken aback. He moved fast, proving Olivia was easily swayed when it came to her feelings. A dirty ruse, although necessary.

"I'd love to dance with you," Olivia said, her eyes lit with blatant admiration.

"It'd be my pleasure." Lance gave her a tight smile.

The following day, while we were doing our kitchen and great hall clean-up chores, Lance was unusually quiet, the harsh sound of clinking dishes adding to the awkward tension. He stiffened anytime we bumped into each other but also made an effort to linger by my side.

I considered Lance a good friend, but his feelings for me continued to gravitate more towards romance. I wasn't sure I reciprocated those feelings. Partly because I couldn't shake

Thomassen. My brows furrowed. Thomassen had told me to stay away last time we'd been together, and I had, but I couldn't deny I was drawn to him. I couldn't get the image of his crinkled eyes and warm blush out of my head. He was a sweetness that felt forbidden.

With the solstice banquet approaching, I craved some kind of clarity. If Thomassen wasn't in the picture, maybe I'd try going to the banquet with Lance. Maybe I'd let him kiss me again and see how things played out. My heart twisted as I weighed my options. Without Thomassen around, I couldn't decide if that's what I really wanted. I didn't know if I could fall for Lance, not when my heart betrayed me with thoughts of someone else. The internal struggle left a hollow ache in my chest.

"You know that bog down the road a ways?" I overheard Peter say to Nora after we were done cleaning the kitchen.

"What bog?" Nora asked with a mouthful of bread, simultaneously sweeping the great hall and eating.

"The one that's said to be cursed," Peter said.

Lance placed his broom against the wall, glancing back at me. "I honestly don't know where he gets these stories from."

"If you follow the tree line out a mile or so from here, you'll find a patch of glowing moss. It's easy to miss, so you have to pay close attention."

"Glowing moss?" I was beginning to think his story was outlandish.

Peter crossed his arms, his expression dead serious. "It's true. The moss is how you know you're going the right way."

Lance snorted. "How would you know this, Peter—sneaking out again?" he asked.

Peter slipped his hands into his jacket, skin flushing.

Lance rolled his eyes and retrieved the broom, helping Nora sweep.

"Glowing moss? What's the importance of that?" Nora asked, her face lit with curiosity.

Peter kept his voice low, leaning so close to Nora that their faces were almost touching. "The glowing moss is a landmark that leads the way to the bog."

"Okay. And?" Nora gave him an apprehensive look.

"The bog is dangerous. A black hole. People have gone there and never returned," Peter continued. "But the legend is that a rare treasure lies within the center of the bog."

"You're making this up, aren't you?" Nora argued.

I shook my head, agreeing with Nora. "I find this story hard to believe as well."

"Neither of you have to believe me, but they say the bog is overrun by banshees. And if you're unlucky enough to run into one, they'll suck out your soul and feed off your lifeless corpse." Peter's grin mirrored Fang's, rendering me momentarily speechless. Nora squealed at his story, which only encouraged him.

The air chilled as Peter spoke. "It's called Blackwood Bog. It's so dark there that you can't see anything. You have to follow the path of the moss to find your way back out, otherwise your soul will be lost there forever."

"Enough horror stories, Peter. Banshees aren't even real. Let us clean in peace. Gods," Lance snapped.

I gaped at Peter. "If this place was real, then wouldn't Alden have warned us about it? You know… with it being so close to here and all?"

"Exactly," Lance said, throwing his hands up.

"Don't believe me? Go see for yourself," Peter said.

"Maybe I will," I answered. "I need an adventure anyways.

This place is insufferably boring." Not only was I sick of being surrounded by walls all the time, but I needed to keep myself busy. If I let myself stop, grief would consume me, and maybe a risky adventure was what I needed. Maybe Thomassen would come to me if he found out I'd sneaked out of the castle.

"There is no way I'm letting any of you leave the castle to seek out some childish story," said Lance. "Besides, Alden would have a meltdown."

"Maybe it's not just a story," I said, hoping to pique Peter's rebellion. "It sounds intriguing either way, especially if there's treasure involved." Could the treasure be the prophecy? That would be *something*.

"Story or not, I don't want you to put yourself in unnecessary danger. There could be Volings about." Lance wrapped an arm around me protectively.

My heart sank.

I held my free fingers behind my back, crossing them as I looked into Lance's eyes. "Don't worry. I won't go."

After Nora left for a playdate with her younger brother, I cornered Peter and convinced him to help sneak me out of the castle. It wasn't like either of us had anything better to do. Peter agreed to help me—with the bargain that he wouldn't rat me out if I talked Nora into going on more than one date with him. Something I didn't mind agreeing to if it meant taking her mind off Finn.

"Wait until midnight. Most people are asleep by then," Peter instructed. We stood in an unused corridor, hidden from prying eyes, an area that saw so little traffic that Alden didn't bother having sconces installed here. It was almost complete darkness. Perfect for plotting escapes.

"Watch the patrol pattern of the guards. It'll help you slip out without getting caught," Peter continued. "I know their patrols like the back of my hand."

"I don't doubt it," I grumbled. Peter didn't know the extent of my history with Fang. Trouble was our middle name. "Tell me which direction to get to the bog."

Peter's face descended into a frown. "You think I'm letting you go alone?"

"Why would you want to go with me?" I countered, my voice raised. The probability of Thomassen showing up lessened with Peter going.

"I'm not letting you have all the fun," Peter said. "Plus Lance would kill me."

"Lance doesn't have to know." My patience was running thin. I wanted to get out of the castle and get far enough to alert Thomassen to my whereabouts. As stupid as my plan sounded, Thomassen had a knack for finding me whenever I was in trouble, and I didn't doubt he'd find me again.

"Are you still drooling or are you gonna answer me?" Peter asked.

I snapped my head towards him. "Huh?"

"I asked when you wanted to go."

"Oh… tonight."

Peter smiled, a devious look in his eyes that reminded me of Fang, crushing my heart into pieces all over again.

"Meet me at midnight in our classroom," Peter said. "Glitch deactivates before that time. Don't be late."

"Done," I nodded.

"Remember, there are guards that patrol at night, but they slow down when it's late."

I waved my hand at him, turning away. "Yeah, yeah. I'll be careful."

After Peter left, I smiled to myself. Little did he know that I was formulating a plan to leave the castle without him.

Chapter 25

A Dangerous Plan

Nora was snoring in bed, tucked under a mountain of blankets, which was my cue to get moving. I had an hour before Peter showed his face, and the last thing I wanted to do was run into him on my way out of the castle.

I hopped out of bed, ignoring the chill, and dressed in black tights and a knee-length black sweater, ready for whatever the night would bring. Grabbing my knapsack, I left the room as quietly as I could manage. Getting around the guards should be no problem. I'd been keeping tabs on where they were stationed throughout the day. Hopefully Peter wouldn't show up early.

I crossed the wooden bridge and made my way downstairs, keeping to the shadows, ensuring every step I took was silent. For once, I was glad for my extra-sensitive hearing ability. If a guard was nearby, I would hear them way before they'd hear me. After finding the door that led to the dungeon area and slipping through, I silently closed it behind me. There was no sign of Peter yet, and I breathed a sigh of relief as I crept down the stairs through the dark hallway, weaving in and out of random rooms as I tried to find the exit.

When I found the exit, I prayed the door would be unlocked from the outside, recalling the metal slab and lock that Arthur so expertly took care of the morning we'd arrived. I grabbed the handle, clenching my teeth as the door opened with a loud creak. I swore under my breath, hoping the noise didn't alert any nearby guards. I listened for any sign that I'd been found out, but nothing happened.

Relieved, I stepped outside. It was colder than I'd expected. I mentally admonished myself for not dressing in warmer clothes or at least throwing on a coat over my sweater. Overhead, dark clouds threaded the night sky, while snow covered every inch of the castle grounds.

The crashing of waves behind the castle trailed up the cliffside in an eerie echo. As I made my way west of the dungeon, I covered my tracks, hardly remembering where Peter had instructed me to go. I recalled the part about the glowing moss being a mile or so out, but cursed myself when I didn't remember which direction that would be in.

Look for the glowing moss.

"Lost yet?" a singsong voice called from behind me.

I startled, my heart damn near coming to a stop. "What the hells, Peter?!"

He approached, snow crunching under his boots. "Where is your coat? You're going to be sick on top of everything else. Dammit, Lance is really going to kill me," Peter grumbled, half-smiling as he took me in.

"That's what you're worried about right now?" I asked angrily, taking a deliberate step towards him.

"You thought I'd be mad? I knew you were going to do this," he told me. "I know you better than you think."

I stared at him in shock. For someone who goofed off ninety-nine percent of the time, he certainly wasn't stupid. I hadn't realized how observant he was. I averted my eyes, chewing on my bottom lip. I needed to lose Peter, but if he was anything like Fang, I was screwed.

Peter uncrossed his arms and squared his shoulders. "Are we going or not?"

"Shh. Keep your voice down. And fine, I guess you're coming along with me," I growled.

Peter took off his coat, offering it to me.

"Thanks," I said, taking it from him. I pulled it on, grateful that it was warm from the heat of his skin.

"I'll lead the way, but stay close," Peter said, wrapping his arms around himself.

I side-eyed him. "You *would* know the way. Why am I even surprised?"

"I don't know why you're surprised either. Out of everyone in this castle, I thought you'd get it."

"Your mother will have you by the ear," I snickered as we trekked forward.

"Not if you don't tell."

Snowflakes fell around us, heavy and wet. The wind picked up, whistling through the trees, icy enough to pierce through the coat I wore.

"If your teeth chatter any louder, we might be discovered," said Peter as he turned to look at me. "We won't even need to make it to the bog for a banshee to discover us if you keep that up."

"How much further?" I whined, forcing my hands into his

coat pockets. I stepped onto a rock that was covered in ice, lost my balance, and planted my face into the snow. Swearing, I wiped the snow off my face, tired of the endless winter.

"You didn't tell me you liked making snow angels with your face." Peter doubled over from laughing so hard.

"Don't make me regret tagging along with you," I chided, face stiff from the cold.

The deeper we traveled into the woods, the more I started to worry. *Where's Thomassen?* Maybe Peter's presence was keeping him at bay. I gritted my teeth, annoyed that Peter had picked up on my deception so quickly and found me before I could make it ten feet from the castle. I stared at the back of his head, tempted to make a run for it, but knowing Peter, he'd probably tackle me.

Peter stopped, and I crashed into his back.

"Told you it was here." Peter knelt near a patch of moss, which glowed so vividly blue that it peeked through the white snow.

My eyes widened. If Peter's story had any truth to it, coming out here was a horrid idea. I took a step back, dimly aware of my surroundings, wondering what lurked ahead. I palmed the talisman in my trouser pocket, calming my nerves, but an impending sense of danger bloomed low in my gut.

"Peter, I don't know about this."

"Oh, come on. Don't back out on me now," Peter said. "I never pegged you for a wimp, Watson."

"I'm not a wimp, but I prefer living." If this was real, then we were both in a shitty position. My senses always picked up on things others couldn't, and I could practically feel the heavy environment weighing me down. I sensed danger not far from where we stood, every particle of my body screaming at me to run away. But my stubbornness had me not wanting Peter to think I was weak, so I continued after him.

I grabbed Peter's arm as he led me deeper into the thick forest. "Shouldn't we turn around?" I tightened my grip.

"I didn't come all this way for nothin."

"Gods, Peter, if we get killed, I will haunt you for the rest of your ghostly life."

"Ghosts don't haunt each other," Peter replied, his tone so unserious that I gawked at him.

I was so close to smacking him. *So* close.

We continued on the path of the glowing moss, snow crunching underneath us. I rubbed my trembling arms, my feet moving like bricks were attached to them, each step heavier than the last. Staring ahead, I spotted something black and oval floating above the ground, positioned between two trees, the edges of it swirling with a darkness that emanated a dreadful aura, a warning perhaps. Shadowy tendrils snaked and protruded from the center of the dark mass, dancing under the moonlight, caressing surrounding branches and snow. The tree's limbs curved inwards, twisting over the dark mass as if creating a creepy portal.

The hells? What's an ominous portal doing here?

The tendrils slithered closer, and I backed away, knowing damned well that couldn't be a good thing.

"What is that?" Peter asked, his voice wavering.

I loosened my grip on his arm as I stared at the dark portal, entranced. Voices spilled out, beckoning me forward, my name whispered as the tendrils reached for us.

We have what you're looking for, the voices said. My blood ran cold. The prophecy. *Come to us.*

I took a step forward, and then another, my skin tingling as the tendrils brushed against my legs. I reached my hand forward, so close. I was almost there.

Someone grabbed my arm and slammed me up against a tree, pulling me out of the trance.

"What *are* you doing here?" an angry voice asked, scaring the hells out of both me and Peter.

Thomassen. He'd come, like I'd suspected he would.

Thomassen swung me around to face him, his mouth set in a hard line and his golden eyes narrowed as he released an exasperated exhale. Yep, he was pissed. As if the portal wasn't scary enough, Thomassen's attitude rivaled it.

"What the hells were you doing?" he demanded. There was no softness in his gaze, no blush on his cheeks. Only white-hot anger as his fingers dug into my skin.

Peter paled. "We were just—"

Thomassen waved a finger at him, and he dropped to the ground.

"What'd you do to him?" I screeched, staring down at Peter, who'd gone completely still.

"I put him to sleep." Thomassen glanced at the portal before returning his furious gaze to me.

"What the—how many gifts do you have?" I asked, portal temporarily forgotten. It was rare for anyone to have more than one gift.

"Answer my question," Thomassen demanded. His grip on my arm tightened, and I cowered beneath his intimidating gaze.

"I'm exploring— h-having an adventure?" I stuttered, peeling my eyes away to look at Peter's limp figure. "With Peter."

Shit. That sounded worse than I meant it to.

"This late at night?!" his voice rose, and he released my arms.

"I was bored," I explained. "Sick of being stuck inside walls all the time." There was *some* truth to that statement.

Thomassen dipped his head until his face was in front of me, his lips close enough to brush against mine. "I knew you were something else, but I didn't realize you were this stupid."

I jolted backward, hurt by his words. "I'm not stupid."

"You really think that because I'm not physically around you, that I don't know what's going on?" Thomassen snapped. "If you and this idiot had kept going, both of you would've wound up dead. This portal—it shouldn't be here. The hells?" Thomassen drifted off, his eyes glued to the dark mass. "I need to speak with my father about it."

My breath hitched. "Why? What's the significance?" My gaze dropped to his lips, lingering there traitorously.

"Think harder, Rue. What else could it possibly be?"

Volings.

"Why didn't Alden warn us of it?" I asked, finding my voice again.

"He hasn't been made aware of it yet, but he will be soon. Once I return you and this dumbass back to the castle," he growled.

"Your father should've been the first one to know about this! I thought he was protecting the castle."

Thomassen turned, running his hands through his damp hair. "My father's unobservant at times. But once he learns of it, it'll be taken care of, and I'll be sure to notify him that two children escaped the castle."

"I wasn't aware we were prisoners," I deadpanned.

Thomassen threw his hands up in the air. "Dammit, Rue, why must you be so difficult?"

Tears stung my eyes, and even though I held them back, that

didn't stop the lump from forming in my throat. Thomassen had every right to yell at me.

"I came out here b-because I'd thought you'd come looking for me," I whispered, voice breaking with a shiver.

"Why'd you assume that?" Thomassen asked, his features hardening.

"You tend to find me when I'm in trouble."

"So what? That's not an excuse to go out after dark, especially with Volings lurking about."

I released a sigh, my eyes watering. "Last time we were together, you told me to stay away, so I thought if I left the castle instead of going to the hidden corridor, maybe you'd come find me instead," I admitted, cheeks heating despite the cold.

Thomassen frowned, shaking his head like he couldn't believe me. "Your logic makes no sense. Do you realize that?"

I hung my head in shame.

"The only reason I knew you were up to something is because you weren't dreaming," Thomassen admitted.

"What?" I asked, taken aback.

"One of my gifts is dream walking. I can enter anyone's dreams. I got curious tonight and realized you weren't dreaming. That's why I came looking. I didn't know you were in trouble, Rue, but I had a hunch you were up to no good."

Dream walking? A gift such as that one was rare. I stared at him, wondering how many times he'd been in my dreams and how I'd never realized it before. Was he there when Fang was attacking me, trying to wake me up?

"How many times have you violated my privacy?" I prodded.

"Gods." Thomassen covered his flustered face with his hands. "This is why I keep to myself. I don't like being around people, especially when they concoct stupid plans like this." Pain flashed behind his eyes when our eyes met again, and my face fell.

"What if I don't want to stay away? I don't want you to only visit me when I'm sleeping," I said.

"Why?" Thomassen snapped. "Why do you want to be around me so badly?"

All I knew was that whenever he was around, I was whole again. I felt safe, and I didn't have to hide my curse. There was something about him that... called to me.

"I can't explain it. I... feel drawn to you. You understand me," I explained, heart beating madly against my chest. We'd shared our secrets with each other. That had to mean something to him. It'd meant everything to me.

Thomassen flushed and averted his eyes, shoving his hands into his pockets. Tension hung in the air between us, and I dropped my gaze to the snowy ground.

"You're a pain in my ass," Thomassen said.

"I'm sorry," I apologized.

"We're going back to the castle, and I'll consider coming around again as long as you stop acting like *this* moron." He gestured towards Peter's sleeping figure.

"Don't be so hard on Peter. He's not completely an idiot." I stared at Peter, grateful that he somehow filled that empty part of me that missed Fang.

"Grab my hand," Thomassen directed.

"What?" A heated blush rose on my cheeks.

Thomassen bent down and grabbed hold of Peter's arm, "Do as I say. Now."

An electric shock bolted through me the second I grabbed his hand, and a cloud of smoke encircled us. When I blinked, we were back inside the great hall.

I gasped for air, my eyes wild as I regarded Thomassen, "How did you —"

He was full of surprises. How unfair for him to have several gifts while I had none. Thomassen panted, anchoring his palms against his knees as he supported himself. At least his magic had limits. He put a finger to his lips, looking behind me. A guard patrolled the hallway right outside.

"Where's Peter?" I whispered, scanning the room for him.

"Back in his room, sound asleep," Thomassen answered. "With no recollection of tonight. You'll be sure not to remind him of it."

I gaped at him, amazed. Maybe he took after his multi-gifted father after all.

"You're incredible," I told him.

Thomassen glanced down at my hand, which was still attached to his arm. "You can let go of me now."

I complied but moved closer to him. "What now?"

Thomassen made no attempt to back away. "Promise me you'll stop putting yourself in unnecessary situations and go to bed at a normal time like a normal person. I don't want to talk about tonight ever again. Got that?"

I backed off and nodded. "Understood. Can you send me to my room the way you did with Peter?"

"If you can get yourself down here without the guards noticing, then you can get yourself back. I have to wake my father and tell him about the portal at the very least, so good luck getting back to your room."

"But —"

Thomassen walked away, each step carving a dagger into my heart.

Chapter 26

Complications of the Heart

THE CRINKLED PARCHMENT REVEALED A HEARTWARMING IMAGE of Puko, a sketch I'd mindlessly drawn as I sat alone on a bench outside the chapel, the bird's face a subtle comfort in my moments of sadness. Puko had become a companion of sorts, an ally I never knew I'd needed nor asked for, but hearing his adorable chirps in my mind somehow calmed my nerves.

Peter hadn't remembered a thing about our trip to Blackwood Bog. He did, however, remember me inquiring about going, so this time, I'd told him no. I didn't want to go and neither should he, especially if that portal was linked to the Volings. Not that Peter needed to know about that little detail.

I rested the back of my head against the wall, my chest tight as I cursed myself for being such an idiot, when Thomassen approached and sat down beside me, rubbing the back of his neck.

"What do you want?" I asked. I wanted to forget him after

last night. He'd made it clear enough times he wanted nothing to do with me.

Thomassen shifted in my direction. "I had a long conversation about that portal with my father last night. Seems he already knew about it and was working on getting it sealed. He also knew about you and Peter."

My hands stilled. "Of course he did." I stared forward, avoiding looking at Thomassen so he couldn't see my pained expression. "Anything else or are you here to scold me some more?"

Thomassen hesitated, and a long silence fell between us before he spoke again. "I was thinking maybe we could try to be friends," he grumbled, a sudden flush blooming across his skin.

My jaw went slack. Hearing the word *friend* come out of his mouth was strange. Shocking even.

"There's no point in being friends," I said dismissively, returning my attention to Puko's sketch. "You've made it clear you hate me."

"I don't hate you," Thomassen said, "but don't take that the wrong way. I never said I liked you either."

I snorted. "Then why are you here?"

"I wanted to tell you, in person, that I'll be attending classes from now on, though I find them rather pointless."

I found that hard to believe. "Why?"

"My father thinks it'd be a good idea to be around other people—make some friends, instead of avoiding people all the time." Thomassen hesitated. "He insisted, more like. Probably to keep you and Peter in line." His gaze held mine, a little longer than expected. There was an emotion there that I couldn't place—one he seemed to be grappling with as he fiddled with his vest buttons.

I dropped my hands to my side, resisting the urge to reach towards him. "I suppose it'll be nice to see you more." I was more excited than I cared to admit, though I was acutely aware that I needed to keep my feelings guarded.

"I suppose so," Thomassen said, the blush across his cheeks deepening. "Try to stay out of trouble." Thomassen stood and walked in the opposite direction, but his gaze lingered, unsettling me, like a wild riptide on a sunny shore. If he didn't like me, why would he stare at me and blush when I caught him? His words were harsh, but his body language betrayed him. Maybe he cared more than he let on.

I lifted my hand in a pathetic wave as he disappeared around a corner, hoping he felt something other than dislike for me, because after all was said and done, there was no denying that I had feelings for him, and those feelings were beginning to run deeper, despite my efforts to bury them.

"Why are you standing here?" Nora asked, joining my side as I waited by our classroom. "Did you eat anything? You left our room in a hurry."

"I'm waiting for Thomassen." After showering earlier, I'd dressed in my best pair of brown trousers and a beige tunic paired with an underbust corset, one that clung to me in a way that made me uncomfortable, but if I was going to see Thomassen today, I wanted to look pretty. I'd taken my time in front of the mirror, combing my brown and green hair into oblivion and adding a rosy color to my freckled cheeks. Leavenfell had done me some good. I'd filled out to a healthy weight, and my hair was less dull.

"Thomassen?" Nora asked.

"The very one. He's going to attend class with us." I glanced at her doubtful expression. "Supposedly," I added with sarcasm.

Thomassen emerged from around a corner and made his way over to us, his chin-length, light brown hair tucked behind his ears in that disheveled manner of his. He dressed casually, in cotton gray pants and a white shirt, instead of his usual dress attire, but it suited him well.

I gave a friendly wave. Nora held my arm as she studied him, her fingers digging into my skin. She greeted him with a friendly smile. "You didn't tell me how gorgeous he was," she whispered in my ear.

Thomassen's cheeks flushed, as if he'd heard her. *Yup… adding super-hearing to his list of gifts.*

"Nora, meet Thomassen. Alden's son. Thomassen, this is my friend and roommate, Nora."

Thomassen offered a hesitant smile before returning his smoldering gaze to me, the corners of his eyes crinkling as he gave me a once-over. It took everything in me not to melt into a puddle onto the floor. My corset suddenly felt too tight, but I resisted the urge to loosen its ties.

"Shall we get breakfast?" Nora asked, her stomach growling. "I can smell the pancakes from here. Looks like Lance's mom outdid herself again."

"Banana and walnut today," I said after catching the delicious scent that hung in the air. The farm workers always outdid themselves.

I led Thomassen to our table, where Lance and Peter sat,

already digging in. Lance waved at me, but the friendly mask came off when he caught a glimpse of Thomassen.

Alden Hall joined our table shortly after, resting a wrinkled hand on Thomassen's shoulder. "I'm delighted to see you joining others your age," he said to his son. "I'm proud of you for taking my advice." He squeezed his shoulder and continued towards his office door.

"Not like I had much of a choice," Thomassen said, but his father had already departed the table.

I glanced at Lance, who'd busied himself with glaring at Thomassen.

"Lance, this is Thomassen." I said, attempting to break the growing tension between them.

"I know who he is," Lance said, his tone flat and disinterested.

I gawked at him, confused by his attitude. "Are you okay?" I whispered, sitting down next to him.

Lance set his fork on the table and walked away, leaving me wondering what I did wrong. I brushed it off as nothing and took a few bites of food, keeping my eyes forward as Thomassen took the seat across from me.

Nora broke the silence. "What's wrong with Lance?"

I didn't know what to say to that. Instead, I apologized to Thomassen for Lance's weird response.

"Not your concern," Thomassen said, taking a bite of his food.

"Thomassen! Hello!" Liessa ran over, flipping her long hair over her shoulder. She wore a low-cut top, practically shoving her large boobs in Thomassen's face as she bent over him.

"It's great to see you again," she beamed. I clenched my fork, wondering how they knew each other.

Thomassen glanced up at her and smiled. An actual smile that paired well with the adorable way his eyes crinkled at the sides.

"Nice to see you too, Liessa."

"How have you been?" Liessa carried on with her conversation with him, and my skin heated as I watched their friendly exchange. Did they have a romantic history with each other? The way Thomassen regarded her with such softness led me to believe they did.

"It's great to see you. Stop by again sometime," Liessa hugged him, and he briefly wrapped an arm around her before pulling away.

"I will," Thomassen replied, and he watched her saunter away. When he faced me again, his expression went blank, but a faint blush rose to his cheeks, and I wondered if that blush was meant for Liessa.

"Did you and Liessa have a thing?" I asked, unable to stop the question from leaving my lips.

Nora, who'd been cuddling against Peter's side, lifted her head from his shoulder.

Thomassen gave me a look of disapproval. "Why does that matter?"

"I was only curious. It looked like the two of you had history." If I could've dug a hole right then and there, and buried myself for having no restraint, I would have. "Sorry for asking."

"Whoever I have a *thing* with is none of your business," Thomassen said coolly, straightening his shoulders.

I didn't know how to respond, so I gawked at him instead, heat rushing to my face.

"Quit looking at me like that," Thomassen snapped.

"I wasn't looking at you like anything," I replied softly, sinking into my chair.

"Then do me a favor and leave me alone," Thomassen ordered, his raised voice spreading across the hall. "Stop prying into my life."

Nora shot a wary glance at Thomassen, her ears drooping. "Everything okay?"

"What's your problem, asshole?" Lance returned to his seat beside me, his expression more annoyed than before he left. "Half the castle can hear you."

"Oy, what are you doing?" I snapped at Lance, covering the side of my face with my palm. I didn't want any more attention on me than there already was.

"I get what this is," Peter said, untangling himself from Nora and leaning forward until his elbows rested on the table. "Rue's jealous of Liessa."

Lance glanced from Peter to Thomassen to me, his expression darkening. He bit his bottom lip, hard enough to leave an imprint.

My jaw went slack. "Peter, that's not—" My scar burned with humiliation. I needed to end this before it spiraled out of control.

Thomassen set his cup down, his sharp gaze falling on Lance. They glared at each other, locked in a silent argument of their own.

"Do you have an issue with Rue or something?" Lance snapped. "What the hells is your problem?"

Thomassen hunched forward, his palms flat against the table. "If you must know, I find her to be an annoyance. She needs to leave me be." He enunciated every word slowly, as if Lance was too dumb to understand him. An insult if anything.

A heavy stillness blanketed the table, dense and stifling, as my fingernails dug into my thighs. Peter glanced my way, mouth open, but I turned my head, desperate to hide the heartbreak I knew was painted across my face. Had I really been that much of a nuisance to him?

"You're lying. I've seen the way you look at her," Lance said, coming to my defense.

Thomassen pinched the bridge of his nose, exhaling. "I don't look at her like anything. Maybe you should hit the books instead of making brainless assumptions." He said sternly, pointing towards the exit.

Red-faced, Lance leapt across the table, grabbed Thomassen by the front of his shirt, and swung his fist at him, but Thomassen dodged at the right moment, throwing curses at him.

"Both of you knock it off!" I blurted, forcing myself out of my seat. Heart racing, I yanked Lance back into his seat and shot him a pleading look. Residents passing by gasped at the sight of us, and for once, I was glad Arthur was nowhere in sight. Peter had no words. Instead, he stared at his older brother in disbelief.

Thomassen ran a hand through his hair, his expression unreadable.

"Thomassen, I—" I met Thomassen' eyes, hoping I could get the message across to him, but I couldn't hold his gaze without something inside of me breaking apart.

I fumbled for the right words to say as images flashed through my mind: the warmth that touched his cheeks whenever he was around me. The lingering gazes. The way his eyes crinkled when they met mine. He'd found me in the room of memories and in the forest with Peter. He'd taken me to his room and shared secrets with me. I'd wondered if he secretly cared for me, but after seeing the way he interacted with Liessa, it was clear I'd misinterpreted him.

A tear slid down my cheek, but I quickly brushed it away, feeling like a damned idiot. "I'm sorry." I didn't know if I was apologizing to Thomassen or myself.

Thomassen tensed, his jaw flexing as he tilted his head away from me. His silence might as well have been a dagger to my heart.

I faced Lance, whose skin had gone pale. "And you. I know you mean well but stop trying to protect me."

"I *will* protect you," Lance argued, his voice breaking. He flung his hand outwards, gesturing at Thomassen. "Because better men wouldn't speak to you that way, me included."

Thomassen scoffed at him.

I brought my fingers to my forehead, closing my eyes as a headache brewed. Though Lance meant well, I couldn't bear to see the pain etched across his face. I couldn't stand to see the hidden meaning behind his eyes.

Thomassen stood. "It's clear I shouldn't have come here," he said, voice low.

Blinking back tears, I squared my shoulders and held my head high. I refused to crumple in front of him. "Then why did you come?"

"My father insisted. I'm sorry to have led you on."

The silence across the table crushed me. I couldn't bear to look at Nora or Peter, fearing how they'd react. Heat rose on the back of my neck, and I forced myself to look at Thomassen, clenching my numb fists against my sides.

A glimpse of regret flashed behind his eyes, but he left without another word.

Chapter 27

The Solstice Banquet

The crackle of the fire was somehow comforting. Puko quietly perched on my shoulder as I sat cross legged on the floor, back in my tower. Nora had joined me by the fireplace, not at all worried about skipping class.

"Peter has a hidden stash of alcohol somewhere. Interested?" She wrapped an arm around me as I stared into the flames through misty eyes.

"Why not," I said, warming my hands as I forced back unwelcome tears. I refused to cry over a boy.

Nora rubbed my back. "I know it sucks, but if it helps, I'm sure he regrets it."

I doubted that.

"Thomassen is so strange," Nora said with a frown. "Plain mean, if you ask me." She tossed a crumpled piece of paper into the fire. There was still a pile of them to our right after I'd gotten back to our room and scribbled a bunch of nonsense in the sketchbook Lance had gifted me.

Nora wasn't wrong. Thomassen's rudeness was something I'd grown tired of, but it no longer mattered since I was determined to bury him in the back of my mind and forget about him entirely.

"Lance though… I can't believe he tried to punch him."

"He was being protective, even if that was taking it too far," I admitted. "It's my fault for trying so hard to be Thomassen's friend. I tried to push him into something he didn't want." I couldn't admit to her that what I'd felt for Thomassen was more than friendship. He'd been so nice to Liessa, but had withheld that same kindness from me, and I wasn't sure what I did to deserve it.

"If you ask me, he's missing out on a great person," Nora said reassuringly. "His loss, Rue. Don't worry about it."

I shifted my body towards the fireplace and closed my eyes, trying to forget it all.

With a sigh, Nora pushed herself up. "Going to grab that drink. We could both use it."

With the banquet looming, excited whispers filled the halls as young girls spoke of dresses they wanted to wear and boys they wanted to dance with. Despite the mood shift of the castle, I wasn't as excited as the rest of my peers. I wasn't much for dancing and dressing up anyways, so who cared if Thomassen disappeared into the void again.

I clenched my teeth, forcing back the wolf that threatened to break out of my skin. Lately, I'd spent too many mornings cursing and brushing my fingertips against the talisman in my pocket.

The talisman brought some relief from my curse, but its effects were dwindling, and I had no idea how to find Shay to fix it. If she really existed, which I'd yet to figure out. If anything, the talisman's fading magic was more proof that magic wasn't permanent.

I forced my legs over the side of my bed, angry that I'd been slacking on searching for the prophecy. Thomassen had been a distraction, but it was time to stop sulking and focus on what I needed to do and not what I wanted. I drew in a settling breath and left my bedroom in search of Nora. Gods forbid I was late for picking out a dress. I'd never hear the end of it from her.

I checked the great hall, my attention lingering on the added golden and burgundy ribbons and autumn leaf decorations that hung from the vaulted ceiling, but Nora wasn't there. Turning back into the main hall, I followed a corridor past where people were setting up the ballroom, peeking into every room that I could.

I made a sharp right turn around a corner when a hand grabbed my arm and yanked me into a dark room. I cried out, punching my unknown assailant.

"Ow," a pained voice said in response.

I stopped swinging when I recognized the voice. "Thomassen?"

A candle flared to life, illuminating the cramped room, stacked from floor to ceiling with cleaning supplies and bottles of wax and detergent. I dragged my eyes over my attacker, confirming that it was, in fact, Thomassen.

"What the hells?" I cursed. "You startled me." I wrapped my arms around myself. I hadn't expected to see him anytime soon, nor had I wanted to. Not after what happened between us. His eyes caught mine as he steadied himself against the wall.

"Rue," he whispered my name, breaking the silence between us. He offered a small smile, despite his tense shoulders.

The memory of our last conversation came rushing back, immediately angering me. Instead of saying anything to him, I turned to leave the room.

"Rue, wait!" Thomassen caught my arm, his touch sending shockwaves through me.

"I don't want to see you," I snapped, shaking him off.

"Please." His tone carried quiet desperation. "Stay. Hear me out."

I stilled, my hand resting on the doorknob. "Why should I bother listening to *anything* you have to say?"

"Because Rue. I need you to know that I'm so sorry, for everything that I said to you, and for how I treated you."

My breath caught. "I'm an annoyance, right? Go bother Liessa, since you can clearly stand her presence over mine." I said with enough coldness to frost over the room. He wasn't going to come back into my life like nothing happened.

"Liessa is an old acquaintance. There was never anything romantic with her." His eyes held a sincereness, but I backed away from him, not falling for it.

"You've hurt me more than enough times." Tears stung the back of my eyes. "I'd been so stupid to think that someone like you would ever care about me."

"I didn't mean a damned word," Thomassen asserted, his eyebrows knitted together. "I was terrible to you, but I'm here now. Begging for your forgiveness."

He's serious.

My stomach sank, like an anchor descending to the bottom of

the sea. A part of me wanted to believe him. Forgive him. But I shook with anger, and I was terrified of trusting him for fear of breaking my own selfish heart.

"You treated me like I was nothing to you, so how will you feel when I do the same to you?"

I yanked my arm from his grasp and reached for the doorknob, but Thomassen grabbed hold of my shoulders and pushed me against the wall, caging me with his body.

"What the hells, Thomassen!?" I snapped, my skin heating traitorously, reacting to his proximity.

His breaths came out in heavy spurts, his hands shaking as he brushed a strand of hair away from my face. He caught my chin in his hands, firm but careful, and I had no choice but to meet his eyes.

"Thomassen, I meant what I—"

His lips were too close, his body nearly flush against mine. "I'm tired of staying away from you. I can't do it anymore, not when I want so badly to be with you."

I barked a laugh. "Have you gone mad? You've made it very clear—"

Thomassen's lips crashed against mine with feverish urgency, pinning me between him and the wall. He wrapped an arm around my back and drew me closer, his warmth drowning any fight left inside me, setting every inch of my skin on fire.

Knees weak, I melted into him, against him. My body trembled, and I wrapped my arms around his neck as he kissed me again, brushing his fingers against the curve of my chin.

He lowered his lips onto the dip of my shoulder. Heat pooled into my stomach when I felt how hard he was against me. Everything I'd wanted to say to him, every heated word, evaporated into the distant corners of my mind, forgotten, as his fingers trailed down my throat, gently grazing my neck.

No. This isn't right.

A soft moan escaped his lips as his hips dug into mine, his hands dipping even lower on my back, stopping near my waistband. His fingers lingered there, his eyes searching mine as he drew his head back.

I pushed him away before things went any further, my own breathing as erratic as his. The fire between us simmered like a candle slowly being extinguished, and I loathed the way I missed his lips against mine. It'd been nothing like when Lance kissed me. This was very different. But pushing him away was the right thing to do.

Thomassen's cheeks flushed with warmth, his hair a tangled mess. His shirt had come unbuttoned, revealing smooth skin prickled with sweat. His appearance was *so disheveled*, but so handsome, tempting me to dismiss my anger. He bent forward, his eyes heavy-lidded and his lips parted. *He's going to kiss me again.*

"Don't." I held up my hand, my heart thumping wildly. "Please don't." *You were so cold to me. You told me to leave you alone.* I bit the inside of my cheek to stop the words from flowing out.

"Why did you kiss me?"

Thomassen's gaze softened. "Because for too long, I've dreamed of kissing you. I haven't been able to take my mind off you. Not since the first time I ever laid eyes on you, that day on the bridge."

My mind flickered back to the memory of the boy I saw in the window my first day at the castle. That had been him? A blush colored my cheeks, my skin tingling from the heat of his hands on my skin. I took another step away from him, an attempt to collect myself, but my body shivered with longing despite my efforts.

The room rattled, catching us both off guard.

"What was that?" I asked Thomassen, bracing my hand against the wall.

He scanned the room, lost in a state of confusion. "I don't know."

I hung my head. "Thomassen, I—"

The door flung open, revealing Nora, her lips curled at the sight of us.

"There you are!" She exclaimed, her eyes lit with amusement.

I backed away from Thomassen, adding distance between us. "I was looking for you," I told Nora.

"Oh, I bet you were." Nora grinned. From the smug look on her face and the perkiness of her ears, she'd seen more than I wanted her to.

"I heard a commotion, but wasn't expecting this," Nora said.

My face heated and I peeked at Thomassen, who was blushing like he'd been caught stealing my virginity.

"Don't worry. Your secret is safe with me. But we need to find a dress for the banquet, remember? Lance's mom has a boutique set up in the ballroom. Nicest clothes I've ever seen."

My head was spinning, and my heart was stupidly thumping against my chest, betraying me. I was still angry with Thomassen, but I wanted him at the same time. *Fuck.*

Thomassen lowered his gaze, his lips twitching. "You should go."

"When will we see each other again?" I asked. "To talk," I added with a raised brow. No more kissing, not until I had a long conversation with him.

Thomassen leaned down until his mouth was right beside my

ear, his hot breath sending lightning bolts down my spine. "Come to my room tonight." Mischief twinkled behind those golden eyes of his, and I had half a mind to deny his request. I wasn't sure if going to his bedroom was a good idea. He planted a kiss on my forehead, weakening my knees. *Curse him for making me feel like this!*

"Oh, come on then," Nora complained with a huff. "You'll have plenty of time to make out later." She grabbed my hand and tugged me from the room. I glanced back once more to see Thomassen smiling at me in a way he'd never shown before. A smile that made me wonder if what had happened was *real.*

I swallowed hard, fighting against my curse, which slowly manifested after the kiss I'd shared with Thomassen. Now wasn't the best time to shop for a dress, not when the wolf inside me was spiraling like this. I entered the ballroom and bumped into Lance, my pulse quickening when my eyes snapped to his entwined hand, Olivia's fingers laced through his. He'd said he would save a dance for her at the solstice banquet, but nothing about holding her hand and hanging out with her. Something about the scene rubbed me the wrong way.

"I can't do this right now," I told Nora in a shuddering breath, giving her an apologetic look after dragging my eyes away from Lance. "I feel an attack coming on, and with how intense they've been lately, I'm worried the talisman won't help." I held a hand over my stomach, the nausea settling in.

Nora gave a subtle nod, understanding in her eyes. She'd

found out about the nature of my attacks thanks to the alcohol she'd brought back to our tower. In a drunken rage, I'd told her all about them, *and* all about Shay and the talisman. Luckily, she was quick to accept whatever I ended up telling her, a friend I didn't deserve but was grateful for.

"Is there anything I can do to help?" Nora asked, placing her hand under my elbow to steady me.

I shook my head. "It's one of those things I can't control, but I'll be fine once it passes."

Nora hung her head but smiled anyway. "I'll bring a nice dress back for you. Promise."

We parted ways, and I exited the ballroom, stumbling into Arthur, who grabbed me by my arms to keep me from stumbling.

"Hey, slow down. You don't look so good." His wrinkles deepened, accentuated by the worrisome expression on his face. His stubble had also grown some, which I found odd since Arthur usually kept it trimmed. I hadn't seen him in a while, not since everything with Fang. On top of that, he'd been extra busy with guard duty, especially with more Volings being spotted as each day passed.

"I haven't been feeling so well these days," I replied, reaching into my pocket to touch the gem. The symptoms dulled before flaring back up again seconds later.

"I can't seem to shake these symptoms," I told him, half-tempted to chuck the talisman out the window out of pure frustration.

Arthur laid a hand on my shoulder. "You're stronger than you know, Rue. You have to fight it."

I stared at him apprehensively. "I don't think you understand how hard this is. I'm scared I might turn."

"That won't happen, so stop worrying."

"I hope you're right." I grimaced, resolved to his denial.

Arthur nodded and brushed past me, but I was sick of the distance between us. The distance that had been there since the meeting with Alden, and since Fang's second disappearance.

I hooked my arm through Arthur's. "Wait."

"What is it?"

"I wanted to tell you that I'm sorry for being a pain all these years. I'm sorry for pushing you for details that you didn't want to give me, and I'm sorry about how we left off after speaking with Alden. I understand now that you were only trying to protect me." I didn't bring up the fact that Alden had written the letter sending me back to the hidden corridor.

Arthur's concern shifted into relief. "You were never a pain, and Rue, I'm the one at fault for a lot of things. I should've been more open with you. For that, I'm sorry."

"I want us to stop avoiding each other. I love you and I can't bear being upset with each other. With Fang gone, I feel so lost." And a lot of the time, I did. I was completely alone, even when I was surrounded by my friends.

Arthur's expression mirrored my own sadness. He missed Fang as much as I did. He pulled me into a hug. "I'm not going anywhere, and I'll always love you like you're my own daughter," he reassured me. "Whenever you feel that way, you come find me. I don't care what time of day it is or how busy I am."

I hugged him back, nestling my head against his chest. "I will. Promise."

My cheeks burned as I sat alone in the empty classroom, trying to make sense of the kiss. I'd been dumb for letting Thomassen touch me that way, but the physical attraction was undeniable. The kiss had burned with such ferocity that butterflies still raged in my stomach hours later. I didn't know if I wanted to melt into a puddle onto the ground like a lovestruck girl or shift into an angry wolf. Maybe both.

Even though Thomassen had apologized and said he hadn't meant it, anger pulsed inside me. He treated me like I was an annoyance, only to wrap me in a passionate embrace later. The whiplash gave me a migraine.

"Rue!" Lance called, and I sensed him approaching.

I swiveled in my seat, my head pounding. "I'm going to be completely honest right now." I scowled, meeting his eyes. "I'm not in the mood to talk to you, much less see you."

"What you saw in there isn't what it looked like," Lance explained, panting as he ran up to me.

"For how long are you going to carry on with Olivia? I thought a dance would be enough, but you're holding her hand now?" I asked, though I knew I was being ridiculous. Who Lance held hands with was none of my business, and it shouldn't have upset me as much as it did.

"She *threatened* my safety and tried to expose me. You of all people should know what that would mean for me if word got out." The people of Leavenfell would be after me with their torches and pitchforks.

I heaved a sigh. "But that's not really what I'm mad about," I admitted, giving him a pointed look.

Lance bowed his head, his jaw hardening. "I know. I shouldn't have tried to punch Thomassen."

"He deserved it," I said.

"Maybe, but it wasn't like me," Lance explained. "I lost control of my emotions. I'm sorry. And there's nothing going on with Olivia besides me doing what I said I was going to do. Olivia came up to me to apologize for her behavior and for spreading rumors about you. I told her she needed to apologize to you, not me. That was when she grabbed my hand, around the same time you and Nora walked in. I have no interest in her. I'm sorry if I gave you that impression. I don't want to lose our friendship."

I exhaled. "I'm sorry too, and everything's good between us. I don't ever want to lose you. You're one of my closest friends." *Not to mention bonded…*

Lance hugged me, crushing me against him. "Let's forget any of this ever happened. Truce?"

"Truce."

After we parted, I went straight to my room instead of meeting up with Thomassen. When the brain fog finally cleared and I had a chance to really think about it, his actions made no sense to me. Thomassen had been cold to me from the moment I met him. There were sweet moments too, ones I clung to in hopes that he liked me, but after the mess in the great hall, I was hesitant to believe him.

I couldn't comprehend how he'd gone from disliking me to pushing me against a wall with his lips smashed against mine and his hands exploring my body. He'd been so cold, only to turn around and shove his tongue down my throat. A lump formed in my throat. As much as I wanted to reciprocate Thomassen's advances, a part of me hesitated. There was no denying my feelings for him, but I didn't want to set myself up for more pain either.

Nora was ethereal. Her hair, entwined with pearls and flowers, was braided into a beautiful updo, some strands of her vivid red hair framing her face. Her gown, made of green silk with a slightly sheer corset and a flowing black lace bodice, was perfect on her.

The dress she'd brought back for me was elegant but simple: backless and made of black silk that cascaded to the floor in one long sweep. The dress was light as air against my skin and hugged me in all the right places, the deep V-neck dipping beneath my breasts in a flattering manner. Staring into the mirror, I flipped my long hair behind my shoulders, admiring the strands as they fell down my back in pretty waves, thanks to Nora's assistance in helping curl them.

We made our way to the ballroom and stopped at the arched doors of the entrance. My breath caught when I glanced inside. Candles hung from the ceiling in glass spheres, casting a romantic glow throughout. Foliage and greenery draped the walls and ceiling, giving the appearance of an enchanted forest, while an oak tree stood in the middle of the room, its branches adorned with ornaments and floating candles. The tree hummed with magic, the air vibrating with its energy.

Alden greeted us at the entryway. "I recommend a dance in the courtyard. You can access it from the doors behind the tree, but please don't wander outside the courtyard's walls and remember that dinner begins in an hour."

I looped my arm through Nora's as we made our way to the doors that led outside. We found ourselves in a square courtyard enclosed with stone fencing, strands of abundant ivy growing up the length of them. Lit glass balls floated above our heads, emanating a soft glow. The gardens in the courtyard were frozen, though the flowers were perfectly preserved in the ice.

My eyes sought Lance, who I found standing next to a dark-skinned, curly-haired girl whose name I didn't know. She was hanging off his arm, a stunning smile spread across her face. When Lance found me, he waved. I waved back, scanning the courtyard for Olivia, who I figured would be waiting for her dance with Lance, but she was talking to another boy with tanned skin and black hair whose name I also didn't know.

Nora searched the courtyard for a man who was way too old for her. "Let's hope I can get lucky tonight."

I raised an eyebrow at her. "What kind of luck are you talking about?"

"A dance with Finn would suffice." She spotted him standing near a table of wine glasses and grinned. "Wish me luck," she said, leaving my side.

I walked to the corner of the courtyard by the overgrown walls, admiring the frozen garden as I passed by. I wrapped my black overcoat around the front of my gown and tied the straps tightly together. The night was cold but bearable without the wind.

"Do you need a partner?"

I faced the familiar voice. "I didn't think you'd be here, not with so many people about."

Thomassen was as handsome as ever, wearing a crisp gray shirt with suit pants and a cozy blazer. His light brown hair fell in front of his eyes the way I liked, and an uncertain smile crossed his angular face.

"You didn't come to my room." He moved to my side and wrapped one arm around my waist.

I pushed his arm away and frowned. "Remember when you didn't like it when I touched you? I'd appreciate it if you kept your hands to yourself."

Thomassen shoved his hands into his pockets. "You were shivering."

"I'm fine," I snapped, averting my gaze.

"Would you like to dance?" Thomassen asked.

"No."

"Are you sure?"

"No," I repeated.

"You're not sure?"

That damned smile lit up his face as I fumbled for a response. He was toying with me, enjoying every second of it, and I hated him for it.

"I don't want to dance with you," I said firmly, holding his gaze.

A dimple formed on his cheek. "You're a terrible liar."

I snapped my mouth shut, my face reddening as Thomassen held out his arm. "Only for a moment. We need to talk."

I grabbed his arm. Probably a dumb idea, but I was interested in hearing what he had to say, even if my gut told me to be cautious around him. Drawing my body against his, Thomassen wrapped an arm around me as we fell into a slow dance, his touch like lightning against the bare skin of my lower back.

"You look beautiful," he said, bringing his lips to my ear. My heart lurched, and I stepped on his foot by accident, which only made his smile deepen.

A few silent moments passed before I peeled away. "You're

not being genuine with me," I said bluntly. "So stop the compli-ments and tell me what this is really about."

Thomassen leaned backward, an air of hesitance about him.

I stilled and planted my fists on my hips. "Why are you being nice suddenly? Why the change?"

"What I said in the great hall wasn't true. I told you this."

I shook my head, not believing a word of his nonsense. "You don't go from being cold to someone to suddenly kissing them in a random storage room."

"I kissed you because I like you, Rue."

My gaze dropped to the ground. "I'm not sure I trust you, so if you're leading me on, stop."

"I'm not leading you on, but regardless, we're stuck together now, like it or not," Thomassen said, extending his hand. He grabbed a strand of my hair, his eyes resting on my green ends, a question in his eyes. Sadness painted his features. He turned his back on me and looked up at the stars. I joined him at his side and stared up at the night sky, annoyed by the whiplash he gave me.

There was a moment of silence as we stared upwards, and I searched for the constellations that Fang and I used to find when we were kids. But—the moon looked larger than I remembered. And there was only one.

Thomassen slowly turned towards me as horror dawned on me. "As you may have noticed, we're no longer in Fennra."

CHAPTER 28

GARDENIA

I SANK TO THE GROUND, DRESS BE DAMNED, AND COVERED MY face with my hands. I exhaled heavily, spreading my fingers as I peeked at Thomassen.

"What do you mean we're no longer in Fennra?"

Thomassen knelt in front of me, placing his hand on my shoulder. "My father took it upon himself to move the castle to Gardenia."

I fumbled for the words to say, rendered temporarily speechless. "H-how is that possible? Did he think no one would notice?"

"I've no idea. Moving castles to other realms was something I wasn't aware he could do until an hour ago, when he thought it important to tell me."

"Again, how?" I pressed. "I've never met anyone like Alden in my life. He can't be a normal wizard." Perhaps that rumble, from the room where I'd kissed Thomassen, was linked to the castle being moved, but I didn't dare bring it up, since I didn't want to remind him of our kiss.

"His parents were related to an ancient bloodline. One tied to the old kings of Fogstone. Their magic passed down to my father. That's the only explanation I got."

"Is that why you have so many gifts?" I asked.

"I only have a *fraction* of my father's magic," Thomassen explained, "but that doesn't mean I know how he does things or why, though I suspect the portal in Blackwood Bog influenced his decision." Thomassen gazed up at the stars. "People don't typically worry about the number of moons overhead when there's a solstice banquet to enjoy. Why do you think no one's noticed yet? My father's a master of creating distractions."

I glanced up again, unable to stop myself from trembling. Gardenia was the only realm in Fogstone where only one moon was viewable instead of two. I didn't know how, but I suspected the fae were behind it. Likely fae magic.

Do Arthur and the other guards know? They had to suspect there was something different about their surroundings while patrolling the outskirts of Leavenfell Castle.

"They know. Knowing my father, he likely made them swear to secrecy," Thomassen said.

I jolted backward. "How did you—"

Thomassen's shoulders slumped. "I guess now is as good a time as any to tell you that I can read your thoughts when we're touching."

I glared at him, unease creeping in. "Stay out of my head." *What else has he seen? Does he know I liked the kiss?* I shivered.

"I wish I could. This has never happened before, not until I met you," Thomassen explained, an apology hanging on his lips. "I don't know how to control it."

Thomassen hesitated, his posture slumping. "There's something else. I know that you've been thinking about the prophecy."

Of course he did.

He drew in a deep breath, pausing as he observed the many expressions crossing my face, most of all, the disgust at knowing he'd been in my head.

"I can help with that," Thomassen continued. "I think the record of the prophecy is in Gardenia somewhere."

"You didn't want to help before," I quipped, recalling our conversation in his room.

"I have my reasons."

Tension filled me. I swayed on my feet. The prophecy could be close, and I didn't know whether to feel excited or nervous about that.

"The prophecy is here?" I asked.

Thomassen nodded, but his eyes were distant. "The very one that you and I are destined to fulfill."

I didn't know what I'd expected to hear, but it wasn't *that*.

"What do you mean *us*?" I asked. I'd already known about my tie to the prophecy, but Thomassen too? My scar burned hot, as if in confirmation.

Thomassen nodded, giving me a few moments to take it all in. My mind was reeling. Why would the prophecy be in a fae realm of all places?

I shook my head. That didn't matter. What mattered right now was that the record of the prophecy that Arthur had tried so hard to keep from me was in Gardenia somewhere, and Alden knew it. This had to be another push to get me closer to it. He'd moved us here of all places, not because of the portal in Blackwood Bog, but because it had to be hidden here, and Alden wanted *me* to find it. And I'd be lying to myself if I said I wasn't the least bit interested in that task. The desire to find it had already been there. Now, a fire had been set inside me.

Thomassen helped me up off the ground, and I grimaced when his skin contacted mine, aware that he could be inside my head that very second.

I forced myself to look at him. "What exactly is this prophecy?"

Thomassen's face fell. "Do you want the long or short version?"

"Short version."

"We're supposedly the fated ones that'll close Vol."

My stomach knotted. Maybe that was why Thomassen was suddenly so keen to stay on my good side. Maybe he'd stopped pushing me away because he knew we were linked to the prophecy.

"Is that why you're telling me you like me? Because of this prophecy we're tied to?" I asked.

"No, Rue. I genuinely like you, and I'm done hiding it, prophecy or not," Thomassen answered, his breath catching when my gaze met his.

"How do we close Vol?" I asked.

"I don't know. The record is supposed to tell us what we're supposed to do, but—" Thomassen averted his eyes, his expression darkening in a way that unnerved me.

"But what?" I pressed, my pulse quickening.

"I don't *want* to find it. Not unless there's a way to change the outcome." Thomassen's face crumpled as he took my hands in his, and I'd never been more scared to see the pain behind his eyes.

"The prophecy said we'd seal the Volings away forever, but it also said that you— you'd die somewhere along the way. And gods, Rue... I didn't want to let myself care. I thought if I kept you at arm's length, if I stayed cold, maybe I could survive it. But I couldn't stop myself from caring, and now I don't know how I'm supposed to face your death."

"There you are," Lance said as he walked to my side. I was sitting alone by an icy sculpture of a rather large... bat? Gargoyle? Something resembling a mythical bat, but not quite so. Whatever it was, its wide, stringy wings arched around my sides, and I took comfort in using the weird sculpture to remain hidden from the rest of the banquet. Even though dinner had started, I wasn't the least bit hungry.

"There *you* are," I emphasized, keeping my eyes averted. I'd left Thomassen's side after a few heated words and stormed off to one of the dark corners of the ice-capped garden, my fists clenched at my sides.

No wonder Thomassen had been avoiding my presence from the start. No wonder he'd been so cold. I wouldn't want to get close to someone who was destined to die either.

"You look beautiful tonight," Lance paused as he took me in. "Are you okay?"

I couldn't bring myself to answer him. Tears threatened my eyes, but I suppressed them, willing myself to stay composed. I'd always been afraid of death, having watched Arthur tend to bodies growing up. It'd been such a bleak job, and I'd never understood why he enjoyed doing it. Imagining myself that way sent ice trickling down my spine.

This couldn't be the end. I didn't have to seek out the prophecy. I didn't have to do *anything* if I didn't want to. But the thought of not doing anything troubled me. I sat there, mulling everything over in my head, eventually coming to the same conclusion. When all was said and done, I knew I'd risk everything, even my own life, to save all the people I cared about. People I'd grown to love. And maybe, just maybe, closing Vol would save Fang.

I buried my face in my hands, shivering when a cold rush of wind cut into my skin.

"What's wrong, Rue?" Lance asked, his tone laced with worry as he placed his hand on my upper back.

"I don't want to talk about it," I told him, glancing up. "I'd rather be left alone for a few minutes. Sorry."

"It's okay. I'll be here if you need me." He squeezed my shoulder and went back to the girl who was waiting for him under the snow-covered gazebo. A smile lit up her features as he approached her, and she took his hand in hers and led him into the crowd of swaying bodies. Their voices grew muffled as the sounds of rambunctious, drunken laughter filled the space between the overgrown garden walls.

I searched for Thomassen in the crowd but only found the gloom of the snowfall.

Peter plopped down beside me and sighed.

"You know," I began with a groan. "There's this thing called personal space. You should try it sometime."

A smile tugged at Peter's lips, and he threw his head back against the cold belly of the sculpture, stretching his legs out in front of him. His hair swept back with the wind, revealing tired eyes and an expression of someone who'd lost the war of love.

"Shouldn't you be dancing with someone?" he asked when he caught me staring at him.

"No," I said, even though I longed for Thomassen's warmth. I wanted so badly to run my fingers through his soft brown hair. I wanted to feel his lips on mine and his hands on my skin. But he infuriated me as much as his father did.

Peter popped a pipe into his mouth, sighing as a puff of smoke left his lips.

"Where did you get that?" I scolded him.

"I nicked it from Alden's office. Don't give me that look. Just this once can't hurt," Peter said.

"You expect me to believe this is your first time?" I asked, catching a hint of sadness in his eyes.

He extended the pipe, offering it to me with a grin. I snatched the damned thing and tossed it onto the wet cobblestone, watching as the pelting snow buried it.

Peter let out a sigh. "What a waste."

"You'll be fine. Now come on." I stood and grabbed Peter's arm, yanking him up.

"Wh-what are you—" Peter stammered, but I shushed him.

"You're going to go ask Nora for a dance," I told him, leading him away from the sculpture. I searched the crowd and spotted her standing alongside Finn. Her stiff posture and bored expression told me all I needed to know.

"Nora needs a guy that's interested in her. Someone who makes her laugh. So go ask her for a dance," I said, pushing him in her direction. "If you really like her, stop giving your attention to other girls, you damned idiot."

Peter broke into a smile. Then he was off, smoothly slipping in between Finn and Nora and dragging her away into the heart of the crowd. He whispered something in her ear, and a huge grin spread across her face, her eyes brighter than I'd ever seen them.

I turned back towards the sculpture, but movement caught my eye, and when my head snapped in its direction, a shiver bolted through me. The garden door hadn't been open before. But now it was *wide* open, swaying with the pull of the wind, moonlight hitting the ground at the right angle, illuminating my worst fear.

An ominous stillness settled into my bones. Standing outside the garden exit was a horrifyingly tall, hunchbacked hyeling, its dark eyes ensnaring me as it curled its lips, showing a mouthful of razor-sharp teeth. The monster watched me, tilting its head. Its hairy fingers gripped the sides of the door, curling around the iron bars, its claws gleaming in the moonlight. It took a deliberate step towards me, and I flinched, my body frozen. When it lurched forward, I cried out, my hand darting to my thigh, retrieving the dagger I'd strapped there.

I slashed forward, the flash of silver slowing the monster as it stopped in its tracks and sniffed the air. Its ears perked up as it let out a low string of yips and calls. *Shit.* I couldn't let this thing in. I sucked in a breath and propelled myself forward, my dagger cutting through the air in an attempt to deter the monster. It yipped and snarled again, showing its teeth as it lifted its hand, its claws lengthening as it moved towards me.

I dropped the dagger and crashed into the monster at full force, taking it outside the courtyard walls and dragging it to the ground with me. My dress ripped, exposing my stomach and bare thighs, but I ignored the freezing cold and slammed my fist into the hyeling's snout. It growled, slashing its claws at my dress, tearing it to shreds as I staggered backwards.

I fell onto my back, stars dotting my vision as pain tore through me. My skin heated and chilled simultaneously as my bones began to crack. I was certain I was about to shift. Throw up first, then shift. I let out a scream of pain, my limbs writhing against the cold ground, giving the hyeling an opportunity to climb on top of me. I swung my fist forward, striking the side of the hyeling's face, but it pinned me down with its powerful claws.

It lifted its arms, ready to strike, and—

"Rue!"

An intense flash of orange light blinded me. When my vision cleared, the Voling had disintegrated into a pile of ash. I coughed, the burning smell stinging my nose, and scooted myself away, pounding my chest with my fist as I cleared my throat. Thomassen knelt beside me, draping his jacket over my exposed skin, a terrified expression on his face. He grabbed my chin, forcing me to look at him while he checked me for any wounds. When he touched me, my curse fell away, the symptoms disappearing entirely. I grasped the front of his shirt and held on for dear life, shaking as though I was going to fall apart.

My breaths came in heavy pants. "I h-had to s-stop it from getting in," I cried.

"What the hells were you thinking? You could've been killed!" Thomassen snapped, pulling me into his lap. I wrapped my arms around him, teeth chattering.

"You should've called for help," Thomassen reprimanded.

"Not tackled a monster twice your size." He tightened his arms around my waist. "But you're brave. I'll give you that."

"I thought we were safe since Alden moved the castle," I said.

Thomassen's jaw clenched. "I guess not." He continued investigating my skin as he gently removed me from his lap. "Are you hurt?"

"I don't think so."

Thomassen wrapped his arms around me again and held me against him, caressing my hair with his fingers. We stayed like that for a while, until I was able to pull myself together.

Thomassen rubbed his fingers across my back in gentle swirls as my head rested on his chest. "No one hears about this, Rue." His head turned towards the crowd. "We don't want to create panic. Not about that hyeling, and not about the castle being in Gardenia."

"I don't know if I can do this," I muttered under my breath.

"Do what?" Thomassen whispered, the heat from his breath against my cheek.

"I don't want to die," I said in a shaky breath.

Thomassen was the only person besides Fang I could tell I was scared. He and I were in this together, after all, until he lived and I died, and I guess that meant that my death wouldn't matter, because everyone else would be safe. They could live the life I've always wanted. *Free*.

Thomassen nestled the side of his face against my cheek. "I won't let anything happen to you. I promise you now and tomorrow, and every day after that. I promise to protect you."

I slumped against Thomassen's chest, gripping onto the front of his shirt, afraid that if I let go, he would disappear forever.

Something inside of me broke as he held me. Even though terror flooded me, a sorrowful void deep enough to imprison me, I was beginning to understand that at the end of everything, one of us had to make it out alive, and it had to be him.

CHAPTER 29

CRYSTALLIZED VISION

"I MET YOU LONG AGO IN A WOODED HOLLOW. A RECURRING dream. You were a wolf and I was dying. But then I was whole again, and you had something to do with it. When I told my mom about it, her expression changed. She was horrified."

Thomassen's voice trembled. "My mom told me the dream was tied to a prophecy, and she was scared that my dreaming about it meant I was tied to it. Later, my father confirmed exactly that… that I was destined to carry it out with a cursed girl. But the only thing that stuck with me was at the end, I lived and you died."

I shuddered but let Thomassen continue.

"That thought… haunted me for years, and I promised myself we'd never meet." Thomassen paused to catch his breath. "But when you showed up on the bridge that day, I was scared, because even though I'd tried to keep away, you still found your way to me." Thomassen confessed. The Solstice Banquet was still ripe with laughter and dancing, but we needed to get away from the noise, so we'd escaped to his room.

"I selfishly tried to protect myself by pushing you away. I thought if you hated me… if you stayed away from me, the prophecy wouldn't be set into motion, but I realized I was wrong, and whether we liked or hated each other wouldn't matter. The prophecy would still come to pass. Regardless, I was drawn to you. I couldn't stay away no matter how hard I tried."

I peeked at Thomassen as his other hand closed around mine. I closed my eyes, listening to his voice, memorizing every tone inflection as he caressed my hair.

"Following your trip to Blackwood Bog, I had to know if you were really the girl my father spoke of, so I went through a clock door, and it took me to the Crystal Realm. I needed a vision to show your face. To show the prophecy." He was shaking, his skin visibly paler, as if what he'd seen scared him to his core. "That realm confirmed my worst fears. The flash of green and brown hair… there was no doubt it was you."

"I want to see it," I told him, sitting up. "If I'm involved in this prophecy, I need to see what you saw," I said, staring up at him. Maybe the clock door would take me there too.

Thomassen sighed, his eyes miles away. "That realm is too dangerous. The lady of the realm will kill you if she finds you there, so I'd rather show you, if that's alright."

"Okay," I agreed.

Thomassen's eyes rolled backward, the whites of his eyes flashing as his eyelids fluttered. The air went cold, and a crystallized cavern took the place of his room. A lake sat at the base of the cavern, and a giant crystal rose from its depths. The unearthly crystal, shaped like a diamond, came to a rest once it fully breached the surface in the center of the lake. The crystal sat atop a curved pedestal made of black onyx. Swirling purple smoke danced inside and around the base of the crystal. Goose bumps rose on my skin as I peeled my eyes away from the crystal and looked at Thomassen, whose eyes were back to normal and fixed on the crystal.

"Go ahead," Thomassen said. "It's safe in my illusion."

I stood and approached the crystal, the water surrounding it hardening to allow my passage. The smoke inside thickened, swirling faster as I neared it. I pressed my hands against it, and the crystal's chill seared my palms. The magic flowed into me, sharp and cold, and a vision caught me in its grasp. Fear ripped through me as images flashed through my mind.

Thomassen on the floor, limp in his father's arms.

The woodland fae.

A sharp-faced fae holding a hand over me, forcing me to shift.

A rotted forest with twisted branches and winding paths.

A soulless man dressed in intimidating black armor.

My lifeless body at Vol's edge, a blood-stained dagger at my side.

I yanked my hands away and turned from the crystal, needing to get as far away from it as I could. But Thomassen was already at my side. The crystallized cavern disintegrated, and we were standing beside his bed.

"Breathe, Rue," Thomassen said, wrapping his arms around me. "I know it's a lot."

"You were dying. I was dead. That man… who was that man?" The words flowed out of me before I could stop them, my heart racing. It was no wonder Arthur had kept the prophecy from me. Those visions were gut-wrenching.

"I know. I saw the same things," Thomassen said, pressing a kiss to the top of my head.

"You were dying. That's not meant to happen." It wasn't

supposed to be him. If the prophecy was right, he was supposed to live. "Is there something going on that you're not telling me?" I asked.

Thomassen hesitated. "The magic inside me is withering. It's why I *look* sick sometimes. I weaken along with it."

So the Netherros's magic wasn't corrupting him. It was killing him, which was even worse than I could ever imagine.

"We have to fix it," I said, my tone desperate.

Thomassen frowned. "Alester took off with the Netherros, and my father hasn't been able to locate him. I'm not sure what's going to happen to me, but if the prophecy is true, I won't die." Thomassen shifted nervously on his feet, his expression flustered. I grabbed his shaking hands. He was as scared as I was.

"We must find the Netherros. Tell me about the dream where you met me, not just fragments."

Thomassen went on to tell his mom's story of the great wolf and the dying boy. He told of how the boy had been lost in the woods, searching for the wolf. How he'd collapsed after finding the wolf. As a last act of respect, the boy offered the wolf an apple, knowing he would be dead soon. The wolf knew the boy shouldn't die, so she laid down beside him and offered up a piece of her soul. Afterwards, the wolf fell asleep, and the boy was whole again. When the wolf awoke, the boy transformed her into a girl.

"It's a metaphor," I told him. "If the story is correct, then I must save you somehow."

Thomassen grimaced. "That's what I've been suspecting, although I don't understand the *soul* part."

"What happens after?" I pressed.

"There's not much else to tell… or rather, it's not known. They set off together on an adventure. The one that would close that dark realm and put away the Volings for good," Thomassen finished. "It isn't known where the journey leads them. All I know is that it will be difficult, and that we need to stop your death."

The weight of what I was destined to do anchored in my chest, like a lingering thunderstorm nestling into my veins. I was petrified at the thought of my own death, but I wanted to save Thomassen. Without the Netherros, the magic inside him would eventually cease. I needed to find Alester before that happened but had no idea where to begin to look. The woodland fae came to mind, since the crystal showed them. Maybe they could tell me where to find Alester.

My thoughts shifted, taking a dark turn. Who was the man with the creepy black armor? Would he be the one to kill me?

As we sat in silence, determination sparked inside me, setting me on a dangerous path. I would search for the Netherros, securing Thomassen's future. I would save him and close Vol for good, fighting with all I had until the very end.

CHAPTER 30

REPERCUSSIONS

THOMASSEN EMERGED FROM THE BATHROOM, A TOWEL wrapped around his waist, water dripping from his skin. From my spot at his desk, I side-eyed his figure, admiring the leanness of his muscles and the smoothness of his skin.

Last night had been the first night I'd felt at home since arriving at Leavenfell, wrapped in arms that made me feel safe after having fallen asleep in his bed. Whenever Thomassen and I were touching, my curse symptoms disappeared. He somehow had the ability to keep the wolf inside me at bay, and I wasn't complaining. If anything, it made me want to stay near him.

Thomassen strode to his dresser, his long lashes fluttering as he searched for something to wear. His cheeks flushed with color as he tugged at his towel. I looked away, blushing like an idiot at his near nakedness. I'd seen Fang naked before, but gods, this was much different.

Thomassen turned, a smirk tugging on his lips. He retrieved an outfit and flung it over his shoulder, walking over to me.

Panicked butterflies scurried about inside my stomach, and I hurriedly turned back to my sketch, my cheeks heating as I tried to remember Gardenia from my vision.

The cozy homes carved into the trees came easily, but I couldn't remember much else about it. I dug further, trying to recall more details. *Something was chasing me, but why?*

Thomassen bent over me, his face inches from mine, and looked at my sketch. I shifted away from him, hunching over the desk. His waist brushed against me, and I spilled ink onto my hand. *Godsdammit, he's way too close.*

"Tea?" He asked.

I raised an eyebrow. "But no book?"

Last night, Thomassen had admitted that a book couldn't be read unless one had a steaming cup of tea to go with it, and vice versa. We'd spent most of the night by the fireplace, and he'd been kind enough to make some for me, before settling into his armchair, a leather-bound book in his hand. I had to admit his tea recipe had the perfect balance of lemon and lavender, but after a few cups, I'd had enough to last me a week.

"I'm not much of a reader in the morning," Thomassen said. "But I'll put on a pot of tea for us."

"I appreciate the offer, but no thank you," I replied, heart racing. I snatched my parchment from the desk and tossing it into the nearby trash bin. I needed to find Shay. If anyone knew anything regarding the whereabouts of the prophecy or Alester, it had to be her.

I pushed myself out of the seat. "I should get going anyways. Nora will have a search party out looking for me and the last thing I need is Arthur breathing down my neck."

"I'll walk you to the door," Thomassen offered, slipping into a white shirt. He gestured for me to turn around. I swiveled, blushing fiercely as the towel plopped to the floor. When he was decent, I caught myself stealing glances. Loose pants and a cotton shirt were a change from his usual suit attire, but he could pull off anything. I resisted the urge to bite my fist, annoyed that I was losing control of my feelings for him.

"I want to see you again," Thomassen said as we embraced.

"Soon," I promised.

I entered my room and bumped into Nora, who was pacing the room with droopy ears. On her bed was a suitcase stuffed with her belongings, only half zipped. It also appeared as though Puko had built a nest of metal and screws on top of it.

That bird.

I froze. "What happened?" Puko landed on her suitcase and added more scrap metal from my storage chest to his nest.

"My mom caught me and Peter in bed this morning, so they're forcing me to move in with them."

"What?" I asked, shaking my head in disbelief while Puko squawked with indignance.

Nora hung her head. "I'm sure you can guess what happened when my mom walked in. Where were you, by the way?"

"Wait, back up." I held up a hand, shocked to hear this revelation from her. "Did you and Peter…"

Nora sheepishly averted her gaze, but her eyes brightened in a way that suggested she didn't regret it one bit. Finn must've been a distant thought by now, but I didn't think it would've happened *this* way.

"I'll kill him!" I balled my fists at my side. "How dare he take advantage of you like that!" Puko flapped his copper wings, squawking madly, as if he were as upset as I was.

"It wasn't Peter's fault," Nora admitted, her glassy eyes flitting to her bed. "He walked me to the door and said goodnight. I was the one who led him inside," Nora said.

I clenched my fists. "I hope to the gods you were careful. Did you use protection at least?"

"Yes, we did."

"Nora…" I began, my tone harsher than I liked.

Nora backed away. "Please, Rue. I don't need more scolding. I've heard enough from my mom. I caused this mess. I'm sorry I have to leave you because of it."

"Nevermind that. Explain why you'd bring Peter into your bed? Of course he wasn't going to say no. It's Peter, for gods' sake," I said, guilt eating at me. I'd pushed Peter towards her and the result was entirely my fault. Now I was losing Nora because of it.

"Why are you mad about it?" Nora asked, tucking a strand of red hair behind her ear. "I really like Peter."

"I'm not mad. I'm worried." And also, a little jealous that she'd taken that step before me, although I'd never admit that to her.

Her face softened, her shoulders slumping as she neared me. "I'm sorry, Rue. About all of this."

I didn't know how to respond, so I hugged her. "We'll figure something out. Maybe your parents won't keep you with them long?"

"I hope so. My dad's going to lose it when he finds out."

"He'd better not lay a hand on you. If he tries, you come right back here and I'll get Arthur involved." I wasn't entirely sure if

Mr. Moore put hands on Nora, but the way she talked about him made me suspicious.

"Thank you for being such a good friend, Rue," Nora cried, pulling me into an embrace.

All I could do was hug her back.

The great hall's usual warmth felt hollow as I glanced at the empty seat beside me, missing Nora. Seeing her in class and defense lessons wouldn't be enough, and I was already dreading going back to my tower alone. Puko hadn't been happy that I'd messed up his nest so that Nora could take her suitcase, but at least it gave her a smile before she departed.

Thomassen stared at the sky through one of the large arched windows, a thoughtful expression across his face. He seemed to be realms away.

"What are you thinking about?" I asked.

"How much I'm sick of snow," he grunted.

I gave him a half-smile. "A warm summer's day would be nice." It had been eternal winter ever since Vol cracked open; sunshine and warmth were rare.

Arthur stopped by the table, his eyes resting on Thomassen. He wasn't smiling. Did he know that Thomassen was tied to the prophecy?

I set my napkin down, "Hi, Arthur. Have you met Thomassen, Alden's son?"

"We've met before," Arthur said.

I didn't like his icy tone.

"I wanted to stop by and let you know that Finn would like his defense students to meet at the stage after breakfast, so don't go running off."

"What about?" I asked.

Arthur shrugged. "Likely patrol teams. We need more of them."

Rorik, smelling of pipe smoke and dressed in a gold-hooded robe, approached the table, meeting Arthur at his side. He mentioned something about having to leave on another trip to Talem, to aid the mortals there, at which Arthur nodded.

I greeted Rorik and wished him well as he readied himself to depart on his journey. Arthur also took his leave, and Lance sat down on my other side with a plate full of food and a cross expression on his face. His mouth was spread into a tight line, and he didn't greet me before he began eating.

"Hey." I touched his arm lightly. "Everything okay?"

Lance ignited with anger, his lips downturned. "As a matter of fact, no."

I let go of his arm. "What happened?"

Lance told me that Nora's father had grabbed Peter by the collar and punched him in the face multiple times, leaving Peter with a broken nose and some crooked teeth this morning. Lance said that if he hadn't stepped in, the damage would've been much worse.

I rubbed my temples. "How is Peter?" I asked, my anger shifting to concern. Thomassen leaned forward, listening in, and I was glad when Lance offered Thomassen a small smile. Maybe they'd gotten over whatever issues they had with each other.

Lance released a sigh. "Peter's fine now. One of the healers patched him up, but I can't believe a grown man would punch a teenager. I know my brother's an idiot, but that's not an excuse.

He should've come to me or our mom about it." He shook his head, his grip around his fork tightening.

My stomach was in knots. I couldn't believe Mr. Moore had attacked Peter, and now Nora had to sleep in the same room as that man. The thought of it made me sick.

"I've also heard that Nora moved into her parents' room. Are you going to be okay by yourself?" Lance asked.

"I... I don't know," I responded, my gaze dropping to my plate.

"If you're scared of being alone—" Lance began.

"I can stay with you," Thomassen cut in.

"No. It's not that. I'm worried about Nora having to stay with her dad. Who knows what he's capable of..."

"What they did is none of her father's business," Thomassen said.

"Mr. Moore should've kept his hands to himself. Now I can't help but worry about Nora." I fidgeted with my blouse, my nerves getting the best of me.

"I'll talk to my father and see about getting Nora back into the tower room with you," Thomassen offered. "If there's anything violent going on, my father will have Mr. Moore removed from Leavenfell."

CHAPTER 31

THE CLOCK TOWER

DROPS OF LIGHT SPILLED ONTO THE STAGE AS THE SUN BROKE through the clouds, casting shadows on the walls.

"Good afternoon," Finn greeted us stiffly, wiping his nose with a tissue. "Let's get into it so we can get out of here faster." He took a wheezy breath and tossed the tissue onto the podium. "A couple of nights ago, a Voling got into Leavenfell."

A few nervous gasps resounded as everyone exchanged tense glances. I froze when the words left Finn's mouth. When my gaze trailed to Thomassen, he gave me a subtle nod. There were more Volings here besides the one the night of the solstice banquet.

"Unfortunately, due to this incident, it's likely the Volings know we're here."

I stole a glance at Lance, whose eyes had widened as he processed this information.

"With that being said, we need to be on high alert. There could be more of them next time." Finn grabbed another tissue and sneezed into it. "Going forward, I want each of you to have your weapon of choice on hand and I would like to organize a few groups to run patrols. I'll allow you a moment to choose your teams, then we'll talk about the details."

When Thomassen appeared by my side, I was glad for his presence. "Who else should we add to our team?" he asked, scanning the room. He caught my eye and arched his brow. "Unless you want just the two of us?"

I hid a smile behind my hand. "I don't think Finn would go for that. Besides, we could use Lance, Peter, and Nora." I glanced at Lance, and he nodded his approval.

"Oliver and Willow might want to join as well," Lance said as he approached us.

"I don't feel comfortable with Olivia joining, and aren't her and Oliver a package deal?" I hadn't resolved my issues with Olivia, and she hadn't yet taken Lance's advice and apologized to me. Plus, if I experienced any symptoms while Olivia was around, she would make accusations again, which could throw my life into chaos, and that was the last thing I needed right now. Olivia and Oliver were out of the question.

"Rue's team will start patrol after breakfast for three hours every day. My team will take over after lunch, and Oliver's team will take over after dinner. Guard duty ends at six, but since we're rotating shifts, each team will only need to do a few hours every day." Finn announced after everyone had chosen their teams.

"What about school?" Oliver asked, his hand raised.

"School is postponed going forward. Your only concerns should be reporting anything that looks suspicious to one of the guards, myself, or Alden. If you have any questions, come talk to me after we're done here." Finn walked to the back of the stage and sat against the wall, pulling out a scroll of parchment and writing down everyone's teams and schedules.

"These patrols should include the hidden corridor. The realms behind the clock doors could act as a crossing point if the Volings discover them," Thomassen whispered.

A chill ran through me. "How would they know about the clock doors?"

"We can't pretend they don't know. Those doors could be an easy entry for them to get into the castle."

The clock tower stood at the end of the castle, overlooking the endless, choppy sea at the edge of the cliff. I stared up at the structure, impressed by the sheer size of it. The ticking was so strong, it reverberated through my ribs, piercing me to my core.

Lance, wearing a gray overcoat over his attire, stared at the massive clock in awe. "Peter would be sad to miss this."

"Nora too," I replied, hoping I'd see her soon. I missed her laugh and the way her ears changed depending on her mood.

I pushed the iron-clad wooden door, and it slowly swung open. Inside, a statue of Alden Hall stood in the entryway, chipped and covered in moss, but standing strong despite its aged appearance.

"Leave it to my father to put a statue of himself in his own clock tower," Thomassen said with a deep roll of his eyes. "I always get second-hand embarrassment when I see it." He stood by my side, and I resisted the urge to hold his hand. Even though Thomassen liked me, small things like holding hands seemed daunting.

"Says it was sculpted by Vaddeus-something. I can't make out the last name." I bent down and studied the inscription, but the last name was gone. I recalled how Alden had hushed Arthur when his name was brought up but knew nothing about him.

Lance crossed the room to the square window and watched the waves crash against the cliffside. The window on the opposite side showed a good view of the watchtower, a spindly iron building with a few guards posted on top of it. My eyes grazed the grounds outside the window, everything appearing the same as it did when I'd first arrived at Leavenfell. It didn't look like we were in Gardenia at all.

"Illusion," Thomassen whispered, reminding me.

"I know. The sea smells different here. Shouldn't we tell him?" I gestured to Lance, and Thomassen nodded.

"What's going on?" Lance asked, his eyes darting back and forth between us.

Thomassen stepped in front of me, crossing his arms. "Since we are in this together, you might as well know. My father moved Leavenfell Castle to another realm."

Lance raised a brow. He took a calculating glimpse of the outside and returned his gaze to Thomassen. "It looks the same to me."

"What you're seeing is an illusion. The banquet was a distraction. We're in Gardenia," Thomassen said.

"The realm of the woodland fae?" Lance asked with a worried tone.

"Yes," I answered for Thomassen.

Lance paled. "Aren't the fae known for their deceit and cruelty? Why would Alden move us to Gardenia of all places?"

"Gardenia is the only realm left that is considered safe," Thomassen said, exchanging a tense look with me, probably thinking about the hyeling we saw the night of the banquet.

"Does anyone else know?" Lance asked.

"Not yet," Thomassen said. "Please keep it that way for now."

Lance gave a sharp nod. "Fine."

We followed Thomassen over to a trap door in the corner. Thomassen yanked on the knob, and a ladder dropped with a loud clunk.

I stepped onto the first rung of the ladder, testing its strength. "It's old but feels secure," I said.

As I ascended, the clock tower's ticking shook me to my core. The climb was long, but after we reached the top, we found ourselves inside a large space that held an intricate network of heavy weights and pulleys. Smaller counterweights rose and fell at regular intervals. The ticking was louder here, the vibrations heavy against my skin.

"The other staircase should be around here somewhere," Thomassen said as he strode ahead. "It should be a thin winding staircase, somewhere in between all these weights, so keep an eye out."

I groaned, already tired from the long walk and climb. My legs were screaming with exhaustion. Lance spotted the staircase across the room, behind a huge counterweight. We climbed up and landed in a room where metal gears linked to the north and south sides of the clock faces. It was probably one of the main mechanisms of the clock itself, but I wasn't one hundred percent positive. I didn't understand how clocks worked, but I didn't need to. My job was to patrol, and we'd have an excellent view of the grounds from the top of the clock tower.

Another ladder led us above to the actual clock face.

Mesmerized, we watched several minutes ticked by. The clock faces, massive marble circles, were adorned with golden stars that framed the roman numerals between them. A gold crescent moon sat at the center of the clock, connecting long, thick hands to the clock itself. We gazed at the grounds of Leavenfell from there, half entranced by the craftsmanship of the clock and half amazed at how far we could see. The illusion only stretched so far. A few miles out stood a dense forest, full of bright flowers and flowing rivers.

When I turned around, I found Thomassen in front of the massive clock face. There was something about him that made my breath catch. His golden eyes shimmered when the sunlight touched them, and his light brown strands lifted with the breeze. When he caught me staring, he gave me a genuine smile that made my heart stutter, and I couldn't help but smile back at him.

Even though darkness was on the horizon, Thomassen was the light guiding my way forward.

Chapter 32

The Realm of Despair

THE TOWER ROOM WAS LONELY, BESIDES THE FLICKERING shadows. I missed Nora's snoring and her presence by the fireplace. I missed her recounting every romance novel she'd devoured and her endless talk about boys. I missed the tea she'd made and the laughs we'd shared. My heart ached as I glanced at the clock. It was past midnight, but I wasn't tired.

I sighed. Our patrol at the clock tower had dragged by. We'd spent most of our time taking turns observing the land surrounding Fennra, or rather, Gardenia, and ended up with nothing to report at all. No Voling sightings should've been a good thing, but I still feared that a storm was coming. If one hyeling had gotten in during the solstice banquet, then there were probably more.

I rested my head against my pillows, my mind lingering on the prophecy, Thomassen, and Alester. I needed to start searching for clues soon, especially if Thomassen was running out of time.

I sighed, bringing my hands to my face, the image of the key taunting me. With my mind made up, I yanked open the drawer. I grabbed the key, then retrieved my bow and quiver of arrows from the chair by the fireplace, along with the dagger I kept strapped to my thigh. Just in case.

Thomassen didn't have to know.

The clock door clicked after multiple failed attempts at opening the damned thing. Once I switched the hands to three o'clock, it swung open, a rush of cold wind smacking into me. I wrapped my arms around myself to keep warm, teeth chattering, and prayed to the gods that this clock door would lead me to more clues and not a boring closet. A sudden flash blinded me when I stepped through, but when my vision recovered, an overcast graveyard enclosed by pointy, looming black gates encircled me, caging me in.

Miles of tombstones, overgrown with weeds and withered beyond repair, stretched into the distance, smelling of damp soil. The wind whistled eerily as I crept forward, soon spotting a gray mausoleum at the far end of a long cobblestoned pathway.

Dread pooled in my stomach as I neared the entrance, and I unconsciously brushed my fingers against the grip of my bow. Shadows clung to the surfaces of the tombstones, hanging over the stones with outstretched tendrils, but I ignored them, keeping my eyes focused on my destination. As I approached the mausoleum ruins, rain descended from the black clouds above. The roof was split in two by what looked like giant claw marks, and engorged, winged worms spilled through the cracks of the stone structure.

With a settling breath, I padded over the jagged threshold and descended narrow, winding steps towards the lower level, my hands bracing the cobwebbed sides of the walls. Eerie sconces emitting pale light dotted the walls above me, and the stairway grew narrower with each step, worrying me that I'd get caught between them.

At the bottom, I set my gaze forward, covering my mouth to stifle a scream. Unease ripped through my body. A coffin encased in ice sat in the center of the damp room, next to a table full of bones and black feathers. An inscription was carved on the top of the coffin:

Beware all ye who enter
Of the monster held within
Olde curse trapped in ice
Hungers for thine wretched skin
Should ye dare set the monster free
Death will swiftly come to thee

My head hovered over the coffin, and I swallowed hard. The large, dark face of something more wolf than human stared back at me, its white eyes open but lifeless. Its snout was frozen in a vicious snarl that displayed its pointed teeth, and its wolfish head was attached to a fur-covered body that resembled that of a human's.

A tap on my shoulder startled me and I notched an arrow with impressive speed. I swiveled, expecting a monster behind me. Instead, I looked into the eyes of a very old woman. Deathly pale with sunken eyes and missing teeth, she was hunchbacked

and wore a hooded gray cloak. Her long, silver hair and pale eyes peeked out from underneath her hood.

Backing away from her, I tripped and fell onto the floor, my quiver of arrows spilling across the ground. I snatched an arrow before it rolled too far.

"What is your business in the Realm of Despair? Who sent you to be punished?" the woman demanded, her voice strong despite her frail appearance.

My back crashed against the wall. "Who are you?" I asked, panting heavily, the air so thin that I could barely catch my breath.

The blind woman didn't flinch, not even at the sound of my drawn bowstring. "I am the caretaker of this guardian, and also the punisher of those that are sent here."

"Punisher?" I asked, my confusion growing. My eyes darted to the coffin behind her, fearing that she would release the beast contained within it. Above, the wind howled, followed by the sound of the ancient trees creaking.

"If you're not here for punishment, then what?" the woman asked.

I shook my head. "The door brought me here. You tell me." To hells with that clock door for bringing me here. I doubted I'd find any clues in a place like this.

The woman considered me for a moment. "I suppose a vision would suffice." She extended her bony hand towards me, tightly grabbing my shoulder. Her pale eyes went pitch black, and I tried to pull myself away, but to no avail. It was like her very essence had latched onto my soul. She forced my eyes open, unnaturally wide, and I gritted my teeth with pain.

The creepy woman disappeared, replacing her presence with brutal images as I stumbled into the darkness of the vision.

Arthur, lying in a pool of blood.

A battle against the Volings.

My knees buckled, sending me to the ground. My skin was tearing, my bones shattering as I began to rip out of my skin, changing into something else. Something I promised myself I would never change into. Excruciating pain ripped through me and I screamed.

This isn't real. I told myself, but my scar burned, the pain intensifying after each image flashed into my mind.

A dagger being held above me by a faceless man.

My body lying in a pool of blood. My eyes open, but unseeing.

A volcano packed with monsters.

A man with blue-black hair.

"Get me out!" I screamed, trying to grasp that old woman in the ruined mausoleum. When she didn't respond, I covered my eyes with my hands.

This isn't real. It isn't really happening.

I screamed again, louder this time, and snapped back into the mausoleum, the vision dissolving as quickly as it came. I was on the floor, clutching the bow to my chest as I coughed my lungs out. The woman released my shoulder and backed away, coughing as hard as I was.

I caught my breath and forced myself to stand, leaning against the back wall for support.

"Why would you show me those things!?" I growled at the woman, who was still hunched over and coughing up droplets of blood. My hands trembled as I brushed dirt from my clothes.

The woman straightened and wiped the blood from her lips. "It is what will come to pass."

"I'm looking for the Netherros, not scary visions," I explained.

"What you're looking for isn't here. Consider yourself lucky I didn't punish you for intruding in my realm." Her eyes lingered on the ice-encased coffin. The wolf's finger twitched, and I shuddered again, queasy at the thought of what death at the hands of that creature would look like.

The old woman picked up a lantern from a stone slab and held it out in front of her, as if she was trying to get a better look at me.

"Consider this warning an aid to your journey, not a punishment. Search elsewhere for what you seek. Now leave."

I didn't need to be told twice. I snatched my quiver from the ground and secured it to the buckle of my pants.

"Don't ever come back here," she said.

I didn't plan to.

The woman vanished and with her, so did the mausoleum. The graveyard twisted around me like a vortex of destruction, and I gasped for air, clutching at my throat. A part of me wanted that vortex to take me with it. To end the fear growing inside of me. But I jolted forward, and the clock door slammed shut, its hands snapping back to midnight. My head spun and I dropped to my knees, drained from the magic of that realm. My scar simmered and I exhaled when the pain went away.

"What the hells, Rue?" Thomassen said from behind me. "What are you doing? Why in the gods' names are you soaked?"

I didn't have a chance to argue because he grabbed my arm and dragged me into his room.

"I'm perfectly capable of taking care of myself," I told him as he pushed me into his desk chair and retrieved a towel.

"Here," Thomassen offered, using the towel to dry me off. A long silence fell between us when he finished, leaving the towel in my lap.

"I couldn't sleep," I admitted, biting the inside of my cheek.

"I know. I went to find you in a dream, and you weren't there," Thomassen said. Nothing ever got past him. "If you're bored, come get me. Don't go through the clock doors alone. They might take you somewhere unsafe."

"Why would Alden put those doors here in the first place?" I asked.

"I don't know. That's a question for my father. Regardless, don't go through them alone."

I tensed, disturbed by the visions the old woman showed me. The only thing they'd done was horrify me. I was still no closer to finding the prophecy or Alester's whereabouts.

"What did you see in there?" Thomassen asked.

"I met an old blind woman in charge of punishment."

"You're lucky you're not dead," he said, letting out a harsh breath. His frustration burned between us, and he shifted away from me with a clenched jaw and pouty lips.

Dammit, he's cute when he's angry.

"I should get back to my own room."

Thomassen grabbed my arm as I turned towards his door. "Let me stay with you. I don't like that you're all alone in that room."

My heart raced as I returned his gaze, words momentarily lost in my muddled brain. If I agreed to it, it would be nothing like how it had been with Fang. I wouldn't be sleeping with a boy that was like a brother. I'd be sleeping with a boy I had feelings for. Being in bed together at night, alone, could end up getting heated. I paused, entertaining the idea in my head.

"I don't know," I said after a minute. The last time I'd fallen asleep in his bed had been an accident.

"Why?"

I raised an eyebrow, hoping he'd get the hint.

"I'm not looking to take advantage of you," Thomassen argued, a blush rising on his cheeks.

"I'm not thinking about that. I'm worried that you want to keep tabs on me more than anything."

Thomassen crossed his arms. "Well, you're not wrong, but—"

"That's all I needed to know," I snapped, tearing my arm from his grasp.

Thomassen grabbed my chin and forced me to look at him. "Rue, let me finish. I told you I like you. That hasn't changed, but I wouldn't mind being with you too so I can know you're okay. I worry about you every night. It's hard staying away knowing what I know about the prophecy."

"Why do you care at all? What does it matter where I'm at or what I'm doing if I'm dead anyways?" Tears stung at my eyes, but I refused to hide them this time. "Just let me go, Thomassen." I didn't care that I was being unfair at that moment. What was the point of being with him if I'd be dead soon anyways? I'd seen myself lying in a pool of blood with eyes that saw nothing. I was running out of time, and he couldn't save me. I doubted anyone could.

Thomassen's expression softened, and he grabbed hold of my hands, bringing them to his chest. "Listen to me. The only person I'll ever care about is you, otherwise I wouldn't be here. I'm as scared as you are, but I'm with you all the way. I promise I'm not going anywhere."

A sob escaped my lips and Thomassen pulled me into his arms, cradling me against his chest.

"I'll always be with you," Thomassen promised.

Alden sat in a leather chair beside the crackling fireplace, the smell of burning wood hanging in the room. The glow of the flames cast dancing shadows across Alden's face, his eyes carrying a grief I was all too familiar with. Fang's laugh echoed in the back of my mind when Alden's pained eyes met mine, but I pushed my sorrow back, for now at least.

After a restless night of sleep following my breakdown with Thomassen, I needed to get myself moving and start looking for the damned prophecy. It'd been hard to leave his arms, but as soon as the slightest hint of sunlight peeked through his window, I'd slipped out of his room in search of answers. If I didn't start looking for clues now, there would be no more friends and no more family. No more Thomassen.

"Rue, to what do I owe the pleasure?" Alden gestured to the chair across from him. He took a long sip of hot tea that smelled strongly of yellowthorn, a rare tea leaf only found in Felroc. Rorik would sometimes bring them to Arthur.

I sat down in the high-back leather chair and propped my legs up on the square table between us.

"You moved the castle to Gardenia," I stated, narrowing my eyes, "meaning there were more portals than the one in Black-wood Bog."

"That's not why you're really here, is it?" Alden asked, a curious look on his face.

"No." I drew in a deep breath and leaned forward, resting my forearms on my thighs."I need help finding the Netherros. I've had no success finding anything concrete that would lead me to it, so I need your help."

Alden glanced back at the flames. "I take it you know of Thomassen's condition."

"Yes."

"You love him, don't you?" Alden asked. "Which is why you want to save him."

I clenched my teeth. It didn't matter how I felt about Thomassen. I would save him even if I didn't love him, because I wasn't a shitty person that left others to die when something could be done to stop it.

I held up my hand. "I *know* you want to save him as well, so please. Where is it?" I asked.

"With Alester," Alden said after a long pause.

I huffed, crossing my arms in front of me, "And where is he?"

"I don't know, which is why I brought you here, to Leavenfell."

I clenched my fists. "That isn't helpful."

"But," Alden continued, "I know someone who might help you."

"Who?" I asked, hope blooming inside my chest.

Alden stood and disappeared into his office, closing the door behind him. A few minutes later, he emerged with a crooked staff no bigger than a tree branch. There was a tiny globe at the tip of it, but it was otherwise unremarkable.

He handed it to me. "The clock door at the end of the corridor, the very one in the center that's hanging off its hinges, will react to this wand. It will open, and when it opens, you will find a portal in front of you. It will take you deeper into Gardenia," Alden instructed me, his tone calm. "It's the only door with a set location besides Thomassen's room, and it will lead you into the Forest of Flowers, near the woodland fae."

I gripped the wand, its power melting into my skin, making the hair on my arm stand up. "What time do I need to set the clock to?"

"No time needed. If it doesn't open right away when sensing the wand, then tap the clock door with the wand three times. That'll do the trick." Alden eyed the staff with a curious expression. "That staff seems to have taken an affinity to you."

"How can you tell?" I arched my brow.

"The way it came to life when you took it from me. You must have wizard blood in you."

"Doubtful."

Alden's eyes darkened. "Regardless, you need to be careful with it," he warned. He leaned towards me, bringing his tone down to a whisper. "Find the centaur called Grahm. Ask for his help."

"You won't come?" I asked, eyeing Alden suspiciously. *Why do I have to do everything by myself?*

"Involving myself could lead to grave consequences," Alden answered.

I huffed with frustration.

"Just be careful," Alden warned. "The fae can be tricky."

"I'll do my best," I promised.

"Also, take this." Alden held out a handkerchief and unfolded it. Inside the silky handkerchief lay a chain made of tiny diamonds. A large emerald adorned the base of the locket. I stared at it in admiration.

"What is it for?" I asked, taking it carefully from him.

"When you meet Grahm, the centaur, offer this as a gift and

he will help you. Centaurs have a deep-rooted appreciation for jewels. It would act as a trade for information."

I shuddered. "He won't hurt me, will he?"

"The centaurs have no interest in humans, other than trading. You should be safe. Take this sack with you. It'll conceal the wand and the gem. There's also a sword in there."

I grabbed the leather rucksack from him, admiring the vintage brown color and many jeweled pockets adorning it, but the bag was reasonably small. "How in the hells did you fit a sword in here?"

Alden's eyes twinkled. "That bag is one of my creations. It can hold many things, despite its size."

I stared at it in awe. "Thanks. I'll make good use of it."

"I'm sure you will."

"One more question—"

The sound of someone crumpling to the floor stole our attention. I whirled around, a cold sweat trickling across my skin when I saw Thomassen, his hand clutching his chest and his skin taking on an abnormal pallor. I shook my head in disbelief. I left him in bed this morning… sound asleep. What was he doing here?

Thomassen was wheezing, his eyes wide as he struggled to breathe. My heart slowed when his head lolled backwards. I rushed to his side, dropping to my knees and elevating his head in one swift movement. He was gagging, blood dripping from the corner of his mouth. I brushed a shaky finger to the side of his neck. *Shit*. His pulse was weak.

"Thomassen!" I shrieked, grabbing hold of his shoulders, terror slicing into me. His eyes fluttered closed and he went limp. Alden hoisted him up, cradling Thomassen to his chest.

I stood, my hands braced against the back of my head in a panic, and Alden's expression tightened with worry.

"What do we do?!" I shrieked. "Is he dead?"

He was fine when I left him. He'd been *completely fine*. There were no signs.

"Alden, what do we do?!" I bellowed, my chest tight.

Arthur entered the great hall, stopping dead in his tracks when he caught sight of us.

Alden's eyes said it all. The magic inside of Thomassen was failing. His brows furrowed, sheer terror painting his features as he raised a hand in the air.

"Go," he demanded.

Chapter 33

The Forest of Flowers

After grabbing a few things from my room, I rushed to that obscure door by the chapel and bolted through it, finding Arthur pacing by the bottom of the spiraling staircase, his arms crossed tightly against his armor.

He better not be here to stop me.

The sconces cast dim light throughout the room, enough so that I could see the frazzled expression on his face as I approached him. Alden must have explained what happened to him after I'd rushed out of the great hall.

"Arthur! What are you doing here?" I asked.

Arthur paused, his expression softening. "I came to give you this." He offered me a carefully wrapped bag, a sandwich and container of water inside.

I took the bag from him, relief flooding through me. "Thank you," I said, slipping the bag into my rucksack. "I don't have a lot of time. I hope you understand."

"I'm not here to stop you. I only want you to know that I'm

here for you. This isn't about my feelings anymore." He paused, "It's about all of us… our future." A tear fell as the words left his mouth. "But it hurts. I can't help but worry about you, *knowing…*"

Tears stung my eyes. He didn't have to say anything else because I knew exactly what he was feeling. He feared I wouldn't come back.

"I'll come back to you," I promised, holding his gaze.

"I'm proud of you, Rue. Your parents would be proud too." Arthur pulled me into a tight hug. "Please be safe."

"I will be." Once I saved Thomassen and the prophecy was set in motion, my chances of seeing Arthur again would be slim. I feared I'd never see him again.

I hugged him tighter, feeling the rhythm of his heart sync with mine. "I love you forever, Arthur." And I did. He was there when my father couldn't be.

"And I love you forever. Don't forget it," Arthur said.

I didn't turn to look back at him as I raced up the tall staircase, skipping steps along the way. I arrived at that old, rusted clock door at the end of the corridor, but it wouldn't open, so I pulled out the staff and tapped it three times, as Alden had instructed. The door groaned eerily but remained shut. Puzzled, I tried again, this time with more force behind the tapping.

The clock door came alive, creaking as it lifted itself back onto its hinges. It swung open, and a warm breeze flowed through the opening, spilling into the corridor. I closed my eyes, whispering a silent prayer to the gods. To help me find a way to save Thomassen. To help me not be afraid of what I might come across.

I spotted the portal. It glowed, like rays of pure sunshine, much different than the portal I'd seen in the bog.

I drew in a deep, settling breath and pushed myself forward. Light blinded me, but only for a moment before I found myself in the warmth of the Forest of Flowers. Vines and flowers encircled every tree, trailing upwards and glowing in the golden sunlight that poured through the spaces of the flowery branches. There was nothing except miles of endless trees and flowers ahead. No sign of any fae, woodland creatures, or centaurs.

The otherworldly redwoods were limber, stretching and twisting around each other in an embrace, but done so in an elegant, deliberate manner. They formed a stunning canopy beneath the sky, the leaves spaced apart enough to allow light to slip through and illuminate the land beneath it. A winding river twisted through the corners of the forest, purple petals floating atop the clear water.

Despite the beauty of my surroundings, dread pooled into my stomach. The forest was too quiet. I stopped, glancing to my right. Something was standing in between the space of two trees. The creature had the body and face of a deer, but feathery wings clung to its sides, and it had two tails. Fascinated, I moved off the path towards it, studying it as its head whipped in my direction. I approached the creature, but it took off into the deeper parts of the forest, leaving a trail of golden dust in its wake.

The dust struck my face so unexpectedly that I inhaled some of it. I coughed and lowered myself to the ground, my eyes suddenly heavy. A ray of sunlight fell over me, warming my face, and I closed my eyes. I wanted to sleep, but I needed to do something—something important. I couldn't remember what it was, but maybe a nap would help clear my head.

As I nestled my head into the soft grass, humming a soft tune, a shadow caught my eye. I whipped my head in the direction of rustling leaves, growing more paranoid, and reached to my thigh, unstrapping my dagger right as a fae landed in front of me.

The tall immortal angrily swiped at my face, but I rolled backwards and righted myself, groggily taking on the defensive stance Finn had taught me. I tried tracking the movements of my attacker, but he was fast, his wings beating wildly as he let out a vicious cry and attempted to grab me. My scar flared as his fingernails scraped my arm, and I ducked and released a counterattack, my dagger missing my target.

"Wait!" I yelled, but the fae growled and flew over me, landing in the trees above and concealing himself within the flowers. I took the opportunity to run for it, but a loud screech rang from behind me. I wasn't getting away that easily. The fae was approaching fast, his thunderous wings closing in. One look back and I was dead.

He flew so close that I could feel the wind from the speed of his fluttering wings. There was no way I was outrunning this thing, so I did the only thing I could think of.

"Help!" I called out desperately. I forced myself to run faster, my lungs screaming in pain. Another bad idea. More fae poured out of the flowered trees and chased after me. It was like the dream that I had, but it also wasn't. I couldn't see their beauty. I couldn't hear the melodic tones of their voices. All I could hear was the furious beating of wings as they tried to catch their terrified prey.

My foot caught onto a thick root poking out the ground and I tripped, falling face first into the grass. I didn't have the chance to look up to confirm I was surrounded by fae that wanted to kill me. By the time my tongue tasted grass, a sack was thrust over my head, and I was yanked upwards. A sharp pain sliced into the left side of my head, and my vision went dark.

I regained consciousness on my side atop a velvety carpet in the middle of a circular room. My hands were loosely tied behind my back, but the sack had been removed from my head. I forced myself into a sitting position and backed up against a wooden pillar. The room was shaped like a dome, the wooden walls smooth, as though the wood was made out of glass. I coughed, my throat parched. I slipped my hands out of my loose restraints and reached for my container of water but couldn't find it. My knapsack was gone as well.

There was a table with a long scroll spread across it, and various pieces of furniture and plush chairs positioned around the room. Bookshelves were carved into the smooth walls, hundreds of old books sitting in the depths of the tree. The smell of wood hung in the air.

My eyes finally rested on a tall fae guarding the doorway. He was more man than creature with his chiseled face and strong jawline. His white hair was tied back, and the toga he wore left little to the imagination, the translucent garment revealing more than I cared to see.

I paused on his abs, my breath catching. A smile ghosted his lips, as if he'd caught my eyes ogling his displayed body. He held a spear in his right hand and my knapsack in his left. He turned around and I blushed, glancing away, knowing that his muscular butt would be permanently burned into my brain.

"She's awake," he called out the door with a husky voice.

My head snapped up when a tall, willowy fae with long locks of lavender hair and silky wings entered the room, her movements deliberate but graceful. *Shay*. She wore a flowy robe made of pearls and white satin, the color complimenting her green eyes. She gave off a magnificent glow, as if the realm itself worshipped her.

Instinctively, I bowed my head.

"What you're searching for isn't here." She extended her delicate hand towards me and helped me up. When her fingers touched me, relief flooded through me.

I forced myself to look at her. Even though the only time I'd seen her was in my dream, there was recognition in her eyes as she studied me, hinting that she remembered me.

"I'm sorry for the way my people treated you." Shay dipped her head, studying me. "It's rare that a mortal stumbles into our realm."

Urgency spilled through my broken voice. "The Netherros. I was supposed t-to meet a centaur called Grahm to help me find it." My chest throbbed. "I'm also looking for a record of a prophecy. Do you know of it? Is it here?" I stumbled over the words but kept my eyes locked on Shay.

"No." The guardian fae stepped forward, placing himself between Shay and myself. "She needs to go back where she came from." His puffed-out chest was practically in my face. I turned my head, heat blanketing my cheeks.

Shay pushed him aside, her features still friendly. She reached into the pockets of her robes and withdrew the diamond necklace Alden had given me. "Her people are already in our realm, just a different part of it," she told the guardian.

She turned to me. "Where did you get this?" she asked, her voice calm as she studied the jewels. "It was stolen from me many years ago by a wizard called Alden."

I blinked, shocked that Alden had stolen something valuable

from the fae. Maybe that was the real reason he didn't want to come with me.

"He told me to bring it to the centaur, as a trade for information," I explained. "I have to save my friend, or he'll die, and the prophecy will fail."

Shay's expression darkened. "Grahm is dead. He was killed by Volings the night we met," she said, confirming she remembered our meeting.

My stomach sank. This couldn't be happening. I needed to find him. Needed to find a way to save Thomassen. I swore under my breath. *Now what?*

"Alden Hall sent you here?" Shay asked.

"Yes," I said. "To save his son."

Shay paused. She waved at the guardian and requested him to leave the room. He began to argue, but she held her hand up and he shut his mouth.

Shay closed the door behind him and faced me. "I will help you. Not to benefit Alden Hall, but because I know your purpose, and I can't help but respect what you're doing." Shay retrieved a small obsidian gem from a nearby shelf and pressed the gem to my forehead. A pleasant warming sensation filled my body as Shay's voice spoke inside my head.

"Go to the Realm of Whispers, a land covered in shadows. The Netherros is there. I will come for you in time, and together, we will find the prophecy."

I clutched my knapsack to my chest and closed my eyes, her warmth enveloping me as I fell away from the Forest of Flowers. Away from Shay. As she slipped into the dark recesses of my mind, an important knowledge awoke within me.

The whereabouts of the Netherros. Shay would open a portal in the Forest of Flowers, one that would lead me to the Realm of

Whispers. The Netherros was hidden deep in the craggy rocks there, guarded by the most feared wizard of all time. Alester himself, the very necromancer Alden spoke of, one who was corrupted by the magic they created.

I opened my eyes, finding myself back in the hidden corridor, but something was very wrong. Peter approached me, pale as a ghost, clutching a hand to his chest. He stopped in front of me, gravely wounded and covered in blood, and doubled over. I caught him before he hit the ground.

"Peter!" I yelled, tapping his cheek in an attempt to keep him awake. He winced, and his eyes fluttered open. *Thank the gods.*

"Try to stay awake!" With Peter in one arm, I used my free hand to dig into the knapsack Alden had given me, unsheathing a sword from the magical bag in one fell swoop.

"What happened?" I shook him, trying to keep him conscious, a battle I was losing. He was slipping, but not before he whispered the last words I wanted to hear.

"The Volings… are attacking Leavenfell."

CHAPTER 34

BREACH

My chest tightened as I bolted down the staircase with Peter. I didn't know how I found the strength to carry him, considering he outweighed me by a ton. I'd wrapped my coat around the gash across his stomach to slow the bleeding. With each step forward, he grew paler, his breathing slower, more ragged. I stopped when he sputtered up a mouthful of blood. If I didn't do something now, Peter was going to die.

Swords clanged in the near distance, but I blocked out the sounds as I gently lowered Peter to the ground and pulled the water container out of my knapsack, lifting it to his lips.

"Drink, Peter."

He groaned, managing to take a small sip.

I surveyed his wounds. His injuries were deep, exposing bone. Part of his torso was crushed. He probably had some broken ribs. His right leg was bent at an awkward angle. The fact that he'd made it upstairs to find me had to have been pure adrenaline. I frantically searched my knapsack, for something—anything that could help. I located the wand and withdrew it, its power melting into my skin as I held it tightly in my grasp.

"Please do something useful." I willed the wand to help Peter. I held it over Peter's wounds and gently waved it, but nothing happened. I closed my eyes, focusing everything I had on healing Peter, calling on every particle of my soul to produce some kind of magic—any magic, to save his life. I waited and waited, until I couldn't wait any longer. I opened my eyes and gasped.

Whatever I was doing worked. The wand vibrated in my hand, the tiny orb at the top of it glowing. Peter's wounds were closing, and his blood was receding back into his body. His leg untwisted and his torso pushed itself back into normal position.

"Oh my gods," I said in awe as Peter healed. The wand continued vibrating, only stopping when Peter looked whole again.

"Rue." His eyes flickered open, disbelief behind them.

The wand sizzled and snapped in half, smoky tendrils releasing into the environment. Whatever I'd done had worked, but now Alden's wand was broken. A pang of guilt ran through me. Maybe the old wand had reached its limit. Hopefully Alden wasn't attached to it.

Loud screams flooded the room, and our heads snapped towards the sound.

When the screams subsided, I peeked at Peter. "I have to go help them, but I need you to stay here. You're still weak."

Peter gave me a confused look as I handed him my dagger.

"In case you need it," I told him.

Without a moment to waste, I burst through the door, sword

drawn as I surveyed the area for Volings. As I turned a corner, more yipping noises caught my ear.

Lance. Arthur. Thomassen. Nora. Please be safe.

Another bloodcurdling scream ripped from the great hall. I dashed through the wide-open doors and immediately plunged my sword into the neck of an unsuspecting hyeling. Blood splattered all over Isobela, who was sprawled across the floor in front of the beast. Her eyes shot to the side of me, and I swiveled and thrust my sword through another hyeling, one that had been sneaking up on us. It dropped dead.

I extended my hand to Isobela and helped her up. "Are you alright?" I gave her a quick once over to check for injuries.

Isobela was shaking, but she nodded. She braced her body against me and let out a deep sigh. "Thank you."

I nodded in understanding but held a finger to my lips. The less attention we drew to ourselves, the better.

"Let's get you to safety." I led Isobela back to the room where Peter was. She sank on the floor beside him and whimpered when I told her I was going back to look for the others.

Dread spread inside of me as I frantically searched for my friends. My first thought was maybe Nora was holed up in the tower room, so I ran to check there first. I stepped out onto the swaying bridge that connected our tower room to Leavenfell Castle and let out a small cry of surprise. Lance, Finn, and a few other men were fighting off a smaller group of hyelings. Lance and Finn were back-to-back, fighting them off using swords and daggers. Hyelings spilled onto the bridge from the opposite side. *Were they in my room!??*

I darted forward to help Lance when a scream rang out behind me. I turned, sword at the ready, as Willow sprinted onto the bridge, a vampire Voling on her heels. The vampire caught her in its grasp and yanked her head back, exposing her neck. I yelled as loudly as I could, trying to get its attention, but to no avail. I wouldn't make it in time.

The vampire reared its head, its fangs lengthening, but before it could sink its fangs in, a stake burst from its chest. The vampire released Willow and crumpled, sliding off the bridge to the ground below. Oliver pulled Willow into his arms and gave me a sharp nod.

"I got her. Help the others!" he yelled before disappearing into the castle.

I glanced over my shoulder at Finn and Lance. A hyeling grabbed one of the guards and tossed him over the side of the bridge. I gasped with horror as he plummeted towards the ground, averting my eyes before he made contact.

"Finn, behind you!" I yelled. Finn swiveled and decapitated the approaching hyeling. Its head fell with a thump onto the planks of the bridge and rolled off. I jumped into the swarm of hyelings, dodging their blows and striking them where I could. Lance leapt past me and brought his sword down through the crown of one of their heads. Another guard I didn't recognize barreled into a horde of them and dragged them off the bridge with him.

No time to stop. Keep fighting, I reminded myself.

One of the hyeling's slashed at my arm, opening a jagged wound. I ignored the pain and skewered the monster with my sword. When the last hyeling dropped, I fell to my knees, struggling to catch my breath. Lance dropped beside me and ripped part of his shirt off.

"That was some impressive fighting," he complimented, using his shirt to bandage the gash in my arm. I needed Arthur's concoction to close that up.

I watched him wrap my wound, wincing from the pain that caught up with me. "Thanks for that."

Lance wiped the sweat from his forehead and glanced behind me, searching for more monsters.

"Where are the others?" I asked frantically. "Nora and Arthur. Thomassen… Alden?" Hopefully, this was the last of them.

Lance shook his head. "I don't know. I haven't seen anyone else. The attack happened so fast —"

I took a deep breath. "It's okay. I'll find them. Check the clock tower. Check *everything* over there."

Lance grabbed my hand, his skin surprisingly soft for how rough he looked. "Stay safe, Rue. Don't jump into a battle you can't win."

I reassured him I would be fine and left to find the others. Inside, the castle was eerily quiet. I covered my nose with my free hand, blocking out the putrid smells.

"Arthur… Nora…" I whisper-yelled, my eyes straining as I looked in all directions. There were far too many corridors and far too many places I hadn't yet explored in this castle. I turned to the ballroom and a wave of relief rushed into my veins at the sight of Arthur at the far end of the ballroom, standing over a dead werewolf. His sword was coated in black blood.

"Arthur!" I waved at him. "I've been looking everywhere for you." I hunched over and placed my hands on my knees, catching my breath.

"I'm glad you're okay," Arthur said, a relieved smile on his face.

"All clear in here?" I breathed a sigh of relief, sheathing my sword.

"I believe so." Arthur sheathed his sword. "The attack… we didn't have much time to react."

"I know." I barely made it in time myself.

Arthur opened his mouth to speak again, but before his lips moved, a werewolf landed on top of him with so much force that the entire room shook. I staggered, blinking rapidly, unable to comprehend what was happening.

There was a tangle of limbs, nails, flesh, and blood on the floor and my heart was hammering against my chest, and suddenly… *suddenly*, I couldn't move.

My feet were cemented to the ground. All I could see and hear and taste and smell was red as the wolf raked its nails into Arthur's fragile flesh. Shredding him into something that should not have been possible, but my eyes could not look away, and my sword was still in its sheath. My eyes traveled upwards to the swinging chandelier. The wolf had been there only a moment ago and now it was on top of Arthur.

Move, Rue!

Finally, my feet cooperated and I was moving forward. I gripped the hilt of my sword as I neared the giant werewolf, screaming Arthur's name and screaming at the beast. Screaming for help.

I lunged at the wolf, aiming my sword at its head, but its front arm slung out with inhuman strength, hitting me in the gut and knocking me to the ground. I clutched my stomach, certain my insides were rearranged as pain ripped through me. Stars danced in my vision as I struggled to catch my breath.

Too slow. The werewolf pinned Arthur's thrashing figure to the ground. I shakily got to my feet, but the werewolf sunk its teeth into his neck.

Barely one second. That was all it took for the werewolf to

overpower Arthur, trying to permanently erase him from this world. From my life. Everything came crashing down around me as I focused every particle of my being on the massive creature. Liquid fire raced through my veins, heating my blood, my skin, as I furiously launched myself on top of the wolf, sword forgotten.

A strength like I'd never experienced before took hold of me as the massive creature snapped its teeth towards my throat. I dodged its attack, propelled forward and dug my fingers into the sides of its head. I wrapped my hands around the base of its skull and yanked upwards with every bit of strength I had.

Its head snapped from its shoulders with a sickening squelch. Black blood poured from the gaping hole between its massive shoulder blades, spilling onto the floor. I tossed its head to the ground, still lost in a scream. Arthur lay on the floor, gurgling as he clawed at his throat, his legs jerking as he struggled.

More Volings and hyelings rushed into the room but stopped at the sight of me, looking from the headless corpse to my blood-covered hands. Silence fell.

Blood stung my eyes, but I glared at them, baring my teeth. My body hurt, but I was ready to destroy all of them. I beckoned them forward, my hand steady as I reached for my sword. My vision blurred, dizziness threatening to take me out, but I held firm. I couldn't take on all of them, but I wouldn't die without a fight. A moment passed, and after sniffing the air, the monsters retreated, leaving me alone in a pool of Arthur's and the dead werewolf's blood. I ran my sword, forged from silver, through the werewolf's body, to ensure it was dead.

It wasn't long before my friends found me sitting on the floor beside Arthur, my hands pressed against his wounds, trying to stop the blood pouring out of his neck. Lance flung his arms around me and Nora burst into tears, dropping to her knees beside me. A fog took hold of me as I bent over Arthur. He was shivering, his eyes widened with shock as he grasped for words, but he couldn't speak. I grabbed his cold hand, shaking and trying to hold it together.

Arthur was bleeding out.

He was dying.

I gazed at his face, devoid of any color, skin already sunken as if in death. Everything around me fell silent until it was only me and him.

"P-promise me, Rue," Arthur said, his voice weak as I held his hand for dear life.

"I promise," I whispered. I held his hand, and an iciness shot through me. "I promise I'll put a stop to them."

It took a long time for Lance and Nora to drag me away from that room, long after a few brawny guards had carried Arthur to the healing ward. I hadn't had the strength or courage to follow them, terrified that I'd have to watch Arthur die. Frustrated that I'd failed in protecting him. I was taken to a separate ward in one of the other towers, located on the second highest floor of the castle, where a healer named Bernice cared for the wounded. Peter, Oliver, Olivia, and Willow were there, all of them sleeping thanks to Bernice's special herbs.

There were more gashes on my arms from where the werewolf had raked me with its claws. Bernice wiped them with an oily substance that stung something awful. I swore as she cleaned up my wounds, biting down on my bottom lip as I slumped into my chair. Lance sat by my side and Nora kept close. Thomassen—I hadn't seen him since I left for the Forest of Flowers, but I hoped he was okay. Alden too.

My question was answered when both walked into the tower. Thomassen had his arms wrapped around himself, his face pale, but he was in better shape than when I left.

Thank the gods. Alden must've stabilized him. Alden looked as though he'd seen a ghost, for good reason. His plan had failed. Gardenia wasn't any safer than Fennra.

"How many casualties?" I snapped at Alden. It was his fault the barrier failed, after he *assured* me it wouldn't.

"Three," Alden stated, his expression grim. "Including Oliver and Olivia's father." His eyes roamed the room until they landed on the twins, his expression somber.

Poor Olivia and Oliver...

"Rue, about Arthur," Alden continued. "His condition is not good unfortunately. I'm so sorry."

I held up my hand, a lump forming in my throat. "I understand. When did the Volings attack?"

"Shortly after you left. Fang was among them."

My heart stopped. I jumped out of my chair, shoving the healer's hands off me, and grabbed Alden by the sleeves of his gray robes. "What did you just say?"

"Fang was among them. He's here," Alden repeated.

"Did he lead them into the castle?" I asked in a panic. "Did he attack us alongside them?"

"No," Alden confirmed. "He did not."

I released a breath, relieved that Fang wasn't trying to hurt anyone. "Then what?"

"He's still here, in the castle. You may talk to him, in time."

"If he's still under compulsion to kill me, then how?" I asked.

It was Thomassen that spoke this time. "We think he's been released from the compulsion."

"How is that possible if Sullivan's still out there?" I asked.

"I don't know, but for now, be glad that your friend is *alive*," Alden replied.

"I have to go see him." If he wasn't under compulsion anymore, then nothing would stop me from going to see him. I stood from the chair and stepped towards the exit. Alden walked in front of me, blocking my path.

"Just because the compulsion is gone doesn't mean I'm making the same mistake as last time. He's currently in a holding cell until we can confirm that he's safe to be around."

"You locked him up?! If he's no longer under compulsion, then why?" Fury boiled over at my seams. If the room hadn't been full of people, I would've had Alden in a chokehold. The magic he held in his small pocket watch cost three lives. And now he had Fang behind bars. Thomassen shot me a warning look, and I swallowed back my anger... for the moment.

Thomassen pulled me towards him. "I'll go with you to see him, after your injuries are tended to. Let the healer do her job, Rue," he said sternly.

I huffed and sat back down into the chair. Bernice gave me a remorseful look and went back to cleaning my wounds. I sank into the chair and closed my eyes, unable to fully process everything that'd happened. In the matter of a few hours, Arthur had been gravely wounded, and Fang had returned. I couldn't wrap my head around either of those things.

I glanced at Oliver and Olivia, my stomach sick over the fact that their dad had been killed. It didn't matter whether Olivia hated me or I disliked her. I wouldn't wish that on anyone.

Peter sat in a recliner across the room, his head bobbing to the side as he slept. His wounds were fully healed, giving no indication that he'd been attacked at all. Thanks to that wand. The magic must have exhausted him though.

"Alden," I began.

Alden acknowledged me, but he wasn't smiling.

"That wand you gave me… it snapped in half after I used it to heal Peter."

Thomassen paled, his eyes darting between me and his father. "You gave her that wand! Why the hells would you do that?" He jabbed a finger at his father's chest. "She could have been killed using it."

"But she wasn't," Alden argued. "I told you, Rue. You had an affinity to that wand, and it seems it allowed you to use it once to save a life."

I shot a wary glance at Thomassen. He threw his hands up and walked out of the room. Alden stared after him.

"Okay, but explain why it broke, which I'm sorry about, by the way," I apologized, turning back to Alden.

"No need for an apology. It was an old wand. Bringing someone back from the brink of death was probably too much for it," Alden said.

It wasn't the explanation I was hoping for, but magic didn't make sense to me as it did for wizards. They could learn magic and wield it, as naturally as breathing, but people like Alden, ancient bloodline or not, never ceased to amaze me and confuse me at the same time.

"Can you please hurry?" I kindly told Bernice my thoughts shifting back to Fang.

Bernice pursed her lips. "I'm almost done, but you should be getting rest after this, miss."

I suppressed a sigh. There was no way I was going to rest, not with Arthur wounded and Fang in the castle.

"Hey." Nora, who'd been beside me, touched my shoulder. "How are you?"

"Terrible." Nausea had been rolling through me ever since Arthur went down.

"I'm going to talk to my parents about moving back in. My mom would be understanding about it, especially with Arthur being wounded."

I grimaced and wiped a tear from my cheek, turning my head towards her. "How are your parents? Benny? Did any of them get hurt?"

"We were barricaded in their room. Nothing got in. We kept hearing them run past, but I think they were looking for someone else."

I swallowed hard, sure she was right. They were probably searching for me or Thomassen, especially if they were in my room. Being that the prophecy wasn't a secret, we were probably target number one.

"It's fine now. Try not to worry," I reassured her.

Nora sniffled, rubbing a tear from her cheek. "It's so like you to comfort others when you're not in the best shape yourself. Take it easy, okay?"

"I will after I see Fang," I replied, my mind made up.

Lance walked over to me, his face pale and covered in dried blood. He hugged me so tightly that I couldn't breathe. Peter must've told him what happened.

"Thank you," Lance said. "Without you, Peter would've died."

"What got a hold of him?" Thomassen asked after entering the room again, his arms wrapped around his waist.

Lance dropped his gaze, face flushing. "I think it was a hyeling. He's lucky to be alive. If not for Rue, he'd be dead."

I closed my eyes, a thread of ice snaking up my spine as I relived the attack. Arthur was almost dead before I reached him. The werewolf had been fast… strong. There was nothing I could've done to stop it.

I pushed myself out of the chair. My brain was a scrambled mess. All I could think about was going to see Arthur and Fang. I wanted nothing else at that moment. Bernice threw up her hands and walked over to another injured person, letting me know she was done with my shenanigans.

Lance caught my hand. "Before you go, there's something I want to tell you. Can we speak alone?"

I eyed him warily. "What is it?"

Lance pulled me from the ward into the hallway, his eyes searching mine, and I could see the despair he held there, and how much it tormented him.

"Please only listen until I'm finished," he requested.

I nodded. "Of course."

"I know you're going through a lot right now, but I need to get this off my chest. Everything between us started because of this wolf bond we share, but I couldn't help falling in love with you along the way. A-and before you say anything, I know you don't feel the same way, but I wanted you to hear it from me, because if I'm dead tomorrow, at least I'll die knowing that I told you. I love you, f-for anything that's worth," Lance confessed, a sorrowful anguish apparent in his broken voice.

My heart burst with overwhelming emotion, so much so that I couldn't stop myself from dragging him into my arms. Guilt dug a hole into my heart. *I'm sorry. I can't love you the way you want me to…*

I buried my face into the crook of his shoulder, breathing in his pine scent. "I love you so much, Lance, but…"

Lance pulled away. "Say nothing more. I understand," he said with a small smile, one that gave me hope that everything would be okay between us.

I placed my palm against his cheek. "I really do love you. You're one of my best friends."

Lance brought his hand up to mine, closing his eyes. "Thank you. That means a lot to me, Rue."

Afterward, we walked back into the healing ward, and Lance took a seat beside Peter. "I'm going to wait here until he wakes up."

"Okay," I said, taking note of Thomassen's pallor and wondering if he'd heard Lance's confession.

Alden tapped my shoulder. "How did it go in the forest?"

"Besides getting kidnapped by the fae and almost concussed, I'd say it went well. I know where to find Alester." *After I see Arthur and Fang, dammit.*

Alden's eyes darkened, but he gave me a subtle nod. "Name the time and we'll go," he whispered.

Thomassen narrowed his eyes. "You shouldn't have made her go alone."

"You collapsed. I had to act fast. We need to find the Netherros sooner rather than later, before…" I stopped myself.

Red tinged Thomassen's cheeks. "Be that as it may, I'm fine now."

"You weren't fine this morning." I huffed and turned back to Alden. "Tomorrow, I'll be working on a way to approach Alester and take back the Netherros, but I want to take a day to recover and see my family, as long as you're okay with that." *And to absorb Lance's confession…*

"That'll do just fine," Alden answered.

I faced Thomassen, closing the space between us, my voice low as I spoke. "I'm not going to stand by and let you die."

Thomassen trembled, his gaze burning with intensity as he locked eyes with me. "Then I want to go with you to find the Netherros."

"It's too dangerous," I said.

"We're supposed to be in this together," he argued.

I contemplated his words. Thomassen was already weak as it was, and traveling into an unknown realm was risking too much.

"We'll talk about it later," I told him, knowing full well I wasn't taking him with me.

Alden turned to the door, his hands in the pockets of his long robe, likely fiddling with his pocket watch. "Thomassen, please accompany Rue to see Fang."

Thomassen nodded as his father stalked out the door.

CHAPTER 35

THE REALM OF WHISPERS

MY SKIN WENT COLD, THOUGH THE ROOM PROVIDED AMPLE warmth. I didn't know what I was expecting, but it certainly wasn't the ghost of a man sitting before me. His eyes were heavy-lidded and rimmed in red, as though he'd been dragged through a Voling battlefield and witnessed multiple horrors. I wrinkled my nose, resisting the urge to cough. The air stank of urine and blood. Fang was lost in his own world, far away from Leavenfell.

"Fang." His name left my lips in a hushed breath.

No answer.

"Fang," I called again.

Nothing, not even a glance. His arms curled around his knees as he folded into himself and fell to his side, whining softly. A light touch on my shoulder turned my attention back to Thomassen, his bleak expression mirroring mine.

"We should leave him alone for now. We don't know all he's been through," Thomassen said. "He's not in a good state of mind."

"He needs a healer," I spat angrily. I desperately wanted to hug him and tell him everything was going to be okay, but I was afraid to approach him, in case he lashed out.

"I will have a healer come to him, but Rue—now's not a good time."

I dropped to my knees, darkness clouding my vision. "I can't lose him, Thomassen. I just can't," I cried. "I don't know if Arthur is going to make it, and now Fang is..."

Thomassen hugged me, his embrace comforting. "I'll ensure the healers do everything in their power to help him, Rue. You have my word."

Fang was moved to the healing ward the following day, but I was banned from seeing him until further notice. According to Thomassen, his healing would be very rough, and it was something I shouldn't be there for, not until he got over the hard parts of it. But I managed to visit Arthur a few times, making sure to hug and kiss him every chance I got. He was never conscious, even when I spoke loving words in his ears. When my eyes grew heavy, the healers shooed me away, telling me they'd come get me if anything changed.

The flames licked at my cheeks, warming me as I scooted closer to the fireplace in my tower room, Nora by my side. She'd moved back in after the attack happened, having stood up to her father and letting him know he didn't control her anymore. We'd spent hours cleaning up the mess the monsters left behind after they'd torn through our room.

"You should have seen my dad's face. He couldn't believe I'd spoken to him that way," Nora said. "Although I wished Benny hadn't heard any of that."

"You did what you had to do," I said, patting her shoulder.

"My mom was surprisingly okay with it. Her only advice was to tell me to be careful when it came to… you know." She blushed, averting her gaze.

"How was *that*, by the way?" I asked. I had zero experience in that department but was curious, nonetheless.

Nora's blush deepened. "Awkward. Neither of us knew what we were doing. But Peter was happy about it."

"Pfft… I bet he was." I stifled a laugh.

Fang and Arthur were constant in my mind, so I was grateful for Nora's presence. She helped calm my nerves, offering a much-needed distraction, especially since I dreaded having to face Alester, a daunting task I couldn't put off much longer. I had to succeed in taking the Netherros from him, otherwise Thomassen would die, and the prophecy would be forfeit. No matter how scared I was, or how hard my life had been up until this point, I wouldn't stop until I pried the Netherros from Alester's cold dead hands.

The wind howled a mournful tune as clouds threaded across the gray sky. I yawned, stretching my arms over my head as Nora rolled over, her arm draping across my stomach. A knock sounded at the door.

"Come in," I called with a yawn.

Peter barged in, his lips twisting when his eyes dropped to find us.

"Did you both sleep on the floor?" Peter gave a lopsided smile.

"Mmm," I responded. It was too early for his obnoxious voice.

"Come on, get up. I brought food." Peter retrieved a crumpled paper bag from his leather pocket.

I pushed myself up, rubbing my eyes as another yawn escaped me. "That's gotta be mush by now," I said, ogling the bag.

"It's still edible," Peter said.

I rolled my eyes. "Fine. Pass it here."

I needed to eat and be out the door. Enough was enough. It was past time for me to grow some damned balls and travel to the Realm of Whispers. I stood and stalked over to my dresser, grabbing the magic knapsack Alden had given me. Nora woke up and moved to her bed, joining Peter as they shared some of the mushy food. While they ate, I changed into clean clothes, the pants fitted close to my skin so I wouldn't have to worry about the fabric getting caught on anything.

"Going somewhere?" Nora asked, pointing to my rucksack, already packed with weapons, a change of clothes, and my water container. I didn't know how long I'd be gone, and I wanted to leave before Thomassen caught up. If Peter was already awake, Thomassen probably was as well. I couldn't risk him coming to find me before I left.

I joined them on the bed and unwrapped the smushed sandwich, taking a bite. The sausage and egg roll didn't look like much, but it sure tasted good.

I swallowed my food, returning my gaze to Nora while

Peter licked his fingers. "When I went to the Forest of Flowers, I was told by the fae that I needed to go to the Realm of Whispers."

Nora scowled, crossing her arms over her chest. "Isn't that one of the dangerous realms located within Vol? You shouldn't be going anywhere near there."

"I understand it sounds scary, but please listen." I went on to explain about the prophecy and my part in it. I also mentioned Thomassen and why he didn't need to know I was leaving without him.

After I finished, Nora shifted closer, fidgeting with a strand of her hair. "You're leaving now?" she asked, her lips quivering. "It seems so sudden."

"Yes," I confirmed.

Peter pushed himself up and sat forward, his eyes meeting mine. "I won't try to stop you, because I know how stubborn you are," he said. *He's one to talk*. "But you'd better kick some ass while you're there, for Arthur and for your friend, Fang," Peter added. "And don't die. Lance would never forgive you."

"I won't," I said. "There's one more thing. Alden will be accompanying me."

Peter let out a low whistle, his eyebrows raised. "You sure that's a good idea? Alden's *old*. That's the equivalent of taking my grandmother into battle with me—and she's been dead a long time."

"Honestly Peter!" Nora rolled her eyes, but a faint smile crossed her face.

My lips twitched. "He may be old, but he's strong. I may need him." I outstretched my hands, holding theirs tightly. "I do have one thing to ask while I'm gone. Please check on Fang and Arthur." I sucked in a breath, heart pounding against my ribs.

"It's so hard having to leave both of them like this, but I have to take care of this now or Thomassen will die."

"Of course we will," Nora promised.

"If we can get past old brood Bernice." Peter's brows furrowed. "That woman is a tank."

"Just come back to us in one piece," Nora said with misty eyes.

I hugged the two of them. "Promise."

Once me and Alden passed through the white portal behind the center clock door, we found ourselves in the Forest of Flowers, another portal hovering before us, just like Shay had promised. This one, its resemblance like that of a rotating storm cloud, was twisted between two redwoods, the branches hanging low, the weight of the portal dragging them down.

My nerves rattled as Alden stepped forward through the cloudy mass, unaffected by the ominous whispers it produced. My eyes slowly adjusted to the swirling darkness enveloping me as I passed through. On the other side, the powerful wind roared, cutting into us so hard that we nearly toppled over.

"What if I don't make it out of here?" I asked after I righted myself, fear bubbling low in my stomach.

"As long as I am alive, Ruby Watson, no harm will come to you. At least until the end," Alden swore.

The end. It sounded so final.

"Don't worry yourself. I will call for help if needed." He gestured at his staff as we pushed forward.

"Who will help?" I asked.

"Shay and her warriors."

We stepped onto a cobblestone path, covered in black soot and pieces of bone. I retrieved a hooded coat from my bag, shivering as I tied it tightly around myself. Dark clouds shrouded the bleak sky while several bolts of lightning struck at once, rattling the ground from impact.

"Stay alert," Alden warned.

I gripped the hilt of my sword. There was nothing ahead except vast open space permeated with floating ash, craggy boulders, and silence. It was a graveyard of bones and ash.

"Keep your head up. We're being followed," Alden whispered.

I stared ahead, goose bumps pricking my skin, trying my hardest not to look anywhere but the path in front of me.

"Followed by what?" I whispered back.

In answer, massive shadows darkened the ground. I followed Alden's gaze to the sky, where three shadowy creatures flew soundlessly above us, black stringy wings spread wide and yellow eyes gleaming. Their long beaks were curved and pointed, their limbs short.

"What are they?" I asked, a lump catching in my throat. Whatever the hells they were, their soundlessness only added to their horror.

Alden held a finger to his lips. "Bonedrills." He gestured to the piles of bones on the ground. "Unless you want to join them, don't make any sudden moves. Don't show fear. They feed off it and will attack us if we show any sign of it," he cautioned.

Alden and I made slow progress through the mysterious wasteland, the cobblestones lighting up in various colors under the pressure of our boots: all shades of reds, oranges, and yellows, resembling fire. The lights cast shadows off every object we passed, living up to what Shay had called this realm: a realm of shadows.

When we turned a corner past a large boulder, I stilled. Hundreds of beings, in various stages of decomposition, paced the wasteland on all sides of us. The crooked, broken way they moved sent shudders through my body. The creatures were gasping, rattling, and wheezing as they slowly lurched in all directions. One passed by me, too close for comfort. I yelped and grabbed hold of Alden's arm.

"What are they?" I said, clutching the hilt of my sword and wanting to throw up from the smell.

Alden didn't face me, didn't so much as look at me. "Rue, keep moving," he whispered, his tone alarmed. "Pretend they aren't there."

I started to pull my sword out of its sheath, but Alden quickly grabbed my hand, stopping me.

"Don't," he warned. "These creatures are beyond our power if we alert them to our presence."

I gaped at him. Were the creatures blind?

"They're corpses… sort of. Not dead, but not alive. Lost between realms," Alden explained. "It's best if we keep moving."

I blinked slowly as we continued to move, my gaze remaining forward until I could no longer see the corpses. I'd be having nightmares for the foreseeable future. Finally, we came to a stop at the base of a volcano. The structure extended into the sky, nearly touching the clouds. Magma wrapped around the volcano in sporadic patterns and crystallized ash sat at the base of the beast. I shivered, taking it all in.

"I can feel him," Alden said. "We're close."

"Alester," I breathed.

"We enter here," Alden said matter-of-factly, pointing to an opening at the base of the volcano.

I stared at the darkness that awaited us, scared to move, but Alden waved his staff in an upward motion until a hovering silver light appeared.

"To guide us," he explained, walking forward into the darkness.

I slipped inside and a wall appeared, closing us in, sealing us from escape. As I turned to ask Alden a question about how we would be getting out of this place, multiple torches roared to life along the walls of the volcano, and Alden's silver light blinked out of existence.

"I've been expecting you for many years, Alden Hall," a cold voice called from the shadows. "And Ruby Watson, I presume?"

We swiveled, weapons ready, and faced a man cloaked in black, eyes as dark as the night sky and shaggy, blue-black hair that fell to his chin. The man sat on a throne made from various bones, flanked by hyelings on either side, their hideous faces hungrily watching us.

Magic tingled my skin from where Alden stood, and I sensed he was getting ready to call Shay.

"Alester," Alden acknowledged grimly, taking a step forward. Tiny creatures I didn't recognize stood alongside the Volings, resembling goblins I'd read about in books long ago, their skin a dark green and eyes unnervingly black and beady.

We were severely outnumbered, our weapons laughable compared to the hundreds of gnashing sharp fangs and claws waiting to snatch us up and tear the skin from our bodies. I swallowed hard, my body trembling.

"Keep calm." Alden's gaze met mine before flickering back to Alester.

I stilled my hands and sheathed my sword, waiting with bated breath for Alden to make a move or give me a signal. I couldn't see how Alden and I were going to make it out of here alive. The exit had disappeared, swallowed by the volcano walls.

"I'd say I'm surprised to find you hidden in a realm within Vol, but sadly, I am not."

Alester stood from his throne, drenched with annoyance. His lips stretched into a devilish grin as he turned his back on us, and I grasped the hilt of my sword. The creatures hissed, a spine-tingling sound that reverberated off the walls and echoed further into the depths of the volcano.

"I wouldn't do that if I were you," Alester said, casting a calculating glance over his shoulder. He let out a high-pitched whistle, and the Volings beside him cackled, a heinous sound that made my blood run cold. They advanced towards us, but Alester held up a fist, and they stopped.

My breath hitched in my throat as I released the hilt and moved my hand slowly away from it. Terror poured into me, but I didn't dare move from where I was standing. Neither did Alden.

Thomassen. I hadn't said goodbye. I hadn't told him that I was in love with him, and now, seeing the mess Alden and I had gotten ourselves into, I feared I'd never get the chance.

Alester's throne was surrounded by a moat of hardened lava and black rock. He lifted his staff, one shaped like a long wolf fang, and muttered in a language I didn't understand. The stream of lava ignited, lighting up the floor of the volcano, streams heating near where we stood. He tapped his staff against the ground again and the lava hardened once more, the brilliant light dissipating.

He gave us a warning look. "One wrong move and you will

be swallowed by this place. There's more than lava here waiting to tear you apart, and I'll gladly watch the both of you get eaten whole."

I swallowed hard, but I'd had enough. If me and Alden were to survive, we needed to act.

"I dare you to try to lay a finger on me. See what happens!" I threatened, my voice taking on an intimidating tone.

Alester observed me, his eyes darkening. He stood tall, his left palm outstretched towards the Volings, like he had them attached to strings. An ugly sneer crossed his otherwise hand-some face. Using his other hand, he lifted his staff and whis-pered an incantation. A golden basin appeared in front of him, towering up towards his chest. He reached his hand inside and retrieved a tiny glass sphere hanging from a thin gold chain. He took off his glove and touched it, and when he did, the sphere hummed to life. The glass sphere glowed with such incredible brilliance that I shielded my eyes with my free hand. Extreme power shed from the tiny sphere, the energy slam-ming into my chest with so much force that I staggered backwards.

I squinted at the sphere. There was a tiny clock inside of it, a telltale sign of one of Alden's creations.

The Netherros.

Alester dangled it in front of his chest, swinging it back and forth. I feared the glass sphere would detach from the chain and shatter on the ground, releasing the power I desperately needed to save Thomassen.

"Searching for this?" Alester's expression hardened as the chain swung from side to side, taunting us.

"You stole it from me," Alden uttered, his posture firm despite his anger. "I trusted you and you betrayed me. Disappeared. You let the magic corrupt you. For what? To diminish the mortal race?"

I stared at Alden, eyes wide, watching the wizard's expressions shift from betrayal to remorse to anger. The magic inside of him scattered like birds being released into the sky, flowing off him wave after wave. That magic melted into my skin, sending electric shockwaves across my skin.

"This magic—we may have created it together, but it chose to remain with me," Alester scoffed. He fastened the Netherros around his neck and returned to his throne.

"It *corrupted* you," Alden corrected, a pained desperation breaking his voice.

"No matter, Alden. You were foolish to bring the girl here," Alester snarled.

I nervously glanced at Alden. "What is he talking about?"

Alden said nothing, seeming to struggle with finding the words to say. Instead, he watched Alester, the hurt of his betrayal evident.

"She doesn't know?" Alester arched his brow. A hint of a sinister smile ghosted his face.

Alden remained silent.

"Know what?" I snapped.

"About Vaddeus Shadowwalker," Alester answered with a poisonous tone.

I glanced at Alden. "Vaddeus?" I'd heard that name before.

Alden became pallid. "He's toying with you, Rue. Don't fall for it." He turned his attention to Alester. "We will not speak of Vaddeus because as soon as we kill you, he will be next," Alden boomed, his robe flowing around him with magic.

I yanked my sword from its sheath and pointed it at Alester, tired of conversation. The Volings inched forward, nearing me, but again, Alester held up his fist, and the Volings stopped.

"You can eat her after I kill her," Alester told them. They yipped at him in response, pawing the ground and hopping with excitement. *Damned fiends.*

I took a few steps forward, but Alden grabbed my arm. "Wait." He prodded me in the back with his staff, and I obeyed him.

Alester approached me, suffocating me with the magic that hung around him, but I didn't dare move. I wouldn't cower to him, no matter how scared I was.

"The girl from the prophecy. How convenient that you would willingly enter my realm. Every Voling across the kingdom has been searching for you." Alester stopped inches in front of me, examining me in a way that made me feel small, as if I wasn't good enough to be tied to the prophecy.

I took a step back. "You speak of the prophecy, but where is it?"

Alester smiled, but it didn't reach his eyes. "The Prophecy of Branches and Blood. It was foretold that a cursed girl and a boy tied to ancient bloodlines would close Vol and bring an end to the destruction of your realms. I assume the Netherros is what you need, because if that boy is dead, then all would be lost." Alester paused for a brief moment, his sharp eyes latching on mine like a rotleech. "Your death is foretold in the prophecy. Do you really want to die for this? Do you not feel any fear at all?" Alester's face softened for a moment, but only a moment, taking me by surprise. It was as though he still had a piece of humanity hidden inside of him, despite the influence of the Netherros's corruption.

"Such a pity that you chose to follow Alden," he said, his vulnerability slipping away, drowned by the evil that ensnared his mind. He pulled away, smoothing his dark hair back. "You understand why I can't give you the Netherros. The boy will die in time, thus ending the prophecy altogether, and mortals will cease to exist."

The Volings exploded with yips and screams. I steadied myself, keeping my head held high even though my scar burned hotter than lava. I only faltered when Alden broke the silence with laughter. A full belly-laugh that rivaled the Volings' cheers.

"You see, Alester—that's where you're dreadfully wrong," Alden said. "We won't be leaving without the Netherros. We will take it by force if we must, and you will die." He stopped laughing and his gaze bore into Alester's.

A menacing energy filled the space around us as Alden called on his dark magic. "You would be wise not to underestimate Rue or myself."

Alester studied Alden, his expression a mixture of amusement and disdain. "There isn't a chance of rebuilding your world if the girl from the prophecy is dead." Alester gripped his staff and waved it over his head, his eyes filled with bloodlust. His staff sparked with horrid black tendrils, and the Volings burst into action.

Alden released me, Shay's name on his lips as he cried out. His staff crackled as he held it high towards the pinnacle of the volcano. A burst of blue light bathed our surroundings. When the light faded, an army of fae led by Shay emerged, dressed in heavy armor made of white steel. The fae collided against the Volings, swords and spears and magic flying about in all directions. The volcano rumbled, the walls vibrating from the sheer power of the attack

Shay ran her spear through a couple leaping hyelings easily, as if they were nothing more than pests. Her army, including the tall, muscular fae I'd seen too much of, chased after the Volings as they disappeared further into the darkness of the volcano, their screams echoing behind them. Spears and teeth flashed everywhere as Alden, and I threw ourselves into the midst of the chaos.

Alester flung spells at my head, but I rolled out the way, barely dodging them. I blocked a hyeling attack with my sword as two of the goblin creatures grabbed hold of my leg and bit into my flesh. I screamed, kicking my leg to shake them off. Alden roared an incantation and the goblins disintegrated.

More Volings descended from the upper chambers of the volcano and dove on top of the fae. Another goblin launched itself at me from the rocky wall above, its mouth opening in a snarl. I thrust my sword forward and the goblin crashed into it, impaling itself. Its body dropped to the ground, black blood gurgling out of its mouth, its eyes distant.

Alden cast spells with his staff, dancing around the Volings gracefully, like we were in a ballroom and not a rumbling volcano. Each spell hit with precision, every target crumpling to the ground in a heap of flesh and blood. I maneuvered around Alden, back-to-back, as we fought off the hungry horde, cutting down Voling after Voling.

Alester's face crumpled into an expression of rage, and he slipped into the shadows, out of sight. Alden slowed his attacks, grabbing hold of my arm.

"We cannot lose him!" He pointed towards Alester, who was disappearing into the darkness with the Netherros.

Teeth clenched, I swung my sword wildly in front of me, cutting a path between the swarm of Volings. Alden struck anything that came within two feet of us, using spells produced by his staff. The rest of the fae formed a barricade with their armored bodies so that the Volings couldn't follow us.

We broke free from the vicious battle and followed Alester into the volcano's depths. I stepped cautiously as we descended a flight of steps carved around the sides of the beast while lava bubbled near my feet.

When we reached the bottom, we found ourselves in a large, smoky chamber. A stream of boiling water ran alongside us, stretching the entire length of the room. Bodies in various stages of decay littered the ground, some floating upside down in the stream.

The stench of death made me gag, but I resisted covering my nose. The smoke crawled into my throat, sending me into a coughing fit as I advanced to the far side of the steamy room.

"Keep your free hand over your nose. Use your sleeves. This smoke will knock you unconscious if you breathe too much of it in," Alden warned.

I followed his instructions and began breathing a little easier.

"It's a spell," Alden told me. "Breathing this particular smoke in through your mouth would kill you slowly. Alester's always been tricky when it comes to magic."

I slipped out of my coat and dropped it to the heated floor. My old leather boots burned, falling apart at the seams as my feet screamed in pain. Sweat poured off my skin as I searched the chamber.

"Stand behind me," Alden ordered. I quickly obeyed, keeping my eyes peeled for any sign of movement.

That looming sense of danger alerted me, but before I could react, the smoke dissipated, and my sword was torn from my grasp. Alester emerged from the smoke as if he were the smoke himself, holding my sword in one hand and his staff in the other. The Netherros hung from his neck.

I faltered, stumbling backward, pain ringing through my skull as he lifted his staff and called on dark magic. I forced a shield up in my head, blocking out the pain from his spell, but my victory was short-lived. Alester struck, twisting his arm and yanking me with magical force until I was dragged before him. My shield went down and pain tore into my skull. I screamed, bringing my hands to my head.

My vision darkened, and Alester ran my own sword through my body, bringing me to my knees. The pain in my head evaporated, shock taking over as I slowly glanced down at the sword protruding from my gut.

"Rue!" Alden yelled in horror.

Blood expelled from my lungs as I met Alester's gaze with a hateful glare. "Fuck you."

Alester backed away from me, his lips upturned as my head began to sway. He turned on Alden and cast a spell so powerful that Alden slammed into the chamber wall across the room.

"Alden," I cried weakly, grasping the protruding sword with slick, bloody fingers, hot pain searing across my stomach. Blood poured from my wound. I struggled to stay conscious.

No—no no no no.

Thomassen...

Nora. Peter. Lance.

Fang... Arthur.

I couldn't die here.

Alester stood by, watching me struggle as I bled out onto the ground. My eyes cut to him, catching the relief that crossed his face, and something that looked like pity, but those quickly faded, replaced by a triumphant smile.

Alden crashed into Alester, knocking him off balance, but he righted himself and swiped at Alester's exposed neck in one swoop. Alden dodged the attack and thrust his hands forward, releasing a gust of powerful magic and sending Alester into the stream full of bodies. Alester coughed up discolored water as he climbed from the stream, but Alden fired off another spell, lifting Alester by his neck and holding him there. Alester clutched his throat, his skin turning blue.

The chain snapped and the Netherros fell from Alester's neck, bouncing a few times but still intact. It came to a stop out of my reach. With a grunt, Alester freed himself from Alden's spell, dropping to the ground and retrieving a wand with the wave of his hand. Alden drew a wand from his robe pockets at the same time, and they began casting short bursts of light at each other, their shouts echoing through the chamber.

A sickening sound echoed and I gasped. Alden had fallen to his knees, wheezing as he clutched a hand to his chest, a gaping wound evident as bright red blood stained the front of his robes, but he called an incantation and the bleeding slowed. Alester neared Alden, moving steadily closer towards his slumped figure. He moved slowly, as if taking his time to savor his small victory. Magic crackled all around him, like streaming lightning bolts as he extended his arms.

Dammit!

I grasped the hilt of the sword and pulled with as much strength as I could muster, biting the fabric of my shirt to muffle my cries as the sword slowly withdrew from my center. The sword came free, shooting stars through my vision. I grasped the hilt as best as I could manage, and with wobbly knees, I forced myself to stand, holding my breath so I wouldn't cry out from the pain. It took every ounce of strength in my body to stand up, hot blood coursing through my veins as my curse threatened to break free. I faced Alester, his attention still fixed on Alden and dragged myself forward as quietly as I could. If Fang taught me anything in my short life, it was that I wouldn't go down without a fight. Both of us were stubborn that way, and if he could survive months in the hands of the Volings, then I could survive this.

With a determined scream, I thrust the sword towards Alester. He swiveled and blocked my attack with a magic shield, his eyes blazing. Alden stood, legs shaking and eyes roaming until they landed on the Netherros. Alester slashed his arm through the air, his spell slamming into the back of my head. I dropped to the floor, the sword clattering to the ground. I slowly forced myself upward, but he pinned me back down with his steel boot, the heel painfully cutting into my skin.

"Get off me!" I yelled, my strength waning. My vision swam in and out of darkness as more blood filled my lungs. The pain in my gut was subsiding, which couldn't be a good sign.

Alden snatched up the Netherros, cracking open the sphere just enough to release a tiny sliver of magic, muttering an incantation as his eyes rolled into the back of his head, his mouth gaping as his head lifted towards the ceiling of the chamber. His voice bellowed, rattling the chamber with frightening power.

The magic inside the Netherros swirled and twisted menacingly before slamming into Alester's back. He staggered, mouth gaping and eyes wide with shock, a large, jagged hole burned into the back of his thick armor. He fell forward, crashing onto the floor as he gasped for air.

Pushing myself upwards, I glared down at him through the dots in my vision. I grabbed my sword and rolled him over with the last bit of my strength, wanting him to look me in the eyes as

I brought an end to his cruel existence. His eyes searched mine, and although he was dying, he was able to speak five rattling words.

"Vaddeus will… come… for you."

"Let him." I brought the sword down to his exposed neck, beheading him. His head rolled a few feet away, blood spurting everywhere. Alester was dead. I tossed the sword aside and crumpled to the ground, unable to hold myself up any longer. My heart slowed, each breath harder to grasp than the last.

Alden rushed to my side, as quickly as someone who was bleeding from their chest could. "I'm going to get us out of here. Hold on." He wrapped my coat around my body, and I cried out in pain when it brushed against my wound. Alden paled, his face crushed with worry, as though he knew I was going to die and there was nothing he could do about it.

At least he had the Netherros and Thomassen would be saved. Some victory had come out of this.

"Rue, keep your eyes open. I'm taking you home."

I coughed up more blood, unable to speak. I'd failed, but maybe Thomassen would fulfill the prophecy without me. He had to.

Thomassen.

His name was on my lips as my eyes fluttered closed.

CHAPTER 36

TO HIDE OR TO FIGHT

ARTHUR WELCOMED ME INTO HIS ARMS. HE WAS WHOLE again, perfect, like he'd never been broken to begin with.

"Rue," Arthur said my name as I sobbed into his chest. "I'm so proud of you."

I pulled back. "But I failed, Arthur. What'll become of the realms?" There were so many questions burning inside me.

"You didn't fail. Not even close." His smile was warm as he gazed down at me. "You don't belong here. It's not your time."

My stomach sank. "That must mean…"

Arthur was dead, and maybe, so was I.

I tore my gaze from him. We were at the edge of an unfamiliar forest, standing by a clear riverside. The warmth of the sun heated my skin as I looked back at Arthur, who no longer had gray hair, nor any wrinkles. It was so peaceful here. Maybe it wouldn't be such a bad thing if I stayed. But I missed home. I missed my friends. I missed Thomassen.

I stared at Arthur, struggling to find the words to say. He

must've sensed that, because he gave me a sad smile and hugged me again. My stomach dropped, the realm tilting around me. When he spoke, both relief and sorrow crashed through me.

"My time was fleeting, but you, Rue—you still have a job to do."

Leaves rustled in the background against the soft breeze. Gravity tugged at me, and Arthur's grip loosened, but I hurriedly embraced him once more, soaking in every final moment. I was hovering close to death, but knowing Arthur, he wouldn't allow it.

"Arthur, what's happening?" I breathed in his earthy scent, taking in everything I could. "If you're dead and I'm alive, how can I see you?"

Arthur tightened his hold around me. He laughed softly, and I turned my head to look at him.

"We didn't know about your gift. Not until now," Arthur beamed. "A rare gift, at that."

"Gift?" It wasn't possible. I'd been born with no gifts.

"You have the ability to cross dimensions, even to the afterlife, and communicate with what's on the other side."

I stilled, dragging my gaze away, everything now making sense.

The dream with the ghostly creature during one of my first nights at Leavenfell, my conversation with Fang at the cliffside overlooking the ocean, my vision with Shay, and now Arthur. Everything had been connected because of a gift I never realized I had.

The pull intensified, and I knew it was time to go.

Arthur buried his face in my hair. "Promise me, Rue." When Arthur was dying in that ballroom, he'd asked me to promise him something. I'd assumed he'd meant stopping the Volings, but now, I knew that wasn't the case.

My eyes filled with tears. I had been so wrong.

Arthur released me for the last time, his eyes full of all the love he had to give. "To live," he said. "Even at the prophecy's end. To *live*."

I woke with a painful yelp. My joints stiffened as I shifted underneath my covers and sat up, shoving my hair out of my eyes. I was back in my own bed, and Alden was standing over me, waving a wand over my body, speaking quiet incantations. His wound was gone, but gauze was wrapped around his shoulder from his chest to his back. Puko perched at the edge of my bed, clicking his beak nervously, his emerald eyes strangely dull, as if he'd been worried.

"You're awake!" Thomassen thrust himself on top of me, earning another yelp of pain as he hugged me. "Gods, Rue. You scared me to death."

My breath caught. "I scared myself too. How am I alive after…"

Alden held the Netherros above me in answer, a smile lighting up his wrinkly face. Even dormant, the Netherros hummed a peaceful tune. He placed it into the palm of my hand. The crystal sphere, glowing with a golden aura, warmed my skin. The small clock held inside ticked softly, barely audible. Amazed, I studied the relic in awe.

Nora came flying into the room, Peter and Lance following

close behind her. She threw her arms around me, shoving Thomassen away, much to his dismay. "You had us all so worried. Don't ever scare me like that again."

I offered a pained smile. "I promised I'd come back, didn't I? I'm safe now."

"Give her some space," Alden warned them. "She needs to recover. It's been a very long day."

Nora ignored him. "You almost died! We heard about everything that happened. All those Volings, the fae coming to battle, Alester impaling you with y-your own sword." Nora's voice broke. "How you pulled the sword from your own body and dealt the final blow." Beside her, Peter's eyes were aglow with admiration.

"You were amazing," Lance said. He wrapped an arm around my shoulder and tugged me against his side. I couldn't help the smile I returned to him.

"Not amazing," I corrected him, my cheeks flushing. "Lucky. Determined and lucky."

"Still amazing," reiterated Thomassen, whose cheeks were as flushed as mine.

"In all my years, I've never seen anything like it. If it wasn't for Rue, I would've died and neither of us would be standing here right now. The quest would have failed. You are remarkably strong, Rue. A true warrior," Alden said.

Puko chirped happily and flew to my shoulder. I patted his head lovingly and faced Alden. "How did we end up back here? How did we escape?"

"Shay found us. When she saw the severity of your wounds, she conjured a portal. One that brought us back home," Alden said.

"Shay got us out of there? What about the other monsters?"

"Dead," Alden confirmed.

I needed to thank her someday. Without her help, I would've died in that chamber.

"Alester mentioned a name. Vaddeus," I recalled.

"Nothing to concern yourself with right now," Alden said.

Thomassen touched my arm, bringing my attention back to him. I looked at him, really looked at him. He was… different, his cheeks full of color and his golden eyes bright. His skin had lost its pallor. I caressed the side of his face, and he melted into my hand, his lips parting as he lost himself to my touch.

"Thomassen, you're…" A tear slipped from my eye as I held a hand to his cheek. He brought his hand to mine, holding it there, as though he couldn't stand for me to let go.

"Everything's okay now. My father used the Netherros combined with his own magic, healing both of us and… just listen." Thomassen pressed my head against his chest. His heart was beating in normal sync with mine. No more humming or ticking. I whipped my gaze to him, shock taking over me. He was going to be okay. He was going to live. Overcome with relief, I threw my arms around him and nuzzled my face into the dip of his shoulder.

"The Netherros will soon fall into your hands, Rue." Alden said, taking on a dark tone. He didn't have to say anything else, because I knew exactly what he meant.

If I had to wield the Netherros, there was a possibility it would corrupt me, but even so, I had to fight against the dark magic with everything I had and hope for the best outcome, if it didn't kill me first. There was still so much to come. But for the time being, Alden tucked the magic sphere into his pocket, until we decided where to go from here.

Thomassen kissed the top of my head. "All that matters right now is that you get some sleep. We'll talk about the rest later, including you leaving me behind," he said. "I may be grateful you're alive, but I'm still mad at you."

In response, I planted another kiss on him, which only made his blush deepen. After catching up with everyone, and confirming that I wasn't, in fact, in any present danger, my friends departed the room to give me some privacy. All besides Thomassen, who remained by my side.

Alden clicked his tongue. "Rue, before I go, I wanted you to know—"

"Arthur's dead," I finished for him. My eyes welled with tears, the weight of his death crushing me as it sunk in. At least I'd had the chance to say goodbye. Most weren't that lucky.

Fang. A knife stabbed through my chest, knowing this would be another blow to his current state of mind.

"I am truly sorry. He was a remarkable man." Alden kept his hand on my shoulder, gently squeezing.

Thomassen wrapped his arms around me, pulling me into his lap. Puko screeched his disagreement and flew back to his little nest of scrap metal and screws on my nightstand.

Alden shuffled away. "I'll return tomorrow. We have much to discuss with plans going forward. But for now, I don't want to burden you with anything more, so please rest."

After everyone was gone, Thomassen slipped under the comforter and pulled me close. I'd missed this. His warmth, his scent. I wanted to melt into him forever.

Thomassen's breath was hot against my ear, his voice soft as he spoke. "Whatever comes next in our journey, I'll be with you every step of the way. I'll do everything in my power to prevent your death."

I angled my head towards him and drew in a deep breath, the weight of what I've been wanting to tell him crushing me, threatening to break loose. He needed to know before it was too late.

"There's something I've been meaning to tell you," I said, fighting against my own hesitance.

"Wait," Thomassen said. "It's important that you hear this from me before you say anything else. I'm so sorry I was such an ass to you, Rue. You didn't deserve it. Not once."

"That's already been forgiven," I said. "I've been —"

"That's not all," he interrupted. "I'm in love with you, Rue. Prophecy be damned… because I am yours no matter what happens. I will never leave your side." He took my hand and kissed my fingers, his eyes locked with mine. "I am yours," he repeated softly. "Now and forever."

My heart throbbed, skipping erratically in the wake of his confession. Thomassen was mine. *Mine*, and I wasn't going to deny myself that happiness. Even if he lived and I died. At the very least, I could say that I allowed myself to love someone so deeply.

"I love you too," I told him, watching his face light up at my admission. "I have for quite some time now." A heated blush crept onto my cheeks as I gently took his face in my hands and rested my forehead against his.

Thomassen was pure magic — the electricity that illuminated the endless storm raging inside of me. His lips crashed against mine as he took me into his arms, his hand cradling my head as we got lost in each other's embrace. I pressed myself against him, needing to claim every inch of him as mine. I hurt everywhere, but at that moment, nothing else mattered. He was perfect. Every part of him was perfect, and I'd be lying to myself if I told him I didn't want him.

Thomassen smiled sheepishly, his cheeks tinted with warmth as he twirled a strand of my hair around his finger. He playfully nibbled my bottom lip, sending butterflies raging through me. I lifted my fingers to the buttons on his shirt, but he gently grabbed my hand.

"I want you. Soon." His words sounded like a promise. "But today, you need to recover."

Reluctantly, I pulled away, my cheeks heating. "You're right," I smiled, holding his gaze. "But when that day comes, Thomassen, I am yours to have."

We remained in bed until well after sunrise, showering each other with feverish kisses and words of affection. Thomassen leaned in for another kiss when a knock sounded at the door. Alden walked in moments later, not waiting for us to open the door.

"Sorry I'm early, but it's imperative to discuss our next move."

I sat up. Thomassen's hand remained on my lower back, supporting me.

"What's going on?" I asked.

Alden fiddled with his pocket watch. "Alester died yesterday, but he was the tip of the iceberg. We still need to deal with Sullivan."

I feared he might say that. Sullivan was out there, biding his time with whatever plan he was concocting, and with Alester dead, Sullivan would be taking action. Alden opened his pocket watch and outstretched his hand, the watch resting in his palm. My eyes landed on the shattered glass of the clock face. I flinched, my skin growing clammy.

"The barrier is gone. The Volings are closing in on Leaven-fell, and I'm certain that Sullivan is in their midst. A storm is coming and we need to fight. I know you need rest, but we need you." Alden handed me my sword. It was cleaned of all traces of blood.

"You are the wolf in this battle, Rue. It's time to let that wolf free."

CHAPTER 37

THE BATTLE OF LEAVENFELL

BOTH FAE AND WIZARDS MET IN THE GREAT HALL, INCREASING our numbers and acting as a ray of hope for the people of Leavenfell. Thomassen stood by my side, squeezing my hand every so often, a subtle reminder that he wasn't leaving my side. Everyone moved towards a massive oak table at the back of the hall and seated themselves, all bundled up and shivering from the cold, the fireplace not doing enough to shake the chill of dread that spread throughout the castle.

Willow stood by Oliver, her head resting on his shoulder, and Nora, Peter, and Lance kept to the back of the table. All around me were those I'd spent the last few months with, and even though I hadn't spent a lot of time with most of them, I'd grown to care about them and our community.

When Alden entered the hall, he stopped before his podium and surveyed the faces in the crowd. "The Volings are gathering outside our walls as we speak. We anticipate they'll attack at dawn, but we've come prepared, with allies and with bravery,"

Alden boomed. "We must thank Shay and Solomon for aiding us in a time of need. Without them standing by our side, we wouldn't stand a chance in this battle for our freedom." Alden gestured at Shay, and she stepped forward, joining his side. Nervous murmurs across the great hall.

Shay moved behind the podium, her hair falling in several layers of lavender braids down her back. Her eyes met mine, a small smile on her lips, and I mouthed a quick *thank you* to her, which she acknowledged with a nod.

"In our realm, it's considered honorable to fight against those with grave intentions. When the Tree of the Wood offered me a vision, one that showed the Volings assembling, I alerted Alden. We came to an agreement, ending our long-time feud." Shay surveyed the crowd carefully, her posture straight despite the wary looks she received. "While we may have our differences, your fight is our fight. Your kingdom is our kingdom. There is no need to be afraid. My guards will be stationed throughout the castle and at every entrance. If the Volings breach before dawn, we'll be ready for them."

When she was finished, Solomon, lord of the wizards, took the podium next. His pale blue eyes matched the color of his pointed hat and robe, and he held a brown staff in his right hand, golden rings adorning each finger. He carried many wrinkles but stood with confidence and strength. He bowed to Alden before facing the crowd, his expression sharp.

"Though many of my kind have fallen into darkness, I'm proud to be standing here, among my people. There may be few of us, but combined, our magic will be useful against the monsters that lurk our kingdom. I'm happy to give aid to my old friend."

A wizard of few words, he reminded me of Rorik in the way

he spoke. I scanned the great hall until I spotted Rorik near the kitchen quarters. He'd quickly returned from Talem following the news of Arthur's death. He caught my eye and offered a smile that didn't reach his eyes. I returned the gesture, missing Arthur as much as he was.

Alden took his place at the podium and gestured to the guards. "To my guards, you are aware of your stations, so please follow protocol. Finn, please work with Shay and Solomon and help delegate where they'll need to be. Sleeping bags will be provided for the rest of you in the hall. Those of you keeping watch need to stay alert. The rest of you get some rest. I presume tomorrow will be a long day."

One by one, everyone walked to the back of the great hall to grab a sleeping bag and a canister of water from one of Alden's guards. Lance's mom handed out sandwiches and biscuits, her overflowing basket emptying quickly.

"Come on," Thomassen said, taking my hand and directing me to the back of the hall. "Let's grab a couple sleeping bags and find a spot to settle down for the night."

We grabbed our supplies and food, but Lance's mom stopped me, her hand on my forearm.

"For you," she said, handing me a small jar. *Arthur's famous healing concoction.* "Bernice gave it to me to pass on to you."

I thanked her and turned away. Despair clawed through me as we searched for a spot to set up the sleeping bags. Thomassen took my chin into his hands as I brushed away my tears.

"You okay?" he asked, dipping his head close to mine.

"Missing Arthur," I said, my chest tight with the scar of grief. I distracted my thoughts by scanning the hall in search of my friends. Peter and Nora had settled close by, and I found Lance approaching his mom with another basket filled with food. When he spotted me, he waved, a hesitant smile pulling at his lips. I waved back, growing increasingly nervous about the battle. My fingers brushed against the bottled concoction in my pocket, a conscious reminder that it was there, in case I needed it. Thomassen watched me with a cautious expression as he laid out our sleeping bags. The sconces on the walls dimmed until the room was dark enough to allow people to settle down, thanks to Alden's timely spells.

"I'm not sure I'll be able to sleep," I said.

Thomassen patted the spot beside him in his sleeping bag. "There's enough room for two."

I slipped in beside him. He wrapped an arm around me as we laid on our sides, our lips close to touching. He pressed his forehead against mine, his soft hair falling across his eyes. Our food lay to the side, untouched. I couldn't eat and I was certain Thomassen was too nervous to eat as well.

"Come here." Thomassen kissed me, his arm draped over my side, but I needed him closer.

I wrapped my leg around his waist, closing the space between us. He deepened the kiss, his delirious urgency stealing my breath. I slipped my tongue into his mouth, drawing a moan from his lips, and he dug his hips against mine, eliciting an embarrassing squeak from my lips.

"Thomassen." My tone came out as a warning.

He let out a quiet laugh, bringing a hand to my chin and rubbing his thumb across my cheek. "I suppose we should get some rest. We both need it."

Exasperated, I gave his nose a gentle flick and rested my head beside his. I closed my eyes, nestling against Thomassen's warmth, but after we went quiet, an obnoxious sound caught my ears. Someone close by was getting some action, and they weren't exactly being quiet about it.

I shot up. Nora was in a sleeping bag opposite us, with Peter's lips smacking against her neck. When I cleared my throat, Peter lifted his head and snickered.

"I'd look away, unless you want a close-up of my ass in a minute."

"Peter!" Nora hissed. "Not happening, and stop being crude." She gave him a sour look.

"But you're so beautiful," Peter argued, drawing her against his body. He pressed another kiss to her cheek.

Nora shoved him off, but her affectionate smile betrayed her. "Not the time or place. What if my parents see?"

I couldn't help the laugh that escaped me. "Weren't you always the one telling others to get a room?" I asked Peter, fighting a smile.

"Pffft… mind your business," Peter joked, gesturing for me to turn around with a wave of his finger.

"I'm trying to, but your sloppy kisses are disturbing my rest. You sound like a dying bogfrog trying to slurp down its last meal."

Beside me, Thomassen laughed.

Nora's grin widened. "She's right, Peter the bogfrog. You're going to wake everyone in the castle."

They continued with their argument, but Thomassen had heard enough, dragging me back under our own sleeping bag and drowning me in sweet kisses until sleep took us.

Morning came too quickly. Thomassen kissed my forehead, his fingers interlaced with mine.

"It's almost time," he whispered. "I overheard Shay speaking to my father. Her guards are readying themselves." Thomassen searched the hall until he spotted his father. "I'll be right back."

I groggily sat up, trying to wake myself with sharp taps against my cheeks. Everyone else shuffled about, packing their sleeping bags and murmuring amongst themselves. The only person stalling was Willow, still sitting in her sleeping bag, tears spilling onto her face. Oliver attempted to console her while Olivia stood awkwardly at the side. I hoped she was alright.

Tearing my gaze away, I quickly changed into black trousers and a black tunic, an armor plate concealed underneath. Once my hair was pulled back into a ponytail, I adjusted the sheath at my side, ensuring my sword was secured. I slung a quiver over my back, and strapped a couple daggers to my forearms, hidden underneath my sleeves. The dagger at my thigh was cool against my skin.

Thomassen returned from his chat with his father and wrapped me in a tight hug. He pulled back, a sad but fiery desperation behind his eyes, caressing my cheek with shaking fingers. "Gods Rue. Every moment by your side deepens the ruin inside me. I can't bear the thought of ever losing you."

I pressed my forehead to his. "Are you okay? What's wrong?"

"I don't want you to get hurt." The tremble of his embrace unnerved me. "I'll tear this entire damned castle apart if that means keeping you from harm."

At a loss for words, I stood on my tiptoes and kissed him, my lips feverish against his as he roughly tangled his fingers in my hair, dragging me against him once more. Only when Alden's voice thundered across the hall, speaking of monsters and violence, did we break apart.

Alden lifted his staff up high, and everyone raised their fists, crying out with cheers. Out of everyone cheering, Peter was the loudest, Nora by his side and as loud as he was. Pride bubbled inside me. My friends were amazing.

The fae stood in a line formation near the front, dressed in steel armor, equipped with their shields and spears. The wizards hung behind, every staff at the ready.

I bit my bottom lip, my muscles tensed, while Thomassen kept his hand on my back. The walls shook as the Volings breached. Swords clanged and bowstrings were drawn as everyone prepared themselves. My heart raced as a terrifying silence followed. Another tense moment passed.

The great arched doors of the castle burst open. Volings bolted in at alarming speed, yipping and cackling as they rammed into the wall of fae. There were hundreds of them, all different races. Finn and his group sprang into action, staking vampires and dodging sideswipe attempts from the goblins. From the back of the hall, a group of guards let their arrows fly, picking off the Volings that managed to launch themselves past the fae's tight wall of defense.

Armor clattering, the fae charged forward and speared anything that crossed their paths, Shay herself a force to be reckoned with. Several Volings fell, but the dead were quickly replaced by a new onslaught of monsters pouring through the open doors. One by one, fae, mortals, and wizards alike took them down, the air heavily scented with sweat and blood.

To my left, Lance fought a pack of Volings that'd gone after his mother. He moved with impressive speed, releasing a silver-tipped arrow with fatal precision through a werewolf's skull. He tumbled onto the ground, regained his balance, and staked a vampire in his next breath. Peter and Oliver came to his aid, and together, they fought off the horde, their weapons a blur as they attacked.

Some hyelings pushed through the fae wall, racing towards us. Catching Thomassen's wary eyes, we unsheathed our weapons and sliced into the approaching monsters.

"Kill the girl at any cost!" A horribly familiar voice boomed.

My blood ran cold. *Sullivan.*

In the next moment, a swarm of vampires surrounded me. At least ten of them. As they closed in on us, Nora shouted my name. Peter left Lance's side, darting our way. Thomassen and I swiveled around each other in a dangerous dance, and I brought my sword down wildly at the attacking Volings, decapitating one while another's claws thrashed at me. Peter staked a vampire that had grabbed me by my legs, nearly causing me to stumble.

Thomassen roared an incantation, coating the ground around us in ice. The monsters slipped and fell, sliding away from us with growls and gnashing teeth. The scene would've been hilarious had I not been fearing for our lives. More Volings attacked, and I took them down alongside Peter and Thomassen, blood splattering all over my face, hair and clothes.

"Rue! Watch out!" Finn screamed from across the hall, flailing his arms above his head. His screams were cut short when a pack of werewolves tackled him to the ground.

Thomassen dragged me to the floor, a great sword narrowly missing our necks. The hair on the back of my neck raised. Sullivan, clad in black armor and carrying the biggest sword I'd ever laid eyes on, stood behind us. He was different than I'd remembered, his onyx eyes sunken and soulless, his skin sallow. He gave me a cruel smile, his fangs lengthening. Two horns poked out from underneath his gray hair, making him appear more beast than man.

I heaved myself upwards, my fingers gripping the hilt of my sword. Thomassen went still by my side, his hand clinging to the fabric of my tunic.

"Good to meet again, Ruby. Did Fang say hello to you yet?" Sullivan said menacingly as he swiped the side of my head with his clawed hand. My vision blurred and I staggered backwards, but Thomassen caught me. I clung to him while regaining my balance.

"I heard you killed a dear friend of mine. Does that ring a bell to you? Did you really think you'd get away with that?"

I launched myself forward, my sword aimed at his neck, but Sullivan grabbed my wrist and tossed me to the ground. I screamed, his touch having burned a hole into my skin, and dropped my sword. Gritting my teeth, I retrieved my weapon, pushing myself to a stand while my limbs rattled with pain. Thomassen lunged at Sullivan, but was tossed across the room, hitting the back of his head against the wall.

"Thomassen!" I shrieked.

He wasn't moving, and before I could make it over to check on him, Sullivan waved his hand and a barrier enveloped us, cutting the rest of the great hall from view. Only the two of us were locked in. Screams, pounding, and clashing steel faded as the barrier solidified. I swayed, uneasy on my feet. Sullivan laughed, a horrible sound that reminded me of all the times he'd laughed as I was tortured inside his little prison in Helm Castle. But he would *never* touch me again.

"Once you're dead—" I crept forward, sword ready, "—make sure to give Alester my regards in whatever afterlife awaits you."

"How humorous that you think yourself capable of killing

me. Unfortunately for you, I'm immortal." Sullivan neared me, his clawed fingers outstretched. "When I'm done with you, I'll go to Fang and finish him. Slowly."

His gaze bore into me, onyx eyes blazing. "I will carry out Alester's plan, and all your friends will die. The prophecy *will* fail, and only the powerful will survive."

Our swords clashed. I propelled forward, keeping my feet light as I slashed at him over and over again, but he blocked every attack with ease. Sweat rose on my skin, my breath ragged, but Sullivan showed no signs of tiring.

"You die today, Ruby," Sullivan snarled.

The barrier split open, disintegrating, and Lance broke through, followed by Alden, Thomassen, and an onslaught of fae warriors.

"The only one dying today is you, you fucking monster." Lance's fist crashed into Sullivan's face, but Sullivan recovered quickly, rubbing the side of his jaw. They danced around each other in a harrowing duel, the space between them crackling with magic, silver and brutality.

Thomassen ran to my side and dragged me from the midst of the battle. "Are you okay?"

"Let me go!" I ordered, but he held tight, his eyes resting on my burned wrist.

"Rue, your arm."

"I'm fine," I reassured him, my head whipping back to the action. Lance staggered—Sullivan was winning. He deflected attacks from the fae and Peter without breaking a sweat. I broke free of Thomassen, snatched the stake from his hand, and launched myself at Sullivan's back, bringing the stake down, but he threw me off easily. My face collided against the wooden floor, and a sickening crack rang through my ears. I was certain my nose was broken beyond repair. I struggled for consciousness as blood oozed down my face, coating my lips.

Once I stood, Sullivan gave a flick of his wrist and I went crashing across the great hall, my back slamming into one of the glass sconces along the wall. Warmth slid down my lower back, but my attention snapped back to Sullivan. Sullivan disarmed Lance, the blow so hard that Lance stumbled. I unsheathed the dagger from my thigh and lurched across the hall, aiming for Sullivan's exposed neck, but he deflected my attack, his claws raking across my skin.

I cried out, dropping the dagger and bringing my hands to my face. Sullivan moved forward, claws outstretched, his eyes dropping to my gut, as though readying himself to disembowel me. I dodged backwards, but Sullivan calculated my next move, catching me by my arm. He grabbed me by the throat and lifted me off the ground, cutting off my oxygen. I spat blood on his face, infuriating him more, his fangs lengthening as he moved in for the kill.

"No!" Thomassen yelled, thrusting himself at Sullivan with as much force as he could.

Sullivan stumbled, dropping me. I clutched my throat and coughed, trying to force air back into my lungs. Thomassen rushed to my side as Lance and the fae advanced on Sullivan again, tearing him away from us.

"Rue, gods, are you alright?" Thomassen braced my shoulders, his expression horrified. "You're covered in blood."

I shook my head, trying to clear the fog. "I'll be fine, but Thomassen…"

He wrapped his arms around me. "We need to get you out of here."

From the corner of my eye, Peter tackled Sullivan at full

speed, making him stagger while Lance jumped onto his back and pounded at his face, his eyes wild with bloodlust. Sullivan bucked, dismantling Lance.

"I won't leave them," I cried. Thomassen helped me to my feet, but a sudden flash of pain behind my eyes buckled my knees, as though a thunderclap had broken loose inside my skull.

"Rue!" Thomassen yelled as I staggered sideways.

The scent of blood hung in the air. I turned my head, my senses spiraling out of control, screaming *danger*, but I was too late. Sullivan impaled Lance with his own clawed arm, digging and twisting it before removing it forcefully, spilling a river of blood onto the floor. Lance stumbled, his knees going limp as he swayed, his expression confused as he tried to cover the gaping wound with his hand.

Time froze with a sickening shudder. Lance fell, bringing the castle down on my shoulders along with him.

"Lance!" His name came out as a hysterical scream. I raced to his side as the fae moved in on Sullivan. My knees gave out, and I dropped to the ground, catching Lance in my arms before he hit the floor, his head falling onto my lap. His mouth hung open as he glanced downward, his expression frozen in pain. Slowly, he dragged his gaze to mine.

A heartbeat slipped by. I held his hand for dear life, frantically searching my pockets for Arthur's healing concoction, but Lance's wound was too deep. I wouldn't have enough to heal him. Lance grabbed my hand, stopping me from opening the bottle. His lips parted as a tear slid down his blood-stained cheeks.

"D-don't. It's...okay." He jolted, his body shivering, the sudden movement startling me.

"I won't let you die," I cried, caressing his face. "I'm right here."

Lance weakly squeezed my hand, the ghost of a smile tugging at his lips. Blood pooled around us at an alarming rate. "Rue, s-so glad… you've been by my side." He released a long wheezing breath, and then, he stilled.

"Lance?" Arthur's concoction slipped from my fingers. I stared down at him in horror, my brain not comprehending what I was seeing.

The bond snapped.

An impenetrable wall slammed down, severing us, until I could no longer feel him on the other side of that pull. A jarring pain tore into my skull, shredding through my body, tearing every single fiber of me into thousands of scattered pieces. When the pieces came back together, they were different, forged from a smothering darkness, pulling my head under the dark waters until the only thing that existed in my mind was his broken image.

Thomassen came up from behind me. His hand pressed on my shoulder, snapping me into action. I snatched up the bottle, opening it and pouring what was left onto Lance, willing his wounds to close and his chest to rise, but nothing happened. I waited and waited, unable to breathe or move or think until Thomassen spoke.

"He's gone, Rue. I'm so sorry." Thomassen wrapped his arms around me, so tightly, as though he was holding all the pieces of me together.

I turned my head. Peter had gone completely still, his eyes darting between me and Lance's body. Something behind his eyes shifted, a heart wrenching pain I couldn't describe, and he launched himself back at Sullivan, pushing past the fae with his sword raised.

A horn sounded somewhere in the distance. I broke free of Thomassen and staggered towards Sullivan, aiming my dagger at his heart. But something inside of me snapped. And everything went as black as the abyss inside my heart.

I paddled myself through frigid waves near a dense but dark green forest. A pack… *no*, my pack of wolves waited on the rocks as I dragged myself onto the cold soil.

A large wolf, black and green in color, came to my side as I regained my bearings. I stared up at the beast, lost to my own sadness. My scar burned with ferocious intensity, threatening to burn the skin around it. My heart raced, thumping heavily in my chest, as the wolf nudged my face with its long snout.

Its voice spoke inside my head.

"You know what to do."

I shook my head back and forth, covering my ears. "I can't."

"YOU MUST!"

I awoke with a start, panting and screaming as my body thrashed and writhed against the wooden floors of Leavenfell Castle. I screamed and *screamed* as my bones cracked and twisted and shattered. My fingers bent at angles that shouldn't have been possible, twisting and snapping, shifting into massive brown paws. Fur spread across my skin like wildfire. My back arched and an otherworldly howl escaped my curled lips.

When I flipped from my back onto my feet, I no longer stood on two feet, but four. I locked eyes with Sullivan, raising my lips in a feral growl. His attacks slowed. He stumbled, taking a heavy step backward, shaking his head.

I collided with him.

CHAPTER 38

AFTERMATH

SOMEONE IN THE DIMLY LIT ROOM WAS SOBBING. I LISTENED, uncertainly, until realizing the broken sobbing was coming from me. My scar ached as I mourned, the air heavy with unbearable grief.

Alden sat at the foot of my bed, his expression somber. He glanced at Thomassen, who slept beside me, then back to me. "I gave him a sleeping potion. He needed the rest."

A tremor ran through me.

He stared off. "I also gave you a sleeping potion, but it seems the wolf inside you doesn't take kindly to potions."

A sob left my lips again, and I curled forward, tears streaming down my face as I brought my hand to the center of my chest. Lance's pull was gone, replaced by an emptiness so crushing, I didn't know how I'd survive. There was no connection. No buzzing warmth. No waves. Only lonely emptiness. My friend was dead.

Alden hung his head. "I'm terribly sorry, Rue. Just know I

understand." He waited quietly, for what seemed like hours, until my tears dried up.

I drew in a deep breath, somehow managing to hold back my tears, though the wound inside me was deep, a relentless ache.

"What happened… after? I think I changed, and then… n-nothing." I don't know how I shifted back into my human form, much less if it disturbed my bones in any way. I observed my limbs. They all looked the same to me.

"After you turned, you attacked Sullivan. It was incredible to witness—your strength. You tore a leg from his body, amongst other inflicted wounds, but unfortunately, he managed to escape," Alden said, his tone grim, and I slumped against my pillows. I'd failed to kill him and now there was a chance he'd return.

"There's another thing, Rue. While you were attacking Sullivan, your snout opened and a black swirling mass, like a storm cloud, emerged. The mass pulsed while you were locked in a howl, and… I swear to the gods, I saw the magic that corrupted Sullivan for so long peel away from his body before embedding itself in the cloud."

Sweat dotted my skin. "What the hells are you talking about? Where did the cloud go?"

Alden averted his eyes, an uncomfortable look in his eyes. "You absorbed it."

I went still. "I-what?!!"

"Calm down. I don't believe it's affecting you. At least not yet. It must be tied to the prophecy, but I'm not entirely sure how. I'm only telling you what I saw."

A shudder ran down my spine. If I'd absorbed some of the Netherros's dark magic, that could mean trouble down the road. I didn't know how to feel about that.

And Sullivan…

He'd gotten away, but if the corruption was gone, had any of his humanity returned? Had he run away because he couldn't face what he'd done?

A thousand possibilities raced through my mind. I couldn't imagine what Sullivan would be like without the Netherros's magic inside him.

"Don't think about it too much right now," Alden said, his tone softening. "I know it's a lot, but one day at a time, Rue."

"So now I'm cursed, *and* I have corrupt magic inside of me," I said. "It's no wonder I'm destined to die."

"Don't speak that over yourself, Rue. We will overcome any obstacle together, even death," Alden said.

"Sullivan got away," I added.

"Yes. Despite that, you killed most of the Volings inside the castle. The wolf inside you—it's a gift. You saved a lot of lives."

As someone who'd been born giftless, being told that my curse was a *gift* was almost laughable. Almost. But something shifted inside me. *Acceptance.* Though others would consider the scar a curse, Alden was right. I had a gift, and a rare one at that. Not many werewolves could shift into humans, after all. I also had the gift of traveling to other dimensions, something I hadn't yet shared with anyone else, but I would when the right time came.

"What of Peter and Nora? Fang?" Peter had to be beating himself up right now. Seeing how he'd attacked Sullivan after Lance died absolutely crushed me, bringing fresh tears to my cheeks.

Alden went gray. "A few Volings managed to escape, but not without hostages. Nora was among them. I'm sorry to have to be the one to tell you."

I climbed out of bed, oblivious to my exhaustion until I stumbled. "They'll kill her." I said with a shaky voice. "We need to find her. Now." I couldn't lose another friend. I *couldn't*.

Alden stood up, meeting me at my side. "We will. In fact, Peter's been ready to go since the battle ended. I had to convince him to wait for you."

"How many others died?"

"Too many to count," Alden replied gravely. "Many fae died, and Shay was wounded, but I know she wishes to speak with you soon. About the prophecy."

"I'll talk to her after we find Nora," I said. "If Sullivan got hold of her—" I shuddered. I couldn't go there. Not now. I sat on the edge of my bed, hollow. Puko flew to my shoulder and nestled into my neck, cooing softly.

After Thomassen had woken, we'd learned that both Oliver and Willow had been killed. I cried for them and the love they'd never get to explore. I cried for Peter and Mrs. Baker, who had lost so much when Lance died.

And *Nora…*

"Where do you think Nora was taken?" I asked Thomassen, who'd remained by my side through it all.

"Probably Vol," he shuddered.

"We'll need to find her soon." I climbed out of bed, not caring that I was mostly unclothed.

Thomassen stood, grabbing my arm. "Woah, slow down. One thing at a time."

I slipped into a pair of trousers, ignoring him.

"You should rest until the funeral," Thomassen suggested. "Going now isn't going to do anyone any good, not in the state you're in"

"Fine, but we leave after." Once Nora was safe, I would put an end to the shadowy realm once and for all.

The courtyard was full of wizards, fae, and humans as Alden listed off the names of the dead at the funeral the following morning. The heavy rain soaked through my clothes, although the cold had long since settled within me.

Each name spoken was a dagger plunged through my heart. When Lance's name was called, I staggered, the reminder of his absence haunting me. His mother stood beside me, sobbing, and I held her hand as tight as I could, fighting the darkness that swirled behind my eyes. *Netherros corruption.* I could feel the sharp edges of the dark magic, prodding my skin from the inside, threatening to break free.

Nora's name was called, but I refused to believe she was dead. Not yet. Not when I had the gift of dimension travel. I was certain I'd be able to reach out to her somehow, if I could figure out how to deliberately access my gift. I turned my head. Peter stood on the other side of his mom, his arm wrapped around her trembling shoulders. When his gaze found mine, it was clear he had one goal. Saving Nora. A ray of hope in a whirlwind of despair. He needed her, and so did I.

Once we found her, I had no doubt that they would remain

by my side until the very end, unless we figured out a way for me to survive. I dreamed of a future with Thomassen, full of happiness and love, comfort and warmth. A future where we no longer feared for our safety.

At the end of the funeral, after Alden spoke parting words, everyone ran inside, desperate to get out of the downpour. Everyone except for Peter, Thomassen, and myself.

I laid a bouquet of flowers at the base of Oliver, Willow, and Lance's graves, and knelt to the ground, my hands resting on Lance's casket. Peter and Thomassen dropped to their knees beside me and together, we sat in silence. I didn't know how much time passed, but eventually, we returned to the warmth of the great hall.

After briefly speaking with Nora's family to let them know of my intentions, they hugged me, including Nora's father, who expressed how deeply regretful he was over his troubled relationship with Nora. He promised that if we found her, he would do everything he could to make things right with her. I wasn't holding my breath, but at least it was a step in the right direction.

Later, I bumped into Olivia, and after a tense moment, I released the grudge I held against her and hugged her, relief flooding through me when she returned my embrace, crying into my shoulder and apologizing repeatedly. I told her how sorry I was for her losses and let her know I'd be there for her, if she ever needed a shoulder to lean on.

At the end of the day, Alden met up with me, Thomassen, and Peter in my tower. The four of us huddled on my bed and waited for Alden to speak.

"We'll be leaving Leavenfell," Alden stated.

"Where to?" I asked before the boys could.

"Solendia."

The realm of commerce, a bustling place with guilds, high fae, and diversity. I'd heard of it from Arthur and had always dreamed of going.

Alden continued, "Shay mentioned that the high fae should know about the prophecy, but it won't be easy to get information out of them. The high fae are tight-lipped and not too friendly. We'll have to find a way to get on their good side."

"What about Nora?" I asked. "We need to find her before doing anything else."

"Vol is not far from Solendia. You should be able to enter under the cover of night but make quick work of it."

"We'll save her," Peter said with determination.

Alden clapped his hands together. "We leave tomorrow at dawn. Be sure to pack what you need."

"And Fang?" I asked. He'd been in the healing tower away from the battle, and last I'd heard, he was safe.

"I'll let Fang know of our departure," Alden said. "I'll allow him to say goodbye."

I nodded. "Of course."

Afterwards, we parted ways to prepare for our journey. According to Alden, the castle would be in very good hands, since Solomon and his followers had agreed to stay, and Fang would be well taken care of. At least until our return.

On the way to my room, Thomassen caught up with me, slipping his hand into mine. "Are you sure you're ready for this?"

I exhaled, clenching my fists, more than ready. "I've shifted into a wolf and cheated death… twice, I might add. Not to mention absorbing Sullivan's dark magic. I'm ready for anything this journey has to throw at me." And I meant it. I had no reason to be afraid anymore, and I swore by the end of it all, I would, at the very least, kill Sullivan and close Vol.

Thomassen smiled. "You're incredible, you know. That day on the bridge, the first time I saw you, I knew I was in trouble."

A smile tugged at my lips. "And why is that?"

"Because I knew that if I didn't stay away, I'd fall in love with the most beautiful girl I'd ever laid eyes on. I knew then that when the time came, I'd do anything to protect you."

I stood on my tiptoes and kissed him as he wrapped me in his warm embrace. "You know… I'd given up on you at one point. I'm glad you found me again."

"I would have searched across every realm and kingdom to find you again, if it came down to that." Thomassen pressed another kiss to the top of my head. "I'm never letting you go."

Hand in hand, we headed to my tower to pack for the next part of our journey. I was one step closer to finding the Prophecy of Branches and Blood. I wouldn't breathe easily until the ancient record was in my hands, but at least Thomassen was by my side.

The relic in my pocket whirred to life. It was time to face my fate, whatever that may bring.

The next morning, as we passed through the exit of the great Leavenfell Castle, a voice called out to me. A smile broke across my face at that wonderful sound.

"You'd better not be leaving me behind." Fang emerged, and as the sun rose, peeking over the grand towers of the castle, I dropped my bags and crashed into him.

In Loving Memory of Joe Mason White, Jr
(1963-2023)

Special thanks to

Kearan and Sawyer Sharkey: My whole world

Patricia Moffett: My incredible and compassionate art illustrator and cover designer

Lucy York: My amazing, detail-oriented developmental and copy editor

Heather "Phoenix" Jackson-Moore: My forever ride-or-die, my sister from another mister, who's always been there for me, no matter how long we've been apart.

Lauren Sweeney: One of my closest friends, who supported me all the way.

Sherry Dovah Mustafa: Beta reader

About the Author

Yuri Sharkey is a dark romantasy writer who incorporates gothic elements into her stories while still maintaining heart and warmth. She is highly fascinated by all things steampunk and strives to add sprinkles of the steampunk genre throughout her works.

When she's not writing, she enjoys spending time with her husband, son (who enjoys anime as much as she does), and three dogs. She cannot function without a bowl of spicy ramen, iced matcha, and tacos.

Her first book, The Clockmaker's Son, was written in honor of her father, who tragically passed away in early 2023.

Book 2 of The Twisted Wolves duology, *The Alchemist's Daughter*, will be released in early 2027. Follow Yuri's website for updates: www.yurisharkey.com